if tomorrow comes

When the world fell apart, all they had was Hope

An end-time story

glen robinson

Pacific Press® Publishing Association
Nampa, Idaho
Oshawa, Ontario, Canada

Edited by Tim Lale
Designed by Dennis Ferree
Cover photo by Harriet Zucker/Photonica

Copyright © 2000 by
Pacific Press® Publishing Association
Printed in the United States of America
All Rights Reserved

ISBN 0-8163-1766-6

00 01 02 03 04 • 5 4 3 2 1

CONTENTS

ACKNOWLEDGMENTS

Thanks to Eric and Céleste, for initially throwing down the gauntlet and then seeing some merit in my ideas.

Thanks to Trish, for her comments and encouragement during the assembly of all this.

Thanks to Shelly, Matt, and Missy, for enduring a grouchy and preoccupied husband and father for the duration of this project.

And:

Thanks be to my Savior Jesus Christ for not only inspiring me to write this, but for His soon-coming reality, which this or any other end-time story can never measure up to.

PROLOGUE

No cars traveled either north or south on Highway 101. The busy traffic that the interstate was known for had gone elsewhere.

Oh, sure, once in a great while a solitary vehicle roared up the six-lane highway unimpeded. The California Highway Patrol wouldn't stop them; they had bigger fish to fry. But on this late afternoon, as the sun disappeared into the red haze of the ash-filled horizon, only the black ribbon of asphalt running north and south broke the endless gray expanse. And one solitary figure. Running.

If there were anyone around to see this person, they might at first miss something very strange and otherwise obvious about this young man. They would most likely notice his muscular but thin build, the ragged coal black hair, and the tattered T-shirt that barely protected him from the strange, bitter April wind. But they would probably have had to look twice to notice that he ran with no shoes.

Mitch wasn't exactly barefoot. A pair of ragged white athletic socks covered his bleeding feet as he ran. The only indication of how far Mitch had already run was the footprints he left behind in the light gray ash that sifted over the asphalt. The prints went back for miles.

He ran effortlessly, as if his mind were in a different place than his body. Mitch let out a deep breath, not even breaking stride. His eyes stared forward, as if looking for something unseen on the horizon. And then he smiled.

* * * * *

The black helicopters were real. Jenny and the others heard them a long time before they saw them. They had escaped from the dogs and the trackers, but they were not likely to escape 200-mile-per-hour machines that could fly over the rain forest and use infrared systems to pinpoint their location within a couple of feet.

And the helicopters were most likely armed, Jenny realized. Jake had told her about the air-to-surface missiles and the machine guns that these fast little helicopters could carry.

She and the others ran, walked, and crawled out of the rain forest and headed for the top of the hill. The strong helped the weak and the children; together they were not likely to move very quickly.

Jenny watched the first of the six helicopters break over the tops of the trees and head in their direction. She thought that if they could get to the top of the hill, everything would be all right. They didn't have far to go, but the group moved so slowly!

She forced herself to look ahead and help the others, rather than looking back at the approaching helicopters. *Just a little bit farther*, she told herself, and saw the top of the hill just ahead of her.

"No. It can't be," she heard a man gasp to himself at the front of the group. When she reached the top of the hill, she understood why. Ahead of her was a cliff that dropped hundreds of feet to the rocks and surf of the Pacific Ocean.

They had nowhere else to run. Jenny finally turned to face the oncoming helicopters.

She took a breath, and smiled.

* * * * *

A rat ran across the rusty floor of the ship's hold. Jake guessed that this hold and this ship had at one time been in pretty good shape. Now they were falling apart, just like the world around him.

It had been two days since they had been sealed into their floating coffin, two days without food or water. He heard someone crying in the darkness. He heard a lot of crying these days. It was easy to become insensitive to the needs of everyone else around you, especially when you hadn't eaten or drunk anything in who knew how long, when you were constantly fighting off bedbugs, lice or rats, or just wallowing in your own misfortune.

You are here for a reason, a voice told Jake. He thought about it and nodded to himself. He had a so-so singing voice, but that had never stopped him from singing when he had something to express. Now he did have something to say, and he opened his cracked lips.

"Amazing grace, how sweet the sound, that saved a wretch like me." His voice wavered out quietly at first, then grew stronger. "I once was lost, but now am found, was blind but now I see."

He sang as many verses as he could remember. By the time he had finished, he realized that his voice was not alone. Singing rose from half a dozen others in the darkness. With no food or water, with disease and vermin all around, behind a welded-shut hatch and tons of seawater, they had defeated discouragement. And that's when Jake smiled for the first time in weeks.

* * * * *

Kris shivered uncontrollably. The harsh April wind that brought gray snow howled outside the dead hollow tree where she hid. A few flakes of the filthy snow filtered down through the opening above her. She took her thin coat and tried to shove it up higher to block as much of the cold air as possible.

She heard the crackling of footsteps outside. Until they

spoke, there was no way to tell whether the noise was one of the search party or the bear she had run into earlier. In either case, it was better to stay quiet. As quiet as a fourteen-year-old girl with chattering teeth could be.

"God, help me. Be with me," she prayed for the umpteenth time, whispering the words as if they were a comfort in themselves. She tightened her grip around her own shoulders, rubbing her skin through the light material of her shirt in her continuous effort to get warm.

As if in answer to her prayer, her father's last words to her came back, just as if he were speaking them for the first time.

And Kris smiled.

* * * * *

Teacher of the Year . . . I never won Teacher of the Year at school, Dan thought. *I wonder what I did wrong.*

It's funny how the mind works, Dan thought next as he lay in a pool of blood on the frozen ground outside the National Guard Humvee. *It's not that I'm disappointed. It's more of an observation than anything else.*

Dan could feel his strength ebbing, as the blood trickled from his head wound. He tried to move his hand underneath himself to get up, tried to move his foot or even his toe. Nothing. He could still see a cockeyed view of a gone-crazy world that ran in panic around him. Feet scurried in all directions, their frenzy quieted by the blanket of pine needles around them and the fact that the gun blast had somewhat deafened Dan. Yet despite the pandemonium, he felt a peace he hadn't felt since—when? He couldn't remember. *It's not long now,* he thought.

Where was Kris? Where were Meg and Mitch? His thoughts were becoming more and more disjointed, and yet he didn't panic. Instead, the sense of calm seemed to warm him. *All is as it should be,* he thought. And he smiled.

prologue

* * * *

Some people believe in coincidence. Those who lived through those final days on earth learned that coincidence was the non-believer's way of explaining providence, the acts of God in humanity's affairs.

And as these five people—Mitch, Jenny, Jake, Kris, and Dan—simultaneously smiled, even though circumstances and thousands of miles kept them apart, their thoughts drew them together. They thought of how close they were to eternity. They thought of the road that had taken them there. And they thought back to a simpler time, a moment just six months before when they had all celebrated Thanksgiving under one roof.

This is the story of five people—a family—who took the road and its journey to completion.

What separates the victors from the vanquished? Maybe it's as simple as a smile of hope when hope seems nonexistent. Maybe it's the ability to see beyond the immediate reality around us and grasp a greater reality.

Maybe it's ... well, read their story. Then decide for yourself.

CHAPTER

1

Click.

"... *with everything on it. Meanwhile, lawmakers in Washington can look forward to another marathon session of congress following the Thanksgiving recess, as the federal deficit and the growing cost of foreign oil stymies their efforts to balance the federal budget. Speaker of the House* ..."

Click.

[Automatic weapons firing, booming explosions] "*He's dead, he's dead! Oh, look at the blood! I'll get you, you son of a* ..."

Click.

"... *and it looks like blue skies throughout the holiday weekend for San Jose and the entire Bay Area* ..."

Click.

"... *the way you look, I have this overwhelming desire to just rip those clothes right off of your body.*"

"*But what about your husband?*"

Click.

"*In light of the Harper Amendment passed just a few days ago, negotiations continue between the Federal Communications Commission, the Department of Education, television executives, and leaders in the burgeoning information industry that may lead to a significant breakthrough . . ."*

Click.

"With just five minutes until kickoff, I predict another one-sided victory for Dallas. After all, with Green Bay's starting quarterback out with a concussion and their front line ravaged by drug convictions, I think backup quarterback Iversen is going to have his hands full."

"Here it is," Dan Lewis said to his brother-in-law, Jake, over his shoulder. "And it looks like we skipped all the pre-game junk, too."

"What a waste," Jake Gallagher responded, sitting down on the couch. "I remember not too long ago when a game between Dallas and Green Bay was an awesome event."

"Well, you never know. Green Bay could still have some surprises left in them. Did you see that tight end run from scrimmage last week in Oakland? Fifty-five yards to tie the game!" Dan took a couple of steps backward toward his recliner, his eyes still glued to the set.

"Yeah, and did you see that hit he took later at the goal line?" Jake responded. "I could not believe that he could even stand after taking that shoulder to the throat."

"Speaking about taking it in the throat, did you get that notice from the IRS about increased taxes?" Dan asked.

Jake shook his head. "I guess my travels with Uncle Sam have kept me ahead of the post office. Even so, it seems with the Harper Amendment passing three weeks ago, those tax increases may never happen."

Dan shrugged. "Yeah, I guess I don't understand that much about the new law. I understand it's to balance the federal budget, and that they're giving the IRS more authority to go after tax evaders, but beyond that—"

"Well, they're also cutting overhead in education and defense, working with the private sector to find new sources of revenue, and pushing to make the U.S. less dependent on foreign sources of energy." Jake shrugged. "I don't know. I've never been too fond of the IRS, but if anyone has the infrastructure and the intelligence sources to pull it off, it's the IRS. If they can balance the budget without raising taxes, more power to them."

Dan shook his head. "I've always been leery of letting government have too much control, even to fix problems—"

A 14-year-old girl wearing jeans and a T-shirt who came up behind him interrupted him.

"*Dadd-e-e*," she whined. "I was going to use the TV for my chat session on the Internet. It's supposed to go on in ten minutes."

"Sorry, Kris," Dan replied with a shrug. "Football is a Thanksgiving tradition." He reached back and grabbed her, pulling her onto him. "Use the computer in the bedroom."

Getting up again, Kris reluctantly wandered into her parents' bedroom and switched the computer on. Within a couple of minutes she was in her favorite chat room with her "friends"—people she had never met face to face but talked to regularly on the Internet.

The discussion was about income taxes, which Kris found boring. She felt torn between trying another chat room and switching the computer off when a familiar user name appeared.

Losergrrl: hi, Kitkat. ;-)

Kris grinned. It was Ginger, her girlfriend from school. *Funny*, she thought, *going to an international chat room to talk to someone I see face to face every day*. She typed back.

Kitkat: hello yourself. How come you're not out killing turkeys or something?
Losergrrl: 'cuz I wanted to talk to you 'bout u-no-who..........
Have you talked to him yet?????????

Kris's mouth became a hard line, and she took a deep breath. Good question. She definitely had a major crush on Brad. Why hadn't she talked to him yet?

Kris's mother, Meg Lewis, swung open the kitchen door and walked across the living room carrying a large plastic bowl.

"I don't know why you continue to watch that game after that player was killed last week," she said to her husband, Dan.

"It was two weeks ago, dear, and it was a coach who had a heart attack on the sidelines," Dan said as she plopped the bowl down in his lap. "What's this?"

"Potatoes. Peel them," Meg said. She paused, then poked her finger into her husband's bulging midsection. "Looks like another couch potato headed for a heart attack."

"Very funny," Dan responded as she retreated to the kitchen. "I'm not that overweight, am I, Jake?" he said after a long minute, staring down at his stomach.

Jake reached over and grabbed a knife and a potato. "Are you asking me to respond as a physician, or a brother-in-law?"

"Both."

"Well then, the answers are yes, you're overweight; and yes, you're headed for a heart attack." Jake looked up from the potato he was peeling and grinned. "Seriously, though, I think you could learn something from your fair wife there. She really seems to be getting in shape."

Dan shrugged. "A lot of good it does me. Between the time she spends at her office and the health club, I hardly see her. Most of the time she's still working when I go to bed, and she's gone to the club before I get up."

Jake dropped his peeled potato in the bowl and grabbed another one. "Well, she's ambitious, that's for sure. The only thing her sister, Jenny, has been working on for the past four months is growing another mouth to feed for the Gallagher household."

Dan reached for a knife and delicately began cutting the skin from a large brown potato. "I can't get over the fact that you will be gone when Jake Jr. shows up. I'm sure Jenny's not real excited about you being thousands of miles away when the baby comes."

Jake sighed. "Yeah, well, the wheels of military progress turn slowly. Jenny wasn't expecting when I signed on for this six-month stint in Antarctica. Besides, it gets me out of the service a year earlier. They put me through med school, and I have to pay them back for that. But I have other bills to pay as well. The sooner I can get a practice established, the better."

"Yeah, but *Antarctica!*" Dan shook his head. "How did you talk Jenny into letting you go on this one?"

"It wasn't easy," Jake said. "When she found out she was pregnant, she wouldn't talk to me for a week. Finally, we agreed that she would spend the last few weeks with her parents back in Illinois. That way if anything happens—" Jake shrugged. "But Jenny's strong, and in this day and age of instant communication, I can just about be near her wherever I am—even in Antarctica."

"So what's going on in Antarctica?" Dan asked. "You gonna do physicals on penguins?"

"Some big corporation has a federal research grant to develop an alternative energy source, so with the Harper Amendment, it suddenly got top priority. It has to do with volcanoes and geothermal energy. Supposed to help the U.S. stop depending so much on foreign oil."

"And what do you do?" Dan asked.

"I make sure no one gets sick, and pick up the pieces if they mess up and blow up Antarctica." Jake winked. "Hey, would you look at that." He pointed at the TV screen. The roving camera had picked out a man behind the goal posts holding a big sign that read "Jesus Christ is coming soon."

In the kitchen, Meg's sister, Jenny, looked up from a magazine she was holding as Meg entered.

"He is so gorgeous," she said, glancing at the photo on the cover.

"Gorgeous is not the word," Meg said. "He's smart, sexy, and worth $150 million."

"And this guy, Simon Esteb, is your new boss," Jenny added. "How will you cope?"

"Well, I guess I'll just have to put in more overtime." Meg looked wistfully into the distance, then grinned at her sister. They both laughed, Jenny self-consciously holding her hand to her abdomen.

"Seriously, Meg, how is your job going?" Jenny asked. "Are you still having Sabbath problems?"

Meg sighed deeply and shrugged. "It's a matter of compromise. I give a little, and they give a little. Right now, I'm available for emergencies, but otherwise I am not available on Friday nights or Saturdays."

"What kind of emergencies could happen at a telecommunications company that couldn't be taken care of during the week?"

Meg snorted. "You'd be surprised. But I just heard that I might be in line for a promotion that will take care of this problem. Dan and the kids and I are keeping our fingers crossed."

A rumbling roar came from outside the front door.

"What is that infernal racket?" Jenny asked.

"That's Mitch," Meg said, shaking her head. "He and his buddies are back from their joyride." She popped her head through the doorway and shouted into the living room. "Dan, tell Mitch to keep it down, please."

Outside, Mitch and two of his friends were debating Mitch's future. Their argument was accompanied by incessant roaring as Mitch adjusted the throttle on his Kawasaki.

"Dude, life would be a lot sweeter if you would just dump that school you go to," said Ivan, a tall, shaggy-haired teen who looked a couple of years older than the other two. "You could surf all day and crash at my place in Santa Cruz at night. And every weekend—par-tee!" He grinned and swayed his hips.

"Yeah, life would be one big joyride," said Flea, a smaller one who stood holding Ivan's Honda as they talked.

Mitch looked up at the two of them. "And who's going to feed us? I hate school, but I've been going there long enough to know that somebody's gotta work. I turn eighteen in a couple of weeks. Then I can quit school, get a job, and get out of here. I hate living here, but I think I would hate starving worse."

Mitch looked at the bike handle and put down his screwdriver. "I think that's got it."

The front door opened behind the threesome. Without looking, Mitch knew it was his father.

"Mitch," Dan said loudly, then repeated a little louder. "Mitch!"

"What!" Mitch responded savagely over his shoulder.

"Would you mind revving those bikes somewhere else?" Dan said.

"Yeah, right," Mitch responded, more to his friends than to his father. "We were just leaving." He tossed his long black hair from one shoulder to the other.

"You just got here!" Dan said. "Dinner will be done in a few minutes."

"Well, Pop," Mitch said, grinning to his dad as he got back on his motorcycle, "you'll just have to enjoy it without me."

Dan stood in the doorway as the threesome roared off down the street. He paused for a long time, then shook his head and returned to the living room.

"I give up," he said, more to himself than to Jake. "I don't know how to get through to that kid anymore."

"Sometimes what it takes is time," Jake told him. "The Holy Spirit can do what no one else can do."

"Yeah, right," Dan said, hearing himself ironically imitating his teenage son.

* * * * *

Sometime later, the family, minus Mitch, sat down to the traditional meal. The Thanksgiving table was decorated festively, and Kris was quietly singing a little jingle to herself as they took their places. But Dan was feeling anything but festive. The conversation with Mitch had ushered him into a chasm of gloom, and as more time passed, the gloom darkened. Finally, Dan looked up and realized that everyone was looking at him, expecting him to lead out with the meal's blessing.

"What? Oh," he muttered. "Let's bow our heads." The others bowed, with a wisp of a smile on Meg's lips.

"Lord, we thank You for, er, something," he muttered, and then paused for a long time. "Oh, God, please forgive us for the mess we make of things sometimes." Dan choked on his words, and Meg jumped in.

"Lord, we thank You for the blessing You have given us this year. Thank You for life and health, for two happy, wonderful children, and for the promise of a future with You. Bless Jake and Jenny and their growing family. Please help this Thanksgiving meal to be but a shadow of another meal yet to come in heaven when we will all sit down together. In Christ's name, Amen."

"Amen."

A long, awkward silence followed the prayer, and then Meg spoke up.

"So who won the game?"

Jake looked over at Dan, who stared, red-faced at his empty plate. "Uh, it's not over yet. Third quarter, but Dallas is ahead 17 to 3." Jake looked over at Meg brightly, as if to change the subject. "I hear you're up for a promotion, Meg. Congratulations."

Meg shrugged as she passed the mashed potatoes. "Nothing's for certain. I hope it comes together. We should know about it by the end of next week."

"Yeah, a raise will come in real handy if I lose my job," Dan mumbled darkly in response.

"Lose your job?" Jenny gasped. "Why? What's happening over at the academy?"

Meg shook her head and held out her hands as if to calm invisible waters in front of her. "Nobody's losing their job," she said. "Dan's just overreacting again. The academy is having a tough time financially, and they're having a special constituency meeting on Sunday to take a look at their options. They've struggled before, and I'm sure the conference won't let them close their doors."

Jake and Jenny looked at Meg and Dan in surprise.

Meg chuckled, dishing up some green peas. "Besides, there is always a need for a biology teacher somewhere. You could teach public school."

Dan shook his head slowly. "I will not teach evolutionary theory, and you know I would have to do that if I went to the public school system."

"All right, all right," Meg said. "I'm sure it won't be necessary anyway. South Bay Academy isn't about to close its doors."

"Can we talk about something more positive?" Kris said, dropping her fork on her plate.

"Why sure, Kris," Jake said. "You were so quiet, we thought you were asleep."

"That's just because you adults talk too much," Kris responded.

"Kris, shame on you," Meg said.

"Relax," Jake said to Meg. "Kris knows she can say whatever she wants to her Uncle Jake." He wrapped his arm around Kris and leaned over to her. "Besides, you *are* going to tell me all about that new boyfriend of yours."

"Boyfriend!" Kris gasped, and Jake laughed. "I don't have a boyfriend," she said quickly. "He's just a guy I know at school."

The phone rang, and Dan got up to get it.

Kris poked Jake in the ribs. "You're a big tease, you know," she said.

"Me?" Jake said innocently. "Why I didn't even—"

"Jake," Dan said, interrupting. "It's a call from—from *Antarctica*."

Jake stood up and dropped his napkin on the table next to his plate. Reaching for the phone, he suddenly assumed his professional voice. "This is Dr. Gallagher."

Dan sat down at the table. "I didn't even know they have phones in Antarctica."

Kris snorted at him. "Sure, Dad. They have live Internet programs all the time with scientists down there. A few weeks ago, I got to ask one of them about the weather there."

Dan looked at Kris in surprise, then at Meg. "Did *you* know they had phone service?"

Meg looked back at him with a slight grin on her face and nodded.

"Well, I guess I'm just dumb."

"Maybe uninformed," Meg corrected him.

"An uninformed teacher is just as bad," Dan said, shaking his head.

Jake stood up and walked to the one side of the room with the cordless phone, listening to the voice on the line.

"Jake, if you don't get down here right away, you'll miss the big show." He could hear the squeak of the chair as Navy Commander Aaron Ridgeway leaned back and put his feet on his desk. Jake knew he was calling from the Antarctic base called McMurdo Station.

"Miss it? I thought we had another week," Jake said.

"Well, you know how these things go. The IRS is pushing real hard, so the brass got together with the executives at Enercorp and agreed that they could move it up. They are still getting resistance from some of the engineers who think it's too dangerous, and they want to get it over with. They're blasting tomorrow."

Jake's voice whistled. "There's no way I'm gonna make it down there by tomorrow, you know that. I'm just now having our Thanksgiving meal here in California."

"Yeah, I knew," Ridgeway chuckled. "I just had to call you up and rib you about it."

"Well, you'll just have to put Band-Aids on elbows without me," Jake said. "After all, you've got a doctor's shingle, too."

"Well, we'll miss you. See you next week."

"Not if I see you first." Jake hung up and turned to look at the others, who sat staring at him.

"What did I do?" he asked innocently.

"Well, you were kinda rude," Kris said.

"Aw, come on. Aaron and I went to med school together. That's how I got the assignment to Antarctica."

Jenny suddenly gasped, and the others looked at her.

Her eyes grew wide, and she got an embarrassed look on her face. "Just a kick, I guess," she said, holding her swollen abdomen.

"I guess Junior is telling us he's ready for pecan pie," Meg said.

"More likely, she's just as uncomfortable as I am to have Daddy so far away," Jenny said, looking up at Jake.

"Come on, Jenny," Jake said. "I'll be on a military base, and you'll be with your parents. Nothing bad is going to happen. Besides, you're as healthy as a horse." Jake stuck his spoon into the Jell-O. "I'm a doctor. I should know."

"Well, you being a doctor doesn't make me any more comfortable with the situation," she said.

"Six months from tomorrow, I'll receive my discharge papers, and we won't owe Uncle Sam any more," Jake said. "We can settle down in Illinois, California, or wherever you want."

Jenny muttered a reply so quiet no one else could hear. She was far from relaxed about his trip to Antarctica. And from the activity going on in her womb, she guessed that their child wasn't happy about it either.

CHAPTER

a hundred and fifty channels, and nothing good on," Dan muttered to himself as he jabbed the remote again and again.

"Well, what do you expect at four-thirty in the morning," Meg said sleepily behind him. "What are you doing up?"

Dan shrugged and rubbed his belly. "Sweet potato pie doesn't go down as easily as it used to. I've been up for hours. I'm also worried about Mitch." He eyed her warily. "What's your excuse?"

Meg rubbed the sleep from her eyes. "I got up to help Jenny and Jake get ready to catch his flight. He's got to drive all the way up to Alameda to catch his plane."

Dan shook his head. "Why can't the military use the same timetable as everyone else, rather than leaving before the sun comes up?"

"Who knows," Meg answered, shuffling toward the kitchen. "By the way, don't forget the pastor will be here at six to pick you up."

"Six? Why?"

"Remember you promised to go out jogging with him?" Her voice came from the inside of the refrigerator, and she reappeared with a pitcher of orange juice. "Don't try to get out of this one. It will do you good to get some exercise."

"Yeah, yeah. Hey, I know this movie," Dan said, pausing on one of the channels. He watched for a moment before realizing that the people talking had no clothes on. "Oops, I guess I don't."

* * * * *

Alameda Naval Air Station appeared in early morning fog as Jake and Jenny pulled up in front of the guardhouse in their rental car. Jake was in his dress whites; the lieutenant commander's bars gleamed gold on his shoulders. Jake returned the marine's salute and handed him his orders. There was a long pause before the marine handed the papers back to Jake.

"That flight to Christchurch has been canceled, sir."

"Canceled?" Jake repeated.

"Yes, sir." The marine reached into the guardhouse and handed Jake an envelope. "The CO was expecting your arrival this morning and said to give you this. Said for you to catch a commercial flight out of SFO later this morning."

Jake tore open the envelope and looked at the orders inside, shaking his head the whole time. The change in orders made no sense, but he had been in the Navy long enough to realize that making no sense was business as usual, and it was the rare occasion when he would get any explanation at all.

"Very well," he said to the marine. He saluted, then drove the rental car forward to the turnaround point, and headed it toward the freeway and San Francisco International Airport.

"Looks like I'm headed south instead of west," he told Jenny. "Flight goes to Los Angeles, then Santiago, Chile."

"South?" Jenny asked. "But don't you *want* to go south to get to Antarctica?"

"Yeah, but all the U.S. military flights that go to Antarctica come through Christchurch, New Zealand," Jake explained.

"SOP, standard operating procedure."

"Then why are they sending you to Chile?" Jenny asked. Jake looked over at Jenny, and she rolled her eyes. "I know, it's the military, so don't ask."

* * * * *

"And you do this every day?" Dan asked Pastor Taylor, huffing and puffing as he struggled to keep up with him.

"Well, I try to," Pastor Taylor said, turning while he jogged in place at a stoplight. "Other things sometimes take priority, but I try to get some exercise in every day—except Sabbath, of course."

"Of course," Dan agreed weakly as he leaned forward and tried not to throw up.

"Look, Dan, this is your first day out in . . . how long did you say?"

"Too long," Dan gasped, sweat dripping from his forehead.

"I want to get you in shape, not lead you down the coronary path," the pastor said. "Let's just jog down here to the park, and then I want to talk to you about something anyway."

Uh, oh, Dan thought. *What did I do wrong now?* He struggled to follow the pastor the half block to the little neighborhood park. Finally the two of them stretched out on the grass.

"Look, Dan," the pastor began, "the church membership is getting older and grayer, and the church board wants to do what it can to get younger people involved in positions of leadership. They asked me to prepare a very short list of members whom I would recommend to add to the board of elders.

"I would like for you to be one of our elders, Dan." The pastor put his hand on Dan's shoulder, and a jolt of electricity went through Dan. *No*, he thought, *not me*.

"I'm honored, pastor, but I can't. I'm not the kind of person that you are looking for. I am still struggling with a lot of things in my life." Dan felt a lump in his throat.

"We are all struggling, Dan," the pastor responded. "The Bible says 'He who says he is without sin is a liar.' I have struggles every day. We don't need elders who are sinless. If that were the case, I wouldn't be able to find anyone to fill the position. What we are looking for are members who are serious about following Jesus Christ, and helping others find their way in a closer walk with Him. You *are* serious about following Jesus, aren't you?" The pastor's eyes bore into Dan's.

Dan stared at the pastor in silence for a moment, then nodded.

* * * * *

In Antarctica, Commander Aaron Ridgeway directed two orderlies who were setting up extra beds in the infirmary at McMurdo Station. A blast of cold air hit them as someone dressed in a parka burst into the room from outside.

"Twelve degrees out there," the man said. "Looks like we're in for a heat wave." Ridgeway recognized the newcomer as Avery Briggs, an executive with Enercorp.

"Speaking of heat waves, Briggs," Ridgeway said. "How is it going over there?"

Briggs shrugged. "Twenty minutes ago they had it unloaded and armed. They have the scaffolding already up on Mount Erebus. It should be ready to go off on schedule."

One of the two orderlies shook his head. "I really don't like the idea of us messing around with nukes, sir, even if it is a little one."

"Look, orderly," Briggs said, taking in a deep breath. "This experiment is important. If it works, it will mean the U.S. will have to depend a lot less on foreign oil, and the IRS won't have to stick it to you in more taxes. You'd like that, wouldn't you? I know I would." Briggs grinned.

"Anyway, don't sweat it. It's a shaped charge, so it will only explode downward. We have the device in a hole almost a mile down. When it blows, we'll hear a rumble and that's it. We've been preparing for this day for five years. Believe me, we know what we're doing."

"That's not what those engineers who flew out of here yesterday were saying," the orderly responded. "They said we were in way over our heads."

"Those three were just upset because they got fired," Briggs said.

Ridgeway nodded. "Briggs is right. We should have about twenty seconds of rumble, and then it will all be under control."

"The government wants this to work, real bad," Briggs added. "And what the government wants . . ."

The orderly looked at Briggs and Commander Ridgeway, then at the clock. "In any case, it should be over in a few seconds."

The four men silently watched the sweep-second hand of the infirmary clock creep up to the 12:00. When it was straight up, they held their breath. Silence.

About five seconds later, the floor began to rumble below them. Ridgeway felt it rather than heard it.

"Twelve, thirteen, fourteen, fifteen . . ." he heard the orderly count. His counting went to thirty, and he stopped. He never reached thirty-one.

A brilliant light like a strobe flashed through the windows on all sides. The men collapsed to their knees and covered their eyes. If they had been outside the building, they would have been instantly blinded.

"What . . . what . . ." Aaron Ridgeway was able to get out before a blast of steam and gas totally flattened the infirmary, the building it was in, and the entire facility known as McMurdo Station. Mount Erebus had exploded sideways, taking with it everyone and everything from the South Pole to Cape Adare, 500 miles away.

The boom was heard as far away as Sydney, Australia and Buenos Aires, Argentina. It was so loud in South Africa that the military was put on full alert, afraid that some new weapon was being tested in a neighboring country.

The blast melted snow and ice for hundreds of miles, then within seconds turned it into steam. The Ross Ice Shelf, hundreds of miles across and thousands of feet thick, exploded into flying icebergs; then it melted, turned to steam, and became a boiling cauldron. The frozen ground throughout that half of Antarctica thawed rapidly, in some places for the first time since Creation. With the permanent ice pack gone, much of the exposed ground was below sea level, and hot ocean water roared inland for hundreds of miles. At the same time, a wall of water 150 feet high roared northward from the ice pack.

On the entire Pacific side of the continent known as Antarctica, the only human beings to survive were on a Norwegian cruise ship that were just embarking for Melbourne, Australia. They survived because they had just turned past Cape Adare and were shadowed from the blast of Mount Erebus by another volcano. They fled for their lives, their radio useless because of the electromagnetic interference caused by the blast. By the time they arrived in port, more than a hundred tourists and crewmembers would be hospitalized for second- and third-degree burns, and the world would know of the most cataclysmic disaster in modern history.

* * * * *

"So you're a doctor, huh?" Jake looked up from his *Newsweek* magazine at the young businessman sitting two airplane seats away.

He shrugged. "That's what my diploma from med school tells me," he replied. Jake looked at the well-dressed man, obviously in great shape and used to the outdoors. "I'm Jake. What do you do?"

"Name's Max. I'm an engineer," he replied with a grin.

"What kind?"

"Bridges," Max answered. "That's why I'm going down to Chile. They've hired our firm to build a suspension bridge down there."

"Sounds fascinating," Jake said. "Say, you'd be probably interested in the project I'm going down to Antarctica for."

"*Antarctica*. And I thought *I* traveled to exotic places."

"Yeah, well, it's my first time out of the U.S." Jake explained. "The Navy is providing support for the Enercorp Corporation on a thermal energy project down there."

"Yeah, Enercorp, good company," the engineer said. "I designed some offshore oil rigs for them a few years ago. But I didn't know they were involved with thermal energy."

Jake shrugged. "Well, this is something experimental. They are doing it in Antarctica for the first time in case anything goes wrong."

"Well, what is it?"

Jake started to reply, but the "fasten-seat-belt" sign came on above them. He reached for his seat belt, but before he was able to latch it, he felt the airplane drop beneath him. The refreshment cart six rows ahead of them suddenly banged into one of the seats, and both flight attendants lost their balance and fell into the laps of passengers.

"Relax, ladies and gentlemen, it's only some unexpected turbulence," one of the attendants said loudly to the passengers.

A moment later, the pilot's voice came over the intercom. "Ladies and gentlemen, I regret to inform you that I have been ordered to turn our flight around and return to Los Angeles. I know that all of you have very important reasons for getting to Santiago as soon as possible, but apparently there has been a disaster there."

The crowd of passengers gasped.

"A tsunami—a wall of water more than a hundred feet high—has hit the coast of Chile, making our flight to Santiago impossible at this time. The tidal wave was caused apparently by a major seismic event in Antarctica."

Jake heard soft crying beginning around him. *Poor Aaron,* he thought with a surge of emotion. *I was supposed to be there with you.*

The pilot's voice continued overhead. "Reports are very preliminary, and the authorities are not releasing too much information at this time. But for those of you who have family or friends in Chile, it's important that we not overreact. We don't yet know how extensive the damage is. Those who wish can use their headphones to access CNN to hear more information about this crisis. Apparently the damage was not limited to the coast of South America.

"In the meantime, it would not be inappropriate for everyone to lift up their thoughts in prayer in their own way at this time."

"I wonder if we can see the wave from here," a young boy said as he looked out the window.

"Kid, we're too far up to see anything," answered an older man. "Remember we are at thirty-five thousand feet."

"We couldn't see anything even if we were at one hundred feet," Max said aloud. "Tsunamis in the open ocean look just like any other swell. It's just when they hit land that they look and act differently. And you never know exactly where they will hit. They are unpredictable—and deadly."

"It's a curse from God, that's what it is," a woman a few rows behind him said.

The blue water below them looked harmless enough to Jake, but he knew that somewhere in that ocean was a force of nature which had already killed thousands and continued to roar northward.

What other port cities will the tsunami head for? Jake thought. How far would the devastation—and death toll—extend?

CHAPTER

Yes, operator, I'll accept the charges," Jenny said into the Lewis's kitchen phone. Then before the operator had time to say "Go ahead," she was urgently shouting into the phone. "Jake, where are you?"

"I'm at LAX," Jake responded from the crowded ticket area. He plugged his left ear with his finger to hear well. "They turned us around before we got to Santiago. Something about a tidal wave."

"Oh, I've been so worried about you!" Jenny exclaimed. "I'm so glad you're safe. Praise the Lord!" She sat down on a kitchen chair while she talked. "So I assume you've heard all about the disasters in the Pacific."

"Disasters? No, all I really know is what I heard on the plane about the coast of Chile, and that wasn't much. This whole place is in a panic. Planes have been rerouted and canceled all over. I tried to find a TV to catch the news, but the crowds here are incredible. I had to wait an hour to get a pay phone."

"Oh, thanks so much for calling and letting me know you are all right."

"Did you think I would do anything else?" Jake said, grinning. "I did try to call the local base here and find out where

I'm supposed to go, since Antarctica is out of the question, but they are in a state of confusion, too." He paused. "What *did* happen in Antarctica?"

"You don't know?" Jenny asked. "CNN says that a volcano down there blew up. It wiped out half of Antarctica and melted all the snow and ice. Jake, listen to me. McMurdo Station is destroyed. Thousands of people were killed, including Aaron."

"Yeah, somehow I knew he was gone," Jake mumbled sadly. "But wait. You said all the snow and ice were melted? That would explain the tsunami, the tidal wave. But you said the south Pacific. Where else did it hit?"

"It hit Tasmania and New Zealand pretty hard. Hobart, Tasmania, and Christchurch were devastated. It hit Fiji and some other islands, and the coast of Mexico around Acapulco. Some earthquakes also hit Peru and Mexico. But they said the whole thing's not done yet."

"Have they checked for survivors at McMurdo Station?" Jake asked.

"No, the eruption shut out all phone and radio service to Antarctica. Normally, rescue crews would come from New Zealand or Chile."

"But those countries are already up to their necks in disaster," Jake thought aloud.

"So where to now?" Jenny asked. "Are you coming home?"

Jake exhaled. "I wish I could, honey. But that's not how the Navy works. I think I will check in at the base in Long Beach. Within a day or two, they should have orders for me. Most likely, they will send me on to Antarctica. They are going to need surgeons for the rescue efforts down there."

"Well, you let me know where you end up just as soon as you get to wherever it is," Jenny said. "I love you."

"I love you, too. Say Hi to your mom and dad for me when you get to Chicago Sunday."

Jenny hung up the phone and folded her arms, hugging herself as she thought how far away the man that she loved was, and how close he had come to being killed. If he had taken the flight to Christchurch, he could have been there when the tidal wave crushed the city. She was still caught up in her reverie when Kris came around the kitchen corner.

"All done with the phone?" Kris asked as she bit into an apple.

Jenny nodded. "That was your Uncle Jake. He's in Los Angeles."

Kris's eyes got big. "Is he back from Antarctica already?"

"He never got there. They turned his plane around before he even got to South America."

"That's too bad," Kris said over her shoulder as she switched on the TV set. "I was hoping he saw the volcano blow up. That would be cool." She switched on the Web interface on the TV, and soon she was scanning through first-hand descriptions of the devastation in New Zealand and Australia. She tried to contact someone in Fiji but couldn't get through. When she tried Chile, she realized that all the reports were in Spanish. Switching to CNN Online, she read for a little longer before returning to her usual chat room.

The discussion centered on only one thing. She lurked in one discussion and read what others had to say, mostly rumor and speculation. Then she saw one discussion between two chatters that interested her.

Fin: I have family in New Zealand. I've been trying to reach them since all this started. The phones are all shut down. No calls in or out.

Marquee: Family? Brothers? Sisters? Parents?

Fin: An aunt and uncle, and my grandparents. And three cousins. They were in Dunedin, south of Christchurch. Don't suppose there's much hope for them now.

Marquee: I heard the wave that hit the coast was over a hundred feet high.

Fin: I didn't need to hear that. I hope they are all right. How could this happen? Where is the loving God people talk about when thousands of innocent people are killed?

Marquee: He must be angry with us. He's punishing us for our evil ways.

Kris couldn't stand it anymore. She typed in her response:

Kitkat: That's silly; just read Matthew 24. Jesus is coming again.

Then she pressed Enter and switched the TV computer off.

* * * * *

The talk at the Lewises' church the next Sabbath started and ended with the disaster in Antarctica. Some members were convinced that the world would end within a few days. Others scoffed, apparently thinking that they knew more than anyone else did.

"There's a specific eschatological protocol that God has to follow," said Dr. Greene, a dentist who led a Sabbath-morning Bible study class and seemed to have an opinion on everything. Dan and Meg were members of his class. "Things have to happen in a particular order. God is a God of order, and he has told us exactly how things will happen. We who have studied the Scriptures won't be caught napping, I assure you."

So you have an inside track on prophecy, Dan thought to himself, watching the well-dressed dentist lead on. *Good for you.*

"It's a sign of the times, I tell you," an older member added, shaking her head. "I give the world two years at the most before Jesus comes."

"Maybe," Meg said. "But we've had disasters before. What makes this one any different?" She looked around the Bible study group. "If this is a sign of the end, I sure don't see anyone doing anything differently."

The older member didn't have a reply for that, but sat back in her seat, perhaps thinking of things in her own life she had not yet resolved.

Seated in the back row, Dan looked at the class and thought about the church's congregation. He could probably go back five years and, except for the large number of young people who had left, could see the same people sitting in the same pews. Then he looked at Meg sitting next to him in her sharp blue outfit. Meg was her usual eloquent self, always seeming to have the right words to say, sympathetic for those who seemed to need it, professional for others who wanted a cordial, distant relationship. *She is so together*, Dan thought to himself. *She should have been asked to be an elder, not me.*

Later, he was still wondering if he had given the pastor the right answer when Pastor Taylor approached him between Sabbath School and church service.

"Are you ready?" he asked simply.

Dan's eyebrows went up. "Ready for what?" Inside, he somehow knew what the pastor was leading up to.

"Your ordination as an elder. I'd like to get it done during church service today."

"Today!" Dan almost yelped. "But doesn't it have to go to church board or something?"

Pastor Taylor grinned, his dark skin glowing with an almost halo effect. "I talked to them before I talked to you. You're signed, sealed, and now I want to deliver you."

Dan stared at Pastor Taylor for a long time. "I feel I'm the victim of some conspiracy. What do I have to do?"

Just before the sermon, Pastor Taylor called Dan forward to the base of the church platform, then called the other elders forward. One woman in her sixties and four men at least seventy years old walked slowly forward. Last to come up was Jonathan Eastham, a retired minister who had served the church as head elder for the past fifteen years. Dan thought about the fights and squabbles that had battered the local congregation over the past few years. Would this church still be here if Elder Eastham had not used his dedication and compassion to hold the congregation together? He watched the frail man in his eighties move forward, rolling the oxygen bottle he had recently started depending on. Even now, he would not accept help in coming to the front. *Strong in spirit, frail in body*, Dan thought. The church waited in silent respect as Mr. Eastham came forward.

The pastor and the elders laid their hands on Dan, and Pastor Taylor said a prayer over him. Dan expected to somehow feel different after the laying on of hands, but all he felt was more responsible. He had prayed a lot between the time the pastor had asked him to serve and this morning. Now all he felt was more need of prayer.

Lord, you've led me to this place for a reason, Dan prayed silently as he sat down. *I don't think you'd put me here if you didn't think I could handle it. Help me handle it.*

The congregation seemed very pleased that Dan had been ordained. Meg patted him on the knee and winked at him. Dan looked down at the kids; Kris grinned at him and waved. Mitch stared straight ahead—*as usual*, Dan thought—but Dan thought he saw a bit of sadness in his face.

"The children of Israel had been delivered from Egypt," Pastor Taylor said as he began his sermon. "They had been led through the wilderness for forty years, led by a pillar of fire at night and a cloud to shade them in the daytime. They had been fed the food of heaven—manna—because the wilderness offered no food. As they came into the Promised Land, God delivered city after city into their hands. Now as they came to finally settle into the land of their ancestors, Joshua was faced with the prospect of leaving them. He was getting old, and he knew that he would die soon. So he called them together at Shechem.

"Joshua reminded them of how God had led them ever since he chose Abraham and led him out of Ur of the Chaldees. He reminded them of miracle after miracle that they had witnessed firsthand. Then he challenged them. We read in Joshua 24, beginning with verse 14:

" ' "Now fear the Lord and serve him with all faithfulness. Throw away the gods your forefathers worshiped beyond the River and in Egypt, and serve the Lord. But if serving the Lord seems undesirable to you, then choose for yourselves this day whom you will serve, whether the gods your forefathers served beyond the River, or the gods of the Amorites, in whose land you are living. But as for me and my household, we will serve the Lord." ' "

Pastor Taylor looked up and paraphrased the next passage: "The people answered, 'We won't forsake the Lord to worship other gods!' And Joshua put it to them again. 'What's it gonna be, people? Who do you choose?' And again the people said, 'We will serve the Lord.'

"And we see in verse 22: 'Then Joshua said, "You are witnesses against yourselves that you have chosen to serve the Lord." ' "

" ' "Now then," said Joshua, "throw away the foreign gods that are among you and yield your hearts to the Lord, the God of Israel." ' "

Pastor Taylor paused and cleared his throat, and Dan felt that the pastor was struggling to say something he thought was important.

"The Holy Scriptures were given to us because many of the instances and situations written here are identical to what we experience in our own lives. Just as it was in the days of the children of Israel, it's easy right now to go along with the program. It's easy to do what everyone else is doing. And sometimes we make promises to God without knowing how hard it might be to keep them.

"Joshua here is laying it on the line because he knew he only had a little time left. You know, none of us know how much time we have left. So if we have something important to do, it's important that we do it *today*.

"Tell your kids you love them *today*. Spend time with your spouse *today*. Make amends *today*. And most importantly—surrender yourself completely to Jesus Christ—*today. Today*, not tomorrow. For there may not *be* a tomorrow."

Pastor Taylor paused again, struggling to find the words that Dan could see were so important to him.

"I want to ask you to stand up, to say as the Israelites did, that you are willing to yield your heart to God; to say that you're willing to throw away all the old idols. But I don't want you to stand unless you really mean it—unless it is a commitment deep down in your bones. Israel answered Yes, but within a few years, they were worshipping idols again. And we can't afford idols anymore. There's no more room for God—and for idols."

Dan stood with the rest of the congregation, many he saw standing apparently out of habit, some with a look of sincerity on their faces. Dan knew that his life was a disaster, yet he sensed that God still saw some merit in him. *OK, God, here it is*, he prayed silently. *Fix my life.*

* * * * *

As Pastor Taylor was speaking in his church, Lt. Commander Jake Gallagher was being called to an emergency meeting in a briefing room at the Long Beach navy base. He entered and saw that the room was filled with navy doctors, including some that he recognized from seminars and places he had served. A rear admiral entered, and they all stood at attention.

"Be seated," the admiral said quietly.

"As of 0533 this morning local time, the Hawaiian Islands were hit by an earthquake that measured 7.7 on the Richter scale, followed by a tsunami estimated to be in excess of eighty feet."

The physicians sat as if hit in the face with cold water.

"Needless to say, the damage is significant, but it's too early to tell how extensive."

Jake tried to read some emotion in the admiral's face, but it could have been carved from stone.

"Some of you have wondered why we didn't have orders for you before this," the admiral continued. "This is why. We knew there was a strong possibility that the tsunami would hit Hawaii, and we wanted to see how much we would need your medical skills. It appears we will need all of you right away."

"Sir, what about Pearl?" someone asked from the back.

"Pearl Harbor was hit pretty hard, but because we knew the wave was coming, we moved most of the ships to the north side of the island. The greatest damage was in Waikiki, downtown Honolulu, among civilians, and on the big island, Hawaii. The Kona Coast was literally wiped clean."

The whispering disappeared.

"Is this the end of the damage, sir?" someone else asked.

The Admiral paused then shook his head. "We still have an active volcano there in Antarctica. And the quakes keep coming. I don't know when this will all end.

"One other thing. A couple of you have asked about bases in Antarctica. I realize they were hit hard, but we are taking care of them. Our priority here—your priority—is Hawaii. Each of you will receive specific orders before you board the plane this afternoon. Dismissed."

California, Antarctica—now Hawaii, Jake thought. *I hope Jenny can keep track of me.*

* * * * *

Dan carried a sense of foreboding into the special constituency meeting at South Bay Academy on Sunday. When he arrived, he realized he was not alone in his concerns. He saw the Bible teacher, Ira Greenhurst, talking to the principal, Alice Shaw, across the gymnasium. Both seemed animated. *They look as though they are afraid for their lives*, he thought.

chapter 3

He took a seat in the back row and watched Alice find her place at a table in the front. Also seated there were Anna Hawkins, the board chair; Hal Woolworth, the conference president; Leon Wallheim, the conference treasurer; and someone in a three-piece tweed suit he didn't recognize, but he assumed was from the local public school district.

Anna Hawkins opened the meeting with prayer, and Dan felt that you could cut the tension with a knife. Anna looked as though she hadn't slept all weekend, and then he realized that the same could be said for Alice and the conference treasurer and the president. Only the stranger looked relaxed.

"Since this promises to be a lengthy meeting," Anna said after the prayer. "I have asked our conference treasurer to begin by sharing the financial picture for the school. When the constituency has had an opportunity to ask questions, we will move on to the business at hand."

Elder Wallheim presented a bleak picture of the finances for South Bay Academy. Dan knew they were bad, but somehow they seemed much worse as he saw them in black and white.

"What it comes down to is this," Wallheim explained. "The majority of parents can't afford the tuition we charge and have depended on the church to help them pay for their children's schooling. The church can no longer afford to support the school. Tithes and offerings are way down, and we just don't have the money. For the past two years, the school has been required to invest more and more in its physical plant, in laboratory supplies and computers—a lot of it just to keep its accreditation. Now it is in a position where it can't even pay its bills. If this were my business instead of a school, I would have shut it down a long time ago."

The gymnasium rumbled with people talking, and Dan saw that individuals were already lining up at the microphone to ask questions. But no matter what question they asked, no matter what suggestion they made, the solution was beyond them. Finally, the line died down, and the board chairman took over again.

"We wanted everyone to see that we have exhausted all other options before we introduced our speaker." *Anna Hawkins' smile looks strained*, Dan thought. "Raymond Harrold is from the state Department of Education in Sacramento. He has a proposal for us that he feels we can live with."

The audience quieted down, each person eager to hear what he would propose. Raymond Harrold strode forward confidently.

"For many years, the California public school system has respected the educational system of the Seventh-day Adventist Church, and your commitment to excellence in education. But we realize that hard times are upon us—all of us.

"Quality education is a priority not only to Seventh-day Adventists, but to all the citizens of California," he said. "It is not in anyone's best interest to see this school close."

These words drew a few Amens and some applause from the audience.

"Therefore, we have set up a special fund for schools like yours to make it through hard financial times, and meet the expenses required to maintain your accreditation.

"We want you to succeed, and we will do everything in our power to make that happen."

Applause broke out through most of the audience, but a few shouted "No! No!" Dan wanted to be happy that there appeared to be a way out of this financial entanglement, but at the same time, a small voice was telling him something was wrong.

Mr. Harrold went on to explain that all bills in arrears would be paid and the physical plant would be upgraded, along with all the new equipment the school needed.

"We will even pay staff salaries as long as it takes for the school to get back on its feet," Mr. Harrold explained.

"What's the catch?" someone shouted from the audience.

"Thank you, Mr. Harrold," the board chair said, interrupting. *She sure looks nervous*, Dan thought. Raymond Harrold sat down at the table, and Anna Hawkins licked her lips before proceeding.

"There's not so much a *catch*, as there is an *accommodation*," she explained, choosing her words carefully. "In exchange for accepting help, we will be required to open our doors to any student who is willing to follow the rules and guidelines of the school, without any discrimination."

That's not so bad, Dan thought. *We pretty much do that now.*

"In addition, we will be able to continue with the curriculum that is unique to the Seventh-day Adventist educational system. But because we will have students from all backgrounds and walks of life, we need to have curricula that are sensitive to those differences."

Dan saw Pastor Taylor creeping forward to the microphone set up in the aisle.

"That sensitivity will not affect the way we teach Bible, or English, or Science," she said. "It will just add alternative viewpoints to class."

Pastor Taylor reached the microphone and tapped on it as if to get attention. "So you are saying that what we are teaching in Science or Bible now is just our viewpoint."

The board chairman looked nervously down at Raymond Harrold, who spoke. "The State of California serves people of all backgrounds, and thus must recognize the viewpoints of many different people."

"So how would this change, say, the way we teach Bible class?" Pastor Taylor asked. Dan had never seen Pastor Taylor angry, but he suspected he would soon.

"In addition to the Christian Protestant teaching about the Bible you normally present, and the specific Adventist doctrines, you would be required to equally present alternative viewpoints."

"Such as Catholic, Mormon, Jehovah's Witnesses," Pastor Taylor said.

"As well as Islamic, Buddhist, and atheist," Mr. Harrold added.

"Unacceptable!" Pastor Taylor said, red in the face. "I can't believe the school is even considering such nonsense."

The board chairman had the look of defeat on her face. "Pastor Taylor, we respect your opinion in this matter, and if there were any other way, we would follow it—gladly. But this looks like the only alternative open to this school."

The discussion went on heatedly for the rest of the day. Opponents of the proposal argued that this was against everything the school stood for. Advocates said that at least Adventist beliefs and doctrines would continue to be taught in the school, even though they were taught in conjunction with opposing beliefs. As the day wore on, and financial realities sank in, the advocates seemed to win more and more support. At 4:30 P.M., the chairman called for a secret ballot from the constituency.

Before the vote was counted, Dan knew what the result would be. As of tomorrow morning, he would be required to teach evolutionary theory in his classroom for the first time in his life.

CHAPTER

ey, what's going on?" Mitch asked Flea as they piled out of Ivan's VW van and looked out at the boardwalk area of Santa Cruz. Barricades were set up, blocking Bay Street ahead of them. Police tape crossed the sidewalk area. Black-and-white police cars were everywhere. A uniformed officer was directing traffic south, away from the beach.

"Haven't you heard, man? Where you been?" Ivan asked Mitch. "Monster waves, dude."

"Yeah, southern California looks like it got nuked," Flea yukked. "Waves came out of Antarctica and laid … them … low."

"Santa Barbara," Ivan said. "Twenty feet of water washed right downtown. Only thing that saved them was the Channel Islands."

"Yeah, Catalina Island is history," Flea said. "Wish I could've seen it."

"So they're expecting this tidal wave here?" Mitch asked.

Flea nodded. "One o'clock is the monster hour." He bumped fists with Ivan. "Scary to inlanders, but some mighty awesome surfing."

Ivan looked at the barricades and the police. "Capitola's

probably got just as many cops as this place. We need to find a place off the beaten path."

Flea thought for a minute, then snapped his fingers. "How about down Cliff Drive out beyond the lighthouse?"

Ivan looked at him skeptically. "Can you get us down to the beach?"

Flea grinned. "No prob, bro. Let's load up."

A few minutes later they followed the parade of cars south, away from the main beach at Santa Cruz and down past the lighthouse. They waited for a lull in the traffic and pulled out their surfboards. Flea started down the path at the edge of the cliff when they heard a voice behind them.

"Sorry, guys. All the beaches are closed. Tsunami warning."

Mitch turned to see a thirty-ish man about four inches taller than himself. He had long light-brown hair that curled almost in ringlets. He was dressed casually in a T-shirt and sweat pants, but carried an air of authority, as if he were used to being obeyed.

"Drop dead," Ivan said, and Flea continued down the trail.

"I guess you didn't hear me," the man said. He reached over and grabbed Flea by the shirt and pulled him and his surfboard back up onto the level surface. Mitch saw the stranger's muscular arms bulge.

Ivan swung his board at the man's head, but he ducked effortlessly and grabbed Ivan's hand, twisting it until Ivan yelped in pain.

"Now I don't want to break your wrist," the man said calmly. "But I will do it to keep you from breaking your neck down there." He stared at Ivan as if waiting for him to challenge him.

Ivan's eyes burned holes in the face of the stranger, and then he gestured toward the van. "Come on, Flea. Let's go."

* * * * *

Jenny waded through the crowd coming from her gate at O'Hare International Airport, her overnight bag in tow behind her, bumping into strangers left and right. She looked for a long time before she saw a woman who had her good looks but a few more pounds and about twenty-five more years, waving to her through the sea of people.

"Hi, honey," her mom said, pushing through the crowd and giving her a hug. The years seemed to melt away, and Jenny felt as though she was a kid again, sharing a room with big sister Meg.

"How are you, Mom?" Jenny said, hugging her mother close.

"Just fine," said Mrs. Abbott, beaming at her younger daughter. She pushed away and looked down at her. "Just look at you! You're already showing! And you've got that glow of someone expecting. How far along are you, now?"

"Four months," Jenny responded, knowing that her mother already knew the answer.

"Four months," Mrs. Abbott repeated. "And that vagabond husband of yours is nowhere in sight. Where is he now?" They walked together to the moving walkway, following the rest of the crowd toward the baggage claim area.

"Last I heard, he was in southern California. But he thought they might go ahead and send him down to Antarctica."

Mrs. Abbott clucked her tongue. "Imagine, him leaving you alone at a time like this. It's not right."

Jenny smiled at her mom. "But he didn't leave me alone. He left me with you."

Mrs. Abbott stared at her, then looked down, apparently a little embarrassed. "I guess I have no room to criticize. Your dad spent ten years in the Marines, then the past twenty years on the police force. I had gotten so used to being alone with you kids. You'd think it would make me more understanding, but all it does is make me more mad."

They continued talking about family as they waited for Jenny's bag to come off the conveyor belt. Jenny told of their Thanksgiving with Meg and Dan, while her mom told Jenny of spending the holidays mostly alone while her father worked a double shift as a police detective.

"It's the same old story," Jenny said. "Daddy's been working extra hours as long as I can remember."

"He's always wanted the best for you kids," Mrs. Abbott responded. "That takes money, and money means more work."

"Sometimes the best is less money and more time," Jenny corrected her.

"Your dad did what he did because he loved you both." Mrs. Abbott sighed. "But you're right. I'm hoping that one of the changes at home will keep him around more often."

"What?" Jenny asked, her eyebrows arching in curiosity.

"We have someone else living with us now. We agreed to take care of your cousin Hank's son, Benji, while Hank is in the hospital."

Jenny squinted and tried to remember. "Hank. That's the cousin who lives in Baltimore?"

Mrs. Abbott nodded. "You haven't seen him since you were little. You used to play so well together. Now he's fallen on some rough times. Got divorced, spent some time in jail, and then got in a car accident. Benji's thirteen. He's a handful, but I think deep down he's a good kid."

As they left O'Hare and got on the Tri-State Tollway headed south, Jenny mused silently on Mrs. Abbott's harmless description of Benji. Something gave Jenny a sense of foreboding, and she wondered if she had done the right thing in coming to Illinois.

Jake, she thought. *I wish you were here with me.*

* * * * *

"There he is," Ginger whispered to Kris harshly at school on Monday. They stood outside the administration office, two freshman girls ogling a cluster of sophomore boys. Kris saw only one boy—Brad—and he had all of her attention. *It's now or never*, Kris thought.

"It's now or never," Ginger said. She looked over at Kris, who felt as though she was withering inside.

You can do this, Kris told herself, and stepped forward, her arms full of schoolbooks. She stepped forward across the crowded hallway, just as two boys came charging down the hall, laughing. One brushed her arm roughly, and her books went flying in all directions.

"Oh!" she cried, and wished she could bury herself beneath the floor tiles. Without looking up at the boys who were laughing at her, she bent down and tried to gather the books together. She reached for the last book, and a boy's hand grabbed it first. Brad held it out to her.

"Looks like you could use a hand," he said.

* * * * *

The projector clicked, and a slide showing an aerial view of the South American jungle appeared before the biology class.

"This is the Amazon rain forest," Dan said aloud from the back of the darkened classroom. "A few years ago, it made up 14 percent of the earth's land surface. Now that's dropped to 6 percent."

A slide appeared, showing huge trucks and workers on barren land, with fires raging in the background.

"Approximately two hundred thousand acres of forest are burned every day—that's 150 acres a minute," Dan explained. "At the present rate, the last rain forest acreage will be consumed in less than forty years."

The next slide showed a tornado ripping through the Midwest.

"Environmentalists have been predicting for years that our freaky weather will grow more and more unpredictable as the world's ecosystem is destroyed—through greed. We need the rain forest, but not just because of the effect it has on the world's weather. Not because of all the animals that will be thrown out of a habitat without it."

The projector showed a man hanging upside down from ropes high in a tree.

"The rain forest is the source of a large portion of the medicines and antibiotics we use today. Quinine for malaria, muscle relaxants, steroids, and anti-cancer drugs all originate in the rain forest. In the future, should the rain forest survive, we may find the answer to AIDS, cancer, diabetes, arthritis, or Alzheimer's among the indigenous plants we are so intent on destroying today."

Dan brought up the lights in the classroom, and spent the rest of the period answering questions from the students. He was in his element talking about plants, and to his relief, none of the questions dealt with evolution. A few questions did deal with the meeting the day before and what would happen to the school.

When lunchtime came for Dan, he headed for the staff lounge, where he opened up his sack lunch and made his usual call to Meg. This time, she was not in her office. Dan left a message on her voice mail and hung up. He was just finishing his lunch when Meg returned his call.

"Sorry I wasn't here," she said breathlessly. "I've been in meetings all morning and just now got back to my desk."

"So it's pretty busy over there," Dan said. "Any more news on the promotion?"

"Yes, in fact, that's a lot of what the meetings were about," Meg said cheerfully. "The boss likes me, I mean, *really* likes me, and as soon as he can get together with the board chairman, he will seal the deal."

"I hope that his liking you is more of a *platonic* like," Dan said wryly.

Meg chuckled. "You don't have anything to worry about, Dan. You're still my man."

Dan laughed then. "Good. Keep it that way."

"What about the changes over there?" Meg asked. "How is everyone taking it?"

"It's like working in a funeral home," Dan responded. "Ira Greenhurst has already told me that he will resign before he turns his Bible doctrines class into a comparative religion class. It's ludicrous. So far, there hasn't been anyone over here enforcing the new system. We'll have to see what happens."

"And what will you do if they insist that you teach evolution?" Meg asked.

"I … I will just have to cross that bridge when I get to it," Dan said.

* * * * *

Pastor Taylor locked the church door behind the last member as Wednesday-night prayer meeting came to a close.

"Goodnight," he said to an elderly woman named Mrs. Carr as he showed her to her car.

"Goodnight, Pastor," the woman said. She closed the door of her old Mercury and pushed the door lock down. *You can't feel safe even in a church parking lot these days*, the pastor thought to himself. A cloud of black despair seemed to hover just above his head. He stood in the darkness and watched the last car disappear down Rincon Avenue.

"Lord," he prayed aloud. "I'm so tired."

He looked down at his big dark hands, his light palms shining in the moonlight. Those hands had dedicated babies, baptized hundreds of souls into the fellowship of believers, and tossed dirt on the coffins of many of the members of his congregation. Now they shook when he looked at them.

"Lord, I have done everything You have asked. Ever since I surrendered my life to You, I have had one adventure after another—some good, some bad. I miss my loving wife, Lord. I long for the day when You will take us all home. And I know it is not far away.

"Lord, I feel I am near the end here. I feel you are telling me to say goodbye to these people. But why? What work could you have for me that I couldn't accomplish where I am?" Pastor Taylor stopped and listened, as if he were waiting for God's audible reply.

Instead he heard a woman's scream.

He looked up and realized that it came from the darkness behind the church. He dropped his briefcase and ran around the corner to where the scream had come from. Two men stood over a young woman on the ground. One watched while the other shoved her down and attempted to tear her blouse off.

"Please … please don't," the young woman begged.

The smaller man looked up as Pastor Taylor approached, but the other, tall, thin man was unaware he was coming.

"Let her go!" Pastor Taylor shouted without slowing down his stride. As the larger man looked up, Pastor Taylor plowed into him, knocking both of them into the gravel a few feet from the young woman. The rapist got up first and started to get away, but Pastor Taylor grabbed him by the lapels and looked at his face.

"I know you," he said in surprise. "You're—"

The pastor's words were cut off as the smaller man plunged a knife into the pastor's side. Pastor Taylor froze as the pain overwhelmed him, and he felt the strength leave his legs.

As he collapsed to his knees, he heard the smaller man say to the larger: "Come on, let's get out of here."

Pastor Taylor watched them run down an alley and turned his face to see if the young woman was all right. She had vanished as well. He looked up at the bleached face of the full moon, and at that moment, knew that he was going to die.

CHAPTER

The news of Pastor Taylor's death came to Dan early the next morning as he was getting dressed for work. Elder Eastham called him from the police station, where he had spent most of the night. Dan didn't even ask why the head elder hadn't asked for help; the word *help* was just not in Elder Eastham's vocabulary.

Elder Eastham explained to Dan what had happened the night before, but the shock of the news made it necessary for him to repeat his story. It wasn't until Dan hung up the phone that reality began to sink in. *Pastor Taylor—my friend—dead! Killed. Murdered.*

He looked around at the empty room and realized that once again Meg was long gone. Seven-fifteen. She would be finishing up her exercise routine and getting dressed, ready for another day with the high rollers. How he wished he could talk to her. He thought back to the way they were when they first got married. Inseparable. His first day at work after the honeymoon, he had called her as soon as he arrived at school. "Did you miss me?" he had asked, even though they had parted not ten minutes before. "Yes," she had answered truthfully. *She missed me.* Now he wondered how much she even thought about him during the day.

The dark cloud of gloom enveloped him as he stumbled through his morning's classes. Again he considered himself fortunate that the issue of evolution had not come up. He had the students spend the morning in biology lab cataloging poisonous, medicinal, and edible plants. It was the subject of his master's thesis, and he loved to discuss it. Over the years, he had earned the nickname "Professor Cattail." One of these days, he hoped to take one of his classes out into the wild and show them how valuable such knowledge could be.

At lunchtime, he was relieved to get his usual phone call from Meg. He felt a bit embarrassed, but dumped on her anyway, telling her of the pastor's death.

"I'm surprised you didn't hear anything about it on the news," Dan said.

"Well, I guess the death of a pastor doesn't make the news these days," Meg said coolly. "Too many other things are happening."

"Maybe so, but he was someone special to me," Dan said. "Remember he was the one who baptized both our kids."

"I remember," Meg said. "I didn't say he wouldn't be mourned. I just said he wasn't important to the news media."

There was an awkward silence, and then Meg spoke again. "I wonder how long it will be before the conference brings in a replacement pastor."

"I hadn't thought about it," Dan said. "Why?"

"It's just that I heard the IRS has been giving churches a hard time about their tax-free status. I would imagine the conference has its hands full right now."

"Where do you get all this information?" Dan asked.

"I listen to the news," Meg said glibly. "You should try it sometime."

"Well, how far are they going to let the IRS go?" Dan asked. "Isn't that what the Revolutionary War was about? Taxation without representation?"

"All I know is that you had better think twice before you do anything to jeopardize your job there at the academy. Tough times are ahead. Think about it."

Dan was already thinking about it. It didn't make him feel any better.

* * * * *

"Oh, look, Dad's home," Mrs. Abbott said as she steered her brown Buick off Ogden Avenue and into the driveway. Jenny notice that her father still drove the same light-blue Datsun pickup he had purchased in the late 1960s. Before she could finish with that thought, the screen door opened and her father appeared. To career criminals his bulldog looks might seem ferocious, but to Jenny and Meg, he was still just Daddy.

She threw open the car door and started to bolt for her father's arms, but her foot slipped on the icy driveway. She almost tumbled out the car door. Her mother reached out and grabbed her left arm, and before she could straighten up, her father was at her side.

"Oops," Jenny said, embarrassed. "Guess I can't hurry out here."

"You forget it gets cold and icy here in Illinois," Mr. Abbott said in a scolding tone as he reached out a brawny arm. "It's wintertime, girl, and you have to protect two people, not just one."

"Yes, Daddy," Jenny said, looking down and taking on the tone of a little girl. Then she grinned and threw her arms up around her father's neck.

"Ooh, it's so-o-o good to be home," Jenny said amidst the prolonged hug.

"Let me go now," Mr. Abbott said, embarrassed. "I got to get your bag."

Mrs. Abbott led Jenny into the house, with Mr. Abbott following behind. Jenny noticed that the house had been painted, but wrinkled her nose when she saw that it still had the same dark wallpaper and ugly green shag carpet that she remember from years ago.

"You must be tired from traveling," Mrs. Abbott said. "Why don't you rest for a few minutes while I get dinner on. We're putting you in Benji's room and moving him into the den. Benji?"

Mrs. Abbott looked down the hallway expectantly, but there was no response. Jenny could hear heavy-metal music playing, muffled through the closed door of her old bedroom. She followed her mom to the door.

"Benji!" Mrs. Abbott repeated, knocking on the door. There was still no response. Mrs. Abbott cracked the door and peeked in. Benji lay on his bed, his head inches away from the speakers of his CD boombox. The freckled, red-haired boy sat up in surprise when he saw that the door was open. Jenny thought she saw an instant of rage behind his eyes, but an instant later the boy quickly recovered and smiled shyly at Jenny and Mrs. Abbott.

"Aren't you afraid of ruining your hearing doing that?" Mrs. Abbott asked him.

Benji stared at them blankly for a long moment, then shook his head. "My dad lets me do it all the time."

Mrs. Abbott sighed. "Your Uncle Bill was supposed to help you get moved into the den. I guess he didn't do it, did he?"

Benji shook his head again. "No, Aunt Sylvia." Benji looked at Mrs. Abbott, then at Jenny. His wide blue eyes looked innocent and appealing on the surface, but Jenny felt an inexplicable rush of fear wash over her as she looked at him. *That's nonsense*, she told herself. *You were thirteen once.*

Mrs. Abbott helped Benji move some items out of his room, clearing out the top two dresser drawers. Mr. Abbott brought Jenny's suitcase in and laid it on top of the dresser.

"Thanks, Daddy," Jenny said. "I can take it from there." Mr. Abbott unzipped the suitcase and left the room. Jenny reached into her suitcase and pulled some clothing out. She opened the top drawer of the dresser and started to drop the clothes into the drawer, then paused. She recognized the dresser as the one she and Meg had shared when they were children. Smiling to herself, she let go of the clothes and reached into the space above the top drawer. For years, she and Meg had hidden messages in the secret space that only they knew existed inside the top of the dresser. Would she find some of her old messages still hidden there?

She felt some papers folded there, and she pulled them out. What she found was not what she expected, however.

Jenny held in her hands the most obscene photos she had ever seen. In addition to the nudity on the pages, the people performed hideous acts she couldn't even imagine were possible. In addition, she noticed that the eyes had been burned out on all the people as if a hot match had touched the images. At the bottom of one page, an obscene phrase had been written there in what looked like a child's handwriting.

She assumed Benji was responsible for these photos. But what did she really know? After all, she had just arrived.

What should I do? she thought.

* * * * *

Jake threw his bags down on his bed and sighed. It seemed as though he had been traveling constantly for days. Then he chuckled. With the exception of the few hours he slept on a cot in Long Beach, he had been. At least he had a place now where he could hang his hat.

He reached for the phone and dialed the number for his in-laws in Illinois.

A few seconds later, he recognized Mrs. Abbott's voice.

"Hey, Ma," Jake said, smiling to himself. She hated that name.

"Hey, yourself, world traveler. When are you going to settle down and make that wife of yours a real home?"

"When the navy lets me," Jake said, laughing. "Is my wife there?"

"Yes, just a second," Mrs. Abbott said. She left the receiver, and Jake could hear her calling for Jenny in the distance. Half a minute later, Jake recognized Jenny's voice, out of breath, but excited.

"Jake! Are you all right? Where are you? Antarctica?"

Jake laughed out loud. "Nope, guess again. I'll give you a hint. I'm about fifteen minutes away from where we spent our honeymoon."

"Hawaii! You're in Hawaii!" Jake had to hold the receiver away from his ear as Jenny almost shouted into it.

"Yeah, but it's not the place you remember," Jake said soberly. "A tidal wave hit Honolulu last Saturday and pretty much wiped out Pearl Harbor and the Waikiki area. I was assigned to a surgical team here. Guess where we will be operating."

"Castle?"

"Yup. The navy has taken over the medical center as a surgical center. I'm working with several people I knew at Loma Linda."

"Is Castle where you're staying?"

"Naah," Jake answered. "The barracks and officers' quarters were destroyed, so the navy has commandeered all the hotels in the area. I'm bunked in a fleabag place about halfway up the Pali. Most of the good hotels were destroyed in Waikiki, and they wanted us high enough that another tsunami wouldn't threaten us."

"Well, I'm glad you're safe," Jenny said. "I guess I can reach you through the navy there?"

"Navy facilities are swamped here," Jake answered. "It would be easier and quicker to reach me through Castle. Just leave a message. Anyway, how are *you* doing?" he asked.

Jenny tried to smile, and it came out a grimace. She started to tell Jake what she had discovered, then stopped. He could do nothing where he was, and she needed more information before she decided what needed to be done.

"Fine, I guess," she finally said. "Home isn't the same as I remember it. I wish I were with you."

"Well, I wish you were here too," Jake said. "But all this destruction means that disease will not be far behind. It would be way too dangerous for you to come and join me."

Be strong, Jenny told herself. "Maybe when things settle down, they will send you somewhere less dangerous, and I can join you."

Jake nodded. "If not, I will send for you as soon as I think it's safe here. In the meantime, be good, and take care of that child of ours."

* * * * *

Kris sat down on the bench outside the library, her favorite place for lunch, and opened her brown paper sack. She felt sorry for herself. Other kids were getting hot lunch—spaghetti today, her favorite—and she was sitting out here eating a peanut butter and jelly sandwich. She loved spaghetti. She hated peanut butter and jelly.

She held the sandwich in her right hand and frowned at it. But no matter how hard she concentrated, it still remained a PBJ sandwich. Then she thought she heard it talking to her.

"Can I share your bench with you?"

She raised her eyebrows in surprise, then looked up. Brad stood in front of her, tufts of his long blond hair falling into his eyes. *He looks like Leonardo DiCaprio*, she thought. Without waiting for her to say Yes, Brad sat down next to her.

"Is that a peanut butter and jelly sandwich?" he asked, pointing at the offending food she held in her hand.

She nodded blankly, sorry that she hadn't hidden it before he saw it.

"I have a cheese sandwich. Do you want to trade?"

She smiled at the thought and handed him the sandwich.

They ended up spending the entire lunchtime talking. Kris couldn't remember anything else that happened that day. She did remember that the walk from the bus stop to the house was like walking on pillows. She barely heard someone else in the house, and realized that Mitch was home early, putting some things in boxes in his room.

She went into Mom and Dad's bedroom—where she could have some privacy—and switched on the computer. Within a minute she was in her chat room looking for her friend Ginger. No Ginger.

She was about to leave the chat room area when she got a message from someone else.

Fin: Aren't you the one who suggested we read Matthew 24 the other day?

Kris looked at the computer screen suspiciously for a moment before she responded.

Kitkat: Yeah, so?
Fin: So my friend Marquee and I want to know if you have any more Bible passages about the end of the world. Do you?
Kitkat: Sure. I know lots of them. Why?
Fin: Would you be willing to meet us back here in two hours and discuss them with us?
Kitkat: Yeah, I'm just a kid, though. I'm not like a pastor or anything.
Fin: That's fine. Talk to you in two hours.

Kris scratched her head. *That's weird,* she thought. *Why didn't they just ask a pastor?*

* * * * *

The dark cloud of gloom that encompassed Dan did not go away. That afternoon Dan had a moment of panic when he returned to the teacher's lounge and found a note. *Your wife called*, it read. *Don't forget Mitch's birthday cake.*

Cake! Birthday! Dan's heart sank as he realized Mitch's eighteenth birthday had come without fanfare and he, the dutiful father, had overlooked it.

When his last class was over, he whipped onto Highway 17 and headed for home. There was a grocery store with a bakery on Camden Avenue not too far away. Mitch liked cheesecake; he'd see if he could pick one up there. A gift would have to wait, unless Mitch just wanted money.

Gloom, depression, guilt. The three emotions stalked Dan relentlessly as he collected the cake, a card, and fifty dollars in cash for his eighteen-year-old son. If relations with Mitch had been bad, this special birthday would not set things any better.

Dan pushed the front door open and was surprised when he realized how quiet the house was. No stereo blasting from Mitch's room.

"Mitch! Kris! Anybody home?" Dan carried the cheesecake and the card to the kitchen table, then turned and listened again. Nothing.

Suddenly Kris appeared from her doorway down the hall.

"Hi, Daddy," she said nonchalantly.

"Hi, Kitkat," Dan said. "Where's Mitch?"

"I think he went somewhere," she responded, sticking her head in the refrigerator. "He left a note over there." She gestured toward the area by the kitchen sink with her head.

Dan grabbed the note and started to read it. He walked across the kitchen to the living room couch and collapsed as he read, his heart beating heavily in his chest.

Mom and Dad,
I'm eighteen now. Legally I can take care of myself,

and you don't have any more say in what I do or say. I have decided to drop out of school and get a job in Santa Cruz. I will be staying with friends there.

Don't worry about me, I'll be fine. I just am tired of everybody telling me what to do. I have to find what's right for me. Maybe I'll be back home one of these days. Maybe not.

Mitch

Dan hardly heard the door when it opened and closed and Meg stepped into the room. *This whole day is a nightmare. It can't be real. Can it?*

"What do you have there?" Meg asked. "Where's Mitch?"

In response, Dan handed her the note. Meg scanned it quickly then read it again. Dan stared across the room.

"What's wrong?" Kris asked innocently.

"He's gone," Dan said quietly. "Mitch is gone."

"What?" Kris asked, her eyebrows going up.

"You did this," Meg said to Dan, crumbling the note in her hand. "You chased my baby away."

Dan said nothing, silently admitting his guilt.

"You and your legalistic view of everything," Meg spat at him. "He knew he could never live up to your expectations. So he left. It's all your fault!" Dan didn't look as Meg stomped out of the room and into their bedroom, slamming the door behind her.

Dan sat on the couch for a long, silent moment, then stood.

"Is she going to be all right?" Kris asked in a small voice.

"Yeah, Mom will be fine," Dan said, feeling very old. "Everyone will be just fine."

An hour later Dan pumped the energy from his body as he ran down the road, until it seemed there was no more to pump. His out-of-shape arms and legs cried for mercy, but Dan gave them none. He kept going.

His face was drawn into an angry, solid rock. Immovable.

Lined and craggy. He could not be hurt. Not anymore. A tear streaked across the side of his face as he ran. Then the tears came in a torrent.

Like a late-night movie, Dan replayed scenes in his mind; angry scenes with his son that he would give anything to erase.

"But I don't want to go to college," he heard Mitch say.

"You *are* going to college—case closed," he heard his own voice respond. "Without a college degree you are nothing."

He could hardly see as he ran on. Instead of the road, he saw the faces of Pastor Taylor and Mitch. He had lost a close friend and spiritual guide, as well as his only son, in one day.

"I would like for you to be one of our elders," Pastor Taylor's voice said. "You are serious about following Jesus, aren't you?"

Dan somehow made his way to the small playground where Pastor Taylor had asked him to become an elder just a few days before. It now seemed like years ago. He sat on the bench for some time before he broke into long, uncontrolled sobbing.

"Oh, God," he moaned finally. "I'm such a fool. But I can't live without Mitch. You've taken so much. What more do you want from me?"

"What do you have?" he heard a voice reply.

He wiped his face and looked up in surprise. "What?"

A well-dressed man sat on the swing, his dark skin shining, and the toes of his wing-tipped shoes carving lines in the sand beneath him. *He looks like a young Pastor Taylor*, he thought.

"What do you have to offer God?" he asked again. "He wants everything, you know."

Dan shook his head. "You don't understand—"

"What? That your pastor was killed and your son has decided to move away from home?"

Dan was taken aback. "Who *are* you?"

"Jim Taylor had a full and happy life. He had given his life to God, and it was up to God as to when it ended.

"And as for Mitch," the stranger continued. "Mitch is becoming a young man. You have taken him as far as you can.

Now he has to figure things out on his own."

"But he's ruining his life! What about college?" Dan asked, exasperated.

"What *about* college? Man, don't you see what's going on here? It's the conflict of the ages coming down to the final days. You either belong to God, or to the army of Satan. College won't do you much good when fire is falling from heaven."

"But—" Dan began, and then stopped. This whole discussion was ludicrous—talking to a total stranger about personal issues that he had no way of knowing about.

"All or nothing, Dan," he heard the man say. "All or nothing."

A strange thought crept into Dan's mind. *Maybe this person knows me better because he's more than just a stranger. No, this is insane.* He turned again to the man on the swing.

"Just who do—" Dan stopped in mid-sentence. The swing rocked back and forth, set in motion by an unseen force. Beneath it, the sand that had been grooved by the toe of the wing-tipped shoes was smooth, with no sign of footprints having disturbed it. And the swing was empty.

Dan sat all by himself in the playground. But for the first time in his life, he knew without a doubt that he was not alone.

CHAPTER

he funeral for Pastor Jim Taylor was held on Friday without fanfare. Dan was surprised at how few members of the congregation actually came. Dan had taken time off from the academy; they had given him a little resistance because Pastor Taylor was not a family member, but in the end they acceded. Dan wondered how many church members had even tried to get time off. He knew Meg hadn't, and he suspected that few others had tried.

Hal Woolworth, the conference president, was there from Modesto, and officiated at the graveside service. Fortunately, the weather remained clear and crisp. *Pastor Taylor would have enjoyed running on a day like today*, Dan thought. He noticed that Elder Eastham was there, even though, from the way he looked, Dan thought he should have stayed home. The strain of the past few days had been tough on him. Elder Woolworth looked as though he had been under a lot of strain as well. First, dealing with the academy. Now, losing the pastor of one of his churches. Maybe the IRS would be the next big problem.

When the service was officially over, everyone left the graveside except Dan, Elder Eastham, and Elder Woolworth. The three of them stood silently facing the graveside as if in communion over some unspoken mystery. *I wonder if this will be the last quiet moment we three have,* Dan wondered.

* * * * *

The sharp chords and screaming voices of Nine Inch Nails blasted from the stereo. Despite his joy at being away from home, Mitch had a headache. Crashing at Ivan's place in Santa Cruz was not the picnic he had envisioned. He had emptied his savings in San Jose for a grand total of $185.35, and half of that had already gone to stock the refrigerator here. Apparently, Ivan believed that providing free rent for Mitch also meant that Mitch should feed the three of them.

Mitch wasn't used to the late hours, the incessant noise, the constant stream of house guests (mostly girls), and the constant stream of profanity that now made up his environment. He kicked a crushed beer can across the room and sighed. Dad was a pain in the neck for sure. But he was beginning to miss sleeping in his own bed, eating home-cooked food, and having control over his environment.

He thought he knew Ivan and Flea. Now he realized that they had intentionally cleaned up their act because of the home environment he was from. With the Christian atmosphere gone, they reverted to behavior Mitch knew his father would call animalistic.

Mitch was drawn from his melancholy reverie by the shrill ringing of the phone. He started to call for Ivan or Flea to get it, then realized they were out. He hit the pause on the CD player remote and answered it.

"Hullo," he answered dully.

"Aloha, bro! Is this the guy they call Mitch?" The voice came across as cheerful, with a slight Hawaiian accent.

"Yes, this is he," Mitch answered, going to the voice he used with his parents' friends.

"I hear you be one bad surfer, bro."

chapter 6

Mitch shrugged. "I hold my own."

"Where you surfed?"

"Zuma, Morro Bay, Stinson. Locally, just about everywhere. Pleasure Point and Sewers are my favorite, I guess. Why?"

"I got a little surf shop in Capitola that's just getting started," the voice said. "Pipeline Surf. Ever hear of it?"

Mitch's heart skipped a beat. "Yeah, I think I went in there once."

"I'm looking for a reliable person to make deliveries and maybe rent out some boards, give local directions. That sort of thing. You interested?"

"Ye-yeah, sure."

"Good. You can start tomorrow. On the way in, do me a favor and pick up a package for me. Here's the address."

One of Mitch's favorite joys was riding his Kawasaki early in the morning, and he was especially happy as he putted east on Capitola Road. He had a job, and he was grateful that the tidal wave had missed the Santa Cruz area altogether. Business was bustling as usual, and he watched tourists, surfers, and beach bums go by.

He looked at the piece of paper on which he had written the address the man on the phone had given him. *2104 Opal Street.* He turned right on Opal, which was really just an alleyway, and followed it past some tiny bare-wood houses, places that were still affectionately know as *pads*, as they had been known in the fifties.

He saw a beat-up old Chevy Nomad, one that he was sure he had seen several times at the beach, and realized that this was the place. He parked his bike and went to the door, rapping on it twice. He could hear ZZ Top's "Sharp Dressed Man" playing in the background.

After a minute, a bearded, beer-bellied man answered the door. His eyes were bloodshot, as if he had just gotten up after a hard night.

"What do *you* want?" the man said, as if looking for an excuse to slug Mitch.

"I'm supposed to pick up a package for Pipeline Surf Shop," Mitch said weakly.

The man's eyes brightened a bit when Mitch mentioned the shop. "You must be new," he said as he turned away from the door and wandered back into the dark house. "Just a second," the man said from a distance.

The man returned with a brown bundle about the size of a loaf of bread. He started to drop it into Mitch's hands, then held it up for a second.

"You be careful with this stuff, kid," the man said hoarsely. "It's worth a lot of money."

Yeah, right, Mitch thought as he rode away with the package. *A guy who lives in a dump like that would have something worth a lot of money. Tell me another one.*

He started to pull out of the alleyway onto the main street when a pickup swerved in front of him. He jerked the handlebars to the right and hit a pothole, almost losing control of the bike.

"Watch it!" he yelled at the driver, and got a stream of swear words in response. He took off again, glad that he had used bungee cords to strap the package down.

It didn't take Mitch long to find the Pipeline Surf Shop in Capitola, and he pulled his bike into the small unpaved parking lot behind the store. He pounded on the door. When there was no answer, he realized that the store hadn't opened yet. He'd have to wait for the owner to show up.

He went back to his bike and unstrapped the package. He popped one of the bungees off. A white cloud of dust puffed up from the cord, and alarm bells went off in Mitch's head.

He took a closer look at the wrapping paper and noticed that white powder was leaking from one end of the wrapping. He ran his finger through the powder and rubbed his finger and thumb together, feeling its texture. *Heroin? Cocaine?*

He'd seen marijuana before, and despite his attempts at

liberation, he was uncomfortable being around drugs in any shape or form. He wasn't sure what this stuff was, but he knew he didn't want anything to do with it.

On the other hand, he needed this job badly.

It took him about half a second to make up his mind. Without realizing it, he reached a turning point in his life.

Strapping the package back on, he revved his bike up and took off in search of the nearest black-and-white.

Three blocks down, he found a patrol car parked in a mini-mall parking lot. He putted up to the car's open window and shut off his bike.

He unstrapped the package and handed it to the policeman, explaining what had happened and what his fears were.

The policeman put his coffee in a cup holder and took a good look at the white powder on the edge of the brown paper wrapping. Finally he took a little on his finger and tasted it.

"I don't know what it is, but it's not drugs," the policeman said. "I don't think you have anything to be worried about."

"What if they are just using this to test me and see if I am reliable as a courier?" Mitch asked.

The policeman laughed. "In that case, you just flunked their test, didn't you?" The policeman started up the patrol car's engine and drove away, laughing.

* * * * *

The day that Mitch turned eighteen and moved to Santa Cruz also marked a turning point in the marriage between Dan and Meg. After his encounter with the stranger in the play-ground, Dan had tried to make up with her, but to no avail. It was as if she were looking for an excuse to sever ties. They went through their usual routine over the next few days, but none of their conversation went beyond surface politeness, and there was no touching except what was absolutely necessary. He got up in the morning to find her gone; she arrived home when he had already gone to bed.

Dan almost expected her to beg out of going to church that Sabbath, but he got up and discovered that Meg was already fixing a big breakfast as if the conflict had never happened. The three of them arrived at Sabbath School a few minutes late and found quite a few cars in the parking lot.

"I wonder if we have a guest speaker this week," Meg said. "I haven't seen this many people here in a long time."

"I haven't heard of anything," Dan answered. "It might be someone the conference brought in since we don't have a pastor . . ." Dan's voice trailed off as the conversation led his thinking into an area where he wasn't comfortable.

They found a space in the back row. Kris went on to the earliteen division, while Meg and Dan walked into the adult class together.

Immediately Dan sensed that the atmosphere of the church was different. No one was at the door to greet them; the guest book stood open and alone. In fact, the lobby was empty.

Dan peeked through the small window on the door to the main sanctuary. "It's dark in there," he said. "Must be showing a video or something."

"Maybe the GC has a special satellite feed," Meg said. Dan shrugged in response and opened the door.

They stood against the back wall in the darkened sanctuary to let their eyes adjust. Dan stared at the screen that towered over the platform in front. On the screen was a man in a dark suit that he didn't recognize.

"I am especially grateful to the president of the world church of Seventh-day Adventists for the opportunity to respond directly to some of the rumors and allegations that have been coming to us from the news media and from concerned Seventh-day Adventist leaders."

"Who is this guy?" Dan whispered to Meg.

As he spoke, lettering at the bottom of the screen identified him as A. G. Hunsaker, assistant director of the U.S. Attorney

General's office.

"What's he doing on the ACN satellite feed?" Meg hissed back.

Hunsaker began speaking again, and the two listened intently.

"One week ago, the Internal Revenue Service, the Treasury Department and the Attorney General's office asked the General Conference of Seventh-day Adventists to make a voluntary freeze of all funds coming into or going out of the United States from the church's assets in other countries. This request was in response to a continued investigation as to the church's eligibility to maintain its non-taxable status here in the United States."

"Uh-oh," Meg said. "Here it comes."

"In the past week," Hunsaker continued, "the flow of assets out of the United States has not only continued, it has *increased* dramatically. Because of this, and the recent Supreme Court ruling that when church bodies are not in cooperation with government agencies they revoke all rights and are subject to fines, imprisonment, or confiscation of assets, we are putting a mandatory freeze on all assets of the Seventh-day Adventist Church. This includes all salaries and benefits of church employees, all bank accounts, and will eventually include all buildings, including schools, colleges and universities, clinics and hospitals, local church headquarters, and local congregational meeting places, as well as all material located within these premises."

An audible gasp escaped from every mouth in the congregation.

"We hope that this action will not be permanent. The investigation may take some time, however. How long the freeze is in place depends on how cooperative and forthcoming officials of the Seventh-day Adventist church are in the coming weeks.

"We wanted to mention this today, on your Sabbath, because we felt it was important to let everyone know up front what was going on. We will be in contact with your local pastor or church leader, as well as local law enforcement officers, in an effort to make the transition as smooth as possible."

"Transition?" Dan asked as the screen went blank and the lights came up. "Transition to what? They can't take over our schools and hospitals! They can't shut down our churches!"

"They just did," Meg said quietly.

Dan watched the whispering of the congregation turn into a dull roar as Elder Eastham moved to the front of the room. He stood before the microphone and called for quiet.

"Now it's important that we stay rational at a time like this," he said weakly.

"Rational!" one man said, standing up. "The government just shut the whole denomination down!"

"Now, that's not true," Elder Eastham said. "Ninety percent of Seventh-day Adventists live in other countries. The Internal Revenue Service can't touch them. We have nine division offices overseas. They will keep the church going during this down time."

"Down time!" the man repeated. "Ninety percent may live overseas, but most of their money comes from North America, and that's been cut off. How long will the church last without money?"

A woman stood. "I don't know about you, but I'm tired of all my money going overseas. What would keep the Adventists in North America from starting our own church here? Those church leaders overseas don't listen to what we have to say. So let's just take our wallets and purses and start an Adventist church for North Americans!"

"You're talking nonsense," Elder Eastham said. "I've dedicated my life to this church, and I won't give up on it now."

"We may be talking nonsense," the man said. "But you're not facing reality. There is no Seventh-day Adventist church anymore, at least in North America. I'm out of here." He pulled on his wife's sleeve, and she and their children walked out the door. Others began to follow, and Dan realized they were witnessing a mass exodus.

"Wait," Elder Eastham said, gesturing for them to sit back down. "We can survive this." He took a couple of steps toward the fleeing members. Suddenly Dan saw him clutch his chest and collapse.

Dan and Meg rushed forward, along with half a dozen other members who had not yet decided whether they would leave or stay.

"It looks like a heart attack," a doctor said as he held Elder Eastham's head up.

A crowd of about a dozen people huddled around Elder Eastham as someone ran to the phone to call an ambulance. Dan huddled with the others, concerned about what was happening to the old patriarch, until he realized that he was the only other elder in the circle.

He stood up and looked around the sanctuary. Most of the people were filing out, some talking angrily with one another, but many just silently staring at the floor as they left. He didn't see any of the elders in the crowd. Who would lead now that Elder Eastham was down?

The ambulance arrived in a few minutes, and Mrs. Eastham climbed into the back after they loaded Elder Eastham in on a stretcher. Dan stood with the small crowd who had stayed with Elder Eastham and watched the ambulance turn the corner and head down the street.

"Well, what happens now?" he asked Meg, who was standing next to him.

"What do you mean, what happens now?" she repeated, looking at him. "The church is gone. It can't function without money."

Dan looked at her and blinked. "Sure it can. It was a movement for almost twenty years before it organized as a church. People met in homes, paid for things right out of their pockets. They didn't have an institution to take care of them.

"And what about Jesus? He was the greatest Minister, the greatest Evangelist who ever lived. And He was penniless. The church isn't done yet."

Meg shook her head, a thin smile on her lips. "That was then, this is now. Nothing can survive without money in this day and age. If you control the purse strings, you control everything. Face it, the Internal Revenue Service has won. The Seventh-day Adventist Church is history."

* * * * *

Jenny waited for everyone in the house to be quiet before approaching her mother. Dad was in the den watching football with Benji; Mom was reading the paper in the kitchen. Jenny stepped in quietly and sat down at the table across from her mother.

Mrs. Abbott looked up from the obituaries and smiled at her daughter. She reached over and cupped Jenny's chin in her hand. "How are you feeling, Jenny?"

Jenny smiled thinly. "Fine, Mom." She hesitated, then began.

"Mom, can you tell me about Benji? What was his home like?"

Mrs. Abbott dropped her hold on the paper and leaned back. "I don't know. I haven't been to your cousin's house in years and years. I know Benji's mom left him when he was little. It was hard on Benji when his dad was in jail for two years. He had to stay in a home for boys."

"Was there any kind of Christian influence in the home?" Jenny asked.

Mrs. Abbott shrugged. "I doubt it. Your cousin never was much for church. We took him a couple of times when he was little, but he never liked it. Why are you asking all this?"

Jenny cringed. "Have you noticed anything . . . strange . . . about Benji?"

Mrs. Abbott sighed. "Oh, well. Benji's thirteen. All children are strange at the age of thirteen."

Jenny looked her mother in the eyes.

"I found some pages cut out of a magazine in Benji's room."

"So?"

"So they had pictures that a thirteen-year-old boy or even a thirty-year-old man should not be looking at."

"You mean, like from a girlie magazine?" Mrs. Abbott's mouth curled into a strange smile.

"No, not just nude women. People doing weird, strange . . . perverted things. Things I don't even want to think about."

Mrs. Abbott shrugged. "Well, honey, you've led somewhat of a sheltered life."

Jenny's eyes flashed. "Mother, I am a married woman. I am carrying my husband's child. I know enough to recognize perversion when I see it. These pictures were . . . were . . . *demented*."

Mrs. Abbott laughed then, and Jenny turned red. *Was this her mother she was hearing?*

"Jenny, Jenny," Mrs. Abbott said. "You are talking about a thirteen-year-old boy growing up in the most secular society in the world at the beginning of the twenty-first century. He just wants to learn about the world. Give him some room to explore."

"Explore! Explore?" Jenny repeated, ready to explode. "I'm going to get those pictures and bring them back here and show you what kind of twisted, perverted exploring is going on under your own roof!"

Jenny jumped up and stomped out of the kitchen to Benji's bedroom. She threw open the top drawer of the dresser and reached into the secret compartment. The hesitation she had felt earlier about exposing Benji's interests had disappeared. As her hand clutched thin air, she realized that the pictures had disappeared as well.

The evening had ended badly, with the conversation between Jenny and her mom going nowhere. Without proof, her mom was more willing to take the position that Benji was innocent than the word of her own daughter. Finally, Jenny went to bed early. Exhausted, she fell into a fitful sleep, with twisted, horrible dreams. Her only salvation was that as soon as she had drifted into a new dream, the old one was forgotten.

The baby started moving violently in the middle of the night, and it woke her up. She opened her eyes, a bit disoriented at first, but took a deep breath and decided to try for better dreams. She almost closed her eyes again, but realized that she was not alone in the room.

In the faint moonlight of the darkened room, she thought she saw Benji standing in the corner, staring at her.

She blinked and looked again, and he was gone.

CHAPTER

Kitkat: For those of you who are just joining us, we are studying Daniel 2—that's in the Old Testament.

Fin: Wait a minute. I thought we were going to study the end of the world. What are we doing in the Old Testament?

Kitkat: Haven't you ever heard of Daniel? He's one of the greatest prophets of earth history there ever was! Are you going to trust me or not?

Marquee: C'mon, Fin. Give the kid a break.

Mat83301: Yeah. Let's see what Daniel has to say.

Kitkat: OK, everybody found it? Fine. This is where the king of Babylon had a dream and nobody could tell him what it meant except for Daniel.

Sweetpea: Because he was smarter than everyone else?

Kitkat: No, because God spoke to him and told him what it meant. Look at verse 31. He talks about a huge statue, with a head of gold, a chest and arms of silver, belly and thighs of bronze, legs of iron, and feet of iron mixed with clay. Then a rock not cut from human hands struck the statue on its feet and smashed them.

Beetlejooz: And the entire statue was destroyed.

Kitkat: Right. Can I continue? If you read later, you will see that the dream is telling the history of the major kingdoms of the world. The head of gold was Babylon, the chest was Medo-Persia, the thighs were Greece, the legs were Rome, and the feet were all the nations that came afterward that tried to unite the world but couldn't.

Fin: But what about Nazi Germany? and Napoleon's France? They were pretty powerful.

Marquee: But they tried to take over the world and failed.

Kitkat: That's right, Marquee. No one has been successful in uniting the world, no matter how hard they try. And no human kingdom ever will.

Marquee: What about the United States? No country has ever had the influence or power that we do right now.

Kitkat: The Bible tells us that many people will try to conquer, or unite the world, but no human government ever will. See what it says about the rock that smashes the statue and ends the history of the world? That's Jesus' kingdom. It's not made from human hands.

Kris waited for a few moments to see if any of the people in the chat room had any more comments or questions. She noticed that the number of people in the chat room had increased from three to eleven. When there were no more responses, she continued.

Kitkat: Now let's flip over to Daniel 7, and we see earth's history talked about using different images . . .

* * * * *

"Man, I am beat." Jake heard the voice of Captain Robert "Robbie" Crownover, his fellow surgeon and roommate as they took their surgical garb off and changed into navy fatigues in the locker room.

"Well, seventeen straight hours in surgery can do that to a

person," Jake answered, sitting down to put on his socks.

"I think I'll go to the room and sleep for twenty-four hours straight," Robbie said. "But first I'm in the mood for a nice thick rare steak."

Jake shook his head. "I think I've seen enough blood for a while. I'm calling home first thing, then as soon as my head hits the pillow, I'm gone."

"Hey, ask your wife if she's heard any more about the volcano eruption," Robbie asked.

"Volcano? You mean Antarctica?"

"Antarctica? No, I mean Sumatra. Happened yesterday. The guy who announced it said they are wondering if that first eruption in Antarctica will cause chain reactions all along the Pacific Rim. Where have you been?"

Jake smiled thinly and threw his scrubs in the laundry cart in the corner. "Do you even have to ask that question?"

A few minutes later Jake sat on his bed and called his wife.

"Yes, I heard about the eruption," Jenny told him. "It has destroyed three towns so far, and the ash is falling several hundred miles away in Jakarta. I'm surprised they haven't told you guys about it over there in Hawaii."

"Well, I've been kinda busy," Jake said, lying back on the bed.

"Of course you have, honey," Jenny said. "I'm sorry. I wish I was there to take care of you."

"How are things there?" Jake asked. "Are you getting along any better with that kid, Benji?"

Jenny looked around the corner to make sure she was alone, then responded quietly. "Something is definitely very wrong here. I tried to talk to Mom about my suspicions, but she's not listening to me. Since then, some other strange things have happened. Frankly, I'm scared."

"Like what?"

"Like the neighbors' cat disappeared, and the next night they found it on their back porch, strangled. Dad found strange symbols and writing spray painted on the wall in the back yard. And like—" She paused, deciding not to tell Jake what she had seen in her own bedroom late at night.

"Go on," Jake urged.

"It's—it's just weird, evil things," Jenny stammered out. "Mom and Daddy have changed as well. They're not the way I remember them. They just seem to let things happen around them without doing anything about it."

"Jenny," Jake began, and she recognized the patronizing, doctor's tone that he used with her when he was about to lecture her. "When a woman is pregnant, often she sees and experiences things that are interpreted differently than were she not pregnant."

"So now *you* don't even believe me," she answered in a hard voice. "I can understand that Mom may not agree, but I thought you of all people—"

Jake closed his eyes and pinched the bridge of his nose. "I am trying to be understanding, Jenny, I really am, but I just got out of seventeen hours of surgery and I am beat and I guess not very patient. I am dealing with a lot of mangled bodies over here; trying to save people's lives. I wish I could have you over here with me, but it's still not safe."

"And you think Downer's Grove, Illinois is safe?" Jenny spat back.

"For now, Jenny," Jake answered quietly, suddenly feeling very, very tired.

"Well, it looks like I'm on my own then," Jenny shot back, and slammed the receiver down on the phone.

Her blood boiling but her heart racing, she strode back through the house toward the room that had once been Benji's but now was supposedly hers.

She lay down on the bed with a heavy sigh and stared up at the ceiling, trying to make herself relax. This excitement and worry was not good for the baby, she knew. After a long few moments of concentrated deep breathing, she felt her heart rate slow. *Now*, she thought, *I have to come up with a plan.*

She felt that the events happening around her were more than just adolescent hi-jinks, and she needed some spiritual support. She pulled herself up to a sitting position on the bed and reached over to the bedside for her Bible. It was the same one she had had since she graduated from high school. She opened it up and gasped.

As she flipped through the pages, she saw that someone had scribbled profanity on some pages with a black felt pen. Other pages had been chopped into pieces with a sharp blade. It appeared that the whole Bible was destroyed.

What now? she thought.

* * * * *

"There were thirteen people in the chat session by the time we finished," Kris said to Brad as they sat together at lunch. "Imagine, going from three people to thirteen in an hour."

"You must be pretty good," Brad said. "I'm surprised so many people would listen to a kid talk about religious stuff. It's always been boring to me."

"Yeah," Kris said. "I never really thought of it as interesting, especially the way they used to teach it in school." She looked down the school hallway as if she were looking for her old Bible teacher. "But this is different. People are interested because the Bible is helping them—helping *me*—understand what is going on in the world and why it's important."

"I don't know," Brad said. "To me, the Bible has always been a bunch of dead guys and dusty old sayings. Rules about what we're not supposed to do. Things like that."

"That's because you only studied when you were forced to. It's like a really good book you look forward to reading, and you get it for Christmas, and you can't wait to open it up and just immerse yourself in it. On the other hand, you wouldn't even crack the cover if it was a school assignment, would you?"

"Yeah, I guess so," Brad said. "I'm more into basketball than reading, I guess. Speaking of Christmas, do you know what you're going to get?"

Kris wrinkled her nose. "I think this is going to be a really low-key Christmas. Mom and Dad aren't getting along, and Dad's afraid of losing his job over at the academy, so I think he's hesitant to spend any money."

"My parents are divorced, and I think I get more presents because of that," Brad said. "They're always competing to show me which one loves me more."

"Well, my parents aren't getting a divorce," Kris said. "They just need some time to work out their problems."

Brad shrugged. "Whatever. Why is your dad afraid of losing his job?"

"With the state running the school, they're saying he will have to teach evolution."

"So?" Brad said. "Thousands of biology teachers teach evolution every day. What's the big deal?"

"He doesn't want to teach evolution because he doesn't believe in it."

"I'm sure there are other teachers that are teaching it and don't believe in it. He's supposed to teach it because it's science." Brad gave Kris a look that made her feel he was beginning to think she and her family were stupid. The look irritated Kris, but it also made her a little nervous.

"Evolution is not science, it's someone's idea of how a universe could exist without God. And since God exists, evolution is a lie." Kris tried to look like she knew what she was talking about, but wasn't sure how successful she was.

"Well, a lie or not, it's what he's supposed to teach," Brad said seriously. "And if refusing to teach evolution makes him lose his job, then I think that's plain stupid."

"And I think you're stupid, Brad Thomsen," Kris said, standing up and walking away from him.

* * * * *

"Quit your job! How could you quit your job?" Ivan yelled over the blasting stereo in their living room.

"They wanted me to deliver packages for them," Mitch said, folding his arms over his chest and leaning against the wall. "Those packages had drugs in them."

"So? You've seen Flea and me smoke grass before, and it hasn't bothered you. What are you, Mr. Clean all of a sudden?"

"You guys smoked grass when I was riding in your van," Mitch answered. "You didn't ask my permission to smoke it, and you didn't ask me to haul your grass for you. I probably should have asked you to stop or let me out. I didn't, but that doesn't mean I have to haul drugs for someone else and risk going to jail for the rest of my life."

Ivan clucked his tongue in disapproval. "What a wuss. This is California. Flea and me got you that job because you don't have a record. The worst they would have given you if you had gotten caught was probation."

"I don't have a record because I haven't broken the law," Mitch said. "And I don't intend to."

"Well, how do you intend to carry your part of the load around here without a job?" Ivan asked.

Mitch inhaled slowly. "Well, first thing tomorrow I'll get another job. A legal one."

Ivan clucked his tongue again. "Dude, you went that route already and wouldn't have gotten the job you had except Flea and me got it for you. Tell you what I think, *Bozo*—" he said sarcastically, and Mitch cringed. "I don't think you're ready to leave home. I think you don't want to hurt your daddy's feelings, so you're just going to wait around and look for someone to take care of you. Well, bro, this is the real world, and you only get what you go out and take."

Ivan looked over to his left as Flea entered the room. "We

have discussed this whole situation, and we think you need to find other housing arrangements."

Mitch looked at Ivan, then over at Flea. "You're kidding. Now?"

"Why not?" Flea said. "We got a chick that's coming over to take your place. She'll buy groceries, she'll do the cooking, and there's always all those fringe benefits." Flea nudged Ivan, and they both chuckled.

"In any case," Ivan said. "You're history."

It didn't take Mitch long to gather up what few things he had. He made arrangements to pick up his surfboard later and packed the rest of his things in his backpack. He decided that he didn't know any other people in Santa Cruz or Capitola he could trust, and he didn't want to go home. He finally decided that his best bet was to go sleep on the beach.

He'd never done it before, and those whom he knew had done it in summer, not December. A light rain started to fall as he headed down Laurel Street on his Kawasaki. Homesickness continued to nag him as he headed for what he knew would be a miserable night on the beach. At best, he could probably find a warm, dry spot under the boardwalk somewhere. At worst, he could get mugged, robbed, raped, or murdered.

He was still wondering whether he was doing the right thing when he spotted Shakey's Pizza on the right. He remembered seeing a "Dishwasher Wanted" sign in the window a few days before. Maybe with luck he could have a job on the same night he lost his other one. Maybe if he was even luckier, they would let him sleep inside somewhere.

Luck just left town, Mitch told himself as he straddled his bike outside the front entrance of the pizza place. He saw a cluster of people filing out the front entrance and watched as the proprietor locked the door behind them. The sign was gone, and he was still standing in the rain.

As he stood there, the Kawasaki sputtered and died. On a hunch, he unscrewed the gas cap. Empty.

"Lord, what else can go wrong?" Mitch muttered, and raised his eyebrows in surprise at himself. He didn't expect to be talking to God; not after the anger he had felt in leaving a godly home.

Home. The word came up again, and he shut it out of his mind.

He stood motionless, trying to decide where to go, when he saw a beat-up Nomad station wagon roar down the street, make a hard left and come barrelling toward him. At first he couldn't believe it was happening, and stood straddling his bike like a deer caught in the lights of an oncoming truck. A second before the car hit, Mitch leaped to the right. He landed on his shoulder and rolled behind a dumpster in the alley next to the pizza shop. The Nomad crashed into his Kawasaki, smashing it into the brick wall across the alleyway from him.

Still stunned, he lay there watching as the Nomad stopped, falling raindrops flashing like fireflies in its headlights. It pulled slowly in front of the alleyway until it blocked the entrance. Mitch's heart began to pound as the car stopped and four large men climbed out. He recognized two: Harpie, the owner of the Pipeline Surf Shop, and the fat, bearded guy from whom he received the package. The other two, one short and one quite tall, looked as though they benchpressed Buicks for a living.

"So sorry it didn't work out, bro," Harpie said to Mitch as they walked up to him. "I had great hopes for you. Now we have to teach you to keep your mouth shut."

"I wasn't going to tell anyone," Mitch stammered, all the time praying inside. "I just didn't want to deliver drugs."

"You already told the cops about the first package," the bearded one said. "We don't want it to happen again."

"It won't," Mitch said, standing up and facing the four men.

Harpie chuckled. "I know." Mitch noticed that his Hawaiian accent had disappeared.

The two silent musclemen grabbed Mitch on either side and pulled his arms behind him. Harpie pulled out a switchblade knife and held it in front of Mitch.

"This is for later," he said, showing him the knife, and put it back in his pocket.

Harpie turned as if stepping away, then punched Mitch full in the mouth. Mitch's head snapped back and connected with the brick wall behind him. He saw stars.

Help me, he prayed silently.

Harpie continued punching and slapping Mitch at random, in the head and in the face. The musclemen loosened their grip, and Mitch slumped to the ground.

The four men then started kicking Mitch with their heavy boots, in the back, in the groin, in the chest and in the head.

"Help me, God," he groaned. "Help me."

"Lift him up," Harpie said, and the two musclemen grabbed Mitch's slumping body and held him up. Harpie reached into his pocket again for his knife.

Through his swollen, bleeding eyes, Mitch caught the sight of a doorway opening down the alleyway a few feet and light spilling outward. A tall man who looked strangely familiar to Mitch stood there.

Harpie turned and looked at the newcomer. "You'll get lost if you know what's good for you," he said over his shoulder to the stranger.

"I guess I don't know what's good for me, then," the man said, stepping toward them.

Harpie started to pull out the knife, and the man threw something at Harpie. Mitch watched a can of fruit bounce off the side of Harpie's head, and Harpie went down.

The two musclemen faced off against the stranger as if they were in some kung fu movie. The stranger stepped in close to the short muscleman on the left, blocked a punch with his left, jammed his open right palm into the short man's chin, forcing his head back, then chopped him with his left hand hard to the throat.

The tall muscleman, seeing the stranger busy with the short

man, stepped forward to grab him from behind. The stranger responded with a side thrust kick to the tall muscleman's chest, which slammed him against the opposite wall.

While the two musclemen were stunned and gasping for breath, the bearded man charged toward the stranger with a tire iron held high. The stranger stepped deftly aside, grabbed the bearded man's arm on its downward swing and slammed the man's fist into the top of his knee. Mitch heard the bones cracking in the bearded man's hand, and the man roared in pain. Holding the bearded man's broken hand with his left arm, the stranger whacked him in the face with the back of his right elbow, and the bearded man collapsed.

The tall muscleman had recovered from the kick and charged at the stranger, who was just finishing off the bearded man. The muscleman leaped, kicking for the back of the stranger's head. Turning while the muscleman was in midair, the stranger ducked and reached for the kicking leg. He shoved the kicking leg high in the air with his left arm and slammed his fist into the groin with his right.

Mitch watched with amazement as the stranger stood in the center of the alleyway with four attackers laid out around him. The light shining from the open doorway made it look as though the stranger had a halo. Mitch couldn't imagine an angel being more welcome than the stranger was at that time.

"Are you OK?" the man asked Mitch, reaching out his hand to help him up.

"I'm fine now," Mitch mumbled through broken, bloody lips. He reached up to the stranger and felt himself being pulled up. It was the last thing he knew as he passed out.

CHAPTER

Mitch awoke with the feeling that he had been fed through a sausage grinder. Every muscle in his body ached. His eyes were almost swollen shut, but he could see some light filtering in through an open doorway. He gingerly turned himself over and discovered that he was lying on a cot in the back room of what looked like a store. He couldn't see anything in the next room, but he heard someone speak and about a dozen voices repeat the words.

He realized that it was daytime. He sat up and groaned with the effort, then sat on the edge of the cot for a long time, giving his body a chance to wake up. After another five minutes, he reached out and steadied himself against the wall and stood up.

He was amazed, but he actually felt better standing up than he had lying on the cot. He shuffled to the doorway that was open only a crack and pulled it open.

Outside the door, he saw a class of what looked like barefooted karate students dressed in black uniforms with a variety of colored belts. In front of the class, the stranger who had saved his life led the class through some exercises. He looked at the open door and at Mitch, and then motioned for another black-belted instructor to take his place.

"How are you feeling?" the man asked Mitch.

"Thanks for saving my life last night," Mitch said through cracked, swollen lips. "I don't know how I can repay you."

"No problem," the man said. "The police in this city aren't worth two licks these days, so we all have to watch out for each other. Besides, you were outnumbered."

"Well, you sure took care of things," Mitch said. "Are you an instructor here?"

"Sort of," the man said. "I own this *dojo*." He reached out and shook Mitch's hands. "Your ID said your name is Mitch Lewis. I'm Reed Marconi." Mitch looked up at the young, curly-haired man, and a light bulb of recognition clicked on.

"You're the guy who stopped us from surfing off the cliff that day."

Reed narrowed his eyes and looked hard at Mitch. "That was you?" he asked.

Mitch hung his head. "Yeah, it was a stupid idea, even if the tidal wave never hit here."

"You're right there. Say, Mitch, you're still looking pretty pale. I think it would be good for you to lie back down." Reed helped Mitch shuffle back to the cot.

"I've had a lot of practice with setting and checking for broken bones in my line of work," Reed continued. "I checked you out after the incident last night, and you didn't appear to have any serious injuries."

"I still hurt awful bad," Mitch said.

"You will for several days," Reed said. "But that's just bruises and strained muscles. The more activity you have, the sooner that soreness will go away." He helped Mitch lie down on the cot and covered him up with a blanket.

"Is there anyone I need to get in contact with?" Reed asked. "Family? Friends?"

Mitch paused for a long moment, and Reed's eyebrow went up again.

"No," Mitch responded finally. "No family."

"Friends?" Reed asked. "Where do you live?"

"I—I just got kicked out of my apartment by my roommates. I don't think they need to know—or care—what has happened to me."

Reed nodded. "I'm sorry to tell you that your bike is totaled as well."

Mitch sighed. "Yeah, I saw it happen." He paused, struggling with an overwhelming feeling of helplessness. "Look, Reed, I am broke. I left home to make it on my own. My friends left me when I ran out of money, and now I am at the bottom looking up. I have no way to repay you."

Reed smiled. "Sounds like a familiar story."

"Yeah, I imagine you see a lot of kids who are down on their luck here in Santa Cruz."

"I was thinking more of the Bible story of the prodigal son. Ever read it?"

Mitch nodded. "I used to hear all those stories every night at family worship."

Reed's eyebrow popped up again. "Sounds like you come from a good Christian background. Why leave?" Mitch didn't answer, but looked away.

"OK, OK, it's not my business," Reed said, sighing. "Tell you what. You just rest up and get well for a few days, and then we'll work out a deal to help get you going again. OK?"

Reed went back to his karate class, and Mitch lay back on his cot and stared at the ceiling. If Reed had not appeared at the right moment, if he had not been willing to intervene, Mitch would be dead right now. He had to show his thanks somehow.

But was Reed the right person to thank?

* * * * *

"I'm right here, Elder Eastham," Dan said, holding out his hand and taking the pale, weak hand of the old man in the hospital bed in front of him.

Mrs. Eastham sat on the opposite side of her husband, the lines in her face showing her worry.

The old man tried to speak, but the words came out only as a whisper.

"Where . . . are . . . the . . . others?"

Puzzled, Dan looked at Elder Eastham, then at his wife.

"I think he's wondering where the other elders are," Mrs. Eastham said.

Dan paused. *Should he lie to the patriarch?*

"The others have given up, left," Dan said. "I tried to call them on the phone after the church service, but they wouldn't even talk to me."

Elder Eastham's face grew grim. "You ... must ... lead."

Dan's pulse quickened. "I—I am not a leader."

Elder Eastham nodded slowly. "God ... has ... chosen ... you."

There's no one left, Dan thought. *They are all gone. The church is gone.*

"The ... church ... will ... not ... fall," Elder Eastham said. "It ... is ... promised."

Dan stared at the old man for a long time in silence, wondering what challenges and inspirations he had seen in his decades of service as a missionary.

"All right," Dan said. "If God can use me, I will let Him."

It will be a miracle, Dan thought. *Only a miracle can save us.*

"I'll come back and see you tomorrow," Dan offered.

"Uh, he won't be here tomorrow," Mrs. Eastham said, slightly embarrassed.

Dan looked at her blankly. "But he's too sick to discharge. Where are they sending him?"

"Home," Mrs. Eastham said. "The medical benefits for church retirees have been frozen. Without insurance, the hospital is unwilling to keep him here. They said he's stabilized; now they need the bed for someone else."

"Someone with insurance," Dan muttered.

"I'll ... be ... fine," Elder Eastham gasped, smiling. Mrs. Eastham grasped his hand and smiled thinly at him.

"Of course you will, dear," she said.

* * * * *

"All right, all right, I'm gonna get informed," Dan said, switching the TV on and settling down in his favorite chair. "No sports, no sitcoms, no reruns. Just good old informative news programming." He used the remote to find the local ABC affiliate station and settled in, daring the TV to teach him something new.

"At the top of the news tonight, Indonesia continues to battle wildfires, hot Santa Ana-type winds, and noxious fumes of gas as the new Bengkulu volcano continues to destroy villages and contaminate the atmosphere."

Dan watched in wonder as the TV showed a roaring inferno of molten lava plod methodically down the streets of a modern city, destroying everything in its path.

"The latest death toll is now estimated at more than thirty-three thousand persons, which makes it more costly in human lives than the disaster at Mount Erebus in Antarctica last month. On the positive side, the earthquakes and tsunamis that were so devastatingly associated with the volcanic eruption in Antarctica have not yet accompanied the eruption.

"On the other side of the Pacific, cities in South America continue to rattle and roll as a series of earthquakes continue to harass the citizens living there. Most recently, just this morning Buenos Aires experienced a temblor measuring 7.2 on the Richter scale. Casualties were light, mainly because so many people have already been made homeless by earlier quakes in the area."

The screen showed a once-proud street that had been reduced to rubble. A young child sat on a street corner and cried, while emergency personnel carried food and other emergency supplies into a devastated church nearby.

"The U.S. State Department continues to receive requests for financial aid overseas, but has been tight-lipped about the possibilities of sending more funds to other countries. Emergency efforts in Hawaii and southern California continue to demand the attention of American military and emergency personnel.

"Meanwhile, meteorologists worldwide are warning of the severe weather disturbances that can be expected in Indian Ocean countries, as well as possible disturbances throughout the globe. India, Sri Lanka, Bangladesh, and Myanmar have been warned of an extended monsoon season."

"Wow," Dan said to himself.

"When will this all end? Some religious leaders are saying this is an indication of God's displeasure with mankind, and leaders of the Conservative Coalition are calling for a unified return to traditional Christian values."

Dan watched a young, well-dressed man addressing Congress and calling for them to lead the country in a national day of prayer.

"Others are blaming the recent worldwide natural catastrophes on those who do not follow the divine principles advocated by our national leaders."

Dan began to feel a bit uneasy as the newscaster's tone took on more of a commentary rather than reporting straight news.

"In any case, the state of disunity among our Christian churches as well as the lack of funds available for emergency care may soon be resolved by actions taken by the Attorney General's office and the Internal Revenue Service. To follow up on this story, let's go to our field reporter, Deanna Carville."

Dan sat up and watched intently as the newscast showed the front of the church's world headquarters in Silver Spring, Maryland.

"Wednesday is normally a busy workday here at the world headquarters for the Seventh-day Adventist Church, a religious sect with more than ten million adherents around the world. But today the parking lot is empty and the doors are locked. Leaders of the Seventh-day Adventist sect recently went head-to-head with the Internal Revenue Service and lost. Now all assets of this fringe group have been frozen in banks, and all facilities have been padlocked. How long will this last?"

The scene showed the reporter interviewing an IRS official.

"The president of the Adventist corporation known as the General Conference promised total cooperation with the Internal Revenue Service, but after we discovered the sheer volume of monies that were being funneled out of the United States, we had to put a stop to it. This is being done as a lesson to show that no church, no matter how powerful, no matter how large, no matter how affluent, can disregard the will of the United States government."

The scene shifted to an interview with a man Dan recognized as the General Conference president.

"The Seventh-day Adventist Church has no desire to come into conflict with the Internal Revenue Service. But ninety percent of Adventists live in other countries, and that money legally belongs to the church overseas. The funds for the North American Division have been held aside as requested. The Internal Revenue Service has ignored our pleas for understanding in this matter, and has refused to even speak to our auditors or our lawyers. From a legal standpoint, the U.S. Constitution and the Bill of Rights are there to protect us from situations like these."

Dan noticed that the president was cut off before he had finished what he was saying. He felt the hackles on the back of his neck beginning to rise.

"Seventh-day Adventists consider themselves a Christian church, even though they base salvation on strict adherence to the Ten Commandments instead of believing in salvation by grace through Jesus Christ. They follow the writings of a nineteenth-century prophet named Ellen White and put high emphasis on extreme dietary practices. Their continued emphasis on the end of the world has led some to militant, antisocial, and suicidal behavior, such as the Branch Davidians in Waco, Texas, and the Heaven's Gate cult in San Diego."

"*No!*" Dan shouted at the television set. He picked up the lamp on the table next to him. Before he could think rationally, he jerked its electrical plug out of the wall, and hurled the large lamp at the TV.

With a jarring crash, the lamp and TV burst into glass and porcelain shards. Blue smoke blew straight up into the air like a mushroom cloud. The boom from the exploding TV shook the whole room.

"What is going on in here?" Meg shouted, running into the room. Kris ran in from the other direction.

"What happened to the TV?" Kris asked.

"Those idiots on the TV are telling people that we are a bunch of lunatics!" Dan shouted back.

"Well, if you keep going around destroying television sets, they'll be convinced you are a lunatic," Meg answered.

"I'm sorry, Meg, I tried," Dan said apologetically, but still very angry. "I wanted to be informed. But if it means wading through the drivel they are promoting as news, I'd rather be ignorant."

He explained what the newscaster had said about the shutdown of the General Conference and the Adventist Church and how they had associated the church members with extremists and cultists.

"Dan, don't be such a baby," Meg said calmly. "Of course there are going to be some negative reports about the church after they tangled with the IRS—*and lost.*"

Dan noticed her emphasis on the last two words.

"Well, I've had enough," Dan said. "No more TV in this house. It's a bad influence."

"Dad," Kris whined. "What about the Internet?"

"You still have access through the computer in our bedroom," Dan said, purposely using the word *our*, even though he had been sleeping on the couch for the past week.

"This won't work," Meg said quietly, shaking her head. "You can't function in our society without a television set. Look at what you learned just tonight from a few minutes of news."

"Rubbish," Dan said. "You want me to wade through an hour of sheep dung to get to a few seconds of worthwhile information. No thanks."

"Dan," Meg said patiently. "I am in electronics. I am in the communications field. You cannot expect me to go through life without a television set in my house."

Dan said nothing, but folded his arms.

"All right," Meg said. "I'm not supposed to say anything, but you need to know this. I have been working for the past six months on a secret project, so secret I couldn't tell you about it. Unofficially, it's part of the Harper Amendment intended to save billions on the Federal Budget. Officially, it's supposed to be unveiled later this week."

Dan said nothing but sat on the couch and listened.

"Sounds cool," Kris said. "What's it about?"

"You know all the hassles the IRS has been going through—and putting people through—trying to balance the budget? Well, this is one of the answers to that problem. It will not only save billions of dollars every year, it will improve the quality of life for all of us."

"What is it?" Kris repeated.

"The government and the major electronics firms have been working together for several years to put all information on a central access site—the Internet—where people of all walks of life can access it.

"I'm not just talking about the random stuff you find on the Internet. I'm talking radio, network and cable television, all the books in the Library of Congress, all the classes necessary to get all the way through school and get a degree in anything you want. It's interactive—and it's free! All you need is your social security number to access it."

"Wow," Kris said.

"So how does this save the country money?" Dan asked, slightly interested.

"Because everyone will have immediate access to the Library of Congress, there will be no more need for public libraries. Immediate access to whatever you want. Kids will get more assistance in school than ever before. And with the interactivity, they plan on teaching through the Internet, eventually cutting back on teachers as well."

"Fewer teachers, fewer libraries. The government will teach us everything we need to learn—or what they *want* us to learn." Dan said. "Great."

"Well, isn't that what the government is there for?" Meg asked. "To take care of us?"

"What if we don't want to be taken care of? What if we want to learn on our own? Maybe even something the government doesn't want us to know?"

"Trust me," Meg said. "It won't happen that way. I'm the one they have lined up to manage it, as the new VP for Media. When our project is officially unveiled, they'll announce my promotion." She reached out and put her hand on Dan's shoulder. "Don't worry. This isn't *1984*."

"Sounds like it to me. Count me out," Dan said. "Look, I've got to get over to the church for prayer meeting."

"Prayer meeting? But the church has been closed!" Meg said.

Dan shook his head. "There are a few old saints who have not missed a prayer meeting in forty years. I'm not going to be the one who is responsible for their first missed meeting." He grabbed his coat and stepped out the door.

The church stood just two blocks off Winchester Boulevard, and Dan made it there in ten minutes, five minutes before prayer meeting usually started. He expected to find several cars in the parking lot. It was empty.

He walked to the front door and found that his key still worked and the door had not yet been padlocked. He unlocked the door and flipped the lights on in the lobby.

He wandered into the sanctuary, his hands in his pockets to keep them warm in the room's chill. A single light shone down on the platform. Dan sat down on the front pew and waited.

An hour later, he was still sitting on the front pew, still alone. *I'm it*, he thought to himself. *Is this the end?*

No, he heard the voice of God inside him say. *It's just the beginning*.

CHAPTER

Mitch found that Reed Marconi was right. Mitch had mainly cuts and bruises, and working out in the dojo helped his body recover quickly. Not only did Reed let Mitch use the cot in the back room of the dojo in exchange for picking up and putting away equipment; he encouraged Mitch to join the others in calisthenics and stretching and coordination exercises.

Within a week, Mitch was keeping up with the rest of the class, and feeling better and better. Reed was a strict vegetarian, stricter than Mitch had ever been, and he promoted healthful living to Mitch as well as to the rest of the class.

Mitch watched the rest of the class and was impressed. There seemed to be a broad variety of people who studied karate under Reed. Some were businessmen who were trying to lose their middle-age spread and lessen their risk of heart disease. Others were teenagers who were either in gangs or had been harassed enough to feel they needed to learn to protect themselves. Many were just people who were looking for purpose in life, for structure and for something or someone to belong to.

In all cases, Reed treated them equally. *For a young, unmarried man, Reed would make a great father,* Mitch thought. He was strict but kind, sensing what each person needed and how far he or she needed to be pushed. He promoted fairness, honesty, respect, and discipline. And through it all, Mitch sensed a pervasive Christian atmosphere in the dojo. Mitch felt as though he had found the place he had been looking for.

After a week, Reed introduced Mitch to a woman named Mrs. Woyczek, who owned a health-food store in downtown Santa Cruz. Mrs. Woyczek put Mitch to work, and in addition to building muscle by stocking shelves and unloading trucks, he began to rebuild his bank account. It all seemed like a dream to Mitch; first to be so close to death, then to have his life working out so ideally.

Thank You, God, Mitch said honestly. *Thank You for sending Reed.*

* * * * *

"I feel like my whole life is coming apart," Kris said to Ginger as they sat outside the school building before school started.

"Well, if you hadn't acted like such a jerk and called Brad stupid," Ginger said. "I don't know what got into you."

"I guess I don't know either," Kris said. "I used to think he was really great. Then when I finally met him, I found out he was better than I ever imagined. I guess he just made me mad."

"Well, that's bound to happen once in a while, but don't make it a permanent thing." Ginger looked up and saw a white Mercedes pull up to the curb. "Don't look now, but that's his parents' car."

Ginger patted Kris on the shoulder. "Do the right thing, girl. Better yet, just forget right or wrong. Swallow your pride and apologize to him."

Ginger ran into the school and left Kris sitting by the steps. Kris watched Brad get out of the car and slam the door. She heard the first bell ring as she watched him walk slowly toward her, his blond hair falling forward into his eyes. He looked at the ground as he walked, as he always did, as if he were trying to work out problems in his head. *Why did I ever say he was stupid?* she asked herself.

He stopped a dozen feet from her, suddenly aware that she was sitting there, staring at him. He immediately lost his air of self-confidence and hesitated.

"Hi," he said, holding his books and binder in front of him with two hands.

"Hi," Kris responded. Pause. "Look, I wanted to apologize for calling you stupid the other day."

Brad held his hand up in front of him. "You don't have to apologize. I need to apologize. I shouldn't have said those dumb things about your dad. Whether I agree or don't agree with what he does, he's still your dad."

"Look, can we be friends again?" Kris asked. She looked hopefully up at his clear blue eyes.

"Yeah," he said. "I'd like that." He reached out and took her hand.

I'd like that too, Kris thought.

"Come on," she said. "We'll be late for class."

* * * * *

Dan had come to the conclusion that he could no longer be surprised, much less shocked, by the strange and sudden changes in his life. That conclusion was confirmed in his mind when the vice-principal called the academy faculty together for an announcement. Ira Greenhurst, the Bible teacher, and Alice Shaw, the principal, had left the school "to pursue other employment opportunities," he told them.

I wonder how soon until they will be saying the same thing about me, he thought.

He sat in his usual spot in the corner of the faculty lounge as the vice-principal introduced Alice Shaw's replacement.

"Jack Burgdorf comes here with an Ed.D. in secondary education, fourteen years' experience as a secondary school principal, and three years at another Christian academy," the vice-principal said. The teachers took turns welcoming Burgdorf, until one of them brought up the courage to ask: "What Christian academy were you at, Jack?"

"I prefer Dr. Burgdorf, since I am the principal," he responded stiffly. "I was at Valley View Christian Academy in Spokane. It's closed now," he said. The faculty responded with an awkward silence.

"Although I have taught at Christian schools and consider myself a Christian," he continued, "my first allegiance is to the school and the standards we need to uphold in order to keep our accreditation and give our students the best education possible. I am aware of the arrangement that the school has made with the state of California, and keeping our obligations for nonsectarian and open education will be my priority. Any questions?"

Eyebrows rose, and mouths stayed shut.

"Then I expect you all to do what you're supposed to. Dismissed."

"Turn out the lights, the party's over," Dan heard the PE teacher sing under his breath as they rose to go to their classes.

"Oh, Mr. Lewis? Dan?" Dr. Burgdorf called above the crowd, and Dan turned to face him as the others filed out.

"It is my intention to sit in and critique each of the teachers in rotation," Dr. Burgdorf said. "I'd like to sit in on your General Biology class in fourth period to begin with. In addition, it has come to my attention that the textbook you are using is deficient in some core areas of the required curriculum. You will need to supplement that. I have taken the liberty of bringing in some support material." He handed Dan a sheaf of papers, the first of which had the heading, "Carbon-14 Dating and the Age of the Earth."

Dan nodded and took the papers numbly. He had no doubt what the man's expectations were.

* * * * *

Fourth-period General Biology class started with a review of a quiz the class had taken the week before.

"Those of you who would like a chance to improve your grade can take the optional quiz this Friday," Dan said to the kids cheerfully. He finished handing out the graded quizzes and answered some questions. Just as he was finishing with his response to the last question, Dr. Burgdorf stepped in the back door of the classroom and took a seat. Dan noticed that the class was distracted, so he interrupted his discussion for a moment.

"Kids, this is Dr. Burgdorf, our new principal. He's here to see what kind of teacher I am and what kind of students you are. You see, teachers are graded too."

Dan smiled as a few kids laughed at his joke. He wanted to pretend that the principal had not given him supplemental material to teach, and he almost called for the students to turn to the next chapter, when Dr. Burgdorf spoke up.

"I'm glad I could join your class this morning, students," he said. "As an indication of the new and exciting direction that South Bay Academy will be taking in coming months, I have asked Mr. Lewis to share some supplemental material with you for discussion."

Reluctantly, Dan handed out the papers he had photocopied. He made no comment as the class studied the papers for a long moment. Finally, a girl in the first row began to laugh.

"This is a joke, right?" she asked, looking up at Dan. "This paper says the age of the earth is four billion years."

"And that human beings have been around for three million years?" a boy in the second row said. "How can they claim that?"

Dan shrugged. "Several methods," he said. "The most common is carbon-14 dating, which the paper tells you about. Based on the premise that the earth has consistently been bombarded with the same level of cosmic radiation from the sun since the beginning, they measure the amount of carbon-14 in fossils, petrified trees, whatever, and determine its age. It is used consistently by the scientific community…"

"But—" the girl in the front row said. "You don't believe in it."

Dan shook his head. "I believe in what the Bible says, that the earth is six thousand years old. Carbon-14 dating is based on the premise that things are today the same way they were a thousand years ago, or a million years ago. It doesn't take into consideration significant changes, or external forces."

"Such as a Creator God?" the girl asked.

Dan nodded. "Or the effect a worldwide flood would have on the atmosphere." Dan looked at the back row and saw that Dr. Burgdorf wasn't happy, but he didn't care. He was a teacher; he refused to share false information with his students.

"For example, it's a scientific fact that the Industrial Revolution brought with it an increase in coal burning in many countries, and with it the carbon in the atmosphere increased. That would have skewed the carbon-14 measurement by itself. How can we assume that the thousands of years before and after the Industrial Revolution had consistently the same level of carbon-14 when we have a historic example that showed the direct opposite?"

Dan looked at his students. "Whatever happens, remember this: science and Scripture can coexist happily. Both of them start somewhere—with a basic assumption that you must have faith in. If you believe in the Bible, you can be true to science as well. It just depends on the assumption you start with—and what you are trying to prove."

Dr. Burgdorf stood up suddenly. "Please come see me when you are through," he muttered to Dan, and stepped out into the hall.

Dan reported to the principal's office after the class, as Dr. Burgdorf had requested him to. He closed the door behind him, and sat quietly in the seat before the desk. The principal was finishing a phone call, and put the receiver back a few seconds later.

"Dan, I would like for you to explain to me why you did not present the material I gave you."

"I did, Dr. Burgdorf," Dan said. "I made copies of the handouts and shared them with the class."

"But you did not support the position of the article or its author."

"That is true," Dan said. "The position the author takes goes against everything I have taught in my class so far this year, and for that matter, ever since I started teaching."

"Mr. Lewis," Dr. Burgdorf said, and Dan noticed an immediate difference in tone. "You are not here to share conjecture, opinion, or belief. You are here to teach science."

"I agree," Dan said. "But we are not only responsible for teaching these kids facts, but giving them the tools to interpret those facts and put them in a proper life framework."

"You are to teach them scientific theory, including evolution."

"I will teach them about all theories of origin," Dan said. "And if they ask me what I believe, I'll tell them and why."

"Creation is not science," Dr. Burgdorf leaned forward in his seat. "Evolution is the only accepted theory for origin in the scientific community."

"Accepted maybe," Dan said, his own voice getting louder as well. "Accurate? No way."

"You will teach evolution as the only scientifically based theory of origin," Dr. Burgdorf stated, his voice like the jagged edge of a knife. "Or you will not teach in this school."

"You can't fire me," Dan said quietly, the blood pumping in his veins. "I have tenure."

"I have the authority to suspend you indefinitely," Dr. Burgdorf said, thrusting his chin at Dan defiantly. "I can keep you from teaching—and keep you from getting unemployment."

Dan stared at the impish little man who had replaced a good friend. "It may be your intention to either turn this school into a public school or destroy it in the process," Dan said. "I won't be party to either one. I quit."

* * * * *

Jenny dropped the plastic bag on her bed and took off her coat. She quickly put the coat away and pulled a red box from the bag. She sat on the bed and opened the box to look at her new Bible, a New International Version with black oxford leather, an index, concordance, and tabs—the works. She was still upset about her old Bible being destroyed—defaced and chopped up—but she decided that since she couldn't find spiritual support from anyone around her, she would have to depend on her Bible—and her God.

Actually, turning to prayer wasn't such a foreign notion to her. With Jake wandering all over the world for the navy, she found that prayer was often the only thing she could do to help support him.

Now she was in a different—and more personal—battle. She not only worried for her parents and her own life; she worried about the future of her unborn baby. Jake had always proven that he could take care of himself, but this baby was totally dependent on Jenny—and she knew she would do whatever it might take to keep that baby safe.

She hated feeling helpless, and Bible study and prayer took that feeling of helplessness away from her. She had learned this in high school and academy, when she was torn between a new awareness of her feeling for Jesus Christ and the pressures of a non-believing family to go back to the life she wanted to move away from. Her only solace was a deep relationship with her Saviour; that is, until He had led her to Jake. Jake was the second high point in her life, and now the baby would be her third. God had blessed her more than she ever deserved, she thought.

She had felt vulnerable living in a non-Christian home, and even more so because of the spiritual assault that came with Benji's extreme behavior. As she studied her new Bible in the privacy of her bedroom, she felt as if a force field of light was growing around her.

A knock on the door interrupted her reverie. Her father's bald head appeared around the edge of the door.

"Can I come in?" he asked timidly. Jenny smiled and waved for him to enter. Anyone who saw him at home would not recognize him as the gruff police sergeant who had been decorated so many times in the past twenty years.

Mr. Abbott came in and sat down on the end of the bed. "How was the shopping trip?"

Jenny shrugged. "I just wanted to replace my Bible." She

showed him the new one, and he admired it for a few moments.

"I came to ask you something, sweetheart," he said finally. "I'm wondering if you have noticed any strange behavior in Benji."

Jenny stared at her father openmouthed. "Dad," she said finally. "Where have you been? For the past week, I have been trying to tell Mom that something is definitely wrong with that boy. Look at this." She pulled her old Bible from her purse and gave it to him. Mr. Abbott flipped through the pages, looking at the slashing and the black felt marks on the pages.

Jenny then told him about the obscene pictures that she had found when she first arrived. "I assumed that Mom would share all of this with you," she said.

Mr. Abbott shook his head. "You'll find that your mother is living in a fantasy world. You and I know that some horrible things are happening out there in the world. I see it every day, whether I want to or not. Your mother doesn't want to see it. She wants to pretend that all people are basically good, that if you wish hard enough, only good things will happen in your life. You and I know otherwise. Don't we?"

Jenny looked hard at her father as if she were trying to read his mind. She reached over and grabbed his arm. "Why all of these questions about Benji all of a sudden?"

"At work, we've had gang activity—sort of a teenage satanic cult, actually—that has shifted geographically in the past couple of weeks. They used to be farther north, up by Lisle, but recently they've been hitting Downer's Grove, Hinsdale, and Oakbrook."

Jenny shook her head. "But Benji's just a kid—thirteen years old. How could he be involved in a gang?"

Mr. Abbott tipped his head to the side and scratched the gray patch of hair above one ear. "These gangs usually recruit kids as early as ten or eleven. And another thing—I called your cousin in Baltimore. He says Benji got involved with some other kids in a juvenile detention center while he was in jail. These kids must have introduced him to all kinds of weird stuff."

"What do we do now?" Jenny asked.

Mr. Abbott took a deep breath. "Your mom's not at home. Benji's in the den. Now is the time to confront him."

Mr. Abbott and Jenny walked into the den where Benji lay sprawled on the floor watching cartoons, while cutting paper into little pieces with a pair of scissors. Jenny watched the cartoon cat chase a mouse with a meat cleaver, whacking at it. The head of the cleaver came off and flew into the air and imbedded itself in the top of the cat's head. The mouse laughed as blood dripped down the sides of the cat's face.

Mr. Abbott stood in front of the TV and switched it off.

"Hey," Benji said, pulling himself up to a sitting position. "I was watching that."

"Benji, we need to talk," Mr. Abbott said, leaning against the TV.

"Why is she here?" Benji asked, gesturing to Jenny.

"She's part of the family too." Mr. Abbott knelt down to Benji's level, making himself less intimidating by shrinking his profile. "Look, I talked to your dad this morning at the hospital. He told me of an experience you had while he was in prison."

"Yeah?" Benji said suspiciously. "So?"

"He said you were part of a gang at the juvenile center in Maryland."

Benji shrugged. "We was just friends."

"What kind of things did you do?" Mr. Abbott asked.

Benji shrugged again. "Just stuff."

"He said that you and your friends killed a dog. Is that so?"

Benji looked up at Mr. Abbott. Jenny noticed a personality change come over him, and saw that light of rage once again come into his eyes.

"No, it's not true," Benji said.

"You and your friends beat up a teacher. Is that true?"

Benji shook his head, still staring at Mr. Abbott. Jenny looked at Mr. Abbott, then Benji, and then the scissors lying beside him.

"Benji, did you have anything to do with the neighbor's cat

being strangled?" Mr. Abbott's face got closer to Benji's.

Benji shook his head again, defiance growing in his eyes.

"Did you cut up Jenny's Bible?"

"No."

"Did you paint graffiti on the wall in our backyard?"

"No."

"Benji, tell me the truth," Mr. Abbott said. "Are these yours?" Mr. Abbott suddenly thrust the obscene pictures Jenny had found in front of Benji. Immediately, Benji grabbed for the pictures, but Mr. Abbott pulled them away.

Wondering where Mr. Abbott had found the pictures, Jenny watched as Benji reached behind him and grabbed the scissors lying there.

"Watch out!" she screamed, and the scissors came up right toward Mr. Abbott's face. Years of police work had taught Mr. Abbott how to react to the unexpected, however. His steel-strong hand intercepted Benji's thrust and grabbed Benji's wrist, squeezing. The scissors fell harmlessly to the floor.

"I'll kill you!" Benji screamed at Jenny and Mr. Abbott. He flailed and kicked, but Mr. Abbott was still much larger and stronger than Benji. He reached into his back pocket and produced a set of handcuffs. In a few seconds, Benji was sitting on the couch, hands cuffed behind him, but still struggling.

"What now?" Jenny asked.

"We have some very good child psychologists on staff that specialize in gangs and satanic cults," Mr. Abbott said. "I'll give one of them a buzz. Chances are, Benji will have to spend some time in a lock-down facility until he gets control of his temper."

Jenny started to respond when she heard the front door slam. A moment later her mom appeared around the corner. She looked at Jenny, at Mr. Abbott, then at Benji.

"What's going on here?" she asked.

* * * * *

"Fired! I don't understand," Meg said, standing in the middle of the kitchen.

Dan shook his head. "Not fired. I quit. But if I hadn't quit, he would have suspended me indefinitely, which would be worse than being fired. I wouldn't be able to teach and wouldn't be able to get another job either. This way I can look for work right away."

"But why quit?" Meg said. "I thought the academy was all squared away with the state coming in to save you."

"The state didn't save anything but themselves," Dan said. "The principal laid it out for me. Either teach evolution or don't teach."

Meg stepped up to Dan calmly and placed her hands on his shoulders. "Dan, I know how you feel about teaching evolution, but I have had to compromise with my job, and it hasn't killed me. Maybe it's time you show some compromise as well."

Dan stared at Meg. "Yes, you've compromised. Yes, you got a promotion. Yes, you are now a vice president and making $120,000 a year. But has it been the best choice for us? I'm not sure."

Meg dropped her hands and stared at Dan. "What are you talking about?"

Dan waved around him at their home. "I am talking about selling out, Meg. How much is your soul worth? Can they buy it with a new TV, a $120,000-a-year job, with the confidence that you know where your next paycheck is coming from? They have you right where they want you, Meg. You belong to them. You don't even know who you are anymore."

Meg's eyes blazed fire. "OK, you want to talk? Let's talk about responsibility. What about your responsibility in this home? How are you going to provide when your self-righteousness keeps you from earning a paycheck? It's not enough that you starve. You have to starve the whole family, too."

"Oh, I don't think the family will starve," Dan said, looking around at the new furnishings in the home. "I think you've prostituted yourself enough to make sure that doesn't happen."

Meg's slap came so suddenly that Dan didn't have a chance to react. He stood staring at her for a long second before she stormed out the front door, got into her car and left.

Dan looked around and noticed that a large, new television sat in the place of the one he had broken.

Sitting in her parents' bedroom, Kris tried hard to ignore the sound of their heated argument. She continued with her Bible study of Revelation 17 as long as she could until she couldn't concentrate anymore. Finally she had to type:

Kitkat: That's all for today. I've gotta run.

She exited the chat room after noting the counter showing that the room had thirty-six occupants. *Maxed out for the second time in a row.* She was about to switch off when she noticed that she had an email:

TO: kitkat
FROM: sysop
We regret to inform you that you will no longer be able to hold your chat session in room number three or in any of the other rooms we have available. Our systems are unable to deal with the overload of requests for this service. Presently you have thirty-six occupants attending your chat session, with forty-four additional users in the standby area requesting access to your chat session.

We suggest you continue your communication with people interested in your topic in one of two ways: (1) individual e-mail that can be forwarded from person to person; or (2) a LISTSERV subscription service that will share e-mail comments with everyone on the list.

We are sorry that we can no longer serve as a site for your chat session. It was one of the most popular we have ever had.

What do I do now? Kris asked herself.

CHAPTER
10

Moonlight shone through the Venetian blinds and drew white lines across the wooden floor of the darkened dojo. Mitch pushed the broom across the broad floor, its bushy head sliding over the brown surface like some alien predator.

He smiled to himself as he worked. He didn't really have to clean the dojo anymore, but he'd grown to like it. His new job had earned him enough money that within a couple of days he would be able to rent a small apartment on his own. He asked himself, however, if he really wanted to move out of the dojo and into an apartment. There was something about the atmosphere here—a sense of security—that he had found nowhere else since he left home.

Home. The word seemed to jump out at him a dozen times a day. It had only been a couple of weeks since he left San Jose in search of his great adventure, but reality had hit him hard. What he had learned had helped him mature very quickly. He was actually even getting to enjoy work.

He was musing on that startling thought when he heard voices coming from Reed's office. It was late. What would Reed be doing there at this hour?

Mitch moved into the lobby of the dojo and straightened the

chairs. Now he could hear the voices more clearly. The door stood partly open, and Mitch stopped to listen to them. After a while Mitch realized that it was a Bible study, and Reed seemed to be the one leading out.

"Well, it's got to be here somewhere," an unfamiliar voice said. "I know my concordance is old and beat up, but I don't think it should make any difference."

Mitch heard Reed laugh. "The Bible hasn't changed in centuries. I don't think it would. But you are not going to find it."

"Well, then where do we get the idea to go to church on Sunday?" a woman's voice asked. Curious about the discussion, Mitch crept up to the partly open door and stood in the shadows watching them.

"The early Christian church originally kept the Sabbath like the Jews did," Reed explained. "But when the Romans started killing the Jews for the rebellion they were fomenting in Palestine, the Christians decided to put some distance between themselves and the Jews. That's why they decided to celebrate the day Christ was resurrected." Reed looked up at Mitch, who hung back in the shadow. "Isn't that right, Mitch?"

Mitch nodded. "That's about the way they explained in school."

Reed stood up and gestured to a chair. "Come in and sit down, Mitch. This is Holly and Ken, friends of mine. We usually have our weekly Bible study over at the restaurant across the street, but the restaurant is closed for their Christmas party. So we decided to have it here."

Mitch took a chair near the door.

"Actually," Reed said, turning back to the couple, "it doesn't really matter on which day we worship, not biblically. Look here at what Paul says." He flipped his New English Bible open to Colossians 2:16 and read: " 'Allow no one therefore to take you to task about what you eat or drink, or over the observance of festival, new moon, or sabbath. These are no more than a shadow of what was to come; the solid reality is Christ's.' " He snapped the Bible shut and looked at the couple.

"Then why do we go to church on Sunday?" Ken asked again.

"Tradition," Reed said. "Nothing we can do or say can save us. Accepting the sacrifice that Jesus Christ made for us on the cross saves us. That's all we have to do." Reed looked over at Mitch, who suddenly felt uncomfortable.

"You agree with that, Mitch?" Reed asked, one eyebrow going up.

Mitch took a deep breath. "Didn't Jesus say, 'If you love me, keep my commandments?' "

Reed's eyes twinkled, and he nodded. "He also said, 'A new commandment I give you, that you love one another.' That's the new covenant. The old covenant was all about law, what we should and shouldn't do. Jesus showed us it was impossible to keep the law and gave us salvation through his death."

"And resurrection," Mitch added. "Don't forget that. Christ's death wouldn't have meant anything if He hadn't shown He had power over death."

"Right," Reed agreed.

"I agree with you that salvation comes only through faith," Mitch said. "But God also promised to make us into new people. His working in our lives as we surrender daily to Him makes it possible for us to live more like Him. He wants us to obey Him. If all we had to do is say we believe and we are saved, then Christianity wouldn't make us any different as people.

"And the Ten Commandments didn't die at the Cross," Mitch continued. "If that were the case, why aren't we out killing and stealing and committing adultery whenever we feel like it? When people say the Ten Commandments aren't valid anymore, they're usually talking only about the fourth one."

"Love is the key," Reed responded, shaking his head. "Love is what Jesus preached, and that is what keeps our society in check."

chapter 10

"I'll remember that the next time I get beat up in an alleyway," Mitch said.

"But what about this passage in Colossians?" Ken asked. "What was Paul talking about?"

"If you look at the context of the chapter," Mitch answered, "Paul was talking about the ceremonial law that Jews observed as part of the sanctuary rituals and sacrifices. It didn't have to do with the Ten Commandments at all."

Reed, Holly, and Ken stared at Mitch in surprise.

"I didn't realize I had such a Bible scholar sweeping my floors," Reed said finally.

The discussion went on for the next two hours. Reed soon realized he had found someone to discuss the Bible with, and Mitch rediscovered truths he had learned throughout his childhood. They were taking on a new significance.

Where is this all headed? Mitch asked himself.

* * * * *

It was late when Jenny heard the car drive up into the driveway and a single car door slam. She threw back her covers and put her robe and slippers on. By the time the front door opened, she was standing in the hallway. Mrs. Abbott stepped through the door, her face looking pinched and drawn in the harsh light.

"Where's Dad?" Jenny asked when Mrs. Abbott closed the door behind her. "Did he have to stay and do paperwork?"

Mrs. Abbott didn't look at Jenny and didn't answer. Instead she walked through the kitchen door toward the cupboard. Jenny watched as she silently reached in and grabbed a cup, then turned to the coffeepot.

"Mom?" Jenny asked, but her mother didn't respond. Instead she walked into the dining area, flipped on the light and sat down at the table.

"Mom?" Jenny asked again, this time a little louder.

"Where is Dad?"

"He's at the police station," Mrs. Abbott responded flatly, staring straight ahead.

"Police station," Jenny repeated. "Is he OK? Did everything go OK?"

Mrs. Abbott didn't respond.

"Mom?" Jenny almost shouted. "Talk to me!"

"I signed a complaint against him."

Jenny looked at her mother blankly. "A what?"

"I signed a complaint that he was abusive."

Jenny shook her head. Had she heard her mother right?

"What he did to Benji was wrong," Mrs. Abbott said, as much to herself as to Jenny. "Benji was just a normal kid."

"Benji was *not* normal," Jenny argued. "He needed help that we couldn't give him. Dad saw what I have been trying to tell you since I got here."

Mrs. Abbott continued to sip her cup of coffee and stared straight ahead.

"Mom, what is wrong with you?" Jenny asked, frustrated. "What are they going to do to Dad?"

"I don't know, and I don't care," Mrs. Abbott said. "He was abusive, and now he's not here."

Jenny shook her head again. This couldn't be happening. It was like something out of Alice in Wonderland. She tried again.

"Mom, you said Dad was abusive. Has he ever hit you?"

Mrs. Abbott thought for a long moment, then nodded slowly. "Once. Three years ago. I was hysterical, so he slapped me."

Jenny frowned. "He slapped you once in forty years of marriage because you were hysterical, and you call that abusive?" Jenny sat down hard. "Mom, I don't believe you."

"He shouldn't have handcuffed Benji," Mrs. Abbott said. "He shouldn't have been so mean to him. Police are mean to kids. You see it on TV."

Jenny stared at her mother. She thought she knew the

woman, but now realized that something was terribly wrong with her.

"This is a lost cause," she mumbled, and walked toward the phone to call the police and find out what she could about her father.

Crash! Glass flew everywhere as a large rock came through the kitchen window and fell into the sink. Dirty dishes exploded into shards, and the noise and confusion made Jenny scream. She threw herself backward against the refrigerator, her heart thudding against her ribcage. In the dead silence following the crash, Jenny heard kids laughing outside in the driveway. She saw a gang of boys running away.

"That's for Benji," one of them yelled over his shoulder.

Jenny stared after them, then turned toward her mom.

"Mom!" she screamed as she saw blood streaming down her mother's face. Mrs. Abbott had slumped over against the wall while seated at the table. Glass had apparently hit her in the face and head, and now she was bleeding from many cuts.

Jenny grabbed some towels and lay her mother down on the floor. She pulled her mother's bloody hair out of her face to see where she was bleeding from, but discovered that there were too many cuts to take care of. Mercifully, her mother was unconscious, as she had never been able to deal with the sight of blood.

Jenny tried to stop the bleeding as best she could and then called 911. The ambulance took ten minutes to get there. By the time the paramedics arrived, there was blood everywhere. Jenny felt as though she was assisting Jake in surgery and suddenly had an overpowering urge to go find him, to be with him.

The paramedics worked on Mrs. Abbott for several minutes and seemed unable to stop the bleeding. They checked her vital signs and finally loaded Mrs. Abbott onto a stretcher. She followed them out to the ambulance and watched as they pushed the stretcher up into the back of the vehicle. Then one of the paramedics turned and looked at her, noticing her obvious pregnant condition.

"Maybe we should check you out as well," the paramedic stated matter-of-factly. "Are you feeling all right?"

Jenny let out a long sigh. "I'm fine, but all the craziness with Mom and Dad has worn me to a frazzle. I'll get Mom's keys and follow you in her car, if you don't mind."

"It would probably be better for you to ride with us, but if you are feeling up to it, we'll wait for you."

Jenny nodded and walked back into the house to lock up and get her mom's keys.

* * * * *

"Ten-hut!" Robbie shouted in the locker room as Rear Admiral Alfred Benhurst, the commanding officer of the operation, entered.

Men dressed in fatigues, scrubs, and some of each stood at attention as the admiral paused for a moment.

"As you were," the admiral said quietly. He looked around the crowded room where Robbie, Jake, and others were getting ready for another marathon surgical session. His eyes finally found Jake lacing his shoes in the corner, and he walked over to him.

"Commander Gallagher, I wonder if I could have a word with you in private," Admiral Benhurst said. He said it as a statement of fact rather than a request, and Jake followed the admiral and two Shore Patrol officers into an adjoining scrub room.

"Commander, do you know a Seaman First Class Steven Auville?" the admiral asked after one of the SPs closed the door behind them. He held up a photo of a young sailor in front of him.

Jake looked at it for a long moment, then shook his head. "I don't believe so, sir. Should I know him?"

"He's one of you," the admiral said. "Adventist, I mean. He even went to Loma Linda University where you were, although he attended for only one year."

Jake shook his head again. "Loma Linda's a big school, and unless he was in med school, well, chances are I never met him."

"Well, he knows you," the admiral said. "Or at least claims to. He normally helps out in the radiology department, and works the Sunday through Friday shift. His willingness to work on Sunday has made it easy for us to let him take his Saturdays— his Sabbaths—off, but with the crisis we are going through, we need every person every day.

The admiral sighed. "He refuses to work on Saturday, no matter what we say about it being a medical emergency. I'm wondering if you will talk to him."

"Me?" Jake echoed. "Why me?"

The admiral smiled. "Isn't it obvious? You're an Adventist too, but you work Saturdays whenever we ask. Maybe you can talk some sense into him."

Jake looked at the floor for a long moment. "Sir, what is his medical position? What does he do?"

The admiral cleared his throat. "He's, uh, he's a clerk. He unloads medical supplies for radiology, logs them in, keeps track of patient records and appointments, that sort of thing."

"Admiral, I am a surgeon," Jake said, looking up at the white-haired commanding officer. "I save lives every day. I justify working on Sabbath because I am doing what Jesus did. He healed people, even on the Sabbath. This seaman must not see his job in the same light. Chances are, if I were in his shoes, I would feel the same way."

"Commander, I consider myself a tolerant man," Admiral Benhurst said. "The United States Navy also has a history of incredible tolerance for people whose religious beliefs con-flicted with their duties." Jake could see the fire beginning to smolder behind the admiral's steel-gray eyes. "That tolerance is rapidly wearing thin, for two reasons. First, we are in a crisis situation where lives are at stake. Second, these cockamamie beliefs are based on a religion that is no longer recognized by the United States government as valid and legitimate."

Jake's eyes grew wide as the admiral's voice grew louder. His mind was spinning with the thought that the Seventh-day Adventist Church was no longer recognized as legitimate, but he kept his mouth shut.

"Now," the admiral continued, his voice quiet again but the tension in it still apparent. "I will make it easy for you and make it a direct order. Commander, following your shift in the surgical suite, I order you to visit the brig in Pearl Harbor and talk to Seaman Auville."

"Yes, sir," Jake said, snapping to attention. "I will do as you ordered, sir."

"Very well," the admiral said. "Carry on. Go in there and save some lives."

* * * * *

The metal door clanged shut behind Jake as he stepped into the visiting room of the navy brig in Pearl Harbor. Seaman Steven Auville sat with his head in his hands, his navy fatigues exchanged for prison garb. *Man, he's just a kid*, Jake thought as he looked at the dark-haired sailor.

He sat down across the table and, as Steven raised his head, Jake held out his hand. Seeing Jake's officer uniform, Steven felt a bit uncomfortable, but Jake shrugged.

"Hi, I'm Jake, LLU School of Medicine, class of 1994," Jake said with a grin. Steven looked at him blankly for a moment before taking his hand.

"Hi, I'm Steve," the seaman said.

"Where you from, Steve?" Jake asked.

"Boulder, Colorado originally," he said. "I graduated from Campion Academy."

"I understand you were at LLU as well?" Jake asked.

"That's what the admiral told me."

"Yeah, but only for a semester. I was in the School of Radiology, but I couldn't keep my grades up. Then I ran out of money, so I worked on my dad's farm for a few years and finally joined up."

"Have we ever met?" Jake asked. "I think I would remember you if we did."

Steven shrugged. "We never were introduced officially, but I remember you."

"You do? From where?"

"You spoke up at a Friday night worship once. The program was about how far we should take our convictions. I remember what you said. You said, 'What is the use of being a Christian if we are just like everyone else? Why would God put us on the earth unless it was to show others what it means to be totally committed to Jesus Christ—not just to an idea, a concept, but to a relationship? Unless we give that relationship the highest priority in our lives, we are living a lie.' I remember you saying that as if it were an hour ago. That statement has stuck with me all these years, and led to my commitment to Jesus Christ just a few months ago."

Stunned, Jake stared at the young man. He didn't remember making the statement, didn't remember seeing the young sailor, nor even going to the Friday night program. But somehow God had used his passing statement to change someone's life.

"I'm supposed to talk you into working on Sabbath, but somehow it seems a bit inappropriate," Jake said quietly. "Rather than me counseling you, it sounds like you should be counseling me."

"I have all the counsel I need right here," Steven said, holding up his Bible. He grinned. "Looks like the navy isn't the happy bunch of sailors they used to be, doesn't it?"

Jake shrugged. "I guess I have had it pretty easy. I haven't had any Sabbath problems because what I do has always seemed to be a twenty-four-hour-a-day, seven-day-a-week priority. There are no options in emergency surgery—you operate or the patient dies."

"But a box of X-ray film can wait until after sundown," Steven said.

"Look, what do you want me to tell the admiral?" Jake asked.

Steven shrugged. "What will they give me? A dishonorable discharge? More time in here? Either way, my Sabbaths are safe. I'll stick to my beliefs."

Jake nodded. "Right. That's the navy way. Want me to get you a good lawyer? Want to see the chaplain?" Jake stood to go.

Steven shook his head. "The navy lawyer has already been here to see me, and the chaplain was busy with all the injured, but he will see me in a couple of hours. I'm set."

"OK then, let me know if I can do anything," Jake said. He shook Steven's hand again and headed out the door, thinking how long it had been since he had read his own Bible.

CHAPTER

i thought you were against television," Kris teased her dad as they sat down together in front of the new set.

"First, I didn't say there weren't good things on TV. I just said it was hard to find them," Dan answered, grabbing her neck in a playful chokehold. "Second, it's not every day that your mother is on TV. Third, you need to keep up with current events. Watching the president's address to a special Joint Session of Congress will help you raise that C plus in social studies to a B minus at least, don't you think?"

Kris didn't have a chance to answer before the TV screen showed the Seal of the President of the United States, and an official-sounding voice intoned, "Ladies and gentlemen, the President of the United States."

Dan and Kris heard applause from the members of Congress and watched the president step behind the lectern and begin.

"It is always a pleasure to bring good news to this nation of ours. I am even more pleased to bring good news in this time of crisis when natural disasters seem to rock every corner of the planet."

Dan thought about the latest report of earthquakes in Japan and China, and shook his head. Thousands dead, billions of dollars spent in disaster relief. Most wondered when it would all end. He didn't wonder. He knew.

"The good news is this: Today I have received a report from the Internal Revenue Service and the Department of the Treasury. The final phase of implementing the Harper Amendment is happening as we speak. Projections indicate that by the end of next year, the Federal Government will no longer be involved in deficit spending. Ladies and gentlemen, we are no longer putting our children and grandchildren in debt!"

Applause exploded from the stereo speakers of the new television set. Cameras panned the audience as senators and representatives alike stood and cheered the president.

"You are watching history, Kris," Dan said. "The U.S. government hasn't been able to pay its own way for a long time."

"I guess this means when I grow up, I won't have to worry about the country owing other countries more than they make— or something like that." Kris scratched her head, not really sure what deficit spending was, or how it affected her.

"That is, if you are around long enough to grow up," Dan said to her quietly. Kris looked up at him, puzzled. "Maybe I'm paranoid," he continued, "but ever since the business with them shutting down the General Conference, I have seen sinister implications all around us. I don't think we will be here on earth long enough for you to worry about growing up."

Kris put her hand on her dad's. "I agree that Jesus is coming soon," she said. "But that doesn't mean that everything that happens has to do with the end of the world."

Dan shrugged. "All I ask, Kitkat, is that you keep your eyes and ears open. Whatever happens, we have to look at it in the light of Bible prophecy."

It was a full minute before the applause on television died down and the president could continue with his address.

"Thousands of dedicated Americans have been involved in this monumental and historic effort; from the lobbyists, senators, and representatives that got the Harper Amendment voted in Congress and approved in last month's election, to the taskforce that worked with the Federal Communications Commission, the Department of Education, and the private sector to put together the nuts and bolts of this proposal. I am pleased to represent the American people when I say thank you to all of you!

"In order to make all of this work as projected, two more pieces of the puzzle are being put into place. First, the taskforce has been working for quite a while to introduce a special benefit that will not only launch our education and communication needs in the twenty-first century, but will save billions of dollars in the process. A new form of communication merging television, telecommunications, education, and the Internet will make it possible for any registered citizen of the United States to contact anyone else via a new network called Internet2. It's a lot more sophisticated than the present Internet, and promises to revolutionize our society. You don't even need a computer to access it; the chips for accessing it are already installed on most modern televisions. Those who don't have a modern TV can obtain an adapter free of charge at any electronics store.

"Effective January 1, you will be able to do all your banking, check out books from the library, enroll in school and take courses, and even do many of the tasks you normally do at work—all from the comfort of your living room. Taxes and fees will be reduced greatly. And all you need to access it is your social security number.

"I love computers, but I don't pretend to know all the details of this system. I will turn the specifics over to the chairman of the Harper Amendment taskforce in just a moment. However, there is one more item to be addressed.

"The Internal Revenue Service has known for a long time that a lot of underground, untaxed commerce was going on—both by U.S. citizens and those living here illegally and then taking the money into other countries. The last effort to obtain these billions of dollars—money that rightfully belongs to the

United States government—will also be the last part of the Harper Amendment. As of January 1, the day that the new Internet2 officially starts, all commerce and financial transactions will be recorded and reported to the Internal Revenue Service. Most stores and businesses already use computers and Internet services for electronic transfer. Either a business code number or social security number will identify the persons making the transactions. Those persons and businesses that are not yet using electronic transfer will be required on a weekly basis to report those transactions as well as the business codes or the social security numbers of anyone involved in the transaction. Failure to report this information will be termed as tax evasion and penalized accordingly."

Dan's eyebrows went up, and suddenly he felt a headache coming on.

"For the most part, Americans will not notice any difference. The IRS has been electronically monitoring commerce in the United States for years. This action is an effort to make that monitoring universal, to make sure everyone is paying the taxes they are legally supposed to pay."

"Wow," was all Kris said.

"Do you understand what he's saying, Kris?" Dan asked, rubbing his forehead.

Kris wrinkled her nose. "Sorta … uh, no."

"What he's saying is that whenever you go to the store now, they will ask you for your social security number. That way, they will keep track of who buys what, and make sure everyone pays their taxes."

Kris shrugged. "What if I don't have a social security number?"

Dan smiled thinly. "When anyone born in the U.S. turns one year old, their parents are required to register them, and they get a social security number. The only people who don't have one are those who are living and working here illegally."

Kris nodded, then looked at Dan. "What if the government

didn't like me, or if I was a criminal? Could they keep me from buying or selling something this way?"

Dan looked at Kris with a small, sad smile on his face. "We'll see," he said. "We'll see."

Dan and Kris continued watching the local follow-up coverage for a glimpse of Meg, who was supposed to be interviewed by the local network affiliate. As the station's new anchor droned on, commenting on the president's address, Dan's headache grew stronger. Finally, he couldn't stand it and headed off to the bathroom medicine cabinet for some headache reliever.

"Tell me if Mom comes on, will you, Kitkat?" he yelled back to the living room as he dug through the medicine cabinet. After a few futile moments, he yelled again: "Do you know where there's any pain medicine?"

"I thought I saw some in Mom's dresser," Kitkat yelled back.

What was she doing in Meg's dresser? Dan asked himself, then decided not to pursue it as he headed for the bedroom.

Meg had left in a rush that morning, and her dresser was covered with clothes she had reviewed and rejected. Dan leafed through the stuff on top and then decided to enter her private domain. Meg was a stickler for privacy, and Dan had always respected it, especially in mail and dresser drawers. But his head was throbbing now, and desperation caused him to toss away his hesitation.

He dug through Meg's top dresser drawer for a few minutes before he found them. It had been years since he had seen them last, but he recognized the foil wrapper right away. Birth control pills. *What was Meg doing with birth control pills?* He thought that his visit to the doctor for a vasectomy right after Kris was born took away the need for them. *Or did it?*

He looked at the foil back and read a recent date. They were new, no doubt about it, and they were not intended for use with him.

He carefully put the pills back and closed the door, his headache forgotten for the moment. Numb, he walked back to the living room just in time to hear Kris say: "Look, there's Mom!"

Dan stood behind the couch and watched silently as the news reporter talked with Meg and Simon Esteb, her millionaire boss, about the new Internet2 system. Dan didn't hear anything that was being said. His eyes were focused on the millionaire's right hand, which rested comfortably on the small of Meg's back.

* * * * *

Payday arrived, and Mitch finally had enough cash to rent the small apartment he had his eye on. It was a few blocks off Laurel Street, within walking distance of both Reed's dojo and his work at the health food store. He walked down Laurel Street toward the apartment complex, the happiest he had been in weeks.

He recognized a teenage girl he had seen sleeping on the beach and trying to hustle change for food down by the boardwalk. He had assumed that she was just another one of the countless prostitutes, addicts, hustlers, and beggars he saw every day. He passed her as she stood in front of an elderly couple, making her usual plea.

"Please, you don't understand," she said with tears in her eyes. "I don't want the money for drugs or booze, or even food. I've had enough. I want to buy a bus ticket to Bakersfield. I want to go home."

Her voice faded as he passed her and headed down Laurel Street toward Bay. However, her words haunted him. He struggled for a moment, then made a sudden left turn and walked into the Greyhound Bus Station.

Five minutes later, he walked up to the girl who still stood at the curb near the retired couple. He reached out and grabbed her hand, pressing a bus ticket into her palm.

"Here," he said quickly. "There's a bus leaving in fifteen minutes."

Mitch left her staring at him in wonder and walked back down Laurel toward the dojo, his hands shoved deep into his jeans pockets, his lips puckered in a soundless, happy tune.

He hoped Reed would let him stay in the back room a little longer.

Reed not only let him stay, but began introducing Mitch to others who were studying the Bible with him. The couple he had met was only one of scores that Reed had contacts with each week. Rather than being upset with Mitch's interpretation of Scripture, Reed welcomed his view and encouraged him to get involved.

Within a week, Mitch had established his own Bible study group, made up of two surfers like himself (although Mitch rarely had time for surfing these days), a couple of teen run-aways, a retired woman, and four black-leathered bikers. They met at the Boardwalk beneath the walkway when the weather was good, and inside the health food store when it wasn't. Mitch felt as if he had been a cold, cobweb-covered gas furnace for years, and someone had just lit the pilot light. He was burning with heat and warmth, and took every opportunity he could to find others to share that warmth with.

* * * * *

Kris was walking with Brad back to class after lunch the next day when she discovered just how much the circumstances around her were changing.

"Hey, what's all the racket?" Brad asked as they look toward a crowd of kids at the stairwell.

"A fight! Some kid is getting beat up," Ginger said over her shoulder as she ran by.

"This should be interesting," Brad responded, quickening his pace. Kris grimaced and followed him reluctantly. She hated violence and avoided confrontation—usually. She followed the crowd slowly and stood at the outer rim. Mr. Kwan, the history teacher, pushed past her and waded into the crowd.

"OK, OK, break it up," he said, pulling three large junior boys off a smaller freshman. She recognized the freshman as a boy she knew named Davey. He had banana smeared on his face and was desperately trying to recover some dignity in front of the large crowd of kids.

"What happened?" Mr. Kwan asked the larger boys.

One of them, a guy named Brice that Kris recognized as their usual spokesman, responded.

"This wimpy kid was complaining about the way the school is being run. He says we were better off when we were Adventist."

Mr. Kwan looked at Brice, then at Davey. "OK, you bigger guys need to keep your hands—and your lunches—to yourself." He laughed and picked some of the food off the freshman's shirt.

"Son, you look like a fruit salad," Mr. Kwan said, and the crowd laughed with him. Davey smiled back uncomfortably, and Kris felt a little nervous herself.

Mr. Kwan addressed the crowd. "Although this school still has Adventist in the name, it is no longer associated with the Adventist Church. We welcome Adventists as students here, but they should not consider themselves special in any way. Adventism is a dead religion. The less said about it, the better."

The bell rang, signaling the end of lunch period, and Brad and Ginger turned to go. Kris, however, stood staring in shock at the dissipating crowd.

"Adventism is a dead religion. The less said about it, the better."

Her head was still whirling when Kris got home that night, switched on her computer, and logged onto the Internet. It would be nice when she no longer had to worry about servers, and all you needed was your social security number to log on, she thought. She wouldn't have to go to the library for research anymore, and if she didn't feel like it, she wouldn't even have to go to school. Everything she needed could be delivered to her e-mail address, courtesy of the United States government.

She opened her e-mailbox and gasped. She had sixty-three e-mail messages. Ever since she had stopped the Bible study in the chat room and had announced that she would answer specific Bible questions by e-mail, every day she had been deluged. She had lost track of how many individuals were sending her Bible questions now. This was a record, however. She would have to figure out something else, she decided.

She was still thinking about her overloaded mailbox when she spied a message that looked as if it didn't belong. She opened it.

To: kitkat; wlReSPace222; losergrrl; hasherman; kkts1234
From: djv
Re: My Declaration of Independence
When I was baptized two years ago, I didn't really know what the pastor meant when he said that the truth makes you free. Today I learned what that was.

Truth is something that is a part of you. If you really believe it, you can't deny it without denying who you are. That's why I will not shut up about what I believe.

Some people say the hardest thing is to stand up for truth when you are being tortured. I think the real test is saying what you think even when people you admire and believe in humiliate you in public, or stand by while someone else does it.

I will not turn my back on my church. I will not deny my Savior.

I will not be quiet.
—Davey

Kris stared at the message for a long while. By the time she switched the computer off and turned away, her face was red, and tears flowed down her cheeks.

CHAPTER

"Hi, Jenny," the familiar voice said over the phone.

"Hi, Sweetheart," Jenny said. "It is so good to hear your voice."

"It's good to hear yours," Jake said. "First things first. How's Junior?"

Jenny chuckled. "Junior's just fine. If you want, I'll put him on the phone for you." She patted her swollen abdomen without thinking.

"Sorry I haven't called more often," Jake said. "Things are still pretty hairy over here."

"Things are pretty hairy here, too. Mom's in the hospital, and Dad's in custody."

"What?" Jake asked.

Jenny updated him on what had happened over the past few days. "Now I'm pretty much here on my own, house-sitting. Just me and the cat."

"It must be pretty quiet, then," Jake said. "You could use the rest after what happened with Benji, I imagine."

"Well, it's not quiet, and the thing with Benji's not over either. Some of his friends are still in the neighborhood. Every time I put out the garbage or go out for groceries, I have to watch my back. The police arranged for a drive-by twice every night, but I'm not sleeping too well."

"I would think not," Jake said. "Look, honey, things will be settling down here soon, and I'll find out how much longer I will be stationed here. Wherever they send me, or if they keep me here, I will send for you."

"Good," Jenny said. "I can't wait. I keep waiting for another disaster that sends you off who knows where else. I'm afraid one of these days the navy will send you off and misplace you."

"I wouldn't let that happen," Jake said. "What's the latest on the disasters in Asia?"

"I was watching the news when you called. It's Alaska now. They are afraid some of the volcanoes in the Aleutians are about to erupt. Some scientists have come up with the theory that the disaster in Antarctica set off a chain reaction. Something about destabilizing the entire Pacific Rim. They say we might have these eruptions and earthquakes for a long time to come."

Jake clucked. "Well, I hope not. There's only so much of me to go around."

Jenny laughed. "And I want all of you, sailor boy."

Jake told Jenny of his encounter with Admiral Benhurst and Steven Auville. "Do you remember Steve from LLU?" Jake asked her.

"All those years are just a blur," Jenny said, shaking her head. "Besides, honey, I have always only had eyes for you."

"Flattery will get you everywhere," Jake said. "But you know, I have been thinking a lot since that conversation with Steven. I wonder if I am as committed to Christ as I was in those days at Loma Linda. Remember that I was going to go as a medical missionary? What happened to those ideas?"

"You were in the navy. Still are. We got married. You knocked me up."

"Well, I just wonder where all that fire has gone," Jake said. "I still love the Lord, and this crisis time has actually brought me closer to Him. But I wonder if I will be able to stand when push comes to shove. Stand like Steve did—is doing."

"I don't know what to tell you, honey," Jenny said. "All I can say is you have to depend on your relationship with Jesus, and not your own willpower."

"Yeah, I know." Jake paused and took a deep breath.

"Well, I gotta go. Let me talk to Junior. I love you."

"I love you, too," Jenny said. She took the receiver and held it down to her abdomen. She could hear Jake's voice coming through the receiver as he talked baby talk. After a minute, the baby suddenly moved inside her.

"Well, Junior knows what Daddy's voice sounds like," Jenny said, returning to the receiver.

"I just hope I get back before Junior decides to enter the cold, cruel world."

"Me too," Jenny said. "Me too."

* * * * *

"I'm home!" Meg shouted from the front entryway as she slammed the door and cheerfully entered the house with her hands raised high above her head. Dan sat on the couch reading the morning paper, and Kris, always the late riser, sat at the kitchen table eating cereal.

"Home! Where've you been?" Dan said. "I thought you were out jogging or at the rec center." He looked at her, dressed in the clothes she usually wore on Sabbath morning.

"I've been to church!" Meg said triumphantly.

"Church!" Kris echoed. "But this is Sunday!"

Dan said nothing, but frowned at her.

"Don't look at me that way, Dan," she said. "It was work related. Simon's parents were here from out of town, and he wanted me to go with them to church. Besides, it was a wonderful service. I hadn't realized what we've been missing going to that stuffy old Adventist church every week."

Dan stood, shaking his head slowly. "I don't understand how

going to a Sunday church service is related to working at a computer company."

Meg waved him away nonchalantly. "Oh, don't worry about it. I was just doing Simon a favor. That's what vice-presidents are expected to do."

"That's what I'm afraid of," Dan muttered under his breath.

"Anyway, their church service isn't anything like what we have in our services," Meg bubbled on. "Their service is *exciting*. It's almost like a pageant. Simon explained to me what this church believes. They really emphasize the power of joining together as Christians, and what the Church can accomplish if we only believe and work together. And they are so *friendly*. I told them I used to attend the Adventist church, and they didn't bat an eye. Said there were several former Adventists attending their service."

"Great," Dan said. "A regular alumni meeting."

"The sermon was incredibly powerful," she continued, hardly taking time to breathe. "This good-looking, well-dressed man explained that the Bible was written by men thousands of years ago. Since they lived in that era, their writing was largely influenced by the time in which they lived. For example, when they counted the children of Israel, they only counted men, since women and children were looked at as property. Much of the Bible was written to keep society—especially women— under control. So it is heavily biased toward men and against women."

"Oh, really," Dan said. He looked over at Kris, who rolled her eyes.

"Not only that, but because of those cultural biases, you have to be trained in sociology and anthropology to really understand what is valid today, and what was intended only for people of that era! It makes perfect sense to me!"

"Mom," Kris said, while Dan shook his head and chuckled. "You're smarter than that. You brought me up to believe that the Bible is true, that we can trust what we read there. Now you are saying just the opposite."

"But it makes such good sense!" Meg said, still excited. "It explains so much that we have not been able to understand for so long. It explains why the world is in such terrible shape."

"The world is in terrible shape because Jesus is coming back—real soon."

"Forget it, Kris," Dan said. "Your mom has lost her marbles."

Meg turned to Dan, suddenly angry and offended. "How can you say I am crazy? I am not the one opening a cold, dead church every Wednesday night and Saturday morning. No one comes. No one will come. Face reality, Dan."

Dan looked at Meg silently and suddenly realized that all the love he had once held for her was gone. Instead all he felt for her was pity.

"I have never been more willing to face reality than now, Meg," he said quietly.

Meg reached out and grabbed his hand. "Then come with me, both of you. See for yourselves what I have been talking about." She looked at Kris, then back at Dan. "See for yourself if I am crazy."

* * * * *

Mitch showed Reed the *kata* he had taught him.

"I'm impressed," Reed said. "You have a talent for karate. You've been here only a couple of weeks and already you are ready to graduate to the orange belt program. Usually it takes about three months."

"You know, if you wanted to, at this rate you could have your black belt in just a couple of years."

Mitch shook his head slowly. "I am still a bit uncomfortable with martial arts. I was raised to be nonviolent. Learning new ways to break a bone or cut off someone's air supply doesn't seem right, somehow."

Reed grinned and shook his head. "Karate is so much more

than beating someone up. It is discipline of body and spirit; it is coordination and balance. It is feeling confident in a dangerous situation."

"Christ can give me that confidence," Mitch said. "And I do realize some of the benefits of karate. I'm just not sure I want to pursue it seriously."

"Just ask yourself," Reed said, punching him playfully on the shoulder. "Where would you be without my karate that night in the alley?"

"Ask *yourself*," Mitch answered, following him into Reed's office. "Who was it that prompted you to go into that alley at just the right time?"

"Touché, my young friend."

* * * * *

"OK, I know it's kinda crowded, but this is the last Bible study we will be able to have before Christmas. I will be out of town for the holidays, and I'm sure many of you have plans of your own as well." Reed looked across the crowded dojo and his eyes settled on Mitch, who glanced at him and looked away.

"This is a bit unusual, meeting in this room and sitting on the floor, but the wooden floors here are not conducive to chairs, and besides, we don't have that many chairs," Reed continued. "What do we have tonight, forty-three? How many of you read my ad in the classifieds?"

Mitch looked up and counted almost twenty hands.

"OK, the rest of you are either regulars from Mitch's group or my group, or are coming in by word-of-mouth. Now I am going to shut up and let Mitch take it from here."

Reed gestured for Mitch to begin, and Mitch cleared his throat. He had never done well in speech class in academy, and this was the largest group he had ever spoken to. *Nervous* couldn't begin to describe the way he felt.

"Uh, we are studying Revelation 14, starting with verse 6.

Holly, you want to read verses six and seven?"

Holly cleared her throat and read, " 'Then I saw an angel flying in mid-heaven, with an eternal gospel to proclaim to those on earth, to every nation and tribe, language and people. He cried in a loud voice, "Fear God and pay him homage; for the hour of his judgment has come! Worship him who made heaven and earth, the sea and the water-springs!" ' "

"What do these two verses tell you?" Mitch asked the group.

Ken spoke up first. "This angel is telling us to obey and worship God, because we are going to be judged."

"It's talking about loyalty to God," Reed said. "Absolute loyalty."

"And the judgment time is now," someone else said.

"That's for sure," added another.

"What about the last part?" Mitch asked.

"Sounds like we worship God because He created us and all the earth."

"Yeah," Mitch said. "Why do we worship God and nobody else? Because He is the only Being that was not created. Everything else comes from the mind of God. God has always been, and always will be."

"Amen," said Ken.

"That also means we should recognize the beauty of the things He created," Mitch added.

"Like the earth that we are destroying," Holly said.

"I'm thinking of something else that originated in Creation week," Mitch said quietly. "Will someone read Genesis 2, verses 2 and 3, please?"

Someone in the back read, " 'On the sixth day God completed all the work he had been doing, and on the seventh day he ceased from all his work. God blessed the seventh day and made it holy, because on that day he ceased from all the work he had set himself to do.' "

The group was quiet for a moment, and then Mitch spoke up. "We worship God because He is the Creator. We are loyal to

Him if we love Him. The Ten Commandments reflect God's desire for us to worship Him on the seventh day, the Sabbath, but He created the Sabbath a long time before Moses got the Ten Commandments. The Saturday Sabbath is for everybody."

Mitch expected an argument from Reed, but Reed sat quietly and said nothing.

"Let's go on. Someone read verse 8 from Revelation 14," Mitch said.

Another voice spoke up and read, " 'Then another angel, a second, followed, and he cried, "Fallen, fallen is Babylon the great, she who has made all nations drink the fierce wine of her fornication." ' "

"What's Babylon?" someone asked. "Wasn't that a country thousands of years ago?"

Reed spoke up. "Let me answer this one, Mitch. Babylon was a great and powerful kingdom a long time ago. Remember Daniel in the lion's den? That was in Babylon. They mixed with lots of other cultures and were so powerful that they blasphemed God. They wanted to rule the world. One night the king was partying and using the holy cups from the temple of Jehovah to drink out of. That same night the king was killed and the kingdom overthrown.

"I think this verse uses that country as a metaphor for a group of people in the last days, perhaps a group that will want to rule or unite the whole world, that will force Christians to 'fornicate,' or merge their beliefs with the beliefs of pagans."

The group was quiet until Ken spoke up. "It sounds like Babylon has either fallen away from the truth, or is going to fall before the true God."

"Maybe both," Reed said.

"OK, Holly, read verses 9 through 12," Mitch said.

" 'Yet a third angel followed, crying out loud, "Whoever worships the beast and its image and receives its mark on his forehead or hand, he shall drink the wine of God's wrath, poured undiluted into the cup of his vengeance. He shall be tormented in sulfurous flames before the holy angels and the Lamb. The smoke of their torment will rise for ever and ever, and there will be no respite day or night for those who worship the beast and its image or receive the mark of its name." This is where the fortitude of God's people has its place—in keeping God's commands and remaining loyal to Jesus.' "

"Wow," someone said.

"Yeah, wow is right," Mitch said.

"Uh," Ken said hesitantly, raising his hand. "If these passages are about the last days, and we are living in the last days, who is the beast?"

"It's, uh, a bit complicated to point out exactly who the beast is," Mitch said, suddenly embarrassed.

"Aw, come on," Ken said. "You got us hooked. If this is such a big warning—and believe me, it is—then we need to know who to look out for."

"Well, look at the text," Reed said. "Right at the end it says the good guys will keep God's commands and remain loyal to Jesus. The bad guys worship the beast and get the mark of the beast on their hand and their forehead, so they can buy and sell."

"How is this beast different than the beast in the previous chapter—Revelation 13?"

"Well, actually there are two beasts in Revelation 13," said Mitch reluctantly. "The first one is the Roman Empire, and the papacy that came out of it. In the Middle Ages, the pope had the power to set up kings and take them down. Then in 1798, Napoleon captured the pope and supposedly destroyed the papacy, but it was reinstated later. That's why it says in verse 3 that 'the mortal wound was healed.' "

"But there are two beasts in Revelation 13," someone said. "Is the pope the second beast as well?"

"No, if you can remember our study of the animal-kingdom prophecies in Daniel 7, they all came out of the sea. That represents established areas where great numbers of people live. Even the beast here in Revelation 13:1 comes out of the sea. But the beast in verse 11 comes out of the earth. That means it's a government or group of people that arises where there aren't a lot of people. It starts out meek, mild, and peaceful, but ends up mighty and speaking like a dragon." Mitch felt all the things he had reluctantly learned in Bible class in elementary school and academy rushing back into his mind; and he was elated.

"Does anyone have any idea what that government could be?"

Silence.

"How about the United States of America?" Reed offered.

The crowd turned and looked at Reed, and Mitch nodded silently. The levity was gone from the group; this prophecy was beginning to hit close to home.

"OK, now what does this American beast do?" Mitch asked.

"It—it has the authority of the first beast—the papacy—and forces people to worship that beast. It makes miracles, including having fire come down from heaven, and makes an image to the papacy. It forces people to worship the image, and if they don't, it puts them to death."

"And it puts a mark on the people who worship the beast— on their forehead and on their hand. And they can't buy or sell unless they have it." Holly finished his thought.

"OK, OK, now," Mitch said. "Let's put what we learned from these three messages together into one message and see what we have."

Reed jumped in from the other side of the room. "We are called to worship and be loyal to God, because He is our Creator, and to observe and recognize the beauty of what He has created, including the seventh-day Sabbath." Mitch raised his eyebrows in surprise.

"We are warned that Babylon, a group of people who want to control the earth, is pulled apart from God and want Christians to blend their beliefs with the beliefs of pagans," Ken added.

"And finally, the United States will enforce a law making us worship the papacy, to go against God's commands, and will put a mark on those who worship them, and will kill all those who do not." The voice came from someone he didn't recognize.

Mitch saw that the crowd was getting uncomfortable. But he wasn't sure if it was because they felt the interpretation of these verses was way off or because it was so relevant to where they were living. After a long, awkward pause, someone in the back raised a hand.

"I have a problem with this interpretation of these verses," a woman said. "I grew up in the Catholic Church, and I have never heard anything about forcing people to worship the pope. Sure, we have been big on trying to get churches to work together, but what's wrong with that? I have never seen anything like what these verses describe happening in my church, and I am offended by anyone who will refer to the pope as a beast."

Mitch inhaled slowly and looked through the corner of his eye at Reed, who was trying hard not to grin. Reed had known this would happen, and Mitch had dreaded it.

"Look, all I know is what I've learned on my own," Mitch said. "And it's not as important that you know who does what as you know what will happen. What will happen will agree with what we have read here. The pope may not be the one to unite everyone and force people to worship together. On the other hand, he might be. What is important is that we see it as a sign that the end is near and remember what it says at the end here: 'This is where the fortitude of God's people has its place—in keeping God's commands and remaining loyal to Jesus.'

"I haven't seen any of this happen yet, either," Mitch said. "But I guarantee it will, possibly in the next few months. What's important is that we all watch with our eyes open, and recognize these events for what they really are."

A couple of hours passed before the group broke up and

people headed home. Mitch went through his usual routine with the dust mop and straightened chairs in the lobby. Reed was still in his office when Mitch finished, so he popped in to say goodnight.

"Pretty good crowd out there tonight," Reed said.

"Good? I was blown away!" Mitch said. "I didn't know there were that many people living in Santa Cruz that weren't out partying this time of night."

"People are tired of partying," Reed said. "The things that are happening in the world have got them thinking—and searching for answers." He gestured for Mitch to sit down. "I want to talk to you about your presentation tonight."

Oh, oh, Mitch thought. *Here it comes.*

"Look, I'm sorry if what I said offended anybody—" Mitch started, and Reed held up his hand.

"We're talking about prophecy that is affecting us here and now," Reed said. "Of course it's bound to offend some people. I'd be afraid if it didn't.

"But what I'd like to know is, where in the world did you learn all this? This is stuff that everyone wants to know right now, stuff everybody is searching for. And here you are, an eighteen-year-old surfer dropout coming up with answers to questions I have been asking for years."

"That's just the beginning," Mitch said. "I wanted to simplify it all because it would take several days to put it all together."

"Where did you learn this?"

Mitch shrugged. "I've gone to Seventh-day Adventist schools my whole life. We study the Bible at home. I used to go to church every Saturday. I'm a big fan of Uncle Arthur."

Reed sat forward in his chair and grew very serious. "Then I have a bone to pick with you."

"What's that?"

"How dare you!" Reed said, suddenly standing up. Mitch sat back, seeing the anger rise in Reed's face.

"How dare you keep this message to yourself, when every-one else is searching and scraping and struggling to find out the answers. God has given you something valuable." Reed pounded on his desk. "No, *priceless!* How dare you not share it with the world!"

"I—uh, I don't know what to say," Mitch said, the hairs starting to stand on the back of his neck.

"Mitch, the Holy Spirit is convicting me to tell you some-thing. Something important," Reed said. "This it is. When you keep such an important message to yourself, you are commit-ting a sin. A *sin!* How many people are you willing to let die without the knowledge you shared tonight? Huh? People are hungry for salvation. Are you going to let them starve?"

Mitch stood in front of Reed's desk and stared at him. He had never seen Reed angry before, and he hoped to never see it again. The message Reed shared fell on him like a collapsing ceiling. He was stunned.

Mitch was still spinning as he lay on his cot and stared at the open door, the moonlight filtering through the blinds into the otherwise empty dojo. God was calling him; there was no doubt about it. God was not whispering anymore. He was shouting Mitch's name. What was he going to do about it?

What was he going to do about it?

CHAPTER

13

December 22 was the lowest day in Dan's life.

That day marked two weeks since he had begun sleeping on the couch. On the surface, it had seemed as though his marriage to Meg had been in relatively great shape until Mitch left, but now he realized that the relationship had been in danger for a long time. Their intimacy had become nonexistent, and for the most part Meg lived her own exciting, challenging life as an up-and-coming corporate vice president—while he led a life that seemed to be going nowhere.

Since that day when he had discovered Meg's birth-control pills, Dan had tried to decide what to do and how to confront her, but in the end realized that he didn't have the desire or the courage for another confrontation. For the most part, it seemed that Meg was oblivious to Dan and the struggles he was going through.

It had also been one week since he had quit his job as a teacher. He had thought he could get a job right away, but a combination of the usual Christmas frenzy and having the word "Adventist" on his resume seemed to end any hopes for a quick solution. For years he had subconsciously tied his own self-worth to his talent in the classroom. Now he had no classroom, and he struggled to determine who he really was.

He also continued to struggle with the loss of Mitch and Pastor Taylor. He felt he was alone, Kris, his fourteen-year-old daughter, being the only person he could really talk to. That is, except for God. He found that he was praying constantly these days. But it was a prayer of supplication, of self-commiseration. He felt no room for praise, but wallowed in self-pity. Sometimes he wondered if God got tired of listening to his whining.

Interestingly enough, it was his dedication to the church that was his last source of hope. Elder Eastham had said that the church wouldn't fall, but he hadn't seen any signs of the church resurrecting itself. Two Wednesday nights and a Sabbath he had opened the doors, with Kris as his only company, and she had come only on Sabbath morning. How could he have a church where there were no members?

Perhaps he was fooling himself, he thought as he lay on the couch Thursday morning and stared at the television. Figures moved across the screen as he stared at it from his prone position. *More news about death and destruction overseas.* He paid no attention to it because he had enough despair of his own. He saw some color and motion out of the corner of his eye and caught a whiff of perfume. Old memories flooded him. The TV switched off, and Dan rolled slowly over to look up at his wife.

"Hi," Meg said softly.

"Hmmm," Dan mumbled, pulling himself up into a sitting position and trying to straighten his pajamas.

"Can we talk for a minute?" Meg said, sitting down on one of stools by the kitchen counter behind him. Dan shrugged.

"I think … I think we need to start over," Meg said, drawing a deep breath. "I know I have been wrapped up in my career for quite a while. I have been pushing for this project and this promotion, and I have neglected my family—and especially my husband." She reached over and cupped Dan's whiskered chin in her delicate hand. Despite himself, Dan felt electricity go through his body with her touch.

chapter 13

"I think we need some time together, and with the holidays coming up this weekend, I think we could do something special," Meg said, smiling. "Why don't we plan to go up to Tahoe and go skiing? With the launch already taken care of, I might even be able to take a few days off." She stood up and drew closer to Dan.

"That will give Kris time on the slopes, and me time to get to know my husband again." She cradled Dan's head up against her, and the electricity he had felt turned into a waterfall of emotion.

"I just have one favor to ask before we leave," she said quietly. "Sunday is Christmas Day, and it is a special day for Simon's—my—church. I'd like you to be there. I'd like you to see for yourself what I'm so excited about. Also there's someone I'd like you to meet, someone you will be thrilled to meet."

Dan's mind whirled. Meg had something going on that she was keeping from him—the birth control pills were evidence of that. Yet she was acting toward him the way she used to, a way she hadn't acted in years. Was there a chance they could pull things back together? Was God giving him an opportunity to patch things up?

But he knew that this church she was attending was bad news. The Adventist Church, empty or not, was the only true church. How could he attend another church, a church that was teaching lies? On the other hand, why attend a church where no one else went?

He pulled away from Meg and looked up at her. She *was* beautiful, more beautiful than he could ever remember. It was wrong to give her up. Now she was giving him a chance to go back to a normal life. *How could he pass it up?*

"I'll tell you what," Dan said finally. "Sabbath is Christmas Eve. I will open the church one last time. If no one shows up, I will know that all of that stuff is over with, and I will close it up and join you at your church." Even as he said it, he felt a sense of wrongness.

Meg smiled broadly and kissed Dan.

"Thank you, sweetheart," she said.

Dan told Kris of his conversation with her mother, about his plan to open the church one last time. Dan could see that Kris felt strange with the idea of attending another church, but grinned broadly when he told her of the trip to Tahoe and how he and her mother would be patching things up. Kris said that she would e-mail all the kids she knew from school that had ever attended their church. Dan in turn got on the phone and tried calling all the old members, including the former elders. Many were not at home, and he left messages on their answering machines. Others hung up as soon as he mentioned the Seventh-day Adventist Church. A few said they would try to come, but would make no promises.

Sabbath morning came, and Dan and Kris woke up to brilliant sunshine. Dan was in an exceptionally cheerful mood, and Kris seemed happy too. Kris serenaded them with Christmas carols as they dressed in their Sabbath finest, and Dan made them a hearty breakfast. Meg, as usual, was nowhere to be seen. Dan knew that whatever would happen this morning would determine the fate of his marriage—and possibly his soul.

These thoughts continued to bounce through his consciousness as they pulled their old minivan into the parking space marked Head Elder next to the church's side entrance. Dan shifted into park and shut the engine off but didn't move to get out of the van. He sat there staring at the church.

Off to the left, he could see the alleyway behind the church where Pastor Taylor had died at the hands of a stranger while trying to rescue someone in danger. Off to the right was the main entrance of the church, still locked and looking neglected after two weeks without any traffic.

Kris sat and stared at her father, trying to understand what he was thinking and feeling. Dan felt rather than saw the immensity of the empty parking lot. He watched the wind sway the branches of a giant pepper tree that shaded the red tiles on the roof of the old church. *Would this be the last time he saw—or entered—this building?*

He inhaled loudly through his nose, raised his eyebrows, and looked at Kris. They stared at each other without speaking for a moment, and then Dan winked at her. She grinned.

"Come on, Dad," Kris said. "Jesus is waiting for us."

They walked around to the front entrance, and Dan unlocked the front door. He almost expected to hear organ music playing and voices raised in traditional hymns.

Tell me the old, old story, he thought he heard a ragged choir singing in the distance. He knew it was only his imagination.

They propped the doors open in front and walked slowly down the center aisle toward the platform. Sunlight poured from the stained-glass window behind them, bathing them in a rainbow of colors.

"God is here, even if no one else is," Kris said. Dan looked at his young daughter and was glad that she was there with him. She was right. This was God's house. As long as someone was there willing to worship, He would be there as well.

They sat in the front pew and waited for a few minutes. Finally, Kris spoke up.

"You know it's not really church service without singing," she said.

Dan looked at her, a small smile on his lips. "You really want to hear my singing? You know I'm tone deaf."

Kris grinned. "God doesn't care."

She opened the hymnal to number 183, and they began singing:

"I will sing of Jesus' love, sing of Him who first loved me, for He left bright world above, And died on Calvary."

Dan was glad that God was patient and tolerant with those who could not sing, for he usually buried his poor singing voice in the midst of the better voices of those around him. Now there was nowhere to hide. He suddenly realized what it was like to come before God with all your flaws, alone. He felt naked.

"Now we need to read a scripture," Kris said. She turned to Hebrews 4:16 and read: " 'Let us therefore boldly approach the throne of our gracious God, where we may receive mercy and in his grace find timely help.' "

Dan paused and thought about what she had read. "I like this one," he said, flipping over to Revelation 3:5. " 'He who is victorious shall thus be robed all in white; his name I will never strike off the roll of the living, for in the presence of my Father and his angels I will acknowledge him as mine.' "

Kris grinned up at her Dad. "Well, what about this one?" she asked, flipping over to Romans 8:35: " 'Then what can separate us from the love of Christ? Can affliction or hardship? Can persecution, hunger, nakedness, peril, or the sword? "We are being done to death for thy sake all day long," as Scripture says; "we have been treated like sheep for slaughter"—and yet, in spite of all, overwhelming victory is ours through him who loved us. For I am convinced that there is nothing in death or life, in the realm of spirits or superhuman powers, in the world as it is or the world as it shall be, in the forces of the universe, in heights or depths— nothing in all creation that can separate us from the love of God in Christ Jesus our Lord.' "

Dan grinned back at Kris as she finished reading the passage. She knew exactly what to read to lift his spirits. He looked around at the empty pews. Somehow he knew things would be all right.

"Dad, can I go out front and watch for cars for a little while?" Kris asked. "I'm afraid some of them don't realize we are open."

Dan looked at her and smiled. "What would I do without you, Kitkat?" He winked at her. "Sure, you go watch for more people."

Kris disappeared into the lobby, leaving Dan alone in the sanctuary. The vast feeling of being alone swallowed him up again. *What irony*, he thought, *being acting head elder in a church with no members.*

"God," he whispered. "I am here. Kris and I are here to worship you. We know you have promised that the church would not fall, but I see no evidence that the church is going to pull through this.

"Where are they, God? Where are your children?" he asked, his voice getting a little louder. "I called them, I encouraged them. I told them not to give up hope. But they have given up. You have called me to be a leader—but a leader of *what?* Of *whom?*

"Lord, I've lost my church, my job, my son—and now I may lose my marriage unless a miracle happens. I need an answer from You, God. I need You to show me what to do. Will You fill these pews again—or will I leave to join my wife in another church?"

Even as he said it, he knew he would never leave the Seventh-day Adventist Church.

Who are you to tell God what He must do? a voice asked him. *If you two are the only ones to worship Him, so be it.*

"O God, forgive me!" he wailed suddenly, falling face down on the carpet. "I have forgotten who is in charge here. Of course, You are right. Of course, You are in charge. I submit myself to Your will.

"Whatever happens, even if they want to kill me, I belong to You," he said, his face buried in the carpet. "If You want me to lead, I will lead. If You want me to worship You in an empty sanctuary, I will do that. Whatever it is, I am Yours."

All or nothing, the voice from the playground came back to him. *All for God—or nothing.*

Tears ran from Dan's eyes as he unloaded his fears, his guilt, and his burdens. Finally he had no more to say; no more tears to cry. That's when he heard the cough behind him.

Surprised, he pulled himself up to his knees and turned to look behind him. Three rows back, an elderly lady he recognized as Mrs. Siebert sat looking at him expectantly.

"It's been a long time since I have seen an elder in this

church really open himself up to God like that," she said. "We all need to do that. That's what He's been waiting for, you know."

"How long have you been sitting there?" Dan asked, more surprised than embarrassed.

"Just a couple of minutes," Mrs. Siebert said. "Sorry I've missed the past few weeks. Been sick in bed with the flu. I didn't think I would ever get well, but God woke me up this morning and told me I had to get over here for church."

Dan walked over to her and hugged her. "God bless you," he said.

"Dad," Kris said, sticking her head in from the foyer. "Someone else is coming."

Dan waited expectantly for a minute until the doors opened slowly and Mrs. Eastham entered the sanctuary.

"Jonathan wanted to be here," Mrs. Eastham said, joining Mrs. Siebert and Dan. "He heard what was happening, but he still doesn't have the strength."

"Bless you," Dan said to Mrs. Eastham, then looked at Mrs. Siebert. *Where would the church have been for the past few years without silver-haired women like these two?* he asked himself.

In response, the doors of the foyer crashed open and what seemed like an army of teenagers strode in quickly. Clad in black leather, some in jeans, others in sandals and cutoffs, the dozen or so strangers walked up the aisle as if they belonged and they knew exactly where they were going. But Dan's eyes were not on them. Instead it was riveted on the young man who led them toward the front.

"Mitch!" Dan shouted, leaping to his feet.

Mitch grinned from ear to ear and opened his arms as his father ran into them. They hugged in the center aisle for many moments, without either one saying anything. Finally Mitch pulled away and looked at his father.

"Mind if we join you for church?" he asked, grinning. "I brought a few friends I met in Santa Cruz who want to learn more about what we believe, and want to get to know Jesus Christ better."

"Mitch!" Kris squealed, bursting through the doors to the foyer and running down the aisle. She plowed into Mitch and Dan and hugged them tight.

"I was outside, and I guess I didn't see you get here," Kris said to Mitch. She turned to her father. "Dad, there is a police car pulling up out front," Kris said after a moment.

In response, the doors opened yet again, and Dan heard the squawky voice of a police radio enter the room. A man in a blue uniform with what looked like a very large gun strapped to his side slowly walked up to the crowd of people.

"Are you the person in charge?" the police officer asked Dan.

"I'm the elder, but God's really the One in charge," Dan answered.

"Do you realize that you are trespassing here?" the officer said. "These doors were closed and locked two weeks ago. How did you get in here?"

Dan shrugged. "As an elder, I have a key to the door. I used it and unlocked the door."

"But that lock was changed two weeks ago," the officer said. "Your key should not have worked."

Dan shrugged again. "It did. That's all I can say."

"God wanted us to meet here," said Mrs. Siebert. "No lock is going to keep us out."

Shouts of "Yeah!" and "All right!" came from the group of teens.

"Well, I don't know what happened to the lock," the officer said, "but I do know that you are breaking the law. You all have five minutes to clear the building. This is now federal property."

* * * * *

"I told you that the church would not fall," Elder Eastham said later that day when Dan, Kris, and Mitch visited him in his home.

"Yes, you did," Dan said, patting him on the hand. Dan could see that Elder Eastham's health had improved and his strength was gradually returning, but he had a very long way to go.

"But, Elder Eastham," Kris said, "the police came and chased us out of our own church. They said we were trespassing. They said we were breaking the law!"

Elder Eastham nodded silently for a moment. "It will get worse. The beast will want to stamp you out for good. Now is the time for two things.

"First, you must wait on the Lord. Pray as you have never prayed before. Study your Bible. Wait for the outpouring of the Holy Spirit—the Latter Rain. When it comes, it will usher in the last push of evangelism this world will ever see.

"Second, you must meet in secret."

He stopped to clear his throat and pull himself up in his bed. Mitch and Dan helped him as much as he would allow them, before he continued.

"Years ago, right after the Second World War, I was a missionary in China," Elder Eastham explained. "The Communists were taking over China, and everything they considered Western, including Christianity, was being cast out.

"We were thrown out of our churches, and the members were persecuted—tortured and beaten. Members were encouraged to testify against their fellow Christians. It was a terrible time, and the church almost died out. But we discovered a way to meet in secret.

"We started meeting in what I called cell churches," he explained. "Each cell was independent of all the others. They would meet several times a week, and would go out and witness and recruit new members every chance they had. But they never let their church get any larger than twelve members.

When they reached that point, they would split off and start two churches with six members each.

"Each church would grow and divide, grow and divide, with its only authority the Word of God and the Holy Spirit. None of the members really knew how many cell churches there were. When someone was captured and forced to testify against his fellow Christians, that cell church would disband; but others would start in its place.

"Only one person knew how many churches there were and where they were meeting," Elder Eastham said. "That was me, and I knew that there were hundreds. I never revealed to anyone who or where they were. It was how we survived the bad times."

Elder Eastham reached over and put his hand on Dan's arm. "These are also bad times, Dan. They will get worse."

Somehow Dan knew that Elder Eastham was right.

CHAPTER 14

"All right, that's far enough."

Dan heard the deep voice rasp through the screen door and then saw the gleam off the shotgun's blue-metal barrel. A jolt of electricity screamed up Dan's spine.

"Uh … I, uh…" was all Dan could utter. He couldn't pull his eyes from the barrel of the over-and-under twelve-gauge double-barreled shotgun. It was a Remington. Dan knew because his father had killed many geese with one. Now Dan wondered if it was his turn to be the goose.

"I have had enough of you religious freaks coming around here trying to peddle your New Age brand of hogwash," the man said. The screen creaked open, and the gun barrel slid out toward Dan, followed by a middle-aged man dressed in slacks and a white sleeveless undershirt.

Dan took a deep breath. *Lord, help me*, he prayed quickly, then began.

"Uh, sir, you have me all wrong. I'm not one of those religious freaks. I'm not into the New Age at all." Dan tried to put on his friendliest smile, which came out looking like a nervous sneer.

"You're not?" the man said, surprised. He lowered the barrel half an inch.

"No, sir," Dan said. "I was just admiring your chestnut tree in your front yard."

"You were?" the man said and then coughed.

"Yeah, I don't think I've seen any others in this area. There are a lot of them on the East Coast, but they don't seem to do well here in California."

The man continued coughing, his gun barrel dropping to point at the ground.

"You know it takes a chestnut tree a long time to grow, especially one as big as the one you've got there. That must be a hundred years old. I can't imagine why no one has written it up in the paper."

Dan paused and watched as the man wiped his mouth after a moment, feeling relieved that the gun barrel was no longer pointed at his chest.

"Sorry," the man said, finally. "I guess I overreacted. Come in, please."

"That's not necessary," Dan said.

"Nonsense," said the man. "I've been rude. Name's Johansen, Ernst Johansen. Sorry about the shotgun. People have gotten really weird lately. What with the big push for this weird new religion and the crazy things people are doing."

"Yeah, I was just admiring your tree," Dan said. "Dan Lewis."

Dan followed Mr. Johansen into his living room, a dark place because all the shades were drawn. Mr. Johansen gestured toward the couch, and Dan took a seat.

"What are you, a botanist?" Mr. Johansen asked.

Dan shook his head. "I used to teach science to high school kids. Now I do yard work for people. This early strange spring has given me plenty of work."

"Yard work? That's a strange change of careers."

Dan shrugged. "Strange times. I…"

Dan felt a queasy feeling and looked up. The small antique

chandelier in the living room began to swing. A second later, Dan felt as if the floor had fallen out from under him.

Brrrrrrooom! Dan and Mr. Johansen looked at each other and realized that they were in the middle of a classic California earthquake. Dust began to sift down from the ceiling. Dan heard a window shatter with a *pow!* somewhere else in the house. Both men were on the floor without realizing how they got there. They tried to crawl to the doorway. Instead they rolled on the floor like two fish out of water.

Thirty seconds later, it was over. Dan had lived in California most of his life and been through countless minor temblors. He knew this one was significant. How significant, he wasn't sure.

"Well, that was fun," Mr. Johansen said, standing up and dusting himself off. Dan heard dozens of car alarms honking throughout the neighborhood, accompanied by howls from every dog within hearing.

Dan shook his head and blew air through pursed lips. "Yeah, like I said, strange times."

"Look," Mr. Johansen said, coughing again. "I know I came down hard on these religious fanatics earlier, but do you think they might have a point? Is God punishing us? Should we all be going to church?"

Dan smiled inside. It didn't take much these days to get conversations around to religious things. Even when someone like Mr. Johansen said he was opposed to religion, God opened a way for Dan to witness.

"Look, Ernst, was it? Do you believe in the Bible? If you read something from the Bible, would you believe it?"

Mr. Johansen grinned. "I'm more likely to believe something I read myself from the Holy Scriptures than something some Druid priest received in vision." He coughed again. "I grew up going to the Lutheran Church, but I haven't been in a long time."

"Here," Dan said, scribbling down a couple of scriptures on a pad he carried. "Look these up, and see what you think." He tore it off. "I also wrote down a prescription for that cough."

Johansen lifted an eyebrow. "Are you a doctor too?"

Dan smiled and shook his head. "I do know plants, however. You can make a tea from the leaves of that chestnut tree to help you with that cough. That's where all of our medicines originally came from, you know. Plants. And that's still where most of them originate today."

Mr. Johansen looked at the sheet of paper and then paused. "I'll try it. Hey, you interested in more yard work? I can't pay much, though."

Dan shrugged and grinned. "Sure. We'll work something out."

* * * * *

Kris fingered a red bookmark as she sat in the cafeteria following her meal. She had another fifteen minutes until classes started, so she sat half watching the students around her and half staring into empty space.

"Hello." Kris felt Brad playfully rap on the side of her head with his knuckle. "Anyone in there?"

Kris smiled wistfully. "I'm not sure anymore," she answered. "I thought I had my life all figured out, and now . . ."

"Now your parents go and get divorced," Brad answered.

"They're *not* divorced," Kris said. "Just separated."

"Right," Brad said. "That's the way my parents started out. Now Dad lives in Pittsburgh. At least you get to live at home with your mom."

"Yippee," Kris responded without enthusiasm.

"Look, it'll get better," Brad said hopefully.

Kris continued to finger the bookmark, a present from her dad at her baptism.

"Hey, Kris," Ginger said behind her. She dropped her books on the table as she spoke. "Did you finish the comparative religion assignment?"

Kris nodded. Everyone was always coming to her for help in their comparative religion class, what used to be called Bible class.

"Well, how did you respond to the essay question?" Ginger asked. "Mrs. Whyte said we could compare notes."

"Comparing salvation in Christianity, Islam, and Buddhism? Simple. Christianity is the only religion in the world where you can't do anything to save yourself." Kris raised an eyebrow.

Brad snorted. "That's not true. What about all those times when they told us that we had to be good? We had to obey or we wouldn't go to heaven."

Kris shook her head. "Don't you understand? That's what we have had wrong for so long. You can't be good by yourself. You can't be perfect. All we end up doing is comparing ourselves to other people. And even the most perfect person who ever lived—other than Jesus—cannot do anything to match up to God's expectation for us."

"Then we are all lost," Brad said. Kris noticed that others were coming over to their table and listening to the conversation.

"No, that's where Jesus comes in. Jesus is the Son of God. Jesus was—*is*—perfect. Jesus died the death of a sinner and conquered death. He died our death. If we accept Jesus' sacrifice, and let His will work in us, we will be saved. Not because we are perfect. Because we are perfect—*in Him.*"

Kris finished the last sentence completely immersed in what she was saying. She looked up and realized that everyone else had stopped to listen to what she was saying. Embarrassed, she dropped her head. Slowly, activity started again around her. A minute later, the bell rang for class.

"So how many people do you have in your Internet Bible class now?" Brad asked as they headed out the cafeteria doors.

"I've lost count," she said as they headed for class.

* * * * *

chapter 14

Another nightmare, Jenny said to herself, splashing water on her face in the bathroom. Getting around was harder and harder these days. Her abdomen had swelled so much that she thought there might be a dozen babies in there. She never seemed to have enough energy, and never could get the sleep she needed.

Her mother had come home to convalesce after the broken window accident. Now Jenny had to take care of herself and her baby and also a mother who couldn't seem to fend for herself. Her face pale and drawn since the accident, Mrs. Abbott for the most part stayed in bed. When she got up, she would pour herself a cup of coffee and sit at the kitchen table, staring out the window.

Jenny had tried to talk to her mother but had gotten no-where. All her mom wanted to talk about was Benji. Whenever Jenny brought up her father, Mrs. Abbott suddenly got tired and headed off to bed. *Dad is the only sane one here*, Jenny thought, tempted to take him up on his offer to let her stay in his new apartment. The incident with Benji was only the capstone on a quiet but long-standing conflict between her parents, she had discovered.

And then, on top of everything, the nightmares had started. *Jake*, she thought, *why can't I be with you?* Even as she thought it, she realized that Jake was dealing with his own nightmares.

That morning's nightmare had been a dilly. Babies all over the house, all with devilish grins and satanic intentions. A baby with a butcher knife had chased her through the kitchen. She could still see its face, even as she splashed cold water on her own face.

"Jenny," she heard her mom call. "Jenny, get me some coffee, please."

Jenny looked at her face in the bathroom mirror for a moment before replying.

"Yes, Mom. Coming right up." She heaved a heavy sigh and dropped the face towel on the vanity. She walked down the hallway and turned into the kitchen, and immediately realized that someone had been there before her.

Flour was scattered over the countertop, as if someone were baking bread or pies. And unmistakable in the flour were tiny handprints, as if left there by a baby.

She stared at the flour and the impressions for several moments, almost without belief. Then she saw the butcher knife on the floor, just below the flour, and what looked like blood around it.

* * * * *

"Faked, all of it," Mr. Abbott said as he looked at the flour and the knife. "Someone made it look like baby handprints, but those aren't handprints at all."

"And the blood on the floor?" Jenny asked, still unnerved.

Mr. Abbott shook his head. "Obviously, you've never been around real blood before. Steak sauce. Would've fooled me. On second thought, it probably wouldn't have."

"Well, how did they know about my dream?" Jenny asked.

Mr. Abbott shrugged. "Can't answer that one, sweetheart." He put his arm around his daughter. "Look, my offer still stands. Come stay with me. The place is small, but I have a semi-comfortable couch. You'll sleep better over there."

Jenny shook her head. "Thanks, but no. Mom needs me."

"Well, then, at least come over for dinner tonight. Spaghetti."

Jenny looked at her dad and nodded. She wrapped her arms around his neck and let the tears come.

* * * * *

"With casualties already exceeding ninety thousand deaths, yesterday's 9.9 earthquake centered in downtown Los Angeles is already the greatest natural disaster in United States history. The death toll is expected to exceed one hundred thousand shortly."

Mitch only partially heard the radio news in the background

as he and Dan struggled to get the last of their belongings down the wooden stairway to the basement of the Eastham home. A single light bulb swung from the wooden beams in the ceiling. Mrs. Eastham had done her best to make the basement homey, but it was obvious from the concrete floor, open crawl spaces, and dust that the basement was never intended as a living area. Nevertheless, Mitch and Dan were grateful for whatever they could find.

They hauled Dan's old trunk down the stairs. Mitch and Dan sweated in the heat, even though it was only late January.

"Why do you hold on to this thing, Dad?" Mitch complained as he fell backwards for the third time while trying to keep hold of the old leather handle.

"You'll thank me someday soon," Dan said. "This has all my lab equipment in it. I haven't used it in years, but something tells me that competent medical assistance is going to disappear pretty fast with the deterioration of society."

As if in response, they both turned to listen to the newscaster's voice coming from the old standup radio in the corner of the basement.

"In response to the California quake, the latest in the series of natural disasters that continue to plague our world, the pope has called for a universal state of prayer from all peoples in all nations. This means that we should all pause at noon this Sunday to pray to our God and seek His mercy.

"The United States government has officially given up. The president's statement this morning, announcing that the federal emergency fund is bankrupt, means that those victims in southern California are at the mercy of those who want to volunteer their time, food, and clothing. But no organized help will be coming from the federal government.

"People, it's time we turned to prayer." The announcer ended with an uncharacteristic five seconds of silence.

Mitch looked at his father.

"It's going to get worse," Dan said. "And then better."

CHAPTER 15

Jenny smiled as she opened the front door of Mr. Abbott's apartment. *Simple and straightforward, like Dad,* she thought. Two old metal chairs stood next to an old card table in the kitchen. Around the corner, she could see that the living room furniture consisted of a beat-up old green couch—her dad's favorite color—and a tiny black-and-white TV. On the wall hung a picture that looked as though it belonged in a yard sale. *Temporary,* was the word that came to Jenny's mind. *Dad's probably thinking he'll be back home before too long.* Of course, she thought, everything was pretty much temporary for her dad.

"*Bon giorno,*" Mr. Abbott shouted out from the kitchen, where he was putting the finishing touches on a green salad. "I hope you like-a my spaghetti, pretty girl." He grinned at Jenny.

"I should like it after having to eat it for the past twenty-five years," Jenny said, grabbing her father around the neck from behind. "Actually, your spaghetti sounds pretty good to me. Junior keeps telling me she's hungry, even though I just ate an hour ago."

"Junior has good taste," her dad chuckled, stirring the noodles in the boiling cauldron. "*He* will fit in well in this family."

"More than that, Dad," Jenny added. "I need something normal—regular—to hang my hat on. Things are so weird—have been so weird for months—that I just need something I can count on." She picked a wet noodle from the spoon he was stirring with and stuck it in her mouth. "Something like your spaghetti."

There is something in certain foods that goes beyond merely good tastes or satisfying one's appetite, Jenny thought. *Some foods—even their aromas—can actually transport you in time and space back to cherished memory.*

Her mother called them "comfort foods," Jenny remembered, and the aroma of boiling spaghetti noodles and homemade sauce brought it home for her. Her dad used to love to cook on Sunday evenings—and often it was spaghetti. It was one of the few days he seemed to make it home at a reasonable hour, and Jenny took comfort in those memories of a complete family.

Jenny helped Dad set the table, and the conversation moved from the preparation area to the kitchen table.

"I made the meatballs as a side dish, since I remembered you are vegetarian now," Dad said quietly.

"Thanks, Dad. You're so sweet," Jenny said. She started to bow her head in prayer and then looked at her father. He smiled faintly and nodded.

"Go ahead," he said. "I'm no good at Grace."

Jenny said prayer for the two of them, and then they began eating with gusto.

"Yeah, I know what you mean when you say things are weird," Mr. Abbott said, continuing with what she had said earlier.

"Used to be, when you had a clear-cut violation of the law you could bring them in to be booked and be sure that they would end up behind bars. Today they not only beat us back to the streets, but the police are openly booed and abused just about everywhere you go. I've gone through three cars in the past month because people have thrown rocks, bricks, and bottles from rooftops as we went by."

"And the court is worse." He dropped his head and shook it sadly. "I can't get a court to convict anyone."

"Is it the judges—or are jails full?" Jenny asked.

"Both, from what I hear. Judges are only concerned about getting reelected, so they are following what's popular rather than what is right. And they're not spending money on jails anymore, so there's nowhere for the guilty to go. Pretty soon they'll be resurrecting the idea of firing squads."

Jenny stopped, startled and surprised. "You're kidding, right?"

Mr. Abbott chuckled a little, then stopped. "It wouldn't surprise me. Some of the guys at the precinct think that would solve a lot of problems. Trouble is, they want to get rid of the religious troublemakers first."

"Troublemakers?" Jenny repeated. "What are you talking about?"

"Well, some of them see all the strange stuff happening in the world. Tornadoes, earthquakes in California, mudslides, and volcanoes—and the riots we have to deal with. They think there must be a reason it's happening. They think the reason is that we're not united in serving God. We have a few "dedicated" individuals—their words here, not mine—who want to bring us back to God as a united, Christian nation. And they think that will solve all these other problems.

"Problem is, they have all these other people who want to do things their own way, the way they think is right."

"The religious troublemakers," Jenny said.

Mr. Abbott nodded. "These are the fundamentalist religions who won't accept or merge with other religions, and the offshoot groups that don't really have an official, organized religion."

Jenny felt an icy chill run down her back.

"Daddy, what about the First Amendment? Isn't it against

the Constitution for the government to stop these other groups?"

"First," Mr. Abbott said, waving his fork in her direction. "One of the first things I learned in police academy was that the Constitution was only as good as the Supreme Court justices that interpret it. The group that's there now will do whatever it takes—legal or otherwise—to get this craziness under control."

"And second?" Jenny asked.

"Second, if a group isn't recognized as an official, organized religion, then they won't have any rights under the law, will they?"

Jenny thought of the news she had seen and heard regarding the now-defunct Seventh-day Adventist Church, and swallowed hard.

"What do you think, Daddy?"

"I think the hard times are upon us, sweetie," he said to Jenny, putting his arm on her shoulder. "And whether it's recognized by the United States government, the Supreme Court or your Aunt Margaret, I want to be on the right side."

* * * * *

"The end is upon us!"

Kris read the words on the web page, along with the words and scriptures that followed. *Well, that's not the way I would have said it*, she thought, *but Marquee never was one for being subtle.* She smiled and shook her head as she thought of all the people she had studied the Bible with who now had their own web pages or hosted listserv programs where an unlimited number of people could communicate over the Internet simultaneously. Thanks to Fin, or whatever his real name was, she now had access to one of the listservs and continued to share what she knew of Scripture with whoever wanted to know. To the credit of her students, most of them had their own Bible study groups now, and many were in theological waters far deeper than she ever dared to enter.

"What are you looking at, sweetie?" The voice behind Kris startled her, and she jumped, almost as if she was ashamed of what she had accessed.

"Uh, nothing, Mom," Kris said, looking up at Meg, who had finally come home from work.

"It's just a web page that one of my friends put together."

Meg squinted at the TV set. "Hmm. Sounds ominous. Is this one of your school friends?"

Kris shook her head. "Someone I met on the Internet. He wanted to know what I believed and knew about Bible prophecy, so I told him."

Meg looked at the screen silently, then shook her head. "Sweetheart, you know we have warned you about the people you might meet on the Internet. There are all kinds of crazies out there, and you have to be careful." She bent down and typed something on the keyboard. A new address appeared on the URL line, and a colorful screen with video and symphonic music appeared before them.

"This is the web page I helped our new church put together," Meg said. "It's a lot more positive and exciting, don't you think?" she asked.

"But, Mom," Kris responded after looking at it for a moment. "It doesn't say anything. It talks about being happy and how God loves us, but it doesn't say anything about what is going on in the world."

"Just give it a chance!" Meg shouted back. Both Kris and Meg were surprised at the outburst that came from Meg, and Meg blushed.

"Sorry, dear." Meg took a deep breath. "We spent a lot of hours making the web page as wonderful as possible without trying to offend anyone. I agree that it needs to address the dreadful things happening in the world, but that will have to wait until phase two of the page."

Meg stood up and snapped her fingers. "Speaking of phase two, I have something for you." She walked back to the front door, and Kris, curious, stood and watched her. Meg picked up a big package and brought it back to Kris.

"Consider it a late Christmas present." Both of them flinched at the thought of the horrible holiday they had had a few weeks before. Christmas Day had been marked by a massive fight between her parents, followed by Dan and then Mitch moving out. Things were a lot quieter now, but not necessarily better, Kris thought. Now Meg was filing for divorce and asking for—and most likely getting—custody of Kris.

Kris tore open the bright blue package and saw the brown box inside with the logo of Meg's company on the outside. She opened it up and saw a shiny new notebook computer.

"Wow! A notebook!" Kris said, carefully taking it from the case.

"Not just any notebook," Meg said. "It's the latest prototype. It has three times the RAM memory, hard drive space, and video definition of the nearest competitor. It's three times as fast. It uses solar batteries that can be recharged by the sun. And look at this—" she pointed at a little red spot on the top of the keyboard.

"That means that this notebook has a satellite modem. Wherever you are, it can connect with the national communication satellites and put you in instant contact with me or anyone else who has access to the Internet."

"Which is pretty much anyone in the world these days," Kris said.

"Pretty much," Meg said, nodding, her hands on her hips.

"Cool," Kris said, thinking of how many people she could share Jesus with now.

"Yeah, pretty cool," said Meg, thinking something totally different.

* * * * *

"I can't find it," Mitch said from the dark corner of the basement.

"Then you aren't looking," his dad shot back. "It's there somewhere. Keep looking."

Mitch stood up, feeling irritated at his father but trying hard to keep his temper under control.

"Look, Dad. I have searched this part of the basement twice, and there is no graphite machine here."

"Mimeograph," Dan said to himself. "Mimeograph. The thing is called a mimeograph."

"Whatever," Mitch said. "I just don't see how something invented in the Dark Ages is going to help us spread the gospel."

Dan stood up, his hands pressing on his aching back. "Look, people were preaching a long time before you were born. Before I was born. The world has not always been the way it is today."

"Thank goodness," Mitch said more to himself than to his father.

"You boys still looking for that old contraption?" Mrs. Eastham shouted down the stairs to Dan and Mitch.

"Yes, Mrs. Eastham," Dan responded. "Your husband said it was stored over in this corner."

"Jonathan hasn't been down in that basement in two years," Mrs. Eastham said, climbing down the stairs. "I was the one who stored it away." She walked over to the opposite side of the basement and opened a cabinet door below some canned fruit.

"Hmm," she said, looking in. "Help me get it out of here."

Dan and Mitch pulled the machine out of the cupboard and took off the black vinyl covering. A rotary cylinder with a rubber blanket and handle on one side reminded Mitch of a miniature printing press.

"It's got all the materials you need over here," Mrs. Eastham said. "All you need to get is some paper—wait, there's some here. Looks as though you are ready to go."

"Thanks a bunch," Dan said to her as Mrs. Eastham went back up the stairs.

Dan stood there, enamored by the ancient mechanism.

"See, Mitch," he said. "This is how they made copies before duplicating machines were invented."

"Uh-huh," Mitch said, unimpressed. "And your newsletter from this machine is going to make the difference in reaching the world with the gospel."

Dan paused in turning the mimeograph handle and looked at his son. "What's wrong with you? I thought you were behind our efforts to spread the gospel."

"Spread the gospel, yes," Mitch said. "But this is plain boring to me. Nobody I know is going to read something printed by this old—dinosaur."

"You'd be surprised what an old dinosaur can do," Dan answered.

"Why don't you do this, Dad, and let me do what I think needs to be done?" Mitch asked.

"Like what? Like hang out with your old friends and get beat up again?" Dan said.

"Hey, I got a lot more people to come into the church getting beat up than you did hanging around here opening the door to an empty church," Mitch said, his voice rising.

"Boys!"

Dan and Mitch heard the word in alarm come from upstairs. They both took the wooden stairs in four leaps.

Mrs. Eastham was standing in the living room, one hand covering her mouth and the other pointing at the television set. On the set was the president of the United States.

"The death toll continues to climb in the latest disaster to hit the United States, the disastrous earthquake in Los Angeles two days ago. Had this been an isolated incident, there would be regrettable devastation and death, but as a nation we would have been able to recover from the blow.

"However, this is only the latest in a series of natural disasters that started last November with the eruption of Mount Erebus in Antarctica and the subsequent earthquakes, tidal waves, and volcanic eruptions elsewhere in the globe. Hawaii has not yet recovered from the tidal wave that hit there two days after the Mount Erebus eruption. Volcanic eruptions have led to cinders in the jet stream. And those cinders have started hundreds of wildfires in Montana and Wyoming. Tornadoes have hit the Midwest by the hundreds. Monsoon floods have hit Florida. Now this earthquake in California.

"No one can reasonably view the earthquake as an isolated incident. Whether you are someone who believes in scientific cause and effect, or a spiritual person who believes in the wrath of God, it is obvious that something must be done.

"But what should be done? I am a God-fearing man, but I am not a spiritual leader. I look to someone that the world sees as a spiritual leader to answers for spiritual problems. For whether you believe our devastation is from scientific causes or from spiritual ones, its resolution can only come from one source. God.

"We must turn our faces back to God. We must humble ourselves before God. We must take time to show our humility before the Maker of the Universe. Only He—or She if you prefer—has the power to make right what is now wrong.

"These are not my words. I do not take credit for them. They come from the leader of the Roman Catholic Church, the largest Christian church in the world, and the undisputed spiritual leader of the world.

"The pope has suggested that all peoples everywhere pause this Sunday at noon for one hour and pray to their Maker for mercy toward the people of earth. These disasters affect us all; therefore we must share the responsibility before God.

"I applaud the pope's suggestion. But I know human nature. People will forget. People will go on with business as usual.

"Therefore I am making it impossible for people—at least here in the United States—to forget. I am hereby mandating that all businesses on U.S. soil, all government operations, military facilities, and other American interests overseas cease from all work at exactly noon local time this Sunday, January 24, to pray and humble themselves before God. Further, I encourage other countries represented in the United Nations to do the same.

"As I already mentioned, we are all affected by these disasters—acts of God, if you will. Therefore we as a nation, as a people, as a human race, must accept responsibility as a whole.

"May God have mercy on us all."

Mr. and Mrs. Eastham, Dan and Mitch stared at the screen, speechless for a minute.

"Did what I think happened just happen?" Mrs. Eastham asked finally.

"It won't be long now, sweetheart," Mr. Eastham said weakly.

Mitch continued to stare at the screen, now showing the network anchor making a commentary on the president's speech. Dan laid his hand on Mitch's shoulder.

"You were right, you know," Dan said to Mitch.

Mitch turned and looked at his father, his forehead creased in worry. This was not like his father.

"That's what God has been trying to teach me all along," said Dan. "We have to reach everyone. We can't use just one way to do it. We have to use every person's talents and special communication skills to reach those they can communicate with best."

"But, Dad, the mimeograph machine is a good idea," Mitch said.

"I agree, it is," Dan said. "For some people. But I am sure you can come up with better ideas for others. From now on, we each do what the Holy Spirit leads us to do. Time is short."

Mitch nodded, his mind reeling with a hundred thoughts. *Too much to do. Time is short.*

CHAPTER 16

Jenny awoke from a sound sleep—the first she had had for a week. She was surprised that there had been no nightmares. Maybe the talk with her dad had helped, she thought, as she lay in the darkness, her eyes half shut in partial sleep.

She had almost taken her dad up on his offer to let her stay with him in his apartment. But she always had trouble getting used to new beds, and she had finally gotten used to this one. In addition, her mother had begun to get up and around, and so the Child Protection Services people had brought Benji back to live with them again.

Benji. The thought of that child made the hairs on the back of her neck stand up. There was something definitely wrong with him, though he was strangely quiet and passive when he arrived back home. Mrs. Abbott had attributed it to medication—she said they were using Ritalin—but Jenny still wasn't sure. She felt very uneasy.

As if in response to her thoughts, she heard footsteps in the hallway outside her door. *Probably Mom or Benji getting a drink of water,* she thought. She lay there for a moment and then realized that the floorboards were creaking heavily as if a large person was walking in the hall. Her heart began to beat faster. *Should*

I see who it is? Benji or Mom could be in danger.

She lay there and argued with herself as the sound of the footsteps continued. *Sure, like a woman seven months pregnant could scare away a burglar,* she thought. *Who am I kidding? Jake, why aren't you here?* She had tried a number of times to call the navy base where Jake was stationed, and even Castle Medical Center where he was doing his surgery work, but with all the disasters throughout the world—and now in the United States—phone service was undependable at best. She hadn't talked to him in what seemed like a long, long time.

The steps continued for a few seconds and then stopped. That was almost worse for Jenny than hearing them. Had the person left?

She waited in silence for a long time, hardly daring to breathe. *I've got to know*, she finally thought. Pulling back the covers, she dropped her bare feet silently to the cold floor.

"Lord, protect me," she breathed as she reached into the closet and pulled out Benji's baseball bat. She turned the doorknob as quietly as she dared and crept out into the dim hallway.

"It's just my imagination," she muttered to herself quietly. She peeked around the corner to her mother's room. Mrs. Abbott was sleeping quietly in her big bed, oblivious to anything that Jenny might consider dangerous or wrong.

"So far, so good," Jenny whispered and turned to check on Benji. She padded down the hallway and into the living room where Benji lay sleeping on his cot.

"It *was* my imagination," she said to herself, suddenly a lot more relaxed. Just to make sure, she decided to check the kitchen. She walked in cautiously, still remembering the incident with the flour and the butcher knife.

She expected the worst. But the kitchen looked the way she had left it a few hours before when she had finished the dishes and turned off the light. The dish towel still hung from the ring by the sink. The counter was completely clean—just as she had left it.

She breathed a sigh of relief.

The phone rang, shattering the stillness. She jumped, startled, then felt relieved that something so normal could be happening again.

She didn't let it ring a second time, but picked it up immediately.

"Hello?" she asked.

Click. The phone went dead.

"Hello? Hello?" she said again. Finally she hung it up.

She took a deep breath and tried to decide how she felt. Angry? Afraid? Confused?

Unsure seemed to be the word most appropriate for her frame of mind, she decided. She walked back through the darkened house to the bathroom and thought about her childhood in this house. Meg always was the leader, and Jenny had been her loyal companion. When Meg thought up grand and often dangerous schemes, Jenny dutifully followed along. When they ended up on the roof of the garage, or in a dark attic, or in the crawlspace under the house surrounded by cobwebs, Jenny never felt afraid. She felt *unsure*.

Unsure because she always thought Big Sister would take care of her and not let her get into danger. When there was danger, she was no longer sure that the trust she had in her sister was valid.

Now she wasn't sure whether she was in danger or not—but she was *scared*. Strange things were happening around her, and she couldn't seem to find anyone who could help her.

She splashed cold water on her face and dried it. She looked at her own reflection in the mirror. A grown-up woman about to become a mother in most people's view, but what she saw now was just a frightened girl.

"God, please help me," she prayed, but for the first time in a long while, she wondered if God was there.

She took a deep breath and headed back to her room. She pushed the door open and looked across the room at the doors of the closet. She gasped as she read what had been written there in red lipstick:

Your baby will die.

* * * * *

Khaki and leather, cotton and chains. Nine young men and women huddled together in a shared apartment, focused on a single chapter in the book of Acts. Books and magazines were stacked everywhere around them, interspersed with Christian CDs. Music from the Christian band Plan C played in the background.

Hope and desperation were mixed in the air; urgent and fervent prayers mixed with praises and hallelujahs. Food surrounded them as well—popcorn, chips, fruit, and enough bottled water to float a battleship.

"It won't work, I tell you," a young woman in the corner said, flipping her blond hair from her eyes. "They were filled with the power of the Holy Spirit. We haven't experienced the latter rain yet."

"But, Gina, how do we know we haven't been baptized with the Holy Spirit?" a young Hispanic man in motorcycle leather asked. "Just because the apostles received a visible manifestation doesn't mean it has to happen that way every time. Besides, we need to do something, not just sit here and wait for the end to come."

"Harley, Gina, just chill for a minute," Mitch said, holding up his hand. "I think you are both right—and wrong. Gina, I agree that the latter rain hasn't come yet, and we need to pray for that. That's what we have been waiting for, Harley. But we need to be doing some witnessing in the meantime. Serious witnessing.

"Now I think this New Church rally thing at the Convention Center is just what we need. It's not yet illegal to speak your mind in public—even about religious matters. On the other hand, we may get some people upset with us. But then, there are stories throughout the New Testament about people getting upset when they heard the gospel. We're not doing anything new."

Several chuckled at that.

"In any case, we need to work on logistics—where, when, and how—as well as an escape route if things get too hairy. It's still too early for all of us to end up in jail."

"Leave the escape to me," said Gina. "I know the area backwards and forwards from my pick-pocketing days."

* * * * *

I am one with God for I am God.
You are one with God for you worship her ways.
We are one with each other, separate and distinct.
For we both seek God, and in doing so, become one with God.

"Aren't they great?" Meg asked Kris, as she turned the volume up slightly on the CD player in her new Porsche 911.

"I think they're kind of strange," Kris said quietly, looking out the window at the people passing by on Alameda Boulevard.

Meg glanced over at her daughter, a look of anger flashing briefly over her face, then resignation. "Oh well, the Flashtones are much better in concert. And if you don't like them, there will be six other Christian bands playing. Plus magicians, jugglers, performing dogs ... they're going to be televising this all over the U.S. and they are even taking up donations for disaster relief."

"Look, Mom, do we really have to do this? I mean, I am not really interested in this event, and I know you are really busy—"

"Kris, just stop it," Meg said sharply. "You haven't given it a chance. You haven't given *me* a chance. There are other things in the world, good things, that you will discover if you just open your eyes and get away from those Internet chat programs you seem to be addicted to."

Mom's probably right, Kris thought. *If I would just give a little, maybe my life would be a little more normal. Maybe I could talk Dad into compromising some. Then we could be a family again.* Her thought was interrupted by commotion ahead.

"Look, what's going on?" Kris asked, pointing in front of them.

"It's the rally. People are lining up to get inside."

"No. There's the line to get inside over there. This is something else."

Meg slowed down and got over in the right lane as they passed the plaza outside the Optimax Convention Center. A crowd of people stood around a man who was speaking to them from the back of a pickup truck. Meg took a closer look at the young man and realized she knew him.

"That's Mitch," Kris said, just as Meg was thinking the same thing.

"People! Listen to me!" Mitch shouted from the back of the pickup. "My friends and I are here to tell you that you have been lied to. We have all been lied to."

Mitch's words caused some of the passers-by to pause and hear what he had to say.

"The message you are getting here is that it's not important what we believe, just that we are sincere, and that we all believe it together. Right? That's ridiculous.

"If someone said that by concentrating we could fly, and if we all held hands and stepped off a cliff we wouldn't be hurt, would you do it?"

"What's in it for me?" a young, sharply dressed man in the front row shouted back. That drew a little laugh.

"See, that's the problem," Mitch said. "We all ask, 'What's in it for me?' If we can see a short-term profit, or have a thrill or a good time, that's all that matters."

Several laughed. "Sounds good to me," one shouted.

"But this whole thing is about God, and how we relate to

Him," Mitch continued. "Are we doing the things we do because we love Him and want to do His will? Or are we doing it because others expect it from us?"

Mitch sensed at that point that the crowd was losing interest in his speech. A few stayed behind, but most headed off for the lines to the rally inside.

"You can legislate religion—even church-going," Mitch said to a bearded man who stood just below him. "But you can't legislate belief in God. It has to come from in here."

The man stared at him for a long time, then turned and walked away.

Mitch watched the crowd leave them and saw the police heading their way.

"Come on, Mitch," Gina said. "This isn't working. Let's get out of here."

Mitch looked at the oncoming police before responding.

"You guys go ahead and split," Mitch said. "This is still a legal assembly. I want to hang around and see what happens."

Shaking her head, Gina and the others ran for the predetermined escape point. Mitch hopped down from the back of the pickup and watched as the patrol cars surrounded him.

"Yeah," he said more to himself than anyone. "I want to see how free this country still is."

Kris and Meg watched from a distance as the police swarmed around Mitch and the pickup. Meg gripped the steering wheel silently as the blue uniforms threw her son against the side of the pickup and handcuffed him. Kris watched in amazement as her mother did nothing to stop the police from driving away with Mitch in the back of a squad car. *Who is this woman?* Kris asked herself silently.

"I hope Mitch learned something there," Meg finally said. "Let them scare him a little. Then I will go down and get him out."

Meg popped the Flashtones CD from the player and stuck it back in the case between the seats. She looked at Kris.

"Don't you ever get the foolish idea of standing out in public and doing what your brother did," Meg said.

"Why not?" Kris asked. "He was saying what he believed. This is still a free country. Freedom of speech is still part of the Constitution, isn't it?"

"Young lady," Meg said, her right hand digging into Kris's arm. "You had better get a big dose of reality. All that stuff they taught you about freedom of speech and religion was appropriate for your grandparents' day, but they are a luxury this society can't afford anymore. Look around you! The world is falling apart. This rally is part of mankind's last hope to hold it all together."

Meg stared at Kris, and Kris realized she no longer knew her mother.

"Mom, you're hurting my arm," she said quietly. Meg stared at her for a moment as if she didn't understand, then let her go.

Mitch and Dad were right to leave, Kris thought. *I have to do what is right—no matter what.*

* * * *

The announcer's voice sounded tinny and small. "Following last week's successful halt of commerce on the nation's first mandatory state of prayer, Congress and the White House have been deluged by calls, letters, and e-mails. What's the nature of all these messages? Senator Pete Hawthorne of Montana tells us:

" 'People know this is the time for our Christian nation to come back to its roots. They see the earthquakes, tornadoes, and hurricanes. They have seen the recent stock market crash. And they believe God is trying to get our attention. And if we are not willing to listen to God, watch out.'

"The latest call is for what some refer to as a Unified State of Appeal. Each church would remain intact and separate, but each would be required to make national spiritual unity their first priority. And it looks likely to happen soon—perhaps within the next few weeks."

Jenny turned down the radio in Mrs. Abbott's brown Buick but continued to listen as she slowly turned right off of Ogden Avenue onto Oak Street and headed for the old Hinsdale Hospital complex. She had noticed that a lot less traffic came through this part of Hinsdale lately, and also the fact that the usually punctual village snowplows hadn't even come to that part of town yet. Across from the massive Adventist hospital was Hinsdale Adventist Church, the largest church in the Illinois Conference, and the church she used to call her home church.

She looked over to the right at the massive stone medical center and noticed that the name had been changed: Hinsdale Community Medical Center. Owned and operated by and for the people of Illinois. *Strange.*

Wednesday night. Should be prayer meeting time, she thought as she looked at the big church. It was dark.

Well, I guess the things I have heard about the Adventist Church are true, she thought. She had missed church for weeks, partly because no one else in her family went, partly because she never felt bold enough to go out on her own in the snow.

She drove around the church, looking for some signs of life. All the lights were off. She was just about to give up hope when she spied an older man shoveling snow from the steps outside the pastor's office.

"I'll bet that's a deacon, or elder...or maybe a pastor."

She needed someone who knew what they were doing on a spiritual level. She didn't know who that might be.

The snow was deep on the parking lot, and she didn't dare try to hike it in her seven-months-pregnant condition. So she pulled into the parking lot and drove as close to the man as she dared, then rolled down her window.

"Can I help you?" he asked.

"Are you a deacon or elder here?" Jenny asked,

The man didn't answer, but walked quietly up to her open

window. He leaned on the car and looked in the window as if scrutinizing her and deciding how he should respond.

"The Adventist Church has been disbanded. There's no such thing as an Adventist deacon or elder anymore."

"And if you were, you probably wouldn't tell me anyway, would you?" she asked. "Tell me, if the Adventist Church is disbanded, why are you shoveling snow around the church walkways?"

A faint smile played over the gray-haired man's lips, and he looked over his shoulder at the church. "Nostalgia, I guess. There's not a lot of traffic around here these days, but that doesn't mean the church shouldn't still look good."

Jenny looked at him and then at the church.

"Look sir, my name is Jenny Gallagher—used to be Abbott. My sister and I used to be members here when I was a teenager. That was about ten years ago."

"Jenny," the man said, still not showing any recognition. "I'm Tom Clavell."

Jenny reached out and shook his hand. "Mr. Clavell, I need help."

She briefly told him of the strange things happening in the Abbott household.

"And you say your husband is in the military in Hawaii?" he asked.

She nodded. "That's why I need spiritual support from a pastor, or an elder—or something," she said.

Mr. Clavell looked off into the distance and scratched his chin.

"Well, if times were normal, it'd be no problem. I'd take you to the pastor or the board of elders and we would deal with it."

"But these aren't normal times," Jenny completed the thought.

"No, they aren't." Mr. Clavell paused. "Tell you what. It's still not illegal to meet in people's homes and study the Bible. I know of a house nearby where you might be able to find some help."

* * * * *

Mitch was tired and scared. He had stayed up all night preparing the street witnessing experience that had for all intents and purposes fallen flat on its face. Then he had been arrested. They had taken his picture, his fingerprints, and done this strange thing called a magnetic scan that burned his hands and face. He was then interviewed for several hours by three different detectives, and left in the interrogation room with his hands cuffed behind him.

He was scared—and angry. He had fantasized as a teenager about a life filled with danger. Now that he was considered dangerous, he found it wasn't that great. Government was one of the few classes at South Bay Academy he had excelled at, and he knew that the police were doing what was unconstitutional. He hadn't been charged with anything. He hadn't been given the chance to call a lawyer. All he had been given was hours of questioning. Who else was involved? they had asked. Where did they meet? What organizations were supporting their effort?

Subversive. That was the word they had used for him. He grinned to himself. So now the truth is subversive. *Well, that tells me a lot about the country I now live in.* They hadn't roughed him up—just tried to scare him—but Mitch knew that his arrest was supposed to be a warning to others who might try to do what they had tried—and failed—to do.

He heard keys rattle in the lock. A second later, the detective who had talked to him last came through the doorway. He walked over to the desk across from Mitch and sat down, ruffling through some papers, as if Mitch wasn't even there. Finally he looked up at Mitch, frowning.

"OK, here's the deal," the detective said. "You don't have any prior arrests, so we are going to release you into your mother's custody. But we want this to be a stern warning to you." He stood up and fished around for the key to unlock his manacles. Stepping behind Mitch's chair, he unlocked the handcuffs, allowing Mitch to stand up.

"Sir, I mean no disrespect," Mitch said as politely as he could. "But I was wondering. What was I arrested for? I never heard any official statement of my charges."

"You weren't arrested," the detective said, stepping in front of Mitch. "You were *detained*. There's a difference."

Mitch raised his eyebrows but said nothing. *Sure felt like an arrest to me*, he thought.

"But, son, let me warn you of something," the detective continued. "These are harsh times, and we all have to pull together to survive them. This country will not stand for people who are promoting *subversive* behavior."

Subversive, thought Mitch. *There's that word again.*

"One more thing," the detective said as he led Mitch out the door and down the hall to the lobby where his mother waited. "Those who aren't part of the solution are part of the problem. And Constitution or not, *those problem people are going to disappear*."

Those last words haunted Mitch as he exited the hallway and walked away from the detective and back to the waiting arms of his mother.

Disappear.

CHAPTER

Doors slammed and music blared outside in the parking lot. Police cars, their sirens screaming through the night, ripped through the neighborhood and were gone. A lonely, drunken sailor, feeling as though life was almost over, sang loudly and off-key to his "date" as he and she walked arm-in-arm back to his room. The clock on the wall ticked on, the hour hand showing eleven, twelve, one, and then two o'clock.

All of these distractions were lost on Jake. He had seen too much. Too much mayhem and death in the surgical suite. Too much anger, hatred, and vengeance even among fellow naval officers. Too much that had been predicted by the Bible. Too much prophecy he had forgotten—almost completely.

As he sat in his Pali hotel room, his roommate, Robbie, asleep a few feet away, the light of a single desk lamp illuminating the pages in front of him, Jake studied his Bible. It was the Bible Jenny had bought for his birthday the year before. She had such high expectations for him, and even though she knew that he loved her, he knew that he had disappointed her as well. First medical school, then his internship, then his naval responsibilities had taken precedence. He had told her that he was pushing to get through more quickly, but he knew that he would always be pushing.

And in the process of pushing, he had forgotten what—or Who—had been responsible for getting him into medicine in the first place.

He flipped another page in Galatians, and his conscience gripped him.

"God," he whispered, closing his eyes and gripping his fingers together tightly. "Sweet Father. I am so lost without You. I have committed myself to You time and again, only to fall back on my own strength each time. Well, no more."

He opened his eyes and looked at the page of scripture in front of him.

"I know that this world's days are numbered. I read it here in Your book and feel it in my bones. And I know that I have let lots of other things get between us, when what I needed more than anything was right here.

"God, I need You in a way I have never even dreamed of," Jake said, tears starting to trail down his face and drip onto the page beneath him. "And navy or no navy, I am Yours—first, last, and always."

The wind began to blow outside his small hotel room.

* * * * *

Several thousand miles away, Jenny sat in a living room with eight people. The initial tension had given way to a warmth and acceptance that she hadn't felt in a very long time. These were her people—she knew that now.

She told the others, at the prompting of the man she had met in Hinsdale, about the strange and frightening happenings that she had experienced in the Abbott household. The group listened quietly while she told of Benji's background, his strange behavior when she had first arrived, her father's arrest and her mother's accident, and the strained relationship between them. She recounted Mrs. Abbott's and Benji's return and the new events transpiring there.

"I have had the police over time and again," she explained to the sympathetic group. "But each time they say there's no evidence to tie it to an individual or a gang."

"The police won't help you," Mr. Clavell said. "They can't."

"Can't?" Jenny said. "Why not?"

"Because this isn't a criminal issue," he said. "It's a spiritual one."

Jenny looked at him and somehow knew that he was right. Deep down, she had always known. The realization slammed down on her like a piano falling from a two-story window.

"I've seen other situations like this one," he continued. "And they always come down to someone getting in too deep with the evil one."

"But why her?" someone asked. "Why is he threatening this woman and her child?"

"There must be a special reason why he hates you," another said.

"So what are we talking about here?" Jenny asked, suddenly embarrassed. "An exorcism?"

He shrugged. "You can call it that if you like, but the modern concept of exorcism is far from biblical. It's not a matter of our strength against Satan's. We'd lose."

The rest of the group grew strangely quiet.

"Brothers and sisters, this is just one manifestation of what is going on in the world today. We have all seen it, and we have chosen to ignore it for too long. Now Satan is pulling together his full strength to use against God's children."

"Lord Jesus," someone whispered.

"We won't call it an exorcism," he said, then took a deep breath. "But the matter is the casting out of demons. And that won't be the end of it either."

He stared at the floor, waiting for someone to speak. No one said anything, so he continued.

"What we need here is no less than the full manifestation of

God's power. Let's pray—and keep on praying until He grants it."

As they knelt for prayer, Jenny heard the wind starting to blow outside.

* * * * *

The music was gone. So were their smiles—and their confidence. Despite all precautions and predictions, Mitch and his group had had no luck in persuading anyone from going to the rally, much less listen to what they had to say about the gospel and the second coming of Jesus. On top of that, the police had arrived and scattered the group.

Now they sat in the living room of the apartment Mitch shared with his new roommates—and stared at the floor.

"You know what our mistake was, don't you?" Harley said. "We should have been more organized."

"Our mistake was depending on our own strength rather than the power of the Holy Spirit," Gina responded sharply. "Like I said earlier."

"Well, what do you want to do now?" someone asked Mitch.

Mitch, still staring at the floor, looked up. "Why are you asking me? Do you think I have all the answers? I'm just a kid that dropped out of school." He picked up the Bible and shoved it into the hands of the man who had spoken.

"Your answer is in there, not in me," he said.

Mitch stood, shoved his hands into his jeans pockets, and turned to look into the kitchen. He stood there for many moments, and the others continued staring at him as if he would come up with the answer.

"We need prayer—lots of it."

Mitch turned slowly and looked at Gina. Then he looked at the others.

No one had to say another word.

And the wind began to blow.

* * * * *

The old man squinted at Dan through his bifocals. "Do you really want to know where all the groups are? Is it safe?"

Dan looked around at the group of leaders that had assembled in the Eastham home. He held up his hands innocently.

"If you leaders don't feel comfortable putting the names of your groups in my hands, I have no problem with that. This was not my idea, and I am not looking for recognition—or more responsibility."

A bald man sitting across from Dan shook his head. "I am still not convinced that this is the best way to organize—or evangelize. I have always been convinced that the mass evangelism rally was the best way. And a cell group of six to ten people just can't support such an effort."

"I agree," Dan said, disarmingly. "But there was a time when mass evangelistic series worked for the church. Now is not one of them—simply because of the logistics of the thing. On the other hand, if one of you wants to take the lead and do something like this, I say go for it."

"Well, what kind of leadership is that?" the bald man said. "I say we argue these things out. Then after some debate we can take a vote. You won't even argue."

"You're right," Dan said. "I am through with arguing."

Several spoke up at once then. Dan simply held up his hands for silence.

"Once again, brothers and sisters, I didn't ask for this responsibility. If someone else wants it, God bless them."

The debate started up again, and then several held up their hands at once. "Let's hear what Elder Eastham has to say," the bald man said.

They all turned to the frail man sitting in the corner in an overstuffed chair. Elder Eastham had lost a lot of weight and color since his heart attack, but they could see that there was a fire in his eyes.

"Here's what I have to say—or what the Bible has to say," Elder Eastham said. "It says, 'When they were all together in one accord, there came a noise like a rushing wind, and the Holy Spirit came upon them.'"

He laid the Bible on his lap, and Dan noticed that for once his hands were not shaking.

"We are all here for the same reason," he said, looking sharply into each person's eyes. "But we are not of one accord.

"As for Dan, God made him a leader—a servant of the people. Anyone want to argue with God?"

Silence.

"But our problem is much larger than that because Dan is not the one who is in charge. God is in charge. Anyone who can't see that doesn't belong here. And that's what being in one accord is all about. Accepting that God is in charge. Doing what He says, regardless of where that leads us. Now who doesn't know that our days are numbered?" Elder Eastham asked. No one responded.

"Then what are we arguing about? Folks, we have work to do. And the first job before us is to prostrate ourselves before the throne of God and accept His leadership in every part of our lives."

The group looked at each other and nodded. As they knelt together, Dan heard the gong of the clock striking twelve, and noticed that the lights were flickering from the storm outside.

* * * * *

Kris could hear the television going in her mom's room, but she kept reading her Bible by flashlight. Mom had insisted that she turn out her lights and go to sleep an hour before. Something urged Kris on, however. God had a very special message for her that night. She just knew it.

And so she read. And prayed. And read some more.

And the wind blew stronger. But the world did not notice.

* * * * *

And in God's appointed time, the saints were gathered together around the world—in ones, twos, fives, and tens. And even though distance divided them, they were unified in prayer and in putting God's will first in their lives. And the power of the Holy Spirit was poured out according to His promise.

* * * * *

The whistling wind became a howl, and then a rumble shook the earth. The rumble awoke Meg, who thought it was an earthquake. She jumped out of bed and ran down the hall to Kris's room.

"That girl," she muttered, as she noticed a glow coming from beneath the doorway.

"Kris," she called as she opened the door. "Are you all— "

Meg stopped when she saw the flame of light above Kris's head and the glowing smile on her face.

* * * * *

Boom! The window in Jake's room exploded as if it had been shot from a cannon. Robbie leaped from his bed as glass showered outward and down to the sidewalk below. He heard a rushing sound like the inside of a wind tunnel, and through his just-awakened eyes he thought he saw what looked like flames of fire dancing above Jake's head.

Robbie rubbed his eyes and looked again. Jake turned and looked at Robbie and didn't say anything. When Robbie's eyes locked with Jake's, Jake's eyes seemed to glow with fire. It was as if Jake had taken his finger and pointed out every evil thing Robbie had ever done and laid it out for the world to see. Robbie knew something significant had happened and that he had a lot of soul-searching to do.

"Jake," Robbie said, his voice quavering. "Tell me what I have to do to be saved."

* * * * *

The flames of fire were seen all around the world. God did not hesitate to point out his faithful children. The outpouring of the Holy Spirit not only showed that they were accepted for the service of their God, but that they had been given incredible power to move people's hearts.

* * * * *

Dan knew in the back of his mind that this would happen eventually. He had even discussed it with other believers. But even Elder Eastham really didn't know what form it would take, or what would lead up to it, or what would follow.

Dan was caught up in prayer more earnestly and intently than he had ever experienced. It was as if he had entered the tabernacle of the Lord and only a thin veil of protection lay between him and the presence of God. And suddenly, with a crash, that veil was torn away.

His first reaction was that he was unworthy. He wanted to hide. That feeling lasted for just an instant as he felt an incredible electricity filling every atom of his being. He heard a roaring in his ears and almost felt as if he was witnessing everything from a distance.

The roaring continued, and he forced himself to open his eyes. Flames of fire danced over the heads of everyone in the room. The power had gone out—from the storm, perhaps, but more likely the power of God—and the flames bathed the room in a yellow glow.

He looked up at the clock. Four-fifteen. Then he looked

around the room at the men and women he had been talking to just hours before. Now they were all living vessels of the Holy Spirit.

* * * * *

Mitch's experience transcended all the others. It was as if the Holy Spirit wanted to speak with an extra portion of power to those who respected it. The outpouring was accompanied by all the windows of the apartment blowing out, all the power for the apartment building going out, and a glow coming from the apartment that people could see from a block away. And once again, every car alarm went off for blocks around.

Mitch felt the Holy Spirit overtake him like the biggest wave he had ever surfed. It rolled him in ecstasy and warmth. He felt loved, protected, and directed. All of his insecurities, low self-confidence, and hesitation were gone.

He opened his eyes and saw that the others had received the same experience. Gina looked into his eyes and smiled. Both knew what the other was thinking without saying a word.

One of the others wasn't so subtle.

Bart leaped to his feet and pumped his fist into the air.

"Yeah! Jesus Christ rocks!"

He ran over the broken glass from the sliding glass patio door and out onto the balcony. A crowd of people had formed around the empty swimming pool below, looking up at the glowing apartment.

"You hear that, people?" Bart shouted at the top of his lungs. "Jesus Christ rocks! And He is on His way back to save us!"

More than one of those listening fell to their knees.

* * * * *

Jenny had joined the group looking for help against the evil within her parents' household. What she got was much more valuable.

The few minutes of prayer turned into an hour, then another, and a third. Suddenly she felt herself lifted off the ground and caught up as if floating in a cloud. Warmth surrounded her.

You are My child, she heard. *You are Mine.*

Reality came back to her as the woman next to her gasped and slumped against her. *She's passed out*, she thought, and opened her eyes to see what she could do to help her.

A roaring filled her ears, and she looked up at the others, bathed in a yellow light. She felt different—peaceful. And then she noticed that her baby was moving—dancing—within her. *She knows God better than I do*, she thought.

And then Jenny was caught up with a new notion. *Would her baby be born here on earth—or in heaven?*

CHAPTER

Kris sat in her usual seat by the window as her comparative religion teacher handed back papers to the class. Kris's mind was miles away. She was brought back to the present by the sensation of a paper being laid on top of her hands. She turned to look and saw only one letter: A big, red F.

"F?" she asked the teacher. "Why?"

The young female teacher flashed a greasy smile. "Because you put the wrong answer, dearie. And if you continue to put down wrong answers, you won't pass this class."

"Doesn't matter anyway," Kris said quietly. "We'll all be gone soon."

"Gone?" the teacher asked. "Where do you think you're going?"

"Heaven," Kris answered innocently. "And you can't stop me."

"Don't give me attitude, young lady," the woman said. "You'll end up in detention."

"Hey, well, Mrs. Whyte, why is Kris's answer wrong?" Brad asked from two rows ahead. "She explained it to us, and it made sense then."

"Because it is based on a dead book," the teacher said. "You can't base a modern religion on a book that was written thousands of years ago."

"What about the Koran? the Talmud? the Bhagavad Gita? Those were written a long time ago."

The teacher shook her head. "That's different. Christianity has new light, different light. It's a western religion that must reflect western lifestyles." She picked up Kris's Bible and held it up.

"This is just a bunch of fairy tales."

Kris began speaking without even looking at her teacher. She spoke quietly, but the other students had begun to key in on what she said. Now when she spoke, everyone heard her.

"All scripture is God-breathed and is useful for teaching, rebuking, correcting and training in righteousness, so that the man of God may be thoroughly equipped for every good work."

The teacher smiled her greasy smile again. "So you are going to believe a dead book rather than a live person, even though that person has been to college for many years, and has studied under Jesuit priests and the Maharishi Yogi?"

"Thy word, O God, is a light unto my feet and a light unto my path."

The teacher was clearly getting frustrated. "But that's all so complicated. How can anyone know what to believe in there? Why can't they write it out in simple terms?"

Kris still didn't look up but continued reciting:

"For God so loved the world that He gave His one and only Son, that whoever believes in Him shall not perish but have everlasting life."

Then she looked up at the teacher.

"You see, Mrs. Whyte, Christianity *is* the only religion where you can't save yourself. And it is simple. 'Believe in the Lord Jesus Christ, and thou shalt be saved.' "

Mrs. Whyte stood staring silently at Kris. Later, Kris thought it was appropriate that the first word out of Mrs. Whyte's lips was a swear word.

"Ridiculous," she said, recovering from her momentary slip. "Students, here is an example of the ignorance of years past, and the mess it has taken this world into. But Kris is convinced that the old way is the right way. Is there anyone here who agrees with her even at the risk of their final grade?"

Kris's mouth went hard as she watched. One hand went up, then another, then a third. Three who still believed.

"Very well," Mrs. Whyte said. "You three and Kris are excused to go see the principal."

* * * * *

The front door of the Abbott house creaked open, and Jenny stuck her head around the corner into the living room.

"Good, Mom, you're here," Jenny said. "I've made some friends, and I want you to meet them." Jenny stepped forward and motioned for the rest of the group to come in.

Mrs. Abbott, who looked as though she had been half-asleep in front of the TV, looked up at Jenny as three people from the Bible study group stepped forward. Benji lay asleep on his cot in the corner.

"Mom, this is Tom Clavell, Angie Adams, and Tutti Schwares. They are friends that I met at a Bible study class."

Mrs. Abbott's eyes grew wide with surprise and then narrow with anger.

"Jenny, you have no right to bring strangers into my house. I've been sick," Mrs. Abbott said.

Jenny stepped forward and reached out to smooth her mom's hair. "I know, I know, Mom, but we think the problems Benji's been having—and maybe your health problems—are more than just physical. Maybe there's a spiritual reason behind them. And you did say to make this my home, too. I am your daughter."

Mrs. Abbott shook away from her daughter. "That's ridiculous. There's nothing wrong with me or with Benji. And even though you are family, legally this is my home and not yours. I'm telling you all to get out."

A voice said, "And I say they can stay."

The voice came from behind Jenny, and she heard the front door shut. A familiar, rugged face appeared.

"Daddy!" Jenny said. "Thanks for coming."

"You're welcome, sweetheart," Mr. Abbott said and then turned toward his wife.

"Helen, this is for Benji's benefit, and for our own sanity. The authorities can't do anything; it's time we found someone who can."

"You get away from me," Mrs. Abbott said, pulling her feet up under her on the couch. "This isn't your home anymore, either."

Mr. Abbott shrugged. "It is in the eyes of the law, at least for now. And I say these people are welcome here."

Mr. Abbott turned to the group and invited them to have a seat. Mrs. Abbott's eyes burned like fire, and she stomped out of the room, slamming the door to her bedroom as loudly as she could.

"Does Mom need to be here?" Jenny asked.

Tom shook his head. "We're here mainly for Benji, but I am sure there is a evil influence here in the household, so we will pray for general protection as well."

Jenny looked at her dad, who sat quietly watching with his hands in his lap.

"Are you OK, Daddy? Do you understand what's going on here?"

Mr. Abbott shrugged. "Spiritual things have never been my area, but you guys carry on. You seem to know more than I do about what needs to be done." He sat back in his chair. "I'll just watch."

Tom looked at the others. "It's just like we discussed. We will pray for the household and build a wall of spiritual protection here. And don't forget to pray specifically for Benji."

Jenny knelt with the others as they prayed. Her heart skipped a beat after a few minutes when her father's big, rough hand slipped into hers, and she realized that he had joined the kneeling circle. They took turns praying, Mr. Abbott kneeling, yet remaining quiet.

After a while they stopped, and Jenny looked over at Benji. He was still asleep and moaned slightly and turned over.

"How long does this take?" Mr. Abbott asked.

"As long as it takes," Tom responded. "I have seen it done— a long time ago and overseas—but there's never a magic formula for it.

"But I am convinced that there is a spiritual problem here."

Mr. Abbott raised his eyebrows and let out a sharp breath.

Jenny looked at her father, her eyes narrowing.

"Dad, I have an idea. What if you prayed?"

Mr. Abbott looked at his daughter in surprise.

"What, me? No. I don't know how to pray."

Tom looked at Mr. Abbott and nodded.

"Jenny's right. There's nothing quite as powerful as a contrite heart coming before God for the first time. Mr. Abbott, if you love Benji, and if you love your family, this could be what we need."

Mr. Abbott looked at Tom in surprise, then at Jenny. Jenny's eyes pleaded with him. He nodded slowly, then bowed his head.

"Uh, God. I don't really have the words . . . I am not an eloquent speaker . . . never have been. But I know there have been many times when I was in trouble on the streets and You somehow protected me and brought me through safely. I have always known deep down that You were there for me."

Mr. Abbott's words came slowly at first, then more easily as he realized he was talking to a Friend who had been there all along through his long career as a police detective. Jenny couldn't help herself. The tears flowed freely as her father's words came from his heart.

"For all the many times You were there, God, thank You," Mr. Abbott continued. "I have never been real good on showing my emotions. I guess it was just the way I was raised. But I know now that You have been with this family for a long time. You have blessed us.

"Now I am asking that You bless us again. Something is wrong in this house, and we need Your help in getting rid of the evil that is hurting us as a family."

Jenny heard another moan from Benji and was tempted to see what was happening.

"God and Father, cast out the demons that are plaguing us here—"

Mr. Abbott's words were interrupted by a scream. Jenny opened her eyes to see her mother in her blue bathrobe, charging the little group on their knees. High above her head she held a butcher knife.

"I'll kill you!" she screamed. Jenny fell backwards, as did the others. Only Mr. Abbott held his ground. He reached up and caught the full force of the blade with one hand. The blade slashed across his palm, and a red line appeared on his hand.

Mr. Abbott ignored the wound, but wrestled his wife to the floor and sat on top of her. He pulled the knife from her grasp and threw it into the corner of the room. Jenny gasped at the blood pouring from her father's hand. She jumped up and ran to the kitchen, grabbing a hand towel.

"Here," she yelled to her father over her mother's screams, and he wrapped his bloody hand in the towel.

"You are all going to burn!" Mrs. Abbott screamed. "You think you are all so holy, but I know better. I know every hidden sin you cherish, every little mistake you made in your life. You think you are worthy, but you will burn in hellfire just like everyone else!"

Jenny's eyes opened wide. "That's not my mother," she said.

Tom nodded. "We've found our demon."

Mr. Abbott was quiet. "Grace was always into some very strange books, and I have caught her doing some strange things recently. She said she was trying to find out what happened to a brother who died when she was little."

"What do we do now?" Jenny asked, looking from her raging mother to Tom.

"We all place our hands on her—Mr. Abbott, you too—and we renounce and cast out the demon within her in the name of Jesus Christ."

The group did as he said, and following Tom's lead, each called for the demon to leave Mrs. Abbott.

Jenny was last. Mrs. Abbott still raged, a fire burning within her that Jenny had never seen, and hoped to never see again.

"You!" Mrs. Abbott said, her bloodshot eyes staring at her daughter. "You think you are worthy to be saved! You think you deserve a loving husband and baby! Well, I know things that you have told no one!"

Jenny hesitated.

"You think Jake loves you. You think that your God loves you! Well, why didn't you tell them about that boy, Chuck? About what you and he did in the back seat of his car."

Jenny gasped, and her face turned red. She looked at the group, embarrassed.

"I was sixteen. I didn't tell anyone about that."

"But I knew," Mrs. Abbott hissed. "Didn't I?"

"God forgave me for that," Jenny whispered.

"No," Mrs. Abbott said.

"God forgave me!" Jenny repeated. She reached out and placed her hands on both sides of her mother's swollen face.

"In the name of Jesus Christ, our Lord and Savior, who died on the cross for the sins of the world, and rose again to reign in heaven, I command you, demon, come out of her!"

Jenny didn't even realize what words came out of her. All she knew was that she was forgiven, and allowed the Holy Spirit to speak.

Mrs. Abbott screamed one more time, her body shaking convulsively. Then she lay still.

Jenny looked at Mr. Abbott, then at the others, then at Tom.

"It's over," Tom said.

The group heard a rustling from the corner. Jenny turned to look at Benji sitting on the corner of the cot, rubbing his eyes.

"Hey, why are you guys making so much noise?" he asked.

* * * * *

Feeling like a fish out of water, Dan stood in the line at the bus stop nearest the Easthams' house. Life was getting more and more complicated. More business transactions involved computers, social security numbers, or fingerprint or even palm scans. At least the bus fare should be pretty much the same.

He looked around at the people in line. About the same as it might have been a year ago, he thought. But then if you looked closer, Dan realized, you'd see the subtle differences.

The tall businessman behind Dan read the San Jose *News*. "Mississippi River flows backwards," the headline read. Dan moved closer to read what it meant, and the man dropped his paper, glaring at Dan.

"Do you mind?" the businessman asked.

"Sorry," Dan answered. "Just curious about the headline there. What did they mean, Mississippi River flows backwards?"

But the man had lifted his paper back into position and was ignoring Dan.

"It was an earthquake in Missouri," the woman in front of Dan said. He turned and looked at her. A reasonably pretty woman, but with a huge sore on the side of her neck.

"The earthquake dropped the elevation several feet, and the water went north instead of south. Very strange."

Dan shook his head. "I hadn't heard anything about it."

The woman laughed. "With so many crazy things going on

in the world, this is just another one of them. Just look how dark it is—all from volcanic ash in the atmosphere. Yesterday, Mount Rainier in Washington erupted. Who knows how many have died from that one."

A voice came from the back of the line. "Yeah, and I heard that cinders from the volcanoes are being carried up into the jet stream. They have started fires all over the place."

Another voice swore behind him. "I wouldn't be surprised if the sun never come up tomorrow."

"I moved to California because it seemed relatively safe," the woman said. "Now I wonder if there is a safe place in the world at all." The crowd saw the bright green Metro bus heading their direction from down the street.

"There is only one safe place," Dan said. "In the arms of Jesus Christ."

The woman looked at Dan for a moment and then laughed. "I suppose you are going to the rally at the Civic Center tonight then. Funny, I didn't peg you for one of the Newbies."

"Newbies?" Dan asked.

"New Age, new Christian Church, whatever you want to call it, one of those guys that believes that if we all just get together and worship God in the same way, we can save the world." The bus doors opened in front of her, and she turned to enter.

Dan took a step to follow her and then paused when he saw a sign in front of him.

"No Cash."

"No cash?" he repeated out loud.

The woman turned and looked at him funny. "Where have you been, in a monastery? You just use your card." She lifted a white card that said "Social Security System" and ran it past a red laser light beside the driver. They heard a beep.

"Sure beats looking for exact change," the driver said, smiling.

"Uh, what if you don't have a card?" Dan asked meekly.

The woman looked at the driver, who shook his head.

"There's one in every crowd," he said. "Just use the keypad there, and type in your social security number. They're making exceptions now, but it won't be long until everyone is going to have to have a card."

"You do know your social security number, don't you?" the woman asked. "The seventy-five cent fare will be transferred electronically from your checking account now."

Dan finished entering his number and pressed the enter key. It beeped.

"But I don't have a checking account," Dan said.

"Don't worry," the woman said. "The government will figure a way to get it out of you. They will take care of everything. They always do."

"You're right," Dan said, as the woman took a seat in the crowded bus. He stood next to her in the aisle. The bus started with a jerk, and Dan clutched the leather strap above him. "I am going to the Civic Center rally, but not for the reason you think."

She cocked an eyebrow and looked up at him. "Business or pleasure?"

Dan shrugged. "A little of both. My ex-wife has been pleading for me to go to one of the meetings. Says there's someone there she wants me to meet. So I am obliging her . . . with a little agenda of my own."

"Sounds interesting," the woman said. "Maybe you're not a Newbie after all. Maybe there is hope for you yet."

* * * * *

Meg looked up from her magazine as Dan and a middle-aged woman with flaming red hair approached.

"I'm glad you decided to come, Dan," Meg said. He looked at her closely, and saw sharp lines on her face that hadn't been there before. She looked as though she had lost weight, and her face had lost some color. "I almost expected you to back out again."

"Meg, this is Clara Winfield. We met on the bus, and she decided to come to the rally as well."

"Great, glad you could come," Meg said, reaching out her hand to Clara.

"From what Dan tells me, I expect to see some exciting things," Clara said.

"Oh, I am sure you will," Meg said excitedly.

"I am sure I will too," Clara said, looking at Dan.

The music was just finishing when they took their seats inside the massive Civic Center. Meg had pulled some strings and gotten them seats within a stone's throw of the front. Around them were local celebrities, including the mayor and his wife, the anchor from the local TV station, and several pro football players from San Francisco. Meg talked to an usher, who found Clara a seat, just a few rows away. Dan settled in and was surprised when Meg reached out and took his hand. Her hands felt like ice.

The musicians exited the stage, and a well-known local pastor took the mike.

"Before our speaker comes on stage, we have had several requests for people to remember loved ones who are having a difficult time. As we speak, the moon outside is the color of blood. The evening sky is filled with what looks like falling stars. Thousands of bright lights are streaming down upon the earth—cinders from the volcanic fire that holds this world hostage. Friends, let's raise our prayers up to a merciful God!"

Stars falling. Moon as blood. Right on time, Dan thought as the program paused for two minutes of silent prayer.

I don't know what I am doing here, Dan thought as they settled back in their seats, *especially since I have turned her down about coming several times. But this is where the Holy Spirit has sent me. Something big is bound to happen.* Dan got his answer half a minute later. The MC gave a dazzling, Hollywood-style introduction for the speaker, and the audience burst into applause. But Dan didn't hear a word they said. His eyes were on the speaker.

He knew it wasn't rational, wasn't logical. But he also knew that logic flew out the window months ago on this planet. The man before him bore an unmistakable resemblance to a man he had helped bury back in November, a man who had been the leading spiritual influence in his life, the man who had died saving someone else from an attack.

Meg gripped Dan's arm, and Dan realized that he had stopped breathing.

"Dan, don't you see?" Meg said excitedly. "It's Pastor Taylor!"

CHAPTER

"It's Pastor Taylor, Dan," Meg hissed. "Aren't you excited?"

Excited was not the right word to describe how Dan felt. *Terrified* was more accurate.

Dan had seen this man lying in a coffin. He had personally carried the coffin to the gravesite. He had seen the coffin put into the earth. And he had seen earth thrown on it—as it should have been.

Dan had not expected to see Pastor Taylor again until the Second Coming. But he was seeing someone—or some*thing*—which looked just like him.

Dan had seen this man preach before—many times. He knew the rhythm of his voice. He knew the inflections that he used. He remembered how he paused before the last word of sentences that he especially wanted to emphasize. And as he listened to this man, he saw all of those things.

Based on what he saw here, *this was Pastor Taylor, the man he knew and loved.* And yet he knew that this was not so. It couldn't be. This was a trick of Satan.

"I been blessed countless times by the hands of God. I have felt death—and He has been gracious to raise me up from the grave. Friends, as you know, I have seen heaven. I have seen those who have gone before, and who wait for us to join them. And I have been returned to you with this message:

"God wants His children to get along. He wants them to worship Him in unison. He wants to save our planet—if we will only let Him.

"Who will stand in the way of God?"

Dan felt the hair stand on the back of his neck as the crowd roared with approval. He had been led there, had expected to do great things in front of these people. But he was out of his league here. Satan was a roaring lion, and he was set on devouring anyone who stood in his way.

I've got to get out of here, Dan thought. He made a move to go, and suddenly felt Pastor Taylor's eyes fall on him. Their eyes locked, and for a moment Dan knew that this *thing* was not Pastor Taylor. There was no love here. Only deception.

That instant of recognition flashed by, and Pastor Taylor's face took on the image of a caring, affable preacher.

"Brother Dan," Pastor Taylor said quietly, reaching out his hand. "You've come. I have been waiting for you."

The thousands of people in the Civic Center shifted their attention away from center stage to a middle-aged, unemployed academy biology teacher in the fifth row who would rather have been anywhere else on earth.

"Come forward, please," Pastor Taylor said to Dan, his hand beckoning him forward. The audience began to clap, which turned into a thunderous applause, then cheering.

Go, a voice told Dan. *It is in my plan.* And Dan did what the Holy Spirit prompted him to do.

Dan waded down the aisle as the mad applause continued. Two ushers appeared from nowhere and escorted Dan to the front, their steel grips on his arms making sure that he went nowhere but to the stage.

Dan's fear slowly dissipated and was replaced by righteous indignation. He took his place standing next to Pastor Taylor, and he thought, *The last time I did this was when I was ordained as an elder.*

The world had changed since then. The world had gone insane.

But not entirely, Dan thought, as he saw Pastor Taylor continue to tell of how he knew Dan. *I have found Jesus Christ, and the Holy Spirit has come over me.*

And as the thought went through Dan's mind, the Holy Spirit did come over him—with power and vengeance. He looked out at the well-dressed mass of people before him and felt nothing but pity for them. And it was at that moment that Pastor Taylor asked him a question:

"I bet you are surprised to see me again, aren't you, Dan?"

Dan stared into the dark eyes of the preacher.

"I have never seen you before in my life."

Pastor Taylor shook with surprise, then pasted another smile on his lips.

"Come on, Dan, we used to go jogging together. Surely you remember that."

"I remember going jogging with Pastor Adam Taylor last fall, but you are not that man."

The crowd hushed and then fell into a low murmuring roar.

Pastor Taylor tipped his head, smiled again, and looked at Dan.

"Then who do you say that I am?"

Dan looked Pastor Taylor squarely in the eyes.

"You are an agent of Satan sent to mislead and confuse these people, and I rebuke you in the name of Jesus Christ our Lord!"

Dan's words rang throughout the auditorium and were followed by deadly silence.

Pastor Taylor seemed to crumble in front of Dan. Finally, he screamed:

"Get him out of here!"

Before Dan could turn to walk away, four ushers had surrounded him. He heard the music start up again hastily and saw bare concrete around him as the ushers dragged him out a back door, down a service passageway, and out into the parking lot behind the Civic Center.

Two of them threw him down onto the wet pavement. The other two stomped on him. Then the four of them left, slamming the metal door to the Civic Center behind them.

All during his escort from the stage, Dan was smiling and laughing to himself. When they left him alone, he laughed aloud.

"God, you scored again!" Dan shouted, lying on the wet pavement and looking up at the cinder-clouded sky.

He would have lain there for several minutes longer, but the lights of a car illuminated his body on the pavement. He sat up and looked at the two figures coming out of the car in expectation.

"Sorry," he said casually. "I was just getting up. I'll get out of your way."

He was grabbed up by steel hands that threw him face down against the car.

"Dan Lewis," a voice said. "You're under arrest."

"For that?" Dan said as they handcuffed him. "Look, I left voluntarily."

"You are under arrest for income tax evasion. You have the right to remain silent. . . ."

And that's just what Dan did. All the way to the local precinct.

* * * * *

Mr. Abbott shook his head.

"Go," he said simply to Jenny. "It's now or never."

Jenny looked at her father, then her mother, who sat sipping tea at the kitchen table. Benji played with dominoes on the other side of the table.

"But you guys still need me," she said quietly.

"The group will watch over them," Tom said, leaning against the refrigerator. "I will watch over them."

"God will watch over us," Mr. Abbott said, winking at his daughter.

Jenny looked at her parents for a long while. It was great to see them sitting there together holding hands, like the old days. Mom was still weak from her ordeal, but there was a radiant glow in both their faces. Even Benji seemed more like a normal kid.

Now the question was where Jenny belonged. Her mind told her she was still needed here. But her heart begged her to find her husband before it was too late. There was no longer a safe place to be in the world. Illinois was just as dangerous as Hawaii. There was no reason for her to wait. Not any longer.

The only thing that worried her was the fact that phone service between Hawaii and the mainland was nonexistent. She hadn't heard from Jake in a month.

She gripped the counter edge and stared at her parents for a few moments, then made her decision. She reached for the phone and dialed a toll-free number.

"Hello. This is Jenny Gallagher. I want to book a seat on your next available flight to Honolulu."

She turned and smiled at Tom, then her mom and dad. She was going to see Jake.

At last.

* * * * *

Jake and Robbie stood at attention in the locker room. Admiral Benhurst was on a rampage again. Not enough supplies. Too many hours in surgery per team. Sick call affecting too many staff members.

"Someone must have stolen his Cheerios this morning," Robbie whispered.

Jake stifled a smile. The admiral was not looking well, Jake noticed. He looked as though he had aged ten years in as many weeks. Of course, he was probably putting in as many hours— or more—as the surgical teams were.

"I realize that your duty has been difficult—sometimes it has seemed impossible. You have done an exemplary job here. The problem has been one of maintaining regular communication and shipments from the mainland. We are mopping up here—and we're almost done. The continental United States is just beginning to feel the brunt of these unexpected natural disasters. In addition, the economic downturn and increased crime has made the situation at home more and more precarious."

Admiral Benhurst walked toward Jake and Robbie as he continued talking.

"That's why Washington feels it is even more important that we, as representatives of the United States government and defenders of the Constitution, demonstrate that we support the decisions that are made there. Whether those decisions are popular or not, whether we agree with them or not, it is our duty as naval officers to support them. Do you hear me?"

"Aye, aye, sir," the surgical officers, including Jake and Robbie, shouted out.

"My yeoman will be bringing around a document for each of you to sign. We think it is important for the officers to take the first step—to set an example of allegiance for the rest of our military."

Admiral Benhurst turned to go, but stopped at the door and turned back to the officers.

"Remember, you are navy. Your opinions don't count. Your personal beliefs don't matter. *Your allegiance does.*"

Jake noticed that the admiral was looking right at him when he spoke.

* * * * *

"It's me, it's me, it's me oh Lord, standing in the need of prayer."

Mitch was not known for having a good singing voice, but he didn't care. He had had a good meeting, and now he was singing to God and no one else. As he walked across town in the late-night darkness, he splashed in the puddles left from the recent storm and thought about how God was using him.

His cell church had just divided into three churches. They met at night twice a week, but it seemed that the church grew too fast to administer under those conditions. Maybe they should meet nightly, Mitch thought.

It was a problem, but it was a good problem to have, especially after the fiasco outside the Civic Center two weeks before. They had experienced the power of the Holy Spirit, and He had directed them to continue meeting people one on one.

And so they had, with phenomenal success. He had seen such changes that he realized he could no longer keep it organized in the way most people viewed organization. The movement had taken on a life of its own.

He was so caught up in his good fortune—his blessings, he corrected himself—that he didn't notice the sound of footsteps behind him. He was almost home. The apartment he shared with two others was just another couple of blocks away. He turned the familiar corner to his alley shortcut—and he heard the steps behind him.

He turned just as an arm with a pipe started coming down on top of his head. Instinctively his body went back to its training. He stepped inside the arm swing, pivoted, and brought the arm up and around. The attacker became the victim, flipping through the air and landing flat on his back.

This is wrong, Mitch told himself after half a second.

Trust me, a voice inside him answered.

He turned to face his second attacker, who had pulled a knife. In the darkness, the attacker looked strangely familiar, but Mitch was more concerned about the knife at this point. The attacker, a smaller man, thrust the knife forward, some-what awkwardly. Mitch had no problem sidestepping the thrust and disarming the attacker with a quick blow to the nerve on the inside of the arm. The knife dropped to the ground, and the attacker clutched his arm in pain.

Mitch stood and looked at his two attackers. The larger one still lay on his back in a puddle of water. The smaller one clutched his arm and moaned.

"You broke my arm," the smaller one said.

"It's not broken," Mitch said. "I just numbed it by hitting the pressure point on the inner arm." Mitch stepped forward and immediately recognized the two.

"Ivan? Flea? What are you guys doing?"

"Trying to rob you," Ivan said, pulling himself up off the wet pavement. "I guess we picked the wrong person."

"For more than one reason," Mitch said. "I'm broke." He stepped into the light.

"Don't you guys recognize me? It's Mitch." He reached down and helped Ivan get up.

"Mitch," Ivan muttered. "We thought you were dead—back in Santa Cruz."

"I'm more alive than you guys are," Mitch said. "More alive than you know. You guys are pretty pathetic. Robbery. What brought you to this point?"

"Bread, dude," Flea said. "We are busted. Ivan got his van repossessed. We both lost our jobs when the economy went south, and we've been living on the streets for almost a month now."

"Yeah, man, you gotta help us out." Ivan held out his hand as if he were begging from Mitch. Mitch thought of how the two of them had thrown him out of their apartment, and where his life might have gone if they hadn't.

"Help you out? Like I said, I'm broke," Mitch said, but in the back of his mind he thought, *I can help you guys in ways you cannot imagine.*

"So you won't help us?" Flea whined.

"I didn't say that," Mitch said. "Come with me. I have a couple of friends I want you to meet. One is named Gina. She works at a bakery, and she gets us all the old stuff for free."

The three of them headed for Mitch's apartment, their footsteps echoing against the brickwork of the alley walls. A lone siren sang off in the distance.

"Sweet," Ivan said. "Who's the other friend?"

"I have this friend who changed my life. His name is Jesus Christ."

As the threesome walked down the alley, an unmarked police car pulled up to the entrance of the alley. The detective in the passenger seat pointed what looked like a radar gun at the three young men. A monitor on the back of the gun showed the three figures in infrared, but Mitch, the middle figure, had hands and a face that glowed bright orange.

"That's him, all right," the passenger detective said. "Magnetic scan registers positive." The detective looked at the number code that printed out on the back of the gun.

"OK, freeze the image and send it on."

The passenger detective pressed a button on the back of the gun, which froze the frame showing the three pedestrians. A computer-enhanced image with accompanying identification data was forwarded instantly to police headquarters where a detailed file was rapidly growing under the name Mitch Lewis.

"That's fourteen today," the passenger said. "This kid's busy."

The driver shook his head solemnly as he put the car in gear. "He won't be for long."

* * * * *

Robbie looked at the document in his hands.

"What you are saying is that not only is this national church unconstitutional, but that it was predicted in Bible prophecy?"

Jake nodded. They sat on their beds back in their hotel room and stared at the documents that had been hand-delivered to them by the yeoman.

"This is the sign given to us in prophecy that the beast was seeking to change the law of God. The Ten Commandments call for us to honor the seventh day of the week. This requires us by law to worship on the first day of the week."

Robbie stared at the document for a long moment, then dropped it next to him on his bed.

"I don't know. We're talking about disobeying a direct order here. Maybe even something worse. After all, what difference does it make what day of the week you worship?"

Jake leaned forward. "The difference is, Robbie, that God made Sabbath on a specific day of the week. No created being has the right—or the power—to change that. Not even the United States government. Besides, it's still against the First Amendment of the Constitution."

"For now it is," Robbie said. "The Constitution has been changed before. They can do it again. Things are so crazy right now, nothing would surprise me."

"Well, I have seen this coming for a long time," Jake said. "And here's my answer."

He took the official document he held in his hands and put it back in the envelope. Then he tore the envelope in half, and then again. Finally he threw the entire mess in the trashcan.

Jake looked from the trashcan to Robbie.

"Your turn," he said.

CHAPTER

an Lewis sat fidgeting in the hallway outside Courtroom 1 of the Santa Clara County Superior Court. He was nervous because he had never been to court before. He had gotten two traffic tickets in his life and paid both by mail. Miraculously, he had never been asked to serve as a juror. And he had never been arrested before.

Even after spending a night in a cell with ten other people, he still couldn't figure out why he had been arrested. *Tax evasion?* He had always been conservative on paying taxes, often to the point of not claiming a legitimate tax break because it looked suspicious. Sure, he might have lost a few dollars in the process. On the other hand, he had never been audited.

But now this. How could he be charged with tax evasion when he didn't have any money to speak of? *They must be trying to get me here for some other reason*, he thought.

Just when he was starting to get nervous again, a Bible passage came to his mind.

"He reached down from on high and took hold of me;
he drew me out of deep waters.
He rescued me from my powerful enemy,

from my foes, who were too strong for me.
They confronted me in the day of my disaster,
but the Lord was my support.
He brought me out into a spacious place;
he rescued me because he delighted in me."

Second Samuel 22:17-20, Dan thought to himself, and smiled.
What can they do to me? To us?

As if in response, the bulky, blue-uniformed police officer a
few feet away came and unlocked the handcuffs that attached
Dan to the bench where he was sitting.

"Your turn, Mr. Lewis," the officer said, his voice full of
gravel. He pocketed the handcuffs and grabbed Dan under his
arm. Together they pushed through the double doors of the
courtroom and went inside.

Dan wanted to pause at the doorway and take it all in. He
had, after all, never before seen the inside of a courtroom. But
his burly attendant thrust him forward down the main aisle, past
the filled spectator area and on to the front of the room.

"Daniel Charles Lewis, social security number 549-98-
0221," the bailiff announced loudly. Dan was thrust into center
stage in front of the judge's bench.

Judge Harriet Schiller, Dan read, and looked at the small,
middle-aged woman who sat in front of him. She seemed
preoccupied as she looked at a computer screen to one side of
her. Suddenly Dan realized she was looking at *his life* on that
screen—his career, his tax background, every credit card he
ever used—everything.

"Mr. Lewis," she began quietly. "This is just a hearing and
not an official trial. In today's court system, we find that making
things informal helps speed things up. Hence the lack of a
prosecuting or defense attorney. Do you agree?"

Dan shrugged.

"Mr. Lewis, do you still live at 1105 Huntington Court?"

"No, Your Honor, not really," Dan said nervously. "That's my legal address, yes. But my wife and I are separated. Now I live in the basement at the home of Jonathan Eastham, at 301 Sharp Avenue."

"Mr. Lewis, what is your occupation?" the judge asked, looking up at him over her reading glasses.

"Uh, unemployed at present."

"You were a high school biology teacher, is that right?" she asked. "Why did you decide to stop teaching?"

Dan took a deep breath. "I, uh, had a difference of opinion on curriculum with the principal."

"And this difference of opinion, as you call it, was so important that you left your job even though you didn't know where you were going to find work elsewhere?"

Dan looked down. "Yes, Your Honor."

"That's saying quite a bit in this economic climate. How long have you been unemployed?"

"Three months, Your Honor."

"Three months?" Judge Schiller echoed. "Has it been fun? Have you enjoyed yourself?"

Dan said nothing.

"Isn't it true that you have indeed started another business for yourself during this time? A landscaping business?" the judge's voice grew louder.

Dan looked at her blankly.

"Landscaping? Uh, no, Your Honor. I tried doing a little gardening for people, but no one could afford to pay me."

"So you got payment in other ways. Right?" the judge cocked an eyebrow.

Dan shrugged. "I don't think you could call it payment. Just tree trimmings, a few vegetables and fruit. That sort of thing."

Judge Schiller looked at her screen and pressed the enter key.

"According to this, you took grass trimmings from one customer and traded them as mulch to another. In turn, they gave you fruit and vegetables. You used some of those and delivered several to the Uptown Mission in Santa Clara, where you also received bread and soup." She looked up. "Is that correct?"

Dan looked at her and then nodded.

"There are also reports of payment in tree bark, roots and leaves, which you have made into home remedies and exchanged for favors with a variety of customers." She turned away from the screen and looked squarely at Dan. "That, Mr. Lewis, is called bartering, and is perfectly legal—but taxable."

"Taxable?" Dan blurted out. "But I was just doing favors for friends in need."

"And in return, they were giving you items that circumvented the United States tax system."

"Uh, uh—," was all that Dan could say.

"Mr. Lewis, where were you two nights ago?" the judge asked.

Dan furrowed his brow. "Where I always am. With friends."

"And the night before? And the night before that?"

Dan looked at her and shook his head. "I—I don't understand. What do my night activities have to do with my tax status?"

"What do you and your friends do each and every night?"

Dan shrugged. "We talk. We read the Bible. We pray." *Where is she going with this?*

"Why don't you and your friends worship with everyone else in a church or in the Civic Center?"

Ah, so there it is. Dan looked in her eyes.

"Your Honor, freedom of assembly and freedom of religion are still a part of the United States Constitution, right?" Dan breathed in through his nose and tried to stay calm.

"For the moment, Mr. Lewis, but this country is concerned about the quality of its citizens. We have a very short tolerance for subversive behavior."

"Your Honor, I beg your pardon, but I don't understand how reading the Bible and praying in someone's home can be considered subversive."

"Mr. Lewis, you are confronted with some serious charges here. Tax evasion in this day and age can get you twenty years in prison. On the other hand, if you demonstrate that you are an upstanding citizen who supports the government, we might be able to make an accommodation."

"What do you mean—*accommodation?*" Dan asked.

"If, for example, you were to provide us with the names of the individuals involved in these nightly subversive meetings, we could find it in our power to grant you a reprieve on the other charges."

But meeting in a home is not against the law! Dan wanted to shout.

Not against the law—yet. Dan felt a chill go up his spine as he stood silently in front of the judge. *She knows something she is not telling me*, he thought. *Something big is about to happen.*

Dan stared at the judge, trying to read her mind by looking at her face. She seemed to wither under his gaze, and the judge began to glance to either side as if wanting to avoid his stare.

"Mr. Lewis, I realize this is a difficult choice you have to make here. Choose to betray your friends and get off, or remain loyal and be tried for tax evasion and get twenty years in prison. I will call a ten-minute recess and allow you to consider your options."

Judge Schiller nodded to the guard, who handcuffed Dan and led him out of the courtroom.

* * * * *

Two thousand miles away, Lt. Commander Jake Gallagher was having troubles of his own. Admiral Benhurst was raging again. And raging was almost too mild a term to use. His face was beet red, and the veins stood out on his forehead. Jake wondered if he was headed for a stroke.

Jake and Robbie stood at attention in front of their lockers as the admiral raged up and down the locker aisles. Much of what he was saying didn't seem to have a point, but the admiral seemed to be generally headed in their direction. It was just like a tornado that wandered across open land until it hit a trailer park. Jake knew that devastation was on its way.

"It's all about honor. Discipline. Service," the admiral almost shouted. "In thirty-five years, I have never had an officer under my command convicted of dereliction of duty or refusal to carry out an order. Much less sedition."

The admiral rounded the corner and turned to stand in front of Jake and Robbie. "That's why I have decided that perhaps I wasn't making myself clear. Perhaps I needed to give the two officers who refused my first command a chance—a lingering opportunity—to redeem themselves and sign General Order 34."

He stopped in front of Jake and Robbie, and Jake's heart went to his throat. *Here it is*, he thought. *Do I really believe all this stuff I have been talking about? Enough to go the distance?*

"Captain Crownover," Admiral Benhurst said to Robbie. "I hope you are well versed in your navy tradition. What can you tell me of the charge of sedition?"

"Uh, sedition, sir, is one of the most serious charges for a naval officer, right up there with mutiny and treason," Robbie responded hesitantly, then cleared his throat. "The official definition of sedition is conduct or language that incites others to rebel against the state."

"Sounds like something you don't want to mess with," Admiral Benhurst responded. "Especially since the penalty over the years has either been life imprisonment or execution by firing squad."

Out of the corner of his eye, Jake could see the sweat beginning to bead up on Robbie's forehead. His own T-shirt suddenly felt very clammy against his skin.

"Now I know that the United States has a history of tolerance of people's individual rights, especially when it comes to religious views." Admiral Benhurst turned and looked at the other medical officers in the locker room. "That will be coming to an end within the next few days. It is imperative that the United States Navy be prepared to back up the decisions Congress and the president pass into law. We must as a people—and as fellow naval officers—stand united in the face of adversity."

Admiral Benhurst turned and faced Jake and Robbie. Jake had never seen him so serious.

"Now I will give you one more chance. Will you sign this document—or do I need to have you taken away in chains?"

God, help him to stay strong, Jake prayed inwardly. *Help me to stay strong.*

"I—I'll sign," Robbie whispered.

"What's that, son?" Admiral Benhurst said, leaning forward, and Jake's heart sank.

"I said I'll sign," Robbie said, tears coming to his eyes. Jake felt like crying as well. The admiral passed from Robbie to Jake, and Jake saw Robbie look to the floor in shame.

"All right, that's one," Admiral Benhurst. "Let's go two for two. Commander Gallagher, you are hereby ordered to sign General Order 34. What is your response?"

Jake inhaled quickly and responded without hesitation.

"No, sir. I cannot. It is against my principles."

"I don't give a fig for your principles. I want your loyalty." The veins once again stood out on Admiral Benhurst's forehead.

"My loyalty belongs to the Constitution which I swore to uphold, and to the God who brought this country into being." Jake said and then stiffened, almost expecting to be hit across the face in response.

"And if that Constitution changes? Are you willing to change?"

Jake pressed his lips together and responded. "If the Constitution and my God are not in agreement, then I will have to choose loyalty to my God. Above all else. Sir."

chapter 20

Admiral Benhurst stared at Jake, and Jake couldn't tell if his expression showed hatred or admiration. A long second later, he looked down and turned away. Jake could see sadness in the admiral's face.

"Put Commander Gallagher in chains," he muttered to the two marines standing at the door. "Take him away."

* * * * *

"Mr. Lewis, you have been given ten minutes to make a decision," Judge Schiller said to Dan. "Are you ready to share your decision with the court?"

Dan looked up at the small woman and nodded.

"Yes, Your Honor. I've decided that my loyalty to my friends and to God is more important that what happens to me. I will not reveal their names to the court."

Judge Schiller looked at Dan without expression. Finally, she unfolded her hands and reached for an official document in front of her, signing it as she spoke.

"Mr. Lewis, you are to stand trial on June 8 in this courtroom on the charge of income tax evasion. Until that time, you are to be held in the Santa Clara County jail with a bail set at ten thousand dollars." She pounded her gavel as if to add emphasis to her words.

As Dan stood in the center of the courtroom, time stopped for him. But a flurry of activity surrounded him. The officer who had manhandled him before came in with another uniformed person. Dan expected to be led off through a side door to his jail cell. Instead, the two of them stood on either side of him, watching the judge.

Dan looked up at Judge Schiller, who was talking earnestly with someone in a suit. Finally she looked at Dan and nodded. She motioned for Dan to step forward.

"Apparently you have friends you didn't know you had," she said. "Your bail has been posted. You are free to go until June 8."

Meg, Dan thought as they unshackled him and he turned to go. *It has to be Meg.*

He waded up the center aisle toward the double doors. It wasn't until he stepped through the doors that he recognized a familiar face.

"Hello, Dan," the man said and smiled.

"Ernst Johansen," Dan said, holding out his hand to shake Ernst's. "The guy with the chestnut tree. How's the cough?"

"All gone, thanks to you," Mr. Johansen said. "And thanks for the spiritual advice as well."

"Spiritual advice?" Dan repeated. "Oh, you mean the scripture—" Suddenly it dawned on Dan who had bailed him out.

"You! You bailed me out, didn't you?" Dan smiled, raising an eyebrow.

Mr. Johansen shrugged. "The charges were trumped up, that was obvious. I couldn't let them put one of the world's last honest men behind bars."

"Well, thanks," Dan said.

"Your thanks may be short-lived," Mr. Johansen said, suddenly getting very serious. "Big things are happening in Washington. You could be back in jail within a few days. Watch yourself."

"I will," Dan said, wondering what the next few days would bring.

CHAPTER

The rock band cranked up the sound another couple of decibels, and Kris covered her ears.

> *Jesus is a friend of mine—hey!*
> *I will help you get to know him—yeah!*
> *We will all be friends together—whoa!*
> *And we will reign on earth—hey!*

Kris wrinkled her nose. *Corny lyrics,* she thought. But she looked around her and saw that the hundred other teens there at Sunday School were enjoying themselves immensely. It wasn't like any Sabbath School she had ever attended. It was more like a party. *Not a lot of direction, just an experience,* she thought. No wonder kids were coming there in droves. They didn't have to change their belief system, just their behavior.

"Come on, let's dance!" Brad said to her, pulling her toward the front of the room, where others gyrated almost out of control.

Kris shook her head. "I don't feel like it," she shouted back over the music. "I'd like to find someplace a little quieter, if we could."

"Sure," he said, coming closer to her and taking her hand. "They are having a discussion in the next room. Let's go check it out.

"You know, after all your talk at school, I'm really surprised to see you showing up here today. After all, it is Sunday."

"Yeah, well, my mom really didn't give me an option. She woke me up this morning, threw a new dress at me, and said we were going to church."

Brad looked down at Kris's dress. "It's an awesome dress."

Kris shrugged and then grinned. "Yeah … I think so, too."

"See, living with your mom is not that bad."

"We'll see," Kris said.

They walked out the open doorway and down the hall to the next room. About thirty kids were sitting around in a living-room-like setting, listening to a young, attractive woman make a presentation. Behind her a large screen TV stood switched off.

"So you can see how unprecedented and historic this occasion is. That's why Congress thought it appropriate to finish up debate and vote it all through today—Sunday."

"What are they talking about?" Kris asked a girl sitting next to her.

"Congress is voting through a new constitutional amendment today," the girl said. Kris couldn't help noticing the girl's splotchy skin and some small lesions on her neck.

"Something about making our church the official, national church," she continued.

Kris wrinkled her forehead and stared into space. The girl's words didn't make sense. She paused for a long time before speaking to the girl again.

"But they can't do that, can they? I mean, what about the First Amendment?" Kris asked the girl, and then realized that the girl wasn't listening to her. She turned the other direction. "Brad, they can't do that, can they?"

Brad shrugged. "I don't know government stuff. Ask me about basketball."

Kris shook her head and looked at the screen in the front of the room. A man in a suit was making a presentation. Words on the screen below him identified him as Representative Hallam McKay from Kansas.

"I find myself standing alone in this issue," he said. "Most of you are calling this a historic event. I call it an embarrassment. This proposed amendment goes against everything that the United States has ever stood for. I have no sympathy for those who would undermine the wishes of the American people. I am not a subversive. But I do believe in the rights of the individual—life, liberty, and the pursuit of happiness.

"Legislating religion is disaster on the fast track. All we are forcing people to do is conform to a way of life. It doesn't change what happens inside them. Going to church will not make them become Christians, or even act more Christian toward each other.

"Look at the statistics. In the past two months, church-going in the United States is up 45 percent. At the same time, crime is up 300 percent. Where is the correlation there? What are we gaining by becoming a totalitarian regime? I am making a public statement right now that I oppose this amendment. I call for those of you with an ounce of dignity and courage to stand with me."

"He's a jerk," someone said from the front.

"Yeah, get real," said the girl next to Kris.

"Jerk or not, he has valid arguments," said the woman in charge. "And those are the arguments that historically have kept the United States from making a move like this in years past. It's refreshing to see that they have finally decided to look past all the rhetoric and do what needs to be done.

"You'll also be pleased to know that at present, Representative McKay is the only one in Congress speaking against the proposed amendment."

"Then why don't they go ahead and vote?" Brad asked, and Kris turned to stare at him.

The woman shook her head. "Because this is such a significant event in our country. They want to make sure every argument is addressed, and every person has a chance to see and hear what is happening."

"But they haven't addressed the arguments," Kris said.

The woman put her finger to her lips, then pointed to the screen.

"Watch," she said.

Representative McKay stomped away from the podium, and another man came to take his place. The screen identified the tall, thin man with long silver hair as Rep. Richard Anderson from Virginia.

"I appreciate the comments that the representative from Kansas has shared with us today. But these arguments are old—older than our Constitution. In fact, I might remind the representative from Kansas that the United States government survived for years without a Constitution. The Articles of Confederation were the laws of the land until 1787. Then when the Constitution was drafted in 1787, it did not include a Bill of Rights. Four years later, in 1791, the First Amendment was added as an afterthought. The drafters of the Constitution didn't feel the need for a Bill of Rights. They realized that people knew their rights and didn't need to be reminded of them. I tend to agree with them. We have added amendments over the past two hundred years, but have we really improved anything? Most amendments have been so timid that they haven't gotten to the root of the problem, and therefore haven't really changed anything.

"The amendment in question today is different. It is bold, brash, and gets to the root of this nation's problem—spirituality. True, you can't control what goes on in people's minds. But you can do the next best thing—make them conform. Make everyone conform.

"Fellow Americans, it is time we all humbled ourselves before God as united brothers and sisters. Enough of thinking for yourself. It's time to join together for the good. And everyone who will not join us will be eliminated."

Eliminated? Did she hear that right? Kris's eyes bulged, and she looked around her at the crowd of teenagers. They applauded and cheered as if their favorite team had just scored a touchdown. Even Brad seemed transfixed.

"This is ridiculous," Kris said to him. "Let's get out of here."

He shook his head without looking at her. "No, this is good stuff. Let's stay."

Kris looked at the ground for an instant, unbelieving. Then she spoke again.

"Brad, this goes against everything they ever taught us in church and in school. This is the prophesied national Sunday law."

Brad smiled, still staring straight ahead. "So?"

"*So?*" Kris repeated. "Brad, what are you saying?"

Brad stopped smiling and looked over at her, apparently annoyed. "I am saying that this is where I belong. Sure, I have been with you for the past few months, and it's been fun. I have heard all the arguments, pro and con. And frankly, I have decided I don't care. All I want to do is have fun."

Kris's mouth dropped open, and she realized she had lost Brad forever.

* * * * *

The light above Jenny's head came on with a *bong*, and she heard a voice through the speaker.

"Ladies and gentlemen, the captain has turned on the fasten seat belt sign. Please return to your seats and prepare for our landing at Honolulu International Airport."

Jenny's heart beat faster. The past few months had seemed like years. She was going to see Jake—finally! She still had not been able to contact him by phone, but she was determined that not even the United States Navy would keep her from her husband. Not anymore. Time was too precious.

In addition, this morning before the flight from O'Hare, she realized that the baby had dropped in her uterus. Delivery was a few days away, a week at the most. What worried her was that Junior wasn't as active as he or she had been in past weeks. With disease and disaster all around her, a competent physician was harder to find than hen's teeth.

She stared out the window and saw the island of Oahu off in the distance. Then she rubbed her eyes. Strange. The island seemed to be dancing.

Just then Jenny felt the plane fall from beneath her. Women screamed, and a flight attendant flew through the air and crashed to the floor of an aisle. Just as suddenly, the plane shuddered and began to climb again. Then it dropped again.

"What's going on?" the heavyset man in the next seat asked aloud. "Are we crashing?"

The plane rocked back and forth, rose and fell, and shuddered for a full minute without any explanation.

The flight attendant crawled back to her seat and strapped herself in. She shouted at the passengers, "Buckle your seat belts!"

One of the overhead compartments opened. Coats, a carry-on bag, and a camcorder bag fell out on the passenger below.

Then just as suddenly as it had started, the air was calm again. Jenny shook herself and looked around her. And then she realized that this was the first time she had really looked at the other passengers. She had been thinking about Jake and nothing else. Now she looked at her fellow travelers.

Most were acting like her, brushing themselves off after the disturbance in the air. But Jenny also sensed something else. Desperation. Hopelessness. All of them seemed as if they were stressed beyond belief, with no solution to their problem.

That's what we have to offer these people. A solution. Hope.

"Ladies and gentlemen, this is the captain speaking," Jenny heard from overhead.

"Sorry about that bumpy ride back there," he said. "We hit some unexpected turbulence. I called ahead to find out what happened, and the news is not good."

Jenny felt as though her heart had jumped to her throat.

"The Hawaiian Islands have experienced a severe earthquake. We don't know how major, really. Unfortunately, there are fires and damage everywhere. Communication between the islands and the mainland is nonexistent. It will be a while before we know how bad it really is.

"Normally our procedure calls for us to turn around and return to the nearest safe airport, which would be San Francisco. But we are five minutes out on approach, and air traffic control assures me that they have at least one strip that's clear. So we are going to land. I just can't promise you what you will see when you get there."

Jenny looked at the floor and shook her head.

* * * * *

Mitch was learning patience, whether he wanted to or not. He was sitting in Eastridge Mall in the food court. Sharing a table with him were three sixteen-year-old girls. He was trying to witness to them, but all they could do was giggle and whisper in response to every question he posed.

"So that's Daniel 2, or at least a brief summary of it," he said. "Do you have any questions?"

The brunette and the redhead continued to giggle. The blonde spoke up.

"Where do you live?" she asked.

Mitch rolled his eyes, as he pretty much figured where her interests were. He pointed to Gina and Harley sitting at another table in the corner. Harley raised his hand and waved.

"I live in an apartment with them. That's Gina and Harley. Gina's my girlfriend," he said. Well, she was sorta his girlfriend, he thought. They spent a lot of time together, and he really liked her a lot. He was pretty sure she felt the same way. They had just been too busy witnessing to think about any kind of relationship.

"Would you ever consider you and your girlfriend getting together for a party?" the blonde asked, twirling her straw in her drink and looking up at Mitch with a grin. "You could even bring Harley. He's kinda cute."

Mitch exhaled slowly. "We're really too busy telling others about Christ to party. Now, let me ask you again. What do you think about what I have been sharing with you this morning?"

The blonde stood up. "We thought you were flirting with us. I thought something was going to happen here. You're good looking, but I think this Bible study is a waste of time." She jerked her head to the others.

"Come on, guys." The brunette jumped up and followed the other without looking back. The redhead was slower.

"I thought what you were saying was interesting," she said shyly. "I wish I had more time to listen to it."

"No one in the world has much time," Mitch said, looking into her eyes. "You only have time if you make time."

She looked at Mitch and then at his Bible. He could tell a battle was going on in her mind.

"I … I'm sorry," she said. "I gotta go."

Mitch watched her walk across the food court to join her friends. She turned and looked back at him as they stepped onto the escalator and disappeared. He looked over at Harley and Gina. Harley shrugged as if to say, "Win some, lose some." Gina smiled that smile which made her look like Drew Barrymore. *I really have to spend more time with that girl,* Mitch thought.

He started to rise to join his friends when he felt a heavy hand on his shoulder and he was shoved back into his seat.

"Sit down, Mitch." The voice was all business.

A middle-aged man in slacks and a polo shirt parked himself in the seat across from Mitch.

"Do you know me, Mitch?" he asked quietly. "Do you recognize my face?"

Mitch looked at the man closely. He looked like many other mall shoppers he had seen. The man could disappear into a crowd and never be missed.

Mitch shrugged.

"I have been following you for two weeks. I work for the FBI."

Mitch nodded. "Right. Like the FBI is going to be following me."

"Look, I can show you a badge if you want, but I want to keep this low profile. It will be better for both of us if no one knew that we were talking." Mitch thought of Gina and Harley across the food court, and his head involuntarily started to turn their direction.

"Yeah, I know all about your friends. Right now it just looks like another Bible study. But I not only know about Gina and Harley, I know about Dolores, Marcus, Flea, Ivan … look, do you want me to go on? I know 'em all. Everyone you have met with in the past two weeks."

Mitch stared at the man. "So?"

"So, ever since that presentation at the Civic Center and your subsequent arrest, you have been tracked." The man drew closer. "Do you understand? Not just followed. Not just watched. *Tracked.*"

Mitch continued to stare. The man reached out and grabbed both of Mitch's arms by the wrists, turning the hands palm-side up in front of them.

"Do you remember what they did to you when they arrested you? The thing with the bright light?"

Mitch looked at his hands and then at the man in front of him.

"Yeah. They put me against this thing like a big X-ray machine. Said it was a magnetic scanner."

"That's right," the man said. "A magnetic scanner. Everyone these days who is detained is scanned. Their skin—hands and face—are given a magnetic code that shows up on special guns like radar guns. The computer can identify you instantly. We can even feed your code into the computer and locate you via satellite."

Mitch shook his head. "This is just so Star Wars–like. I mean, who am I? Just a kid out telling people what he believes."

"That's why you're dangerous. You are telling people the truth. You're a subversive. The government won't stand for it. They have a file on each and every one of your friends. And they have a big, thick file on you."

The man reached over and grabbed Mitch's wrist so tightly that Mitch's hand began to grow numb.

"One more thing," he hissed. "Right now, Congress is voting through a new constitutional amendment that will make what you are doing completely illegal. As soon as that happens, there is going to be a roundup. You and your friends have been tagged and will be behind bars in a matter of hours."

"What do I do?" Mitch looked at the man, and then at his friends, who were talking and didn't see him look at them. "I mean, I have put so many people in danger. How many people have I talked to in the past two weeks? I don't even know."

"I do," the man said. "Three hundred and fourteen."

"What!" Mitch said. "I could never warn that many."

"You're right," the man said. "So don't worry about them. You did what you had to do; that is, tell them the truth. Look, I've been listening to your conversations and arguments and Bible studies for two weeks. You're not a bad kid, and you don't deserve to go to prison. So just get out while you can. You and your friends."

Mitch started to get up, but the man motioned for him to sit.

"I have something for you," the man said. He pulled out a small bottle of clear liquid. "Use this with a stiff brush. Wash your face, scalp, and hands real good with this stuff. It's acid. It will take the outer layer of your skin off. Hurts like the dickens. But they won't be able to track you anymore."

Mitch pocketed the stuff, and started to say something to his benefactor.

"Listen, I—"

But the man had left.

CHAPTER

22

AMENDMENT 28 TO THE CONSTITUTION OF THE UNITED STATES: "The rights and privileges afforded by the Constitution of the United States of America are guaranteed only to citizens of the United States. Citizenship is determined by (1) birth or naturalization; (2) allegiance to the government of the United States exclusively; and (3) allegiance to the National Unified Church of the United States and observance of Sunday, the first day of the week as the Lord's Day, a holy day of rest."

* * * * *

Kris pedaled her ten-speed as fast as she could. The news was ringing through the neighborhood. She could hear the president's address on every car radio she passed, and through the screen door of every home. Every person on the street seemed to know. The world had changed dramatically—for the worse. It had finally come.

She thought about the new amendment. She didn't completely understand the significance of what Congress had voted into being. She did know that forty-four out of fifty state legislatures had approved the amendment and that the president had immediately signed it into law. She also knew that it was bad news for anyone who didn't believe in the Unified Church or in worshipping on Sunday.

Now it was late Sunday evening, and she was in search of Mitch. She knew that lately on Sunday evenings he had been meeting with a group of kids who played basketball at the academy. He'd play for a while and then the group would almost always end up in a Bible study. She hoped that he was there so she could warn him. On the other hand, maybe he already knew and was on his way to a safe place—if there was such a place.

She rounded the corner of Rincon and Dot avenues and sped into the parking lot. Sure enough, a small group of academy guys were playing basketball.

"Hey," she yelled when she got close enough. "Hey, have you guys seen Mitch?"

The kid with the ball paused below the rim and looked at her cautiously, as if trying to decide whether he should trust her or not.

"It's OK," she said, jumping off her bike and laying it down as she got close. "I'm his sister."

The teen looked at her then glanced purposefully over at a brown sedan that was parked across the street. Without turning her head, Kris saw the two men inside and understood.

"No, Mitch's hasn't been around," the teen said loudly. "You might try the mall, although I heard they're shutting that down on Sundays now."

"Look," Kris whispered. "It's really important that I find him. You would understand if you knew what was going on."

"Yeah, we heard about the new law," the teen said. "Ain't our problem." He turned his back on Kris and went back to his game.

Kris sighed. Her brother was around here somewhere, she was sure. And she was pretty certain that this kid knew where he was. But whether it was to protect him from the guys in the car or for some other reason, he didn't seem too cooperative. As she turned to go, another boy picked up her bike.

"Try the stairwell," he whispered quickly and stepped away

from Kris. She almost nodded, then caught herself. She needed to contact Mitch, but the police or whoever was in the car had no doubt heard her say who she was. If she went to Mitch, they would find him.

She walked her bike down the sidewalk adjacent to the school, all the while looking back as if she were watching the game. Finally she rounded the corner and saw that the car had not yet followed her. She pushed the bike quickly behind a hedge and jumped over a small concrete wall and down into the lower level of the split-level school building.

She heard the car start up and drive past; then it accelerated down the street. She carefully poked her head over the edge of the concrete wall and saw the brown sedan roaring away down the street and around the corner.

"Mitch!" she hissed. "Mitch!" The long shadows of evening made the lower locker level of the school quite dark.

"Over here," she heard a voice from the stairwell. She picked herself up and ran to the familiar voice.

Mitch was sitting on the stairs, dressed in an old T-shirt and jeans. But she almost didn't recognize him. His hands and face were beet-red and blistered. His hair, once jet black and magnificently thick, looked ragged and stood on his head in clumps. He looked up as she came to him. He stood and hugged her.

"What happened to you?" she asked, looking at his hands and wrinkling her nose. "You look like you've been in a fire."

"No, it's acid, and it's a long story, one we don't have time for right now. I suppose you know what's happened."

"Yeah, I rode over here first thing when I heard. I'm on my way to Dad's. I don't even plan on going home at all." She pulled off her backpack and showed him a change of clothes, her Bible, and her notebook computer.

"Well, where are you guys headed?" Mitch asked.

"To the mountains, I suppose," Kris said. "Although I don't know how we will get there. Dad's old car gasped its last breath a week ago, and we don't have any way to get gas anyway." She looked at her brother. "You're coming too, aren't you?"

Mitch shook his head. "I've got three hundred friends who are being hunted by these guys as we speak. I have to do whatever I can to warn them. And there's someone else. A girl named Gina. I have to make sure she's safe."

Kris started to argue, then realized that there was no way she could be sure that she and Dad would be any safer than Mitch would.

"Where . . . how . . . when will I see you again?" Kris asked.

Mitch smiled. "Don't worry. I will find out where you are somehow and come and join you. If not, then I will see you when it is all over."

Kris looked at her big brother.

"When it's all over," she repeated. "You mean, when Jesus comes."

Mitch shrugged. "I guess that's all we have to look forward to. And that's a lot. That's really what all this is about, isn't it?"

Kris clutched her brother and hugged him for dear life.

"I love you, Mitch," she said.

"I love you, too, Kris," he said, tears coming to his eyes. "Tell Dad not to worry. Tell Dad I love him. Tell Dad . . . he'll know. There's just not enough time for everything."

Kris looked up at him, the tears wet on her face.

"Soon we will have all the time in the universe," she said. "Soon we will be with Jesus."

"Now we see as through a glass darkly," Mitch quoted. "Then we shall see him face to face."

"I . . ." Kris started, and realized she had no more words to say. She turned and walked up the stairs to her bike, got on it, and rode away.

* * * * *

Dan didn't own much, so he knew it wouldn't take him long to pack. A couple of changes of clothes, a few family mementos, and he was ready to go. He started to leave the Easthams' basement for the last time when he caught sight of the framed picture of Meg he still had standing on his makeshift dresser.

He hesitated. Were they still married? Did she still care? Well, whether she still cared or not, he did. She was still his wife in his eyes until he decided otherwise. He grabbed the small picture and shoved it into his bag.

"Kris," he muttered aloud. "Where is she?" He looked around the empty room as if he might find her there. She had told him nothing that would lead him to believe that she would be meeting him there. Yet somehow he knew she would. At least he hoped so.

"Mrs. Eastham," Dan yelled up the stairs as he climbed up to the main floor. "Are you and Elder Eastham ready to go?"

He looked around the kitchen and saw that nothing had been disturbed. No one was in sight.

"Ma'am?" he asked aloud as he wandered from room to empty room. Finally he realized that she was in the bedroom with her husband, and he knew that something was wrong.

He cautiously approached the bedroom door and peeked inside. Mrs. Eastham sat on the side of the bed by her husband, holding his hand. Elder Eastham's eyes were closed, and Dan sensed that the old man was no longer breathing.

"He took a nap this afternoon and just didn't wake up," Mrs. Eastham said quietly.

"He's done a lot for all of us, for the whole church," Dan said to her, putting his hand on her shoulder. "He deserves a rest."

" 'It won't be long now,' he kept saying. I guess he knew more than the rest of us."

"Mrs. Eastham," Dan said. "The police will be here any minute. We have to leave."

Mrs. Eastham shook her head. "I'm an old woman. I would only slow you down. There's not much they can take away from me now. I will stay with my husband."

Dan opened his mouth to argue and stopped when he heard the kitchen door slam and feet run across the floor toward them. Kris poked her head in the door. When she saw Elder Eastham on the bed and noticed the sadness in the room, she started to back out without saying anything.

"It's OK, dear," Mrs. Eastham said. "He's just sleeping until Jesus comes."

"Mitch isn't coming," Kris said quietly, looking from Mrs. Eastham to her father. "He says he has unfinished business."

"I suspected as much," Dan said, sighing. "I guess it's just the two of us on the road, Kitkat."

"But, Dad, the minivan died two weeks ago. You told me yourself."

Dan sighed. "Yeah, I know. I was waiting for God to send a miracle."

Mrs. Eastham reached over and grabbed her purse. "You want a miracle?" she asked as she dug through her purse. Finally she found a set of keys and thrust them out in front of Dan.

"Here's your miracle," she said. "Of course, you may not think it's much of a miracle when you see it. It's a 1962 Volvo. Pretty homely little car. But it runs and has three-quarters of a tank of gas. At least it did when I ran it a week ago."

Dan and Kris looked at Mrs. Eastham, then at each other.

"Let's go," Dan said.

Mrs. Eastham watched Dan and Kris pull out of the driveway and around the corner onto Winchester Boulevard.

"Dear blessed Jesus," she prayed. "Keep them safe. Help them to find a haven where they can continue to worship you in their own way. Watch over Mitch as well."

She looked over at the body of the man who had been her husband for fifty-eight years. "And thank you for giving me such a wonderful husband and a wonderful life. I don't think I could ask for any more than what you've already given me."

As she prayed with her eyes open as if talking to a lifelong friend, she saw the three police cars pull up in front of her house. Six uniformed men jumped out and headed for her door.

"Jonathan, you were right," she said. "It won't be long at all."

* * * * *

Too late, Mitch thought as he looked at the swarm of police cars that surrounded the Pruneyard Apartments where Gina, Harley, and he had lived for the past two months. From his vantage point at the 7-Eleven store on the corner, he watched in the darkness as they brought Harley out to a squad car in handcuffs and put him in the back seat. Then, surprisingly, the police officer left the vehicle and went back into the building.

He's probably looking for me—or Gina, thought Mitch, as he crept forward through the parking lot, keeping out of sight behind the parked cars.

So far, so good. Mitch was able to reach the back of the black-and-white without being seen. He crouched behind the vehicle and listened to the radio squawking inside. Holding his breath, he reached up and lifted the handle to the back door. Surprisingly, the door opened. He looked inside.

"Mitch!" Harley hissed. "What are you doing here?"

"Rescuing you," Mitch mumbled. "Where's Gina?" He looked at Harley and realized that he had been handcuffed to the vehicle.

"She didn't come home from her bakery job, thank God," Harley said. "If she had, she'd be right here."

"Then there's still a chance to save her," Mitch said. "But first, I have to get you out of here." Mitch fingered the shiny handcuffs that held Harley captive.

"Forget it, man," Harley said. "That's tooled stainless steel. I had a set of handlebars on a bike made out of that stuff. Rolled and totaled the bike. Didn't even scratch the handlebars."

"Maybe if we could find a set of bolt cutters," Mitch said. He started looking around the vehicle.

"Just leave me," Harley said. "Save yourself. Get the word out. People still need to hear the good news. There is still a chance for a lot of people."

Mitch kept looking as Harley talked. He started to look in the squad car next to them until he realized that an enormous German shepherd occupied the back seat. Miraculously it had not yet started barking, but watched the two men carefully. Mitch decided to not tempt the dog, however.

"Look, let me go take care of Gina," Mitch finally said in frustration. "Maybe she's got some tools in the back of the bakery."

"Yeah, you do that," Harley said. "Save Gina. One more thing, Mitch. Remember where I stashed my Hog down on Monterey Road. The old garage there? If things get tight, use it. It should have enough gas to get you wherever you need to go."

Mitch felt ashamed for leaving Harley, but he didn't know what else to do.

He started to say something, then just shook his head.

"Keep the faith," Harley said, lifting his chin in salute. "Jesus is coming."

"Hey, hold it right there," a voice yelled at them from a distance. Mitch looked up and saw three blue-uniformed San Jose police officers running toward him, their right hands over their holstered sidearms.

Mitch didn't even wait to shut the car door, but bolted across the parking lot and toward the 7-Eleven. Before he reached the convenience store, however, he saw a patrol car pull into the parking lot in front of him. Lights appeared everywhere, and sirens started to sound in front of and behind him. Impulsively, he ran to his left and straight out into the busy traffic of Bascom Avenue.

Like a frightened rabbit, Mitch charged straight ahead into the traffic. He knew that if he thought about it logically, he would just throw up his hands and surrender. So he allowed instinct to take over. He ran blindly into the oncoming fifty-mile-an-hour traffic and prayed that his guardian angel would protect him. The sound of sirens was replaced by the screaming of tires and car horns honking. Mitch ran, leaped, and dodged, and somehow made it across the busy street. He didn't know how far behind the police were. He didn't look behind him to find out.

Ahead on his left was the Foster's Freeze where he had met

Harley. He charged through the parking lot and leaped over a wooden fence that separated it from a residential area. Once again, Mitch began to hear sirens wailing, and he knew the police were not far behind.

He ran across a plush backyard lawn and leaped another wooden fence on the other side. The next yard had a pool. He ran around it and leaped the third fence. Mitch was purposely leading them away from his intended goal—the shopping mall and the bakery where Gina worked. He should have been traveling north instead of east. But he also knew that the old Dry Creek was ahead. Once he got there, he could follow it north to Campbell Avenue and cut back to the mall. In the meantime, the patrol cars couldn't follow.

Then a police helicopter appeared out of nowhere. It began sweeping the backyards of the homes with a powerful searchlight. Suddenly he felt naked beneath its penetrating beam. He hid beneath the edge of a small shed as the helicopter passed over. As soon as the beam passed, he grabbed the top of the fence and started to pull himself over.

"Woof!" Mitch looked down into the face of the biggest dog he had ever seen. It didn't look happy to see him, either. Mitch hesitated, then let himself back down into the yard.

Suddenly, the back porch light came on. An overweight man in his fifties opened the back door and looked out. Mitch could see that the man was on a portable phone.

"Yes, he's here in our back yard, officer," the man said. Mitch didn't wait another second but ran parallel to the fence and out the gate into the front yard.

He got to the street and began running. Ten seconds later, he heard the sirens again.

It's gotta be around here somewhere, Mitch thought. He had grown up in this neighborhood and had played in the old creek bed many times. Since then, however, they had moved across town, and the area had become built up with higher priced homes. *What had happened to the old creek?*

Then Mitch realized what had happened. They had turned the dry creek bed into an underground storm drainage system. And when he realized that, police or no police, he knew what he had to do.

With the sound of the patrol car's siren loud in his ears, he saw one of the oversized storm drains coming up at the edge of the street. Without missing a beat, he leaped headfirst into the dark opening. He didn't know what would await him, but he knew it had to be better than any alternative the police had for him at this point.

His back hit the edge of the concrete slope, and he slid down the angled wall into the darkness. He could hear the police siren on the street above him.

"He jumped down the hole, I tell you," Mitch could hear the officer above him tell the others on the radio. Mitch knew that gave him very little time. Within minutes they would have all ways out blocked. He had to move fast—and in total darkness.

Fortunately, there hadn't been rain in San Jose since the previous November. The drought and heat had distinct disadvantages, but at least it kept the storm drains dry and free of vermin. He held out his left hand and felt the rounded edge of the storm drain, then moved ahead as quickly as he could.

After what seemed like an eternity, he could finally hear heavy traffic above him. He tried to envision the local layout in his head and figured it must be Campbell Avenue. He thought there was a bridge there and had planned on getting out at this point. Above him he could see two pinholes that indicated a manhole cover. He just hoped it opened up in a safe place.

He climbed the metal rungs on the side of the concrete storm drain and pushed up on the manhole cover with his shoulder. It popped open, and he looked up.

Mitch was pleased to see that the manhole cover actually opened on a cul-de-sac that faced Campbell Avenue. He pulled himself out of the storm drain and into the light of a street lamp.

Mitch looked down at his hands and felt his scraggly hair. He wouldn't be much to look at, but Gina's safety was more important than how he appeared. There would hopefully be time for other things at a later date.

He walked out on Campbell Avenue and realized that he had lost the police. He looked behind him and saw the police helicopters searching the neighborhood he had left behind.

It was only half a block to the Pruneyard Shopping Center and the bakery where Gina worked. There were only a few cars left in the lot, and Mitch realized this would be the last Sunday there would ever be cars here. The new law made Sunday shopping illegal.

He jogged across the lot and onto the sidewalk that surrounded the outside mall. Mitch walked quickly down the sidewalk, all the while feeling that he was being followed. It now made no difference to him if he was arrested. All he wanted was to know that Gina was safe.

He could see the bakery light on ahead. Three shops to go. He quickened his pace. That's when he heard the sound that chilled his blood.

"OK, freeze. You're under arrest."

The voice came from behind him. Sirens began wailing across the parking lot. He hesitated and then ran.

Mitch didn't see the Taser darts that flew through the air and hit him squarely in the back. Through the convulsions of the electric shocks, he was vaguely aware of the crowd that surrounded him. He was able to see as the police officers pinned him to the ground and twisted his arms behind him, that Gina had slipped out the bakery door and into the edge of the crowd.

Despite being bruised and beaten, handcuffed, and thrown into the back of the patrol car, Mitch was smiling. Gina was gone. She was safe.

CHAPTER
23

The ugly gray Volvo crunched slowly up the gravel road. Dan ran and then walked behind it as it moved more and more slowly.

"OK, pull it over to the side," Dan shouted to Kris, who sat behind the wheel. She turned the wheel hard to the right, and the Volvo found a place to rest—for itself and the person pushing it along the road.

"Let's take a break," Dan huffed to Kris, who got out of the car and joined him in the shade of an oak tree.

"Daddy, you've become a hunk," Kris said, looking at her sweating father as he leaned against the tree.

"Yeah, right," he said. "You just don't want to have to push that car to town."

"No, I'm serious," Kris said. "You look like you've lost fifty pounds, and you've got all that hard muscle now."

Dan shrugged, smiling. "A far cry from last Thanksgiving, eh? That day seems like a lifetime ago, even though it's been only four months." He looked around him at the bleak landscape shimmering in the unusual March heat.

"Did you ever think it would be like this?" he asked. "The end, I mean?"

Kris shrugged. "I didn't really think about how it might be. I kinda took it for granted that things would continue the way they always had."

"That's what most people thought," Dan said. "That's why they weren't ready."

Dan spoke as a red-and-orange tow truck came over the hill they were headed for. On the truck door were written in peeling letters: "Mariposa Towing and Repair."

"Gotta problem, mister?" the man shouted from his open window as the tow truck stopped in the opposite lane of the narrow highway.

Dan nodded. "It's a friend's car. It was doing fine, then just died on us. We still have a quarter of a tank of gas. I don't understand."

"I'll take a look-see," the man shouted back. "Could be the timing chain, or it could be something as simple as a stuck gas gauge." He cranked his wheel over and pulled in behind the Volvo on the side of the road.

"Name's Rick Ferree," the mechanic said to Dan after he stepped out of his truck and joined the two. "I own the only mechanic's shop and gas station in town that's still in business." He shook Dan's hand, then climbed into the driver's seat and tried to start the car. When it wouldn't start, he popped the hood and poked his head into the engine well.

"Dad, can I ask a stupid question?" Kris said quietly. "How are we going to pay to get the car fixed when we don't even have enough money for lunch?"

"The Lord will provide," he answered. "My grandma used to say that all the time, and I didn't really appreciate her attitude. That is, until recently. If it makes you feel any better, pray. But I already know that God's going to take care of us."

Kris looked at the dying trees and grass around her. "I know that God is going to take care of everything, including lunch. I just wish He would hurry up. I am hungry."

Dan took a few steps to one side of the oak tree he had been leaning against, reached down and picked up a couple of acorns. He held them out to Kris.

"Very funny," Kris said.

"Pigs and squirrels love them," Dan teased. "Actually, if you leach out the tannic acid, they make a pretty good flour that you can bake with."

He looked around and noticed a pine tree nearby. He walked toward it, looking at the ground the whole time. Finally he reached down and picked up a pinecone. He pulled the cone apart and pulled out a pine nut. Popping it in his mouth, he crunched down and smiled.

"Mmm good," he said. "Have you ever eaten pine nuts before?"

Kris shook her head, and Dan broke some more nuts free from the cone. He handed them to her. She picked one out and looked at it suspiciously, then put it in her mouth. She was surprised that she liked it.

"As I have said for years, plants are a primary source of medicine. But wild plants offer many possibilities for food sources as well. Cattails are a great food source, so are dandelions. There's skunk cabbage. And then there are all kinds of berries—thimbleberries, blackberries, huckleberries. But you know all of this. You got your honor in wilderness survival back in Pathfinders, didn't you?"

Kris shrugged. "That was three years ago. An eternity."

Dan and Kris looked up and saw that Rick the mechanic was standing behind the Volvo looking at them.

"All fixed up. It was just a wire loose on the coil."

Dan stepped forward. "I've got bad news. I have no money. None."

Rick wiped his hands on a rag and grinned.

"Shoot, with the world the way it is, most people don't have any money. Besides, there's no charge. It was just a loose wire."

"Well, thanks, Rick. You're a godsend."

Rick cocked his head. "Maybe it's you guys that are the

godsend. Did you mean what you said about plants being medicine and all? Do you really know that much about plants?"

Dan nodded. "Sure. I taught high school biology for years, and my master's thesis was on medicinal properties of plants right here in the Sierra Nevada."

"Well, then," Rick said. "We got lots of plants in this area, and we got lots of people who need help. What we don't got is people with education. The doctors and teachers took off weeks ago. Since then, we've had nothing but problems."

"I'm not a doctor—" Dan began.

"Sure, I know that," Rick broke in., "I'm not asking for you to play doctor. Just teach people how to use nature to take care of themselves."

Dan paused, then nodded. "I'm sure we can arrange something."

Forty-five minutes later Dan and Kris's Volvo chugged through the entrance of Wawona SDA Camp. Dan and Kris knew it by that name, although the sign identifying it had been removed. They drove down the rutted driveway for a short distance until they came to two posts on either side of the road. A heavy chain with a padlock ran from one side to the other.

"Wait here," Dan said and stepped out of the car. Kris sat in the passenger side and watched Dan walk into the camp and disappear through the trees. About five minutes later, Dan reappeared with a man in his seventies who looked as though he had lived in the outdoors all his life.

"Kris," Dan said as he led the man to the car. "This is Mr. Brewster. He's been the caretaker here for the past couple of years. He's going to let us in. We'll be staying at the camp for a while."

Kris wondered how long *a while* would be.

* * * * *

The earthquake victim had had part of a wall fall on her. As a result, her pelvis had been crushed. Most of her vital organs were not functioning. In addition, she had been buried in debris for two days. She stank from oil and concrete dust, from untreated wounds, and from her own waste.

Jake looked down at the teenage girl and sighed. *Not a chance, not in these circumstances,* he thought. Triage wasn't easy, especially in a major disaster, but someone had to do it. He breathed a prayer over the still form, then sighed. He pulled out a red tag and put it on her, then motioned for an orderly to move her.

"Over there," he said, gesturing. "Next."

The next patient was an Asian man with a makeshift bandage wound around his head and over one eye.

"What have we got here?" Jake said to the man, lifting the bandage gingerly.

"Not much," the man said. "I just got knocked in the head by a pole."

"Well, it doesn't look real serious, but you never know with head wounds," Jake said, looking at the deep cut on one temple. "Yeah, looks like you need some stitches, and probably something for the pain. Any problems with dizziness? Blurred vision?"

The man shook his head nervously, and then Jake noticed that the man was clutching something in his hands. A book. A red book. A light went on in Jake's head.

"Whatcha got there?" Jake asked casually, nodding toward the book.

"Something I was reading when the earthquake hit. It's a book that means a lot to me," the man said. He lifted it up, and Jake read the title. *"The Desire of Ages."*

"Ever heard of it?" the man asked Jake.

* * * * *

Jenny held her abdomen and tried to be patient. The tropical heat was making her nauseous, and the line of people searching for loved ones stretched on forever. She had taken the navy bus to Pearl Harbor. She quickly learned that the earthquake had leveled all the buildings there. The administration there was working without power, without computers, and with makeshift tents as their only shelter.

Because Jake's orders for Hawaii had come in the wake of the first earthquake, Jenny thought it would be easy to find him. But she had had no luck.

Now she was at the ruined Castle Medical Center. She looked up at a huge crack that ran from floor to ceiling and wondered if the whole hospital would come down if that wall collapsed. In another time, the building might have been condemned as unsafe. But in this day and age, there didn't seem to be a single safe building on the island of Oahu. People here were making do, just as other people were making do all over the world.

She looked ahead and realized she probably had another hour in line. She sighed. Then she looked over at a young black doctor who was giving instructions to a couple of orderlies. The name sounded familiar—Crownover. And then it clicked.

"Excuse me," she said to him, waving. He looked up at her. "Are you Robbie?" she asked.

"Do I know you, ma'am?" he asked, stepping forward.

"No, but I think I know you," she said, smiling in relief. "I'm Jenny Gallagher."

Robbie's eyes opened wide, and he looked at her again. "You're Jake's Jenny?" Then he took another look at her swollen abdomen. "Of course you're Jake's Jenny."

Jenny's heart beat faster. "I'm trying to find Jake. No one seems to know where he is. Can you tell me?"

Robbie's smile disappeared from his face. He grabbed Jenny by the arm and pulled her out of line and over to the side where there was less traffic.

"Jake . . . uh, Jake's been arrested," Robbie said quietly. "He wouldn't go along with what he calls the national Sunday law, what we refer to here as General Order 34." Jenny thought Robbie looked sick.

"Well, then, he's in the brig. Right?" Jenny thought hopefully that at least she would know where he was, and that he was safe.

"The brig at Pearl is rubble, just like about every other building on this island," Robbie said. "They have him under guard, but they are taking advantage of his medical and surgical skills. Last time I heard, he was down on Waikiki at a special MASH unit set up where the International Marketplace used to be."

Jenny remembered their honeymoon, and how they had wandered through the International Marketplace, enjoying the music and brash colors. Now it was a field hospital.

"Thanks," she said to Robbie, and turned to leave. Robbie grabbed her arm.

"Jenny, I know you've been in hospitals before. That's a frontline triage site. You are going to be exposed to the most horrible injuries imaginable, not to mention diseases of every kind. It's not really the best place to be when you're pregnant."

"Look," Jenny said, pulling Robbie's hand from her arm. "I have been through all kinds of turmoil and been without my husband for four months. I have just flown seven thousand miles. I am going to him—now."

Robbie drew a deep breath and nodded. "Then do me a favor, will you? Tell him ... tell him I'm sorry."

Jenny took one last look at Robbie and saw what looked like the face of someone who knew he was beyond hope.

* * * * *

"Jake?" The voice cut through the craziness of the triage unit, and Jake's concentration was broken. He looked up, and across the cots and countless bodies, he saw someone who looked familiar.

"Jenny!" he shouted. He started to run toward her, then

realized that he was in the middle of treating a patient. In addition, there was the marine private with the sidearm standing right behind him.

Jake didn't have to worry. Jenny was there and all over him in a heartbeat. They kissed, oblivious to the medical team standing and staring at them, oblivious to the heat and the stench, oblivious to everything but each other. They held each other for a long, delicious moment until Jake pulled away and looked at her.

"Look at you!" he said. "You're huge!" Jake looked at her and snapped his fingers. "That's right, the due date is next week."

Jenny smiled at her husband. "Junior wanted Daddy there for his arrival."

Jake suddenly remembered where he was, and the insanity of it all. He looked over at the rest of the team.

"Guys, this is Jenny, my wife."

They nodded, obviously jealous of the chance to have a loved one with them. "We figured there was some relationship," one doctor said, motioning to her state of pregnancy.

"Yeah, well," Jake said, looking around, and pulling off his rubber gloves. "Can I have a break to talk to my wife?"

The other doctors nodded and then motioned to the marine.

"Five minutes," the marine muttered. "Over there." He gestured to a broken park bench outside the tent area and confusion of triage.

"Jake," Jenny said as he pulled her toward the bench and the two of them sat down. "Jake, what is going on? I heard you were arrested. For sedition?"

"Jenny, what are you doing here?" he asked, ignoring her question. "Why didn't you stay in Illinois where it was safe?"

"Safe?" Jenny said. "First of all, Illinois was anything but safe. Second, I felt I had an obligation to be with my husband. That's you, in case you've forgotten."

Jake shook his head. "I haven't forgotten. Believe me, I

haven't forgotten." He kissed her again. Then he shook his head.

"But you can't stay here, Jenny. As bad as it was the first time, it's ten times worse now."

"Can't stay!" Jenny said. "Where are you going to send me? The North Pole? Look, there's nowhere safe on this planet now. Illinois has its crazies running at you with butcher knives, and California has drought and earthquakes. I know Hawaii is dangerous, but you're here, and I came so the baby could be born close to you."

Jake reached out and took her hands.

"Jenny, listen to me. The national Sunday law has passed. I have been arrested for sedition, which in this day and age is a capital offense. If you stay, you will be arrested as well. They will take our baby and use it against us—try to get us to go against God. Do you want that?"

Jenny looked at Jake, tears starting to come to her eyes.

"Now, there's this man I met. Pastor Sato. He was a patient here yesterday. He used to work for the Hawaii Conference. He has a boat, and he is taking a select few to the island of Kauai. There's a small colony of people back in the rainforest. That's where I want you. That's where I want our baby to be born. And if I get out of this in one piece, I will join you. Just as soon as possible."

Tears ran down Jenny's face as she looked at the man she had tried so hard to be with, only to be sent away from him again.

"And if you don't get away?" she asked, not wanting to hear the answer. "What then?"

Jake took a deep breath. "Then it will only be a little time and we will be together again. Forever."

CHAPTER

he forty-foot sailboat *The Promise* rose and dropped, pitching and yawing in the heavy seas. Strong winds pushed her rapidly across the water, but each forward advance was like the jagged jerk of a dull saw through wood. *The Promise* was making good time, but the passengers aboard her wished they had never gotten on board.

Six men and women huddled and prayed inside the small cabin while the captain and his first mate struggled with sails and rudder. Only one passenger seemed calm through it all. Remarkably, she was the pregnant one.

Jenny had finally resigned her fate to God. She had decided to stop fighting. For months her one battle had been to reunite with her husband before the baby was born. Now she knew for sure that that would not happen. The baby would be born within days, and Jake wouldn't be there to see it. He might never see it.

Never. She pushed the word from her mind. *Never* won't exist in heaven, except in phrases like "never sin," "never fear," "never cry." Whatever happened to her, whatever happened to Jake, was temporary. Time was marching on, and the Second Coming would be here soon.

"Hurry, Lord Jesus," she whispered.

In response, she felt fluid trickle down her leg, and a sharp pain hit her abdomen, causing her to collapse to the small bed. *Not yet*, she prayed. *No, not yet. Please.*

* * * * *

The small huddle of children cheered as, by candlelight, two women spooned out the last of a large tub of rainbow sherbet into bowls. Each kid grabbed a bowl and ran to sit down and devour the treat.

"They think it's Christmas," Dan said, pushing through the cafeteria's double doors into the kitchen. A group of men and women were sitting around the big preparation table, their faces illuminated by a dozen candles.

"Let them enjoy it," Mr. Brewster said. "With the electricity gone, that will be the last ice cream they taste for a long time—probably ever. From here on out, it's strictly pioneer time. Fortunately, you people are relatively experienced in wilderness living. We've even got two Master Guides here." He gestured at an elderly couple at the end of the table.

"Dan Lewis knows his plants and will be responsible for stocking us with medicines and edible foodstuffs."

"With some help, of course," Dan added.

"Yeah, you just tell us what to pick and we'll do it," the elderly woman said.

Dan nodded to her, then turned back to the rest of the group. "That brings up another issue. I realize that the national Sunday law has passed, but my studies tell me that there will still be conversions, still more baptisms. Now more than ever, people are searching for God. What are we prepared to do as far as evangelism is concerned?"

The others looked at each other. "Evangelism? How?"

"There are still people in Yosemite National Park," Dan

said. "People who have come—like us—to try to escape the craziness and disease in the cities. And there's something else."

Dan told them of his contact with the auto mechanic in Mariposa. "He wanted someone to come and show the people there how to use nature for medicine and food. I intend to do just that—and more."

"What about gas?" Mr. Brewster asked. "All the vehicles are pretty much out. Most people didn't bring extra; they didn't think they would need it."

Dan shrugged. "The Lord will provide—as He always does." He looked around the table at the tired, thin adults gathered there. "I know you've all been through a lot. But there are people out there who will die without salvation unless we help them. How about it? Is there time for one last push?"

* * * * *

"Don't push, Jenny," an old woman named Abigail said to Jenny. "It's still too early. You're dilated to only about four centimeters, so you still have a little ways to go. Breathe. That's good."

Jenny tried to relax as the waves of pain swept over her and the sweat dripped from her face. She held the hands of two other women and reclined in the old dentist chair they had set up for her. She barely remembered their landing on the north shore of Kauai and the quick trip to the remote refugee camp in the rain forest. By the time they had arrived at the cluster of camouflage tents, she was already into heavy labor.

She took a deep breath, one of the few she knew she would get before the contractions came back. She looked up at Abigail and smiled. Within minutes of meeting her, Jenny had fallen in love with the old woman.

"I'm so glad you are here," Jenny said as one of the attendants wiped her face.

"We're glad *you* are here," Abigail said to her. "And I'm glad

God has decided to bless us with another birth before He comes. You know, I have been delivering babies as a midwife for forty-seven years. Must be thousands of them. And I am still overwhelmed with the miracle of birth whenever it happens."

"Well, I'll be glad when this birth—ohh!" The pain hit Jenny and interrupted her mid-sentence. "It hurts! Please Abigail, help me!"

The wall of pain overwhelmed Jenny, and she felt as if she might pass out. Even as she spoke, her vision seemed tinged in red. Her whole body throbbed.

"Let's take a look," Abigail said, looking down between Jenny's legs. "Yes, yes, I see." Jenny saw Abigail rise up again with a look of alarm on her face. She motioned to one of the women who held Jenny's hands. The woman came over, and Abigail whispered to her. The woman shook her head and Abigail frowned.

"Jenny, your baby is in trouble," Abigail said to her calmly. "The problem is, we don't have any doctors here with us. I've been a midwife for a long time, but I always know when to call in a physician."

"What—what are we going to do?" Jenny gasped.

"We—why, we're going to pray," Abigail stammered. Jenny watched her close her eyes, and then in turn Jenny closed hers. The close communion she had gained with her Savior almost eliminated the pain, and Jenny hung on every word Abigail said.

"Lord Jesus," Abigail prayed. "Here we are, out in the jungle, hiding where we can worship You in our own way. We need You here with Jenny and her baby. We need You now."

A wall of pain swept over Jenny, and she screamed. Abigail opened her eyes and looked closely at Jenny and the coming baby.

"OK, Jenny, it's time. We're there," she said in a strange quiet voice. "Now push."

The pain overwhelmed Jenny, and she felt weak.

"Push!" Abigail repeated.

Jenny took a deep breath and tried to push.

"*Push!*" the old woman shouted at Jenny. With a mighty heave, Jenny pushed with all her might.

Jenny felt relief as the baby left the birth canal and fell into the waiting arms of Abigail. Jenny relaxed and waited for the cry of her new child.

"What is it?" Jenny said hopefully. "Is it a boy or a girl?"

"It's a girl," Abigail said without emotion.

"Hannah," Jenny said. "Her name is Hannah."

Jenny laid back and stared at the ceiling of the tent. *Hannah*, she told herself. *If only Jake could have been here.*

"Jenny," she heard Abigail's voice call. "Jenny, I need to talk to you."

"Where's my baby?" Jenny asked. "Where's Hannah?" She looked around and noticed that the other two nurses had left, and she was alone with Abigail.

"Jenny, sometimes there are complications and things don't turn out the way you expected," Abigail said, the age lines in her face suddenly prominent. "Many times, only God knows the reason why."

Jenny wanted to ask what was wrong, but the words wouldn't come. She looked at Abigail, and her tears began to flow.

Abigail began to cry too. "Jenny, Hannah was born dead."

The words fell on her like a heavy door, and for many moments all Jenny could see was darkness. Abigail knew enough to stop talking. Nothing else could really be said.

Jenny and Abigail cried together for a long time before Jenny spoke again. "We're almost home, Abigail. Just a few more days and then heaven. What does it matter if I have to wait until then to have Hannah with me?"

Abigail looked at Jenny and stroked her hair. "An angel will bring your baby to you and put her in your arms."

Jenny sniffed and looked at Abigail. "I want to see her."

Abigail nodded and left the tent. In a minute she came back bearing a small bundle of cloth. She carefully held out the tiny bundle to Jenny and pulled the blankets away from the baby's face.

Jenny looked at Hannah, and surprisingly, felt more at peace. There was no indication of pain or trauma in the baby's gray face. Her small eyelids were closed as if she were asleep, as Jenny knew she was.

"Sleep, my darling," Jenny said to Hannah. "Soon we will be together."

* * * * *

The loud harsh buzzer went off, and the metal doors slammed open. Mitch followed the other prisoners into the cellblock. He was still in shock. The satisfaction he had felt when he knew that Gina had escaped had lasted only a few minutes. He had been processed once again in the police station, led before a night court judge, been found guilty of breaking the national Sunday law—a felony—and been subsequently bused off to Vacaville State Penitentiary.

Gone was the reward of knowing that he would be a martyr for the cause. Now he was confronted by the reality of prison life. Tough men—and women had confronted him—over the years. These around him were the toughest he had ever seen. And he was locked in the same building with them, presumably for the rest of his life.

The hackles rose on the back of his neck. He reached up and felt where they had shaved his head. Gone was the black shaggy hair most people had recognized him by. In its place was dark fuzz with tufts where the barber had missed a strand and left it.

The loss of his hair hadn't been his only humiliation. He had been cavity searched when he arrived in prison; something he had heard about but couldn't imagine until he had experienced it. Then he had stood naked in the middle of the inspection room with nine other new inmates until they received prison garb. Finally the new group was ushered into the cellblock.

Now he looked up at the animal-like men caged in this, his new home. Some screamed a constant stream of obscenities. Others cried and begged for mercy. Others tried to get him to look their way.

"Fresh meat!" someone shouted from the upper level of cells.

"Hey, sweetie," someone else shouted. "Wanna be my girlfriend?"

"Animals can smell fear," his friend Reed had told him. It seemed like decades ago. "Professional fighters can sense it as well. You have to compensate for your fear. Be a rational being. Confront it. Only when you look it in the eyes will you be in control."

In his mind Mitch went over the words from long ago, and for a moment as he walked, he almost thought he heard Reed's voice. Then he was sure he did.

"Mitch!" he heard through the cacophony of noise. "Mitch, it's me!"

Mitch looked to his left and saw what looked like an old man in one of the cells. Then he saw the familiar build of the man. Could it be Reed?

While he was wondering, he was shoved into a cell to his right. Only a single bulb in the ceiling lighted the small room. A big, burly man with a full beard and a T-shirt lay on the bottom bunk. Mitch stood at the doorway and stared at the man as the metal door clanged shut behind him.

The big man stared back at Mitch.

"What are you looking at, kid?" he asked.

Mitch said nothing.

"So I guess you're my birthday present," the man said, rubbing his hands through his beard. "Did you know it was my birthday?"

"No, sir," Mitch said, clearing his throat.

The man continued to stare at Mitch, and Mitch felt very self-conscious.

"Don't call me 'sir,' " the man said. "Sir's only for daddies and teachers. I don't look like either one of those, do I?"

Mitch shook his head.

"Boy, that's some sunburn you got there," the man said. "How'd you get that?"

"Acid," Mitch said. "I put it on my skin so they couldn't track me with the magnetic scanner."

"Magnetic scanner," the man repeated, "Yeah, that's how they got me. But they caught you anyway, didn't they?"

Mitch nodded. "But my girl got away."

The man nodded. "That's good."

The big man sat up in the bed, and Mitch saw that he had two fingers missing on his right hand and a scar on that arm.

"Shoot, you look like my kid brother up in Idaho," the big man said. "Ever been to Idaho?"

Mitch shook his head.

"Haven't missed much," the man snorted. "I grew up in Shoshone. 'Bout as much in the middle of nowhere as you can get. Other parts are purty, tho'." He reached out a massive hand to Mitch, who took it.

"Name's Dan. Dan Hadley."

"My—my father's name is Dan," Mitch said.

"Well, I guess that makes us related," Dan said, laughing. "You look like my kid brother, and I have your daddy's name."

"Yeah, I guess so," Mitch said. He dropped the blanket and spare clothes he had been carrying onto the upper bunk, then turned and looked out the cell door.

"Lights out," he heard from down the hall, and saw the lights dimming in the cellblock. He looked across the block to the cell he had passed a while ago. Was that Reed he had seen? Or was it his imagination? Would tomorrow reveal anything new?

"Yeah, we'll get along just fine," Dan said. "As long as we don't talk about religion or politics." He lay back down on his bunk and belched.

Religion or politics, Mitch thought. *OK, God, what is your plan for me here?*

* * * * *

Abigail stood with Jenny and the others as Pastor Sato led them in a song, then officiated at the funeral for Hannah. It was still very soon after Hannah's birth, but Jenny insisted that she stand at the graveside.

Jenny had felt torn away from her husband Jake, then tortured by the birth and death of her first and only child. But she felt a warmth among these people that she had never felt before. And she knew that this was where she belonged.

But that wasn't right either, she thought. None of them belonged here. And that was what they all had in common. These were people who belonged in another place, face to face with their Creator. The ragged tents, the dirt on hands, knees, and faces, the cuts and bruises given to them by the rain forest only emphasized the rightness of what they were doing.

There was nothing to hold them back now, she realized. Not possessions. Not loved ones. Not life itself.

All that remained was the final act in the Great Controversy.

These thoughts ran through her head as she took a handful of dirt and scattered it over the small bundle of rags that covered her baby. She looked down at Hannah and smiled.

"It won't be long," she whispered. "Not long at all."

CHAPTER 25

*Y*ou've got mail.

Kris left her fifth online Bible study that morning and opened her e-mail box. She sifted through the hundreds of e-mails for names she was familiar with. *They need to invent something that automatically throws out unsolicited junk mail*, she thought. Then she grinned. If she knew her mother, she had probably already invented it.

She paused in her browsing and hit the Options menu on her new computer. She selected E-mail Filter and typed in the names of several people she had corresponded with in the past few months. Then she paused before adding her mother's e-mail address to the list.

She pressed Enter and saw the computer automatically reduce the list to twenty-three messages, a manageable size even for her. But then she saw one message that immediately caught her attention. It was from her mom.

Dear Kris:
I don't know where you and your father went. I won't even ask why you left so suddenly. I just want you to know that I miss

you and want you back at home where you belong. Somewhere this religion business has confused you. Nothing is worth separating the family as this has done.

She's got a point there, Kris thought. *Religion was really the reason the family fell apart.* She read on:

Maybe you are afraid that you will be arrested if you come home. Maybe you are still not sure if you are ready to join the Unified Church or not. Well, be assured that I have special connections in the church, corporation, and government. You could have all the time you needed to make your decision.

It's amazing how much happier people are now with the new law. Everyone worships together and works together. We all have the same goals. And soon God will come, and we will reign here on earth with her.

This is stupid, Kris thought, and moved to delete the message. Then she paused. *I'm not going through a server or even a regular phone line. I'm using a satellite. They shouldn't be able to trace this message. Should they?* She hesitated, then typed a quick message and clicked Send.

I love you, Mom.

* * * * *

"OK, this is our fifth class," Dan said to the group gathered in the city hall. "Who can tell me some medicinal plants that live in this area, and what they are good for?"

"Nasturtium," someone shouted from the back. "It's good for healing."

"Right," Dan said. "It's a natural antibiotic."

"Walnut," someone else said. "It has potassium, which is good for the brain and nervous system."

"OK," Dan said. "But both the plants mentioned so far are domestic plants that have been brought in. What about some of the plants indigenous to this area?"

"Witch hazel," someone suggested.

"Brier hip," another said.

And Dan listened to the group recite plants that God had provided to mankind for thousands of years. *We've come full circle,* Dan thought. *For so long we thought we didn't need God or what He provided; now we learn that the only things we needed were the things that God supplied.*

And the audience seemed to sense this without Dan stating it aloud. Mankind needed God. Not the God that was being fabricated by society; not the limited God that was conveniently put in a box and tucked away when propriety called for it. Mankind needed a full-sized, all-powerful, all-present, all-knowing God. The real thing.

As a result, the classes were resulting in some informal Bible studies. Dan was careful never to promote the Bible studies. Instead, the students who studied the Bible with him in turn found those they trusted and shared it with them. The group had been growing for a couple of weeks.

But now Dan was concerned. As he looked out over the crowd, he saw several key faces were missing.

"Something wrong?" Rick Ferree asked, looking around him. Rick had been his first Bible student and was now teaching students of his own.

"Where's the mayor?" Dan asked. "And Mrs. Dunsmuir? And the Lukotskys?"

"Yeah, we's thinning out," Rick said blandly. "Must be the bugs going around."

"Bugs?" Dan asked. "What bugs?"

Rick nodded. "That's right, you haven't been down to the valley lately. They got bugs down there that will drop you cold. Old bugs like cholera, dysentery, bubonic plague. Only difference is, antibiotics don't stop 'em. In fact, seems that the new diseases like antibiotics."

Dan stared at Rick openmouthed. "Bubonic plague? Cholera? In California?" he asked.

"Sure," Rick said, and others agreed.

"That's nothing compared to what's happening in the Midwest," a woman in the back said. "I heard something about the Midwest Aquifer—I guess that's it. Don't know exactly what it is, though."

"It's the giant underground lake that exists under the entire midwestern United States," Dan explained. "It's where all the artesian wells in that area get their water. What about it?"

"Well, they say that all the geo-something activity has gotten the aquifer contaminated. Poisoned."

The others muttered in agreement. Dan frowned and shook his head.

"That seems a bit strange. Geothermal activity shouldn't contaminate the water base. It should purify it."

"Maybe an earthquake happened and something bad like man-made chemicals got into it," Rick suggested.

"Or bacterial warfare," suggested someone else. "Or maybe radiation."

"In any case," the woman said. "They got people dropping all over the place. Dallas had so many people dying they couldn't bury them all. Lincoln and Omaha are pretty much ghost towns."

"It's the last plagues," someone said.

"It's some sort of plague," Dan agreed. "Let's just hope the diseases stay in the valleys."

* * * * *

Mitch's first week in prison seemed like a year. It helped a lot that Dan, his roommate, really liked him, and tended to take care of him. There were more and more vicious-looking men around him. Mitch didn't wander too far from Dan.

After a week he started to relax a little, and continued to look around for Reed, or the person he had thought was Reed. He was surprised that he had not seen him before this. He was sitting in the exercise yard, his back to Dan, when he felt a hand on his shoulder. Instinctively he reached up and twisted the arm holding him and swung with his other hand, ready to push the person off-balance and make him vulnerable.

He paused when he saw that the other person was Reed. Reed stood laughing at Mitch. His long blond locks had been shorn, and white stubble had replaced them. But the build was the same, even if he was a little thinner, and Mitch saw that his biceps were still massive.

"Reed!" Mitch shouted, grabbing him and hugging him. Dan jumped up as if to protect Mitch, but Mitch waved him down.

"Dan, this is a friend," Mitch said. "Besides, he would tear you in two. He is a third-degree black belt karate instructor."

"Was an instructor," Reed corrected him. "Now I am a full-time Bible instructor."

"Bible," Dan said, clenching his fists. "Don't give me none of that religion."

"Chill, Dan," Mitch said. "Reed, that's cool. I assume you've got a class started here?"

"Of course," Reed said. "But things are a bit different. You've got to keep it low key. Remember, the government runs this place, and they have a vested interest in everyone here buying into their brand of religion."

Mitch nodded.

"Tell you what," Reed said. "Come sit at our table in the cafeteria tonight and see how the discussion goes. You'll learn that there are lot of searching people in here as well."

Mitch punched Reed and agreed. *Just like old times*, he thought. *Almost.*

That evening, Mitch was eager to get to the cafeteria. "Come on, Dan," he said impatiently. "The cafeteria will be closing before we get there."

"Just a minute, just a minute," Dan said, brushing his long hair back. "OK, how do I look?"

"Beautiful," Mitch said sarcastically. "Now let's go." They stepped out of their cell and walked quickly down the cellblock to the end of the hall where the cafeteria was located. Before they got to the door, Mitch realized something was wrong. A roar came from the room, and a dozen people stood in front of the door.

"What's going on?" Mitch asked.

"Fight," a tattooed inmate at the door answered. "Someone was talking religion, and someone else tried to stop him."

Mitch hopped up and down before he saw a glimpse of Reed surrounded by four men with knives.

"It's Reed," Mitch said to Dan. "We've got to get through this crowd."

"No problem," Dan said, pushing ahead like an icebreaker.

"Outta the way," Dan said, pushing with one arm while Mitch followed in his wake. Dan cut through the crowd, and Mitch was inside the cafeteria within a minute. He was amazed by what he saw.

He had known that Reed could fight. He had never seen him under these conditions. Even in the alleyway, Reed seemed to be above the abilities of his competition. Now he was fighting for his life. And he was winning.

Ten men lay at his feet as he stood on top of the cafeteria table and whirled to face each attacker. One would charge in with a knife and fall back with a broken arm. Another would hurl a plate and charge ahead, only to be thrown across the room with the force of his own charge. Finally, there was only one more man to face.

A massive man with a jagged, homemade knife faced Reed. On the surface, it seemed as though Reed didn't stand a chance. But everyone in the cafeteria saw the pile of attackers surrounding Reed. Finally, the last attacker took a long look at Reed and dropped his knife.

Reed smiled. "Smart man."

Boom! The blast came from the other corner of the room. Mitch watched Reed fall from the table, a huge red hole suddenly appearing in his back. Mitch looked at the guard who held the still-smoking .357 Magnum pistol.

"If you want something done right, you got to do it yourself," the guard muttered.

The cafeteria cleared quickly, the other inmates eager to put distance between them and the guard with the gun. Mitch pushed forward to where Reed lay on the concrete floor, blood everywhere around him. Some of his friends from the Bible class huddled around.

"You're late," Reed said to Mitch. Mitch nodded to his former instructor.

"I'm glad you're late." Reed reached up and grabbed Mitch's lapel. "You know what to do." He blinked, then closed his eyes for the last time.

Mitch shook himself as if he weren't really living this nightmare. *It couldn't have happened. Not this way. Not Reed.*

"What do we do now?" one of the men in the huddle asked aloud.

"Leave it to me," Mitch said. "Like he said. I know what to do."

* * * * *

Dan looked at the sparse crowd in the city's community center. Where there had been fifty just a few weeks before, now there were eight. One or two of them coughed constantly. Another left quickly halfway through the presentation.

Finally, at the end, Dan opened a folder with some hand-made certificates. He read off the names. By many of the names he wrote "Deceased." On others he could only write a question mark.

"This is our graduation of sorts," he told the small group. "You've learned everything I have to teach you."

"No, we haven't," Rick corrected him. "We've learned about plants, and how they can make you live better. But we really came here because we saw something in you, something we wanted."

Rick stood and looked out over the others and at Dan. "We came because we wanted to hear about your God. Tell us about God."

Dan looked down and cleared his throat.

"Uh, Rick, I've told you about my God. I've shown you what the Bible says. I've taught you to pray. I've shown you the plan of Salvation. I've talked about the Sabbath." Dan shrugged. "What else do you want?"

Rick looked at the others, then back at Dan.

"We want to be baptized."

* * * * *

Mitch had taught Reed's Bible class everything he could in as short a time as he could. Thankfully, they absorbed his Bible knowledge like a sponge. Mitch's biggest handicap was his lack of a Bible. He was sure there was a law somewhere about a prisoner's right to have a Bible, but the guards made sure no Bibles could be found anywhere. Mitch started writing Scripture on his cell walls, bathroom and shower walls and anywhere he could find. As quickly as he wrote it, he found, it disappeared.

Mitch's second handicap was that he was being watched. He knew it. The authorities knew what he was in there for. And the day after he contacted a prisoner and gave him some spiritual support or Bible information, that prisoner would disappear, apparently moved to another cellblock. On the negative side, Mitch had no idea how much information the inmate was absorbing. On the positive side, whatever he absorbed was then most likely shared with the inmates in other parts of the prison.

One evening Mitch was sitting on the top bunk, mulling over the challenges Reed had left him, when Dan came into the cell, his face drawn into a very sober stare.

"Word has it that the Man is tired of your religion talk," Dan said, standing in the doorway. "A new law is coming down. Tomorrow they plan on frying any of you who don't shape up and join the Big Church."

Mitch looked up at Dan. "It was bound to happen sooner or later."

Dan's interest picked up. "Really? How did you know it was going to happen?"

"Because I study the Bible, or I did, until they took mine away." Mitch dropped off his bunk and walked over to Dan. "I know you don't like religion talk, Dan, but that's what all the craziness in the world is about. Religion. God."

Dan rubbed his chin and sat down on his bunk. "I ain't had nothing but trouble over religion. My daddy was a drunkard and got chased out of town by churchgoers. My momma never got nothin' good from the Christians in our town. And my kid brother and I got stepped on every day of our lives by do-gooders."

"That's just people, Dan," Mitch said. "You see it here. Good people, bad people. Don't judge God by the sinners He's trying to save." Mitch walked over to Dan and carefully put his hand on Dan's shoulder.

"Look, big brother," Mitch said, and saw that Dan softened when he used the term. "Let me tell you what I know. Forget what's happened before. Listen with an open heart and mind. Then after you've heard what I have to say, you decide if it's all trash or not."

Dan rubbed his chin again and looked up at the young man with the stubbly black hair. Whether he agreed with his beliefs or not, he had grown to love the kid.

"What about this business of them frying you Christians?" Dan asked.

chapter 25

"That's tomorrow," Mitch said, waving his hand. "The Bible says 'Today has enough worries of its own. Let tomorrow worry about tomorrow.'"

"Sounds like a good idea to me."

* * * * *

Dan walked down the dark streets of Mariposa, looking for houses with their lights still on. It was late. He knew that. But that was just the point. It was late. People were dying. The end was coming—no, it was here. Every soul he contacted was potentially another soul saved, another soul brought to Christ.

He found a house with the light on. He walked up to the door and pounded on it. No one answered. He looked in and realized that there was a body lying on the floor. He tried one more time. When there was no answer, he left and walked down the street to the next house. No light. He continued down the street.

To the next house. And the next one. And the next one.

Until there were no more houses.

And finally it was time to go home.

CHAPTER

26

Arguably, the happiest moment in a Christian's life is the moment of baptism. Conversion comes at another time and has its own significance. Service and sacrifice have their own rewards. But baptism is the act of publicly declaring that we are new creatures dead to sin and alive to the power of Christ and the Holy Spirit.

Thus it was that Dan, Kris, and the followers who had found shelter at Wawona SDA Camp celebrated the last mass baptism in the history of the world. Hundreds came from area towns to be baptized in the frigid waters of the Merced River. As it had been since January, the weather was incredibly hot—more like August than April. Just as they had for months, Dan and the others recognized that there was no longer such a thing as "normal" and had learned to accept whatever happened.

"Incredible, isn't it?" Dan asked Mr. Brewster as they stood on the dirt road and watched the trucks and cars drive up from Mariposa and the valley. "Just goes to show that when you think hope is gone, it reappears. Probation hasn't closed yet, at least not for these people."

"Disconcerting is more the word I was thinking of," said Mr. Brewster. "I can't imagine how we can keep our location secret with this many people coming up here."

Dan shook his head. "They all know the danger they are putting us in. Besides, the camp is a couple of miles from here. I have faith that things will work out. This is God's will. I know it."

Mr. Brewster didn't reply, but his face continued to hold the worried look that Dan had realized rarely left. They watched the line of cars drive up the winding dirt road. When no more cars were in sight, they left to join the others.

Dan had been an elder and acting pastor, and Mr. Brewster and one other man were ordained ministers. The three of them officiated in the baptisms.

Dan waded out waist deep to a sandy pool they had selected beforehand. The other two men were about seven feet away on either side of him. Rick Ferree was the first to join Dan in the freezing water for baptism. As Rick and two others waded out, the group of people on the shore spontaneously started singing "Shall we gather at the river."

"Rick," Dan began, "I've only known you for a few weeks, but you've grown to be like a brother. I will always remember that first time we met, when God let our car break down so we could meet."

"Yeah," Rick responded. "Praise God for loose wires."

"I won't linger long on this moment, Rick, because we have a lot of people waiting to be baptized and this water is freezing," Dan said, and the audience chuckled. "And so because of your profession of faith in the saving power of the Lord Jesus, and your willingness to follow Him wherever He might lead, I now baptize you in the name of the Father, the Son, and the Holy Spirit."

As Dan plunged Rick into the icy blue waters, his mind went back to that day when he was twelve in Stockton, California. He had expected his life to change with that one act. It had changed, but not with one act, and not in the way he had expected. It had taken years for God to guide him to this point. *How ironic that I would be baptizing others like this*, Dan thought. The follower had become the leader, and all because of his willingness to follow Christ wherever He might lead.

Rick and the two others rose from the water to cheers and

applause. Before they had climbed out of the water, three more had waded out to take their place.

Kris had gone with the children to a walking bridge above the baptismal pool so that they could see well. She crouched with nine primary and kindergarten children, looking through the ropes of the suspended bridge. One after another they watched the adults go into the water and come back out.

"When I get to be older, my mommy says I can be baptized too," a little boy said. Kris smiled at his comment.

"Yeah, I want to be baptized so I can go to heaven. 'Cause I love Jesus," another boy said.

"You don't have to be baptized to go to heaven," Kris said. "Being baptized doesn't save you. It just shows others that you love Jesus and that you want Him to change you and make you clean."

"I want Jesus to make me clean," a little girl said.

"Me too," said another.

"Look," one kindergarten boy said, pointing down the narrow valley. "Army trucks."

Kris looked in the direction he pointed. A cloud of dust was billowing up in the distance from several vehicles headed their direction. And leading them was a Humvee painted camouflage brown.

"We've got to warn the others," Kris said to the children. "Let's shout as loud as we can. Maybe they'll be able to hear us."

"Look out! Trucks coming!" they shouted, but soon realized that the roar of the river made the sound of their voices disappear.

Dan had baptized his fifteenth candidate and was getting numb. But he was really having too much fun to notice or care about his physical condition. He looked up at the crowd waiting for his next candidate and then at the bridge where Kris had taken the children of the colony.

Kris was waving her hands and pointing down the valley at something. He turned and noticed a cloud of dust heading their direction. Alarm bells went off in his head, and he turned to look at Mr. Brewster. The worried look was still there.

The three pastors stood with their candidates in the deep water as the military vehicles pulled up and surrounded the group. From his low angle, Dan could only see three military-style vehicles, one with a machine gun mounted on the back, and two carrying soldiers. He was sure there were more, but how many he couldn't say.

Dan looked back at Mr. Brewster, who motioned with his hand to stay put. Dan took a deep breath and held onto the candidate, a woman in her fifties, just to make sure she didn't do anything rash.

He watched the troops fan out—National Guard, he suspected—along the river's edge and hold their M-16 assault rifles where the crowd could see them. Finally he saw a face that looked familiar. It was Meg.

She had lost weight—more than she could afford. She wore a dress that had always looked good on her. Now it hung on her limply, as if she were a wire clothes hanger. On her face she wore a heavy coat of makeup. And she had pockmarks on her skin as if she were just getting over some disease. But the eyes were the same. Intelligent. Sharp. Cold.

"Hello, Dan," she said casually. "Want to come out of the water? You're all under arrest."

Dan looked up at the rope bridge where Kris and the children had been watching. No one was there.

"This is a sacred act we are doing here," Dan said. "Mind if we finish?"

"This is a sacrilege, Dan," Meg answered. "Only the Unified Church can baptize, and the new law that just passed makes what you want to do punishable by death."

"In the eyes of man it's sacrilege," Mr. Brewster said. "In the eyes of God it is a sacrament."

"Get out of the water," Meg said. "Now."

Dan started toward the shore, but a look from Mr. Brewster stopped him. "Because you love the Lord your God, and accept His sacrifice—" Mr. Brewster began, holding his candidate's shoulders.

"This is your last warning," Meg said. "Sergeant."

The soldier nearest Meg at the river's edge raised his weapon and pointed it at Mr. Brewster. Mr. Brewster didn't hesitate.

"—I now baptize you in the name of the Father, the Son and the Holy Spirit." Mr. Brewster dropped the candidate into the water. At that instant, Meg spoke one word.

"Fire."

Three bullets blasted from the muzzle of the assault rifle and penetrated the chest of the old man. The bullets missed the candidate completely because she was under the surface of the water. Mr. Brewster died instantly.

Dan watched in a trance as the body of Mr. Brewster, the man he had talked to just moments before, floated face down in the pool, clouds of red blood billowing around his body. No one dared move, not even when the body floated out of the pool and drifted downstream.

"Now, just to be nice, I will repeat myself one last time," Meg said quietly. "Get out of the water."

* * * * *

Run. That was the word that came into Kris's mind when she saw the military vehicles pull up to the baptism site. She repeated it to the children.

"Run," she said to them. "Jesus wants us to run."

The ten of them ran off the bridge, away from the crowd and into the woods on the other side. Kris had no idea where they were running to or what she would do with nine children. All she knew was that she had to get out of there right then.

* * * * *

"Commander James Gallagher," the marine said to Jake as he approached the surgical table. "You are to come with me."

Jake looked up wearily at the marine in battle gear. "I'm not done here. There are more wounded to take care of."

The marine flipped the safety off of his rifle. "Yes, you are, sir. All medical activities by you in this vicinity are to cease and desist immediately. That is an order directly from the Admiralty. You are under arrest."

Jake sighed and stood up. His back ached, his head throbbed, and his fingers were numb from sewing stitches. But he had been saving lives. At least they had let him do that much. Now they were taking even that away from him.

He pulled his gloves and hat off, threw them down on the table, and looked around. All the other doctors had gotten sick or just run away from fright. Now there was no one else left to care for the injured.

"What will become of all these wounded?" Jake asked the marine.

"That's not your concern, sir."

Apparently that's not the navy's either, Jake thought as the marine led him out of the tent.

* * * * *

Jenny had had a few weeks to recover from the ordeal of the delivery of her stillborn child. During that time she'd gotten to know the others in the refugee camp quite well. Most of them were senior citizens who had once served their church as missionaries, colporteurs, or teachers. A few teenagers and children also inhabited the camp. She seemed to be the only person in the thirty to fifty age range.

The group had set up camp in the remotest region of the island of Kauai. This area had once been a haven for marijuana farms. What made the area so inaccessible were the steep canyons, large amounts of rainfall, and correspondingly dense growth. To the north was the Na Pali Coast. To the south lay the Waimea Canyon, what some called the Grand Canyon of the Pacific. All supplies had to be packed in by horse, mule, or backpack. The camp was founded by Charlie Chu, a new convert who had been a drug lord years before and knew the area thoroughly.

Charlie had established lookout posts throughout the area. The camp itself was in a low hollow, with running water and supplies available in a nearby cave. The camp was surrounded by tree platforms from which lookouts could keep an eye on the surrounding countryside.

One morning before dawn, Abigail awakened Jenny. "Get dressed," was all she said. Jenny dressed herself and exited the tent. Instead of the usual cheerful group, she was greeted by whispering in the darkness.

She stumbled through the dark to the table where the others had congregated. "OK, it's happened," Pastor Sato was telling the others. "They've passed the international Sunday law. Those who won't bow to the beast will be killed if they are found. It's our purpose to make sure we are not found."

He rolled out a map and pointed at it with a penlight. "There are supplies buried at several sites in this area. The weather is mild enough that we won't need to worry about cover or protective clothing that much. But we do need to keep a low profile.

"This group is way too big to keep hidden for very long. So we are going to break it up into three groups. Charlie will take group one to the west. Mr. Hamui will go south toward the canyon. I will go with Abigail to the east.

"Stay low. Stay hidden. Keep praying," Pastor Sato said.

* * * * *

Mitch and Dan talked all night. As had happened many times before, Mitch found himself listening to sordid stories of a childhood filled with pain, abuse, and heartache. Toward daylight Dan was sobbing like a little baby. And by the time roll call came around, Dan was ready to surrender his life to Jesus Christ.

Mitch was exhausted—and elated. Every victory for Christ he was involved in made him more prepared for whatever the devil had to throw at him. And he knew the devil would come calling sooner or later.

Mitch and Dan went to breakfast and then to their work assignments without fanfare. It seemed like business as usual. Half an hour before lunch, the loudspeaker called for the inmates to assemble in the exercise yard.

Here it is, Dan thought. *Well, come on, Satan. I'm ready for whatever you throw my way.*

Mitch and Dan had different work assignments, so when everyone gathered in the yard, Mitch was surrounded by men he didn't know. He looked around him, and as usual the wall of the yard was thoroughly guarded, and each tower had guards with guns. In front of the yard was the warden. He pulled out a megaphone and began to speak.

"As of midnight last night, anyone who worships on any day other than Sunday, or worships outside the guidelines of the World Unified Church is subject to immediate execution. We have a list of people who have either been sent here because of subversive religious activity or have been involved in religious activity in this facility. If you are on this list, you have one last chance. Submit to the World Unified Church or be executed."

The warden read the list of forty-three names. Mitch heard his own, then recognized several others he had met with.

"What is your answer?" the warden asked after he had read the list of names.

Mitch waited and watched. Who would respond? To his surprise, he heard a familiar voice respond in song.

"I have decided to follow Jesus." Dan's voice came from the other side of the prison yard in a beautiful baritone voice. "I have decided to follow Jesus; I have decided to follow Jesus. No turning back. No turning back."

Mitch opened his mouth in surprise. He didn't realize Dan knew the song, much less could sing as wonderfully as he did.

Another voice joined Dan's. And another. And still another. Soon more than the forty-three were singing the song. Mitch saw hardened men with tears in their eyes as they sang.

"Shut that man up!" the warden said. Instantly three different guards fired their shotguns at Dan, and he collapsed in a heap of smoke and blood. The music faltered and died. Satan had killed the music.

* * * * *

Jenny had very few possessions to take with her. She packed her Bible, her toothbrush, and a change of clothes into a daypack, and she was ready to go. She was surprised at how many were ready just as quickly. She held a small girl while a grandmother gathered up the last of her things. Holding the three-year-old girl seemed like the natural thing to do, and Jenny hugged the girl as long as she possibly could until the little girl protested.

"Too tight," she murmured. Jenny reluctantly watched her run back to her grandmother and take her hand, then smiled as the girl came back and reached out to Jenny for her hand.

"Family," the little girl said. "We a family."

Jenny looked at the old woman, who smiled. "Yes, we are a family."

Light was just breaking over the treetops when Pastor Sato called for his group to move out. Jenny was pleased to see that Abigail was part of her group.

They watched the other two groups follow pathways to the west and south, then turned onto their own winding path up to the ridge above the camp. They paused at the top and looked back. Jenny couldn't help but think of the little body that was buried there.

Oh Hannah, she thought. *So close.*

"Back," she heard Pastor Sato say, and she stepped under a large banyan tree that stood on the ridge. She heard a buzzing coming in from the north and watched as two small black helicopters zoomed in at tree level and roared over the camp. They banked and returned to the camp, apparently looking for signs of life.

"Let's get out of here now," Pastor Sato said.

Jenny took a step forward, and watched as the ground fell from beneath her feet. She collapsed to the ground, as did all the others.

* * * * *

Dan watched Mr. Brewster's body drift into the main current and float rapidly downstream. Then he turned to follow the others toward the shore.

Kris, I hope you got away, he thought. He looked down and realized for an instant that the water had stopped flowing.

He looked up and saw that the trees around him were dancing. The people on the bank were dancing—falling and being thrown in the air. And then he realized what was happening.

Earthquake.

Before he had a chance to react again, he felt the rocks beneath his feet jar loose, and he fell into the water. The current caught him, and he went under. He choked on water, spluttered, and came up for air. When he did, he realized that he was already twenty feet farther down the river. The soldiers on the bank were either flat on their backs or trying to keep their balance. No one noticed that he—and several others—had gotten away.

* * * * *

Mitch stared at Dan's lifeless body.

"Gather up the rest of these imbeciles and bring them up here," Mitch heard the warden say. Guards appeared and shoved Mitch and the others forward. They lined up the prisoners against the wall and stepped back. Mitch had no doubt what would come next.

"Ready," the warden said, and the guards raised their weapons.

"Aim," came his command. Mitch tried to think of something brave to say or sing, but his mind was blank.

Father, into your hands—

Mitch felt his stomach go queasy and realized that the world was moving. He watched as the guards dropped their weapons and fell to the ground. The rest of the inmates were falling as well.

Mitch turned and realized that the wall he stood in front of was cracking and shattering. Alarms began to sound around the prison. Mitch took several steps away from the wall and collapsed to the ground. The guards on top of the wall fell and were crushed by the crumbling stones of the wall. The towers collapsed and fell. Men were running, falling, stumbling, crying, and laughing.

Within seconds, inmates had picked up weapons, and guns were going off in all directions. The ground was too unstable for anyone to aim with any accuracy. Guards and inmates shot at each other. Mitch realized he had to get out of there if he wanted to stay alive.

He turned and saw that the wall behind him had collapsed, and that the high electric fence was a twisted piece of metal. Inmates were already running across the parking lot, so he knew there was no power coming to the fence. He leaped across the stone rubble behind him and ran for the parking lot. He didn't stop until he was well across the main street outside the prison.

He turned and looked behind him and realized that no one was chasing them.

He was free.

CHAPTER

Mitch thought about Dan and Reed as he ran from the prison. He had never been in a more dangerous—or strange—place. Inmates were running in all directions. Some ran toward the residential area of town, presumably with the intent of robbing, raping, and killing. Others ran toward the freeway and the train yards. Mitch ran away from everyone else. Since everyone seemed to be headed toward civilization, Mitch headed for the open countryside.

After a while his running slowed to a jog, then a fast walk. As he walked, a plan formed in his mind.

Mitch had to find Kris and his dad. Obviously they would have taken off for the mountains. That was what Kris had mentioned. But which way? West to the Santa Cruz Mountains and Big Basin? South to the Big Sur Wilderness? North to Oregon or the Klamath River?

Plants, a voice told him. *Your dad studied edible plants.*

Fine, he thought, but how does that tell me where he is?

Think about Pathfinders. And plants.

Still confused, Mitch continued walking down the empty road toward the mountains. Half an hour later, he heard a horn honk and saw a familiar van pulling up behind him.

"Ivan? Flea? What are you doing out here? How did you get your van back?"

"Prayer, dude," Ivan said. "We prayed that God would give us some money so we could bail out the van after it was repossessed. And just like that, presto, we got a job at a Safeway, stocking food."

"And the manager was a Christian, man, so we told him our situation," Flea added. "That we had a brother stuck up in Vacaville unduly imprisoned for his beliefs." Flea chuckled. "Not only did he bail the van, but he gave us gas to get up here and back home. Ain't that righteous?"

"So you just drove up here and happened upon me on this back road?" Mitch said, shaking his head.

Ivan shook his head. "We've been cruising around Vacaville for a couple of days, waiting for something to happen. Sure enough, the mighty quake came, and God spoke."

"And we knew you were likely to head for open country rather than the city, so here we are!" Flea said, laughing.

"Amazing," Mitch said.

"Whatever works," Ivan said. "So where to?"

Mitch scratched the short black hair on his head. "Monterey Road, south San Jose. I got a Hog to pick up."

* * * * *

The South Fork of the Merced River flows strong year around, and even with the drought that California had suffered through the past winter, the flow kept Dan from making land for several miles. It wasn't until he got to Wawona Village that the current began to ebb and he was able to pull himself out.

He tried to think rationally and make plans. The truth was, he hadn't envisioned things happening this way. As naïve as it sounded, he had expected to have advance notice that the authorities were coming, and then he and Kris would make an orderly retreat to some predetermined site where they would hide in some warm, tidy cave until the Lord came.

But not this. Headlong flight had separated him from everyone he knew or would ever know. Including Kris. Not only that, but the river had dragged him right into town. He stepped out onto the sidewalk, his best clothes a dripping mess.

He had no clue which way to turn, so he did the first thing that came to mind. He stepped into an alley and bowed his head in prayer.

"Lord, my life is in Your hands. Do with it as You will. But right now I could use some dry clothes and an idea of which direction to go. And I surrender Kris—and Mitch—into Your safekeeping. Amen."

A chill wind blew around the wrecked shack that had once been a Laundromat. *Strange*, he thought. *It had been hot before the earthquake. Now it felt like fall was coming.*

He stepped out onto the street and saw what was happening. People were digging through the rubble of various buildings. At first he thought they were trying to rescue people trapped inside. Then he realized that these people were looting the stores.

One elderly man stepped forward a few doors down with a shotgun. He waved it at a looter, who promptly knocked him down and took his shotgun.

I've got to get out of here, Dan thought. *This is madness.*

A young man rode up to Dan on a bicycle, his face pockmarked with scars. "Here," he said. "Take my bicycle." He thrust the bike into Dan's hands and ran around the corner of a pharmacy. Seconds later, he heard shots fired and saw the man drive out from behind the pharmacy with a small pickup loaded with packages.

Dan looked down at the bicycle and realized that a bike made more sense than trying to get away on foot. On the other hand, had the person who left it intended to give it to Dan? He was mulling over this possibility when he heard a muffled shout.

"Help me," he heard a woman's voice say. "Help!"

The voice came from inside the Laundromat—or what was left of it. The entire façade of the building had collapsed, and the sides had buckled. Dan was amazed that anyone could remain alive in such a tangled mess.

He dropped the bicycle and ran to the building, looking for an entrance somewhere.

"Hello," he shouted. "Are you in there?"

"Help me!" the woman repeated. "I'm in here!"

Dan began pulling boards back, trying to expose some entrance to the wrecked Laundromat. In the meantime, the looting continued around him. After a while, he realized he needed to get help. Some of the boards and building materials would take several people to move. On the other hand, the longer he stayed, the more likely he was to be captured.

He looked around. Two young men were walking briskly across the street, talking. They didn't seem to be part of the looting.

"Hey, you!" Dan yelled. "I need some help. There's a woman trapped in here. Help me move these timbers!"

The men glanced at Dan and waved him off, continuing their brisk walk. Dan ran over and planted himself directly in their path.

"Look down inside yourself," he said to the two men. "Isn't there a shred of decency left in you? I need your help for five, ten minutes, and maybe we can save someone's life!"

The men stopped talking and looked at Dan strangely. Then they looked at each other and nodded.

"Ten minutes," one muttered.

Dan led the two men over to the Laundromat. Together they were able to move the heavy rafters from the building. Finally they tore away the shingles from the roof, making a hole through which Dan was able to crawl.

Without a flashlight, Dan had to feel his way through broken glass, torn timbers, and collapsed washers and dryers. It was very slow going. He stopped every few minutes and listened for the woman's voice or sounds of breathing or crying.

Finally he found her in the back of the Laundromat. She had run for the bathroom when the earthquake came, and made it to the doorway. The wall had collapsed, and the beam had her pinned to the floor. Dan found a two-by-four that he could use for leverage and soon had her free.

The way back was easier. Someone outside had found some flashlights, and Dan dragged the injured woman back toward the light. He could also see the obstacles and avoid them as they crawled. Within a few minutes, he had moved her to the hole they had cut in the roof.

It had gotten dark in the time that Dan had been inside the wreckage. The wind he had felt earlier had gotten colder and stronger. Dan pushed the woman forward and then followed her. The first thing he noticed was that the looting had stopped, and Dan realized why. The flashlights were held by National Guardsmen, who had already arrested the looters.

Two soldiers pulled Dan from the wreckage. He was tired, cold, wet, and filthy. He was also under arrest.

* * * * *

The headlights from Ivan's van shone on the wreckage of the old garage on Monterey Road. The big wooden doors had been padlocked, but the earthquake had torn them loose from the front of the building. Mitch pushed them open without much difficulty and looked inside.

He hit the light switch and realized that the power was out. *The earthquake must have been everywhere,* he thought, and vaguely remembered reading about a worldwide earthquake being another sign of the end.

Mitch picked his way through the trash and debris to the back of the garage and found something covered with a water-proof tarp. Pulling it back, he saw what he was looking for. It was Harley's chopper. Behind it were two gas cans.

Mitch looked back at Ivan's van. "We got it," he shouted back to them, and then realized that the van was empty.

Curious, he walked back toward the van and looked outside. Ivan and Flea had walked back toward the street and were looking off into the eastern sky. Mitch had a strange feeling and went to join them.

The night sky in the east was boiling with colors. Reds, oranges, yellows. Mitch thought he heard something like beautiful singing coming out of the night sky as well.

"He's here," Ivan said, falling to his knees.

"Who's here?" Mitch asked.

"The radio said that Jesus has come," Flea said, laughing and hitting Mitch on the shoulder. "He's in Denver."

Mitch looked at the colorful sky and felt very strange.

"Guys, there's a passage in the Bible that says every eye shall see Him," Mitch said. "This isn't Him. This is the other guy."

"Are you kidding?" Ivan said. "This is the real thing. I know it. I feel it. How can you ignore this after everything you've said for the past few months."

Mitch moved between his friends and the horizon they were staring at. "That's exactly why I am ignoring it. The Bible says Satan will come pretending to be Jesus. Is this all it takes for you to be fooled? A radio broadcast and a light show?"

Ivan stood and grabbed Mitch by the shoulders. "Dude, we gotta see this, man. Sorry you don't believe. But before I go, there's something I gotta tell you. Something that's been eating at me, man, for a long time.

Ivan looked down, then at Flea, who looked suddenly embarrassed. "You know that preacher, Pastor Taylor, that your Dad liked so much?"

Mitch nodded. "The one who was killed outside his church. Why?"

Ivan looked at Flea again, then at Mitch.

"I … we … Flea and me … are the ones," Ivan said quietly, then he began crying.

Mitch put his arms around his friends. Flea was crying too.

"I'm sorry, man," Ivan said, weeping. "I'm so sorry."

"It's all behind us, guys," Mitch said. "I forgive you. God forgives you. And I am sure that Pastor Taylor would have forgiven you too." He pushed away and looked at his friends, who were still blubbering.

"But what's important now is that we ignore this business in Denver," Mitch said. "That's the Antichrist. He is there to deceive you. You've been deceived enough already. We're headed for Yosemite."

"Yosemite?" Flea asked. "Why?"

"I was trying to figure out where Dad and Kris would go, and I remembered that my dad did some graduate work up there at a camp the church used to have. They're likely to head that direction."

"But the police probably know about that place too," Ivan said. "What makes you think they would still be there?"

Mitch shrugged. "I don't know. All I know is I gotta try."

Mitch filled up the tank on the Harley-Davidson motorcycle and pushed it out of the old garage. He straddled it, flipped the switch on and cranked it over once. It roared into life.

"Now you guys follow me," Mitch shouted to the two others. "We're going north to 580, then east, then south on 101. Everyone else should be going north to Sacramento and over the mountains toward Denver. You'll be tempted to go with the crowd. Don't do it."

Ivan and Flea nodded.

"We're with you, bro," Ivan said.

Mitch's motorcycle roared down the driveway to Monterey Road, and he turned right, headed for the nearest onramp for 680 North.

He checked in his rearview mirror every few miles as they traveled north along 680. A few miles before the 580 turnoff, traffic started getting heavy. Mitch noticed that all the cars were traveling north toward Sacramento. He concentrated on not getting hit on the big motorcycle. When he turned back to his mirror a few minutes later, Ivan's van was nowhere in sight.

A few miles later, he turned onto 580 and slowed to let them catch up. Finally he pulled over and waited fifteen minutes for Ivan's van to appear.

It never came.

Ivan and Flea were headed for Denver.

* * * * *

Kris had always been in a hurry to become an adult. Now she wondered why. An adult would know what to do in this situation. Instead, there she was, a fourteen-year-old in charge of nine, six- through twelve-year-olds, running and hiding in the mountains from the army and the police.

She followed instinct and headed as far away from the baptismal site as she could. As far as she knew, everyone else who had been there had been captured and arrested—including her dad. She had heard the shots fired right after they left. Now she couldn't get those shots out of her head.

They had been hiking for three hours and now it was getting dark—and cold. The hot day had turned into a bitterly cold night. No matter how much danger they were in, she knew she would have to find shelter, build a fire, and find food and water for these children very soon.

She pushed the little ones as fast as she dared. A couple of the older boys helped her by carrying one of the smallest kids for short distances. At least they weren't arguing with her or objecting to her leadership, she thought. Apparently they all understood how much danger they were in.

The path they followed led over a ridge and down into another valley. A hiking sign they passed said, "Crescent Lake, 2 miles." Kris knew that they would have to stay close to some source of water, but that also increased their danger. She also knew that they would have to stop very soon.

Finally they came to a ridge overlooking Crescent Lake. At the edge of a clearing on top of the ridge was a small cabin that Kris guessed was used for emergencies. *Well, if this isn't an emergency*, she thought, *I don't know what is.*

She led the group into the darkened cabin and sat them down on a cot.

"I'm cold," the littlest one said.

"Me too," said another. "And hungry."

"OK," Kris said. "First we get a fire going. Then we figure out something to eat."

She asked the two oldest boys to look through the shelves and see what they could find to eat. Because she was the only one with even a light coat on, she volunteered to go out and find some kindling for a fire. She picked up two wooden matches on a shelf by the door and put them in her pocket as she went out the door.

Normally, it would have been hard to find kindling near the cabin with so many backpackers traveling through. In addition, Kris was faced with a moonless night. After fifteen minutes of searching, she had found only a few dry twigs, some pinecones, and some needles.

"This is ridiculous," she said, looking up at the dark sky. She shivered and decided that they would have to do until morning.

Her shiver turned into something more serious when she heard a car door slam. It came from the direction of the cabin. She hurried as quietly as she could back to the clearing, stopping at the edge.

Across the clearing was a Humvee filled with uniformed men. They were shining flashlights into the cabin. Peering back at them through the glass window were three pairs of children's eyes.

"OK, we've found the children," Kris heard one of them say into his radio. The men stomped into the cabin.

Alone, Kris thought, and turned around and headed back into the woods.

CHAPTER

Losing the children was a mixed blessing, Kris thought as she hiked along the trail in the darkness. On the one hand, for a while she had felt that God was giving her the responsibility for their care, and she had bungled it by allowing them to be captured. As a result, she struggled with terrible guilt. Because of her, those children were now probably going behind bars.

At least they're alive, she argued with herself. *I'm not qualified to take care of little children, especially under these conditions. I'm only fourteen, after all.* Logically, she knew that she would do better on her own, and that lifted a burden from her shoulders. Emotionally, she still felt guilty.

She hiked through the night, stumbling through the darkness and shivering uncontrollably at times. She heard helicopters fly overhead, and once or twice thought she saw bright searchlights shining down from the sky. *How could they know I'm out here*, she wondered. Then she wondered if there were others hiding out there.

By midnight she had passed Crescent Lake, pausing only to get some water and forage for some food. She continued on, this time turning north toward Buena Vista Lake. The moon came out about 2:00 A.M., a fat orange crescent that seemed to be there specifically for her company.

She arrived at Buena Vista Lake just before dawn. Exhausted, Kris found a pile of logs that were stacked on the lake's edge. She climbed inside the maze of timbers, crawled as far back inside as she could, and immediately fell asleep.

She awoke in the late afternoon, shivering again. The day was very gray. She looked out through the timbers and realized that she had left a trail of footprints that led out of the forest, across the sand and directly to where she was hiding.

I've got to do better than that, she thought. She shivered, and then realized that she was starving. *Water, food, shelter*. She went through the mental checklist for wilderness survival. *Staying hidden comes first*, she reminded herself.

She peered through the logs and tried to determine if there were any people around. A lone helicopter flew across the horizon to the south, but it was so far away that Kris knew she couldn't be seen.

What about spy satellites? Fire station lookouts? Random backpackers? Kris caught herself and realized that she was getting paranoid.

"I can't stay in here forever," she whispered to herself. And yet she couldn't bring herself to climb out of the tangle of logs. At least, not yet.

"Jesus," she prayed. "I'm scared and I am hungry. I don't know whether I am more hungry than scared, but I know that You will take care of me if I let You. I need You to bring me something to eat."

She opened her eyes and looked out over the lake, somehow expecting a miracle vegeburger to drop out of the sky. Instead, she heard a squeak behind her.

She turned and looked into the opposite corner. There was a tangle of fishing line, feathers, and fiberfill she guessed was from some sleeping bag. It was a rat's nest.

She got closer to examine it. Pulling back the top and peering inside, she saw that the mother rat had babies and was nursing them. Amazingly, the rat didn't seem to be concerned about Kris being there. Kris watched her for a while, then saw something shiny on one side. She reached in and pulled out a foil package that was still sealed. Inside were two cookies.

Her heart beat rapidly, and her stomach prepared itself for its first food that day.

"Thank you, Mrs. Mouse," Kris said, bowing to the rat. "Thank You, Jesus." She ate the two cookies and looked for more. There were none.

"Well, I guess four cookies is too much of a miracle to ask for," she said. She stood up and scanned the area outside.

It was getting close to sundown, and she was getting restless. She needed water, and she wondered how safe she was where she was hiding. Her answer came when she looked out and saw two men in uniforms carrying rifles step out of the woods and walk toward the lake.

She waited until sundown, then walked quietly down to the lake and got her drink. Then she started hiking north again.

* * * * *

They're all headed for Denver, Mitch thought as he walked along empty Highway 101 South and looked for a ride. The chopper had done fine until Mitch had taken 580 east and dropped south on 101. Whether it was from dried-out parts or from bad gasoline, the bike had started hesitating and stuttering at that point. He had pretty much coasted through Modesto, but just south of Turlock it sputtered and died for good. Mitch tried to clean out the fuel line and the spark plugs, but nothing helped. After half an hour he left it on the side of the ash-covered road and started walking.

He saw plenty of cars, but they were all headed in the opposite direction. Mitch didn't worry, however. After a month of having the walls of a maximum-security prison around him, it was just enjoyable to be in an open space, able to travel in any direction he chose. Besides, he had the Holy Spirit for company.

"They're all gone," Mitch thought aloud as he walked. Dad and Kris, Reed, Harley and Gina, Ivan and Flea, Dan. Mom. Mitch thought about his mother the longest. He felt a longing to crawl up into her lap and hear her sing "Jesus Loves Me" to him as she used to when he was growing up. He used to listen to her read *Uncle Arthur's Bedtime Stories* and *Great Stories for Kids*. Now he knew that he would never get a chance to talk to her about Jesus. He most likely would never see her again.

He was alone. And he felt very alone, especially when he thought of the people he loved and had lost. He was sliding into a depression thinking about it as he walked when an old pickup with a camper slowed down and stopped on the road next to him.

"Need a ride?" asked the old man behind the steering wheel. Mitch saw an elderly woman seated beside him.

"Sure," Mitch said, and ran around the front of the truck to the other side.

"I'm Ed Blacker, and this is my wife Barbara," the old man said, holding his hand out for a shake. "Where you headed, son?"

"Name's Mitch. I'm headed for Merced," Mitch answered. "Then east to Yosemite."

"Well, we can take you as far as Merced," Ed said, putting the truck into gear and driving back out onto the road. "We're headed south."

"What's in Yosemite?" Barbara asked.

"I've got family up there," Mitch said.

"Family?" Barbara repeated. "I would think you would be headed to Denver like everyone else."

"We're not into the craziness like everyone else," Mitch said. "I think there's going to be a big disappointment when people get there."

"I agree," she said. "Ed and I have had enough. We are headed up to our son's cabin in the mountains east of Fresno."

She turned and looked at her husband.

"We're going up there to die," she said simply.

Ed nodded as Mitch stared at the couple.

"Die?" Mitch repeated. "Did you say die?"

Barbara nodded.

"We've seen and done pretty much everything there is. Our son died two days ago, and now our family is all gone. There's not much to live for anymore. Even this Christ they say has come in Denver. Sounds more like Hollywood to me than anything else.

"I just want to find a quiet place and find some peace for a few days before I die," she said.

Mitch stared at the couple for a moment before saying anything.

"Mr. and Mrs. Blacker, are you church-going people?"

She shook her head. "We've never had much use for church. Seems like a waste of time, especially the way the government's been pushing it in the past few months."

"What about the Bible? Have you read the Bible?"

"No," she said. "Never did. I have respect for people who do read it."

"Well, that's something I have started doing in the past few months," said Mitch. "Reading the Bible. A lot. And sharing what I have learned with those I come in contact with."

Barbara looked at Ed, then back at Mitch. "So what have you learned?" she asked.

Mitch gave the old couple a short Bible study, focusing on the plan of salvation, the Sabbath, and what Daniel wrote about the last days.

"And you can see how all that's happening fits into Bible prophecy," Mitch said finally.

"Yes," Barbara said. "It's amazing." She looked at her husband again, as if a hidden message was being passed from one to the other.

"Dear," she said to Ed. "I need to find a restroom. I think

there's a restaurant coming up soon. Let's pull over."

Mitch saw a giant lemon appear on the horizon and then the sign attached to it. "Best Lemonade in California. Only 95 cents."

They pulled into the parking lot, and Mitch let Barbara out to go into the restaurant. "Come on," Ed said to Mitch. "I'll treat you to a lemonade."

Mitch hadn't eaten since he shared a peanut butter and jelly sandwich with Ivan the night before, so lemonade sounded good.

They went into the small restaurant and found a seat. There were no other customers in the place. The waitress brought them lemonades, and they sat there a while sipping through straws. Finally Ed stood up.

"Barbara's taking her time back there," he said. "I'd better go check on her." He disappeared into the back of the restaurant, leaving Mitch alone in the dining area. He sipped on his lemonade and finished it off. Five minutes later, he was still alone.

This is very strange, he thought. *I'd better check to make sure they haven't left.* He stood to leave and realized that the cashier, the waitress, and the cook had left as well. While he stood there wondering about it, the front door opened and a Madera County sheriff's deputy walked into the restaurant.

Mitch looked at the man and immediately recognized the expression on his face. The man casually pulled his revolver from his holster and pointed it at Mitch.

"Come with me."

Mitch looked at the man and realized that this man had used his gun before and was ready to use it again. He didn't want to give him any excuse to pull the trigger though. Mitch walked quickly past the deputy and out the door.

"Back here," the deputy said, motioning toward the back of the building. Mitch wondered where they were going, but obeyed. They walked to an alleyway between the building and a small power station. A dumpster blocked the view from the highway.

"Stop," the deputy said to Mitch. "Now take off your shoes."

"Take off—" Mitch started to ask.

"Just do it, kid." Mitch unlaced his prison-issue black low-topped shoes and placed them side by side next to the deputy.

"All right, kneel," the deputy said, waving to the blacktop. "Over there."

Mitch knelt and began to pray.

"That's it. Pray, kid," the deputy sneered. "We've tried warning your kind. We've tried putting you behind bars. I'm sick of messing around. Let's see if your God can put you back together after I've splattered your brains all over this pavement."

Mitch prayed for courage and kept his eyes closed. He heard the hammer click back on the deputy's revolver. Mitch knew that he would hear a blast, and the next thing he would see would be the face of Jesus Christ.

"It's not so bad," Mitch whispered, his eyes still tightly closed.

"We'll see," the deputy said.

In the next instant, Mitch felt a whoosh, a sense of power, and a blast of light. The deputy behind him screamed, and Mitch heard the gun clatter to the pavement. He opened his eyes just in time to see something bright with wings flash around the corner of the building.

Go, a voice told him. *I have set you free.*

Mitch saw the deputy unconscious on the ground. He got up and ran for the highway, and didn't look back.

* * * * *

The marine pushed Jake along the walkway of the old ship. Jake had been beaten with a rubber hose and twice strangled just enough to make him go unconscious.

"I guess you guys are done with me," Jake said.

"Shut up," the marine said and backhanded Jake across the face. "We're done with you, all right. You'll wish we would have shot you when we are finished, though."

They pushed through several entryways and made their way into the bowels of the ship. Jake was amazed that the ship stayed afloat as he looked at all the rust that had accumulated on the old bucket.

They finally came to a hatch in the floor of one of the engine rooms. The marine opened the door and pointed to the opening beneath him.

"You're the last one, slime," he said. "You know what we are going to do with you?" he asked. "After we throw you down in this hold with the others, we are going to weld the hatch shut. Got it? *Weld* it shut. No one will ever open it again.

"One more thing. This ship looks pretty rusty, doesn't it? It is. We are planning on taking it out and sinking it. Not only will you never get out of this hold, you'll never get out of this ship. And you will die slowly, knowing that you are buried alive at sea."

Jake stared at the man, then shook his head.

"Enjoy it now, jarhead," he said. "In just a little while, you will be crying like a baby when you see the glory of the King of Kings."

The marine grabbed Jake and shoved him down the ladder into the dark hold below and slammed the hatch behind him.

* * * * *

The guardsman's fist slammed against Dan's cheek, jarring another tooth loose. Dan looked down at his white shirt and tie and realized that he couldn't tell what color it was anymore.

"Are you ready to cooperate?" the young man asked.

Dan shook his head. "I don't even remember what the

question was anymore."

The guardsman turned the chair around and shouted into Dan's face.

"Your daughter," the man said. "We want to know where your daughter is."

"Sorry," Dan said through broken lips and jagged teeth. "I have no idea."

"You think you're so clever, don't you," the guardsman said, and backhanded Dan across the face for good measure.

"Smarter than you," Dan said quietly. "At least I'm on the winning side."

"Winning?" the guardsman said, laughing. "You sure don't look like you're winning to me."

Dan shook his head. "You don't have a clue, do you? You don't even know what the stakes are. Now I understand why Jesus said, 'Father, forgive them, for they know not what they do.'"

"Why, you pathetic little—" The guardsman reached out to hit Dan again, but a voice stopped him.

"As you were, soldier," Dan heard Meg say. The guardsman backed down and gave Meg some space to come before her husband.

"We won't be needing any more help from this man," she said to the soldier while staring Dan in the eyes. "We've located the girl—my daughter. Satellite photos show she's halfway up the slope of Mount Starr King, just a few miles from here. Let's go get her. But first, take care of him."

"With pleasure," the marine said, pulling his pistol and cocking it.

Meg started to leave and then she stopped.

"On second thought," she said, looking back at Dan. "Bring him along. He may come in handy later on."

CHAPTER

The black helicopters were real—and tenacious. Many square miles of dense rain forest had helped Jenny and the others in her small group to elude the dogs and the trackers. But they were not likely to escape 200-mile-per-hour machines that could fly over the rain forest and use infrared systems to pinpoint their location within a couple of feet.

And the helicopters were armed. Twice they had attacked the group as they followed a path over a ridge, exposing the hikers to the air. On the first attack, the group had escaped without any casualties. On the second, three people had died, including Abigail.

Pastor Sato had led them in great circles, hiding and running, hiding and running for several days. Jenny understood the strategy. He was simply buying time until the inevitable happened.

Above all, they prayed. Sometimes they stopped to rest and automatically fell into prayer bands. Sometimes two would clutch each other as they hiked and prayed for encouragement. Jenny found herself praying constantly—as she ate, as she hiked, even as she slept.

But for all the prayers that they lifted up to God, Jenny

missed something significant. For some reason, she did not receive the feeling of reassurance that normally she received with her prayers. She knew that God was there. But that was based on past experience, not on anything she felt or saw in the here and now.

They had lost contact with the other two groups after that first morning. For all they knew the others could be captured, dead, or like them, still running. But the helicopters didn't give up, and so Pastor Sato kept them moving.

This afternoon, the group was nearing its end. They had been on the move for hours, had had little to eat or drink, and were running out of places to run or hide.

Pastor Sato led them to the edge of the rain forest and into the grassland beyond. "Over this hill," he urged them. "Over this hill, and we'll be safe."

She and the others ran, walked, and crawled out of the rain forest and headed for the top of the hill. The strong helped the weaker ones and the children, but together they were not likely to move very quickly.

Behind them, Jenny watched the first of the six helicopters break over the tops of the trees and head in their direction. Somehow she knew that if they got to the top of the hill, everything would be all right. They didn't have far to go, but the group moved so slowly!

She forced herself to look ahead and help the others, rather than looking back at the approaching helicopters. *Just a little bit farther*, she told herself, and saw the top of the hill just ahead of her.

"No. It can't be," she heard Pastor Sato gasp. When she reached the top of the hill, she understood why. Ahead of her was a cliff, tumbling hundreds of feet below to the Pacific Ocean.

They had nowhere else to run. Jenny finally turned to face the oncoming helicopters.

She took a breath and smiled.

"A mighty fortress is our God," she began to sing. "A bulwark never failing." Suddenly she realized she didn't know the rest of that verse and faltered.

"Our helper He amid the flood of mortal ills prevailing," Pastor Sato answered in his tenor voice. He smiled and looked over at Jenny.

"But still our ancient foe, doth seek to work us woe . . ." The rest of them joined in on the song.

And Jenny watched the six black helicopters with their machine guns and air-to-surface missiles fly right at them and past them at 200 miles per hour. She turned with the others to watch the helicopters disappear over the horizon of the Pacific Ocean.

Another miracle had saved her life. Another miracle had proved that God was still in control. Another miracle demonstrated His love for her.

". . . on earth is not his equal." The song carried over the sound of the waves, the gulls below them, and the disappearing deadly helicopters.

* * * * *

The Humvee took the road out of Wawona Village and headed toward Glacier Point. Five miles before getting to the famous lookout, the vehicle carrying Meg, Dan, and two soldiers turned to the right and headed down a fire trail, away from the ridge. Dan had a general idea where the driver was headed. He had backpacked the area when he was in graduate school and had even taken Mitch and Kris up there years before, when they were in Pathfinders.

Dan couldn't understand how Kris could have gotten halfway up a mountain as monstrous and barren as Starr King. Wilderness survival called for staying close to water because water meant not only liquids but food sources as well. Apparently Kris was headed away from the lakes. Dan thought about it a little harder. Maybe she had done it because the military was too heavily concentrated around the lakes.

The Humvee pulled into a bivouac by the stream at the base of the mountain. Dan saw three large tents with a table in front of the first. Meg stepped out, followed by the driver and the soldier who was watching Dan. Dan struggled to get out the door, his hands cuffed behind his back. The soldier jerked him out the door by the arm, and Dan almost fell. The soldier jerked again, and Dan stumbled forward.

Meg walked directly over to a table where a map had been laid out. Two officers stood looking at the map, and she listened as they talked about the situation.

"She's the last one," the older officer said. "We have the entire area staked out, but she's so small that she can hole up just about anywhere. Resourceful, too."

Meg looked over at Dan, who smiled thinly at her through his bruised face and bleeding lips.

"She has a resourceful father," she responded blandly. "But she's still naïve. Ever wonder how I knew they were up here? Every time she used that laptop computer I gave her, our satellites pinpointed her. I knew exactly where she was." She shook her head, then looked up the mountain slope. "What about the loudspeakers?"

"We have speakers set up here, here, and here," the officer said, pointing at the map. "We suspect she's in this area. There's a thick patch of blackberries in there, and she could climb under them and we'd never find her."

The other officer cleared his throat. "We had a casualty," he said. "One of our soldiers ran into a black bear and got mauled. After that, we told the troops to give the bear a wide berth."

"Shoot it," Meg said simply.

"What about preserving the planet?" the younger man said. "We have orders to keep from disturbing wildlife at all costs."

"Not at the cost of letting this child go," Meg said. "Shoot the bear."

* * * * *

Kris shivered uncontrollably. The harsh April wind that brought gray snow howled outside the dead hollow tree where she hid. A few flakes of the filthy snow filtered down through the opening above her. She took her thin coat and tried to shove it up higher to block as much of the cold air as possible.

She heard the crackling of footsteps outside. Until they spoke, there was no way to tell whether the noise was one of the search party or the bear she had run into earlier. In either case, it was better to stay quiet.

It was funny. She felt a lot more welcomed by the bears than she was by the human beings outside. She had stumbled across the bears early that morning when she was looking—as usual—for something to eat. The two bears had been crossing the creek below where she now hid. The mother bear seemed to sense that she was hungry. She had turned and headed up the hill from the creek. Kris had followed her to the big patch of blackberries. She had climbed underneath the thorny branches and had her fill of the sweet fruit. She had almost fallen asleep when she heard the bear roar and a man scream. That's when she'd decided to keep heading up the mountain. *They'd expect me to follow the creek. Instead I will go up the mountain and wait for them to pass me by.*

About half an hour later she'd found the hollow log. Now her main goal was to stay quiet. As quiet as a fourteen-year-old girl with chattering teeth could be. She heard whistles, dogs, and helicopters outside.

"God, help me. Be with me," she prayed for the umpteenth time, whispering the words as if they were a comfort in themselves. She tightened her grip around her own shoulders, rubbing her skin through the light material of her shirt in her continuous effort to get warm.

"Kris," she heard her name called over some sort of loudspeaker. "Kris, this is Mom. I've come to take you home."

"Mom?" Kris whispered. "Mom, is that you?"

"Honey, you're cold and hungry. We have warm food, blankets, and whatever you need. But we don't know where you are," the voice said. "Show yourself. Show yourself, and we will send someone to come get you."

Kris was confused. That was her mother out there, *her own mother*. Why was she hiding from her? Why couldn't she just go home and get warm and dry and get food to eat?

Because she hates Jesus, she told herself. *Because she wants to take life and hope away from everyone. That's Satan talking. Don't listen to him.*

Kris whimpered and clutched herself a little tighter.

"She's not buying it," the older officer said.

"But I'm her *mother!*" Meg said, stomping her foot. "Wait till I get my hands on her."

"Uh, ma'am, maybe she would respond better to her father," he said, gesturing to Dan, slumped against the front of the Humvee. "You said he might come in handy."

"Right," Meg said, walking briskly over to Dan and pulling him upright. "Dan, dearest, I have one more task for you to do for us before you are done." She led him over to the microphone and amplifier they had set up by one of the tents.

"Now our daughter is up there," Meg said to him, pointing up the mountain. "She's cold and hungry, probably suffering from exposure. You can be a good father and help us get her down here so she can be taken care of. Or you can fight us and suffer the consequences." She planted herself in front of him and stared into his face.

Dan looked at Meg, the woman he had shared a home with for nineteen years. She had been beautiful. He could still see her the way she was when they were dating. She was always the athletic one, the smart one, and he always wondered why in the world she would give him the time of day. His mind flashed through their marriage, the births of Mitch and Kris, the purchase of their first home, the fights they had had, and the wonderful time they had had making up afterward.

He had looked forward to growing old with her, to playing with his grandchildren. Now he saw that it was all a lie. And he realized that the woman he had fallen in love with was dead and gone forever. This woman was a shrieking monster. Worse yet, she was a murderer and an agent of Satan.

She had given him a decision to make. He had decided what he would do before she had even asked him. How he would do it was another question. In any case, he realized that it was likely the last thing he would ever do on earth.

"OK," he said to Meg quietly. "OK, I'll talk to our daughter."

He limped over to the microphone and reached up to steady himself with the stand.

"Kris," he said as feedback squelched loudly. "Kitkat. This is Dad. I have only one thing to say. Honey. Listen to me carefully." He licked his dry lips before continuing.

"No matter what happens, hold onto Jesus. He's on His way."

Dan heard a low growl behind him that he realized was coming from Meg. She charged forward, a light of insanity burning in her eyes. Without hesitation, she reached into the younger soldier's holster and pulled out his automatic pistol. She held it out in front of Dan's face and pulled the trigger.

Kris heard her mother's plea. She heard her father's words. And then she heard the gunshot that she knew signaled the end of her father's life.

"Just You and me now," she whispered. "Just You and me now, Jesus."

CHAPTER

30

*T*eacher *of the Year. I never won Teacher of the Year at school,* Dan thought. *I wonder what I did wrong.*

It's funny how the mind works, Dan thought as he lay in a growing pool of his own blood. *It's not that I'm disappointed. It's more of an observation than anything else.*

Dan could feel his strength ebbing, as the blood trickled from his head wound. He tried to move his hand underneath himself to get up, tried to move his foot or even his toe. Nothing. He could still see a cockeyed view of a gone-crazy world running in panic around him. Feet scurried in all directions, their frenzy quieted by the blanket of pine needles around them and the fact that the gun blast had somewhat deafened Dan. Yet despite the pandemonium, he felt a peace he hadn't felt since—when? He couldn't remember. *It's not long now,* he thought.

His thoughts were becoming more and more disjointed, and yet he didn't panic. Instead, the sense of calm seemed to warm him. *All is as it should be,* he thought. He felt his heart beating slower and slower. And then it stopped.

* * * * *

chapter 30

Suddenly he heard music. He was waking up in his own bed. No, this was music like he'd never heard before. Angelic music. Fantastic.

He opened his eyes. He still lay on the pine needles, beside the Humvee, but things were vastly different. Everything around him was dark, but the sky was lit up like the Fourth of July. Better. Like a million Christmases.

He lifted his head and looked up. Brilliant beings filled the sky. Power surged through him, and he knew he belonged up there with them. And then he saw Him. *Him*.

Jesus was the reason Dan had gone through everything. And yet Dan knew he had really gone through nothing at all. Everything he had, everything he was, belonged to the God that was coming to the earth. Right then. That very instant.

Dan stood and glanced around him. There was nothing here worth looking at or worrying about. All answers were found, all problems solved. This was the end and the beginning.

"Yes!" Dan yelled, and his feet lifted off the ground. He was flying, but he didn't feel a sensation of hanging at all. *All is as it should be*, the voice said once again.

"Yes, Master," Dan said as he rose into the air. "All is as it should be."

* * * * *

Kris heard a distant rumble and thought at first that the military had brought a cannon to fire at her. Then she thought it was approaching thunder. Then she realized it was something else. Something wonderful.

She pulled her jacket away from the entrance of the hollow log. Brilliant light poured into her hiding place. Then she heard the music—fantastic, unearthly music.

"He's here," she whispered. "He's here!"

She climbed out of the log faster than she could have thought possible and looked up. The sky was full of angels. She

313

had never seen a real one, of course, but there was no mistaking these powerful beings for anything else. The world seemed to dissolve and collapse around her, and all she could do was look up.

"Jesus," she whispered. "Here I am."

And in response, her feet left the ground and she rose heavenward.

* * * * *

After the helicopters flew over them and disappeared, Jenny, Pastor Sato, and their small band realized they had nowhere else to go, and no reason to go there. God was in control, and it was up to Him to make the next move. They kneeled in a circle and waited for the Last Event.

Maybe Hawaii was the first place on earth where the cloud like a man's hand could be seen. If so, the small group might have been the first human beings on earth to see Jesus' second coming.

Jenny had seen many Fourth of July fireworks displays. Now she realized that the most fantastic special effects display imagined by humanity could never begin to compare with what she was witnessing.

First came the lights and the thunder. The clouds rolled and peeled into shades of pink, red, orange, and black. The thunder crashed, but she didn't see any lightning.

Then the earth itself responded to the challenge. The ocean boiled and spewed onto the shore beneath them. The ground shook and trembled. Trees collapsed and exploded into fire spontaneously. Ash and fire spewed from every mountaintop. But Jenny and the others were unafraid. Their salvation was here.

Angels appeared—huge, powerful, brilliant beings. Jenny was at first intimidated by them, then fascinated. They roared past the small circle of believers, each on some important mission, many singing as they flew.

Then one angel flew directly toward them. Jenny watched the angel in fascination and realized that it was coming to her. She waited for it to speak.

"Rejoice," was all it said. It held out a bundle of white cloth and placed it in Jenny's arms.

Jenny caught her breath and opened up the blankets. Hannah looked up at her mother and smiled. Jenny had never seen a more perfect baby and had never been more full of joy.

"Thank you," she started to say. But the angel was already gone.

Before they realized it, the cliff they were on crumbled beneath them and they rose into the air. Jenny looked at Hannah, at the others, and then up toward the face of Jesus.

"I'm coming, Lord," she said.

* * * * *

Jake had fallen into a state of lethargy. The oxygen in the sealed hold was almost gone, and the men's singing had stopped hours before. They were well below the surface of the ocean, he was sure of that. He could feel the pressure on his eardrums.

I will cast your sins into the depths of the ocean, he thought. *Now I know how very far that is.*

He heard rats squealing in the darkness. He heard water dripping somewhere. Then he heard something else. It was the sound of tearing metal.

Light poured into the hold from above them. Jake shielded his eyes and wondered if he had died.

"Get up, sleepyheads!" a bright shining being said to them from above. "The day you have waited for has come!"

Jake felt new energy come into his ragged body, and he stood. For the first time he was able to look around him, and he saw that there were nearly a hundred men in the hold of the old ship. Some had died and were reborn into strong, young men.

Others, like him, were changing as he watched.

Jake looked up again and realized that angels were his rescuers. There was no upper area to the old ship. Instead a giant tube of light rose straight up through the rusty ship and the seawater above them. Beyond he could see a sky filled with bright light.

"Come on!" the angels said, beckoning for Jake and the others to follow. Jake leaped and found himself flying through the tube and into the air. He rose into the sky and realized that the world was in chaos. The land and the people on it were collapsing, dying. The sky, however, was filled with believers traveling up, a cloud of light coming down, and angels flying in all directions.

"Jake!" he heard a familiar voice call. He looked to his right and saw his wife carrying something.

"Jenny!" he responded, and they moved toward each other. She reached out and handed him something—a baby, *his* baby.

"This is Hannah," Jenny said simply. "We have a story to tell you."

"In time," Jake said. "We now have all the time in the universe."

* * * * *

Mitch felt as though he had the best seat in the house. He was still walking down the abandoned highway when the cloud approached, the lights started, the angels appeared. Strange things happened. People rose through the air all around him. Mitch assumed they were people who had died in years past, now granted new life.

The cloud drew closer and closer, and Mitch suddenly realized that he was still walking in the direction of Yosemite. *It's not there anymore*, a voice told him. Mitch imagined Half Dome collapsing, the Three Sisters crumbling, El Capitan catching fire.

"Awesome," he breathed. "Totally awesome."
And then it was his turn to rise into the air.

* * * * *

Time takes on new meaning when forever and eternity become part of your daily vocabulary. Thus it was that Mitch really didn't know how long it was before he found Gina and Harley, Dan, Reed, and the others. The entire trip to heaven was like a party gone crazy, however. Mitch not only saw old friends as well as Kris and Dad, Jake and Jenny—and the new baby—he met people he had only read about in books. The fascinating thing for Mitch was that, as much as he talked to people and learned from them, he wanted to know more about them. And in every single case, their story came around to how they were saved by Jesus Christ, the King, the Messiah, and the Savior of Mankind.

Dan looked for a long time for two special individuals, however. And perhaps it was providential that he found them at about the same time. One he had seen many times and on him had based many of the major decisions of his life. The other he had met once.

"Pastor Taylor," Dan said quietly as he flew up behind the dark man in his suit.

"Dan!" Pastor Taylor shouted, hugging him. "It's just Adam, there's no need for pastors up here."

"OK, Adam, there's someone I want you to meet." Dan gestured to another dark being some distance away.

"I see you took my message at the playground to heart," the dark-skinned angel said.

Dan nodded. "What I don't understand is why you look so much like Adam."

The angel grinned. "My choice. You see, up until his death, I was Adam's guardian angel. Because you were so close to him, I thought my appearance would have more impact with the

317

message I had to share. Apparently, it worked."

"More than you realize," Dan said. "I owe you a lot."

"All praise goes to He Who sits on the throne," the angel responded.

"Amen and amen," Adam said.

"So what happens next?" Dan asked.

"Everything," the angel replied. "Everything happens next."

EPILOGUE

"And that's the story of my family," eight-year-old Hannah said, folding her hands in her lap as if she had completed some masterful task. A hummingbird flitted around her golden blond hair, and she shook her head to chase it away.

"How do you know so much about what happened?" a little dark-skinned boy asked her. "You weren't there. Not really."

"I was too there," Hannah insisted. "Besides, my cousin Kris told me everything. She's a writer. She tells lots of stories about people and how Jesus and the Holy Spirit do miracles. Someday I'm going to be a writer too." A lion roared in the distance.

"I want to be a musician," another little boy said, pulling on the sleeves of his robe. "I want to play the tuba."

"There are lots of songs to be played, that's for sure," Hannah said. "Uncle Dan sings all the time, and every time he sings, it seems like it's a different song than the time before."

"Well, there are lots of stories to be told, too," the first boy said.

"That's right," Hannah said. "We'll never run out of things to do here." She smiled a perfect smile and looked out at the manicured lawn with the people, angels, animals, and creatures from a million other worlds walking with each other in perfect peace.

"But right now I want to go see King Jesus," Hannah said.

"Me too!" said one boy.

"Me three!" said the other, and the three of them ran across the grass toward the Crystal Throne.

IF YOU ENJOYED THIS BOOK,
YOU'LL ENJOY THESE AS WELL

Eleventh Hour
Céleste perrino Walker and Eric Stoffle. A religious coalition with a strong political agenda. A movement for all churches to "get together." Believers doubting whether or not holding on to a few "different" beliefs is worth being ridiculed by the world—especially by other Cristians. *Eleventh Hour* is an end-time story showing God's people facing the ultimate crisis.
0-8163-1649-X. Paperback. US$12.99, Can$19.49

Midnight Hour
Céleste perrino Walker and Eric Stoffle. Midnight Hour is the heart-thumping sequel to Céleste perrino Walker and Eric Stoffle's *Eleventh Hour*—an end-time drama that reads like today's head-lines. With time winding down, the world hurtles toward certain destruction. But while the wicked seek to blame and destroy the Remnant for their misery, God's faithful discover peace, hope, and courage.
0-8163-1698-8. Paperback. US$12.99, Can$19.49.

The Orion Conspiracy
Ken Wade. The Orion Conspiracy is unlike any end-time story you've ever read. It portrays earth's final days in a context that is as contemporary as tonight's TV news or the latest computer software. This page turner is guaranteed to challenge you, surprise you, and encourage you to think about and get ready for our Lord's soon return.
0-8163-1179-X. Paperback. US$11.99, Can$17.49

Order from your ABC by calling **1-800-765-6955,** or get online and shop our virtual store at **www.adventistbookcenter.com.**
- Read a chapter from your favorite book.
- Order online.
- Sign up for e-mail notices on new products.